LEGACY

LEGACY

Ekaterine Nikas

little **FOX**

Long Beach

Published by Little FOX
PO Box 91593
Long Beach, CA 90809

ISBN: 0989189317
ISBN-13: 978-0-9891893-1-6

This book is lovingly dedicated to my late father Theodore and my son William.

Prologue

London, April 1806

The room was not empty.

Catherine realized the fact too late. She had come to this out-of-the-way chamber in search of air and a brief respite from the jostling, overheated throng who were making Lady Henson's rout such a success. The room had shown all signs of being vacant. No tapers were lit, nor was any fire burning in the grate. Yet as Catherine's eyes adjusted to the meager illumination provided by filtered moonlight, she made out a shadowy figure—no, two figures entwined in an embrace so all-consuming neither had taken note of her entrance.

Cheeks burning, Catherine backed toward the still open door. She tried not to hear the soft moans the lady uttered, tried not to see the intimate caresses the gentleman's ungloved hands bestowed. She was trespassing unforgivably and had to remove herself before her trespass became known. At least she was ignorant as to the identity of the amorous couple; in the dark room, both their faces were swathed in shadow.

She had almost escaped when someone passed by in the hall behind her with a candelabrum. The light illuminated the scene for the briefest of moments, but it was enough for Catherine to recognize the lovers. Stunned, she fled the room. Grasping her skirts with trembling hands, she hurried back toward light and sanity, but by the time she reached the crowded staircase, her vision was blurred by tears.

She ran full-tilt into someone and looked up to find a gentleman who, though his face kept wobbling out of focus, appeared to be scrutinizing her with alarming intensity. She braced herself for his ire, but he slid a strong arm around her and forged a path down the packed staircase and into a truly empty chamber: the library. Safely ensconced in a chair and armed with the blurry gentleman's handkerchief, she gave in to a storm of weeping. Only after the storm was over did she realize her rescuer was still in the room, standing quietly by the mantel, waiting.

"Better?" he asked gently as he crossed to stand before her.

Wiping her eyes, she looked up at him and saw him clearly for the first time. Though almost of an age with her father, he was an exceedingly handsome gentleman with broad shoulders and a trim waist. A mane of silver hair framed his expressive face, and he gazed at Catherine with eyes of piercing blueness.

"Yes, thank you, sir. I am quite recovered now, and most grateful for your assistance." Despite her very real appreciation, her tone was stiff, for she was sorely embarrassed to have behaved in such a manner before a stranger.

His finger lifted her chin. Once again she was staring into that startling blueness, but this time she also noticed the tightness around the mouth, the deeply scored lines of some long-standing hurt etched around the eyes. "You wish me to leave." It was a statement, not a question, but she heard the small sigh. "You are right. It would do you no good to be found closeted alone here with me." He started for the door.

"Sir, please! Wait. It was kind of you to guide me here so that I might be alone ... or rather so that I might have privacy—oh, drat! What I truly mean to say is — "

He had turned to face her, a smile twitching at his lips. "You see, Lady Catherine, it is impossible to cast my actions in a favorable light. Still, if you are not distressed by my presence here, I am tempted to disregard the conventions just this once," he paused, his tone amused, "and remain to enjoy the pleasure of your company."

"Sir, how do you come to know my name? We cannot have met, for I am certain I would not have forgotten you if we had."

His blue eyes twinkled. "No? I am gratified to hear it."

His charm was like a well-banked fire that chased away the cold. Catherine could not help it; her lips curved into an answering smile.

Something constricted in the man's face, and his expression sobered. "You are right, we have not met before. And yet — " He took her two hands in his and gazed at her face with a sad intensity that checked her impulse to pull away. "And yet," he repeated softly, "I knew who you must be the instant I set eyes upon you."

"I do not understand."

"I know my dear, but let us set that puzzle aside for the moment. There is another matter of greater import I wish to discuss with you. Who or what sent you running into that crowd with tears in your eyes?" He spoke quietly, but there was an undercurrent of anger in his voice that warmed Catherine's heart. Before she knew what she was about, the story poured out of her in a torrent.

"I only desired a little air," she repeated wearily at the end of her tale. "I would never have seen them else." Her voice trailed away as the scene rose again before her eyes. Phillip, her beloved Phillip, trailing kisses down her stepmother's white bosom while that treacherous but beautiful lady ran her small hands possessively through his hair. Catherine stared down at her own gloved hands and thought of the times uncounted she had wished she dared reach up and brush back one of her fiancé's wayward locks with an ungloved finger. How green she had been. How blind and naive! An angry tear slipped down her cheek.

Her companion reached out and wiped it away. "Come. Enough. These are much too precious to waste on such a fool!"

She looked up, suddenly wondering what had possessed her to confide such an intimate and sordid tale to this stranger. Admittedly, she had suffered a shock, but why hadn't she simply swooned and been done with it, instead of exposing her family and name to such terrible scandal? For this man knew who she was, and therefore who her father was, and what had she done but revealed her father to be a cuckold and her stepmother a—no, she ought not use that word even in her thoughts, though it was lamentably apt.

"Please, child, do not look so stricken," the stranger urged gently. "You have nothing to fear. I would sooner pluck out my tongue than say anything that might cause you harm. Much as it might tempt me to call young Farleigh out for hurting you so, no one will ever learn of this night's events from me."

Catherine felt weak with relief. "Sir, I thank you. For your reticence and your kindness and most of all for your concern for me. You are a stranger, and yet you have acted as a friend to me at a time when I sorely needed one."

"My dear, your gratitude alarms me. Are you so friendless that you must rely on strangers for support?"

How was she to answer such a question? Admit that she had no one to call upon but a father who ignored her, a stepmother who despised her, and a fiancé who betrayed her? Catherine bit her lip and was silent.

"By God, Trenwich has much to answer for!"

Catherine felt renewed alarm. "You and my father—you are acquainted?"

His expression grew bleak. "We were friends. Once. We had a falling out."

Catherine was curious, but dared not pry further. Instead, she asked in a low voice, "Sir, what you said before—about Phillip being a fool. Did you mean it?"

His gaze seemed to bore into her very soul. "He's lost you, hasn't he?"

Catherine swallowed hard. "Yes," she answered hesitantly. "Of course."

For a moment the gentleman's gaze grew unfocused, as if he were regarding some distant scene invisible to the eye. Then his attention returned to Catherine, and he looked down at her with an expression that almost broke her heart. "Then there is only one man in England who has ever been a greater one."

Suddenly there were voices outside the library door.

"The time has come for me to depart," he said, scanning the room hastily. "It would not do for us to be found here together."

"But I do not even know your name!"

He bowed. "Forgive me, my dear. George Henry Vincent St. John, at your disposal." He lifted her hand quickly to his lips. "And now, if your reputation is to be preserved, I must execute a quick retreat." So saying, he crossed to the casement window, opened it, and disappeared into the dark, leaving an astonished Catherine to stare after him.

Even she, ignorant as she was of much of the gossip among the ton, recognized the name she had just been given: George St. John, the infamous Marquess of Ryde, in his day one of the most notorious rakehells in all England.

Catherine stood there for some time gazing after him, wondering where a hardened rake had learned to look so sad.

Chapter 1

Staffordshire, November 1811

A flash of lightning seared the night sky as Andrew George Martin St. John, sixth Marquess of Ryde, rode wearily into the courtyard of Trenwich Castle.

For a moment, bright light illuminated the crenelated outline of the massive structure, affording Ryde his first glimpse of the old earl's home. Then darkness flooded back, reducing the castle to a towering shadow. Ryde slowed his horse to a walk and stroked the bay's neck in a gesture of reassurance as thunder rolled toward them with a crash. As if some cosmic signal had been struck, the rain, which moments earlier had been but an annoying trickle, began to pour from the heavens in a cold deluge.

Ryde swore under his breath. Why had no one yet come to guide his exhausted mount to the stables? He swiped at the rivulets of water streaming into his eyes and searched for the outbuildings. Suddenly a stable boy appeared from the shadows. Even in the darkness, Ryde could sense the lad's curiosity. Had no word been given that he was expected? The hour was late, but surely Trenwich had known he would not tarry in coming.

He slid stiffly from the saddle and tossed the reins of the dripping horse to the boy. "See to it that he is well fed and curried. I rode him hard, and he carried me well." Ryde finished off the injunction by dropping a coin into the boy's free hand, then turned and started for the castle's entrance, suddenly afraid. He had ridden for a night and a day to get here, but what if he were too late and found the door already draped with mourning ribbons?

To his relief, the large oak door was bare. Ryde knocked and then knocked again, as the wind-lashed rain continued to douse him. The door finally opened. The butler eyed Ryde coolly from the top of his rain-soaked hat to the tip of his sorely muddied boots. "Your business, sir?" The man's insolent tone set the damp hair on the back of Ryde's neck bristling.

He took a deep breath and—recalling his late mother's cease-less criticism of the ungentlemanly passion so often displayed by his unfortunate father—managed to keep his temper. "I am the Marquess of Ryde," he pronounced in carefully controlled syllables. "I am here to see the earl on a matter of some urgency."

"His lordship is ill," replied the butler curtly, "and is allowed no visitors. You will have to return another time." To Ryde's amazement, the heavy oak door began to close in his face.

This was too much. As Ryde slid a boot into the breach, the tight rein on his temper snapped. "Perhaps I have not made myself clear," he said, all his pent-up fear turning to anger. He shoved the door back until the odious butler was pinned against the entryway wall. "The earl is expecting me. I will not depart until I have spoken with him. If he is too unwell to be disturbed this evening, you will inform the countess of my arrival and ask that I may speak with her."

Ryde released his hold and strode away toward a set of double doors. "I will await your mistress in here," he said, entering a dimly lit but well-furnished drawing room. He slammed the doors shut behind him and grimaced. *Damn*, that the behavior of a servant should cost him his self-control! Then his gaze fell upon the wet stain spreading rapidly across the worn Axminster carpet beneath his feet, and his grimace turned to a rueful smile. *You were a fool,* he chided himself, *not to delay your grand exit long enough to toss the insolent wretch your hat and coat. With any luck he might have drowned in them.*

Cheered fleetingly by the thought, Ryde stripped off his wet hat, gloves, and many-caped greatcoat and laid them on a footstool near the hearth. Then he collapsed into a chair. He might be tired, sodden, and cold, but sometimes he found it damnably difficult to quell the fiery humors that coursed through his veins by birthright.

Lady Catherine Denton pushed the library steps farther to the right and climbed up again. Surely she had seen that copy of The Castle of Otranto on this shelf? Or was it the one above? She stood on tiptoe and peered at the dimly legible spines of her father's neglected volumes. Dust and damp were taking their toll; the countess's servants saw little need to waste their energies on a chamber their mistress never entered. There had been a time when Catherine's father had cherished Trenwich's library, but that affection, like others, had dimmed with the years. Now he seldom visited it, and his disregard was taken as a signal for neglect.

With his illness, however, had come nostalgia for reading, and since the earl was too weak to partake of the pleasure himself, Catherine was summoned to her father's bedchamber each afternoon to read to him. They had just completed Robinson Crusoe, and her father had surprised her by requesting the tale of the cursed Prince Manfred and his suffering family. Catherine was bewildered by her father's choice, as he usually disdained such gothic fare, but she was determined to honor it. That was, if she could find the dratted book.

Ah, there it was! Catherine reached up to pull the green and gold volume from its hiding place. Suddenly a cool draft of air caused the thin muslin of her gown to eddy and flutter about her legs. She turned to look over her shoulder. She had not heard the door open, but there stood Simpkins, his gaze fixed on her exposed ankles, a faint leer curving his sagging mouth.

Catherine was tempted to hurl the book at the impudent butler's head, but she knew if she did so it would be she, and not the wretched Simpkins, who would be called to task when her stepmother returned from Hilliard House in the morning. Simpkins was one of her stepmother's servants, one of the many who had been installed at Trenwich when the countess had realized the graveness of the earl's illness would necessitate a lengthy stay in the country. Simpkins was devoted to the countess and obeyed her in all things. If on occasion he was insolent to Catherine or some hapless visitor not yet established in the countess's good favor, that was hardly a fault to merit the countess's consideration.

"Well?" Catherine demanded, retreating down the steps and wrapping her shawl tightly about her. "What is it?"

The butler's dark eyes narrowed. "A gentleman, my lady. He has just arrived and desires to speak with you."

"A gentleman? At this hour? What possible business can he have here? And why should he wish to see me?"

Simpkins shrugged his narrow shoulders. "I cannot say, my lady."

Her hand clenched on the soft folds of her shawl. "Who is the gentleman? What name does he give?"

The sagging mouth twisted grimly. "He claims to be the Marquess of Ryde."

"Lord Ryde?" she exclaimed in disbelief. "Here? After all this time?" She turned and stared unseeing at the door. "Where is he now?"

"In the Elizabeth Parlor."

She forced the urgency and excitement from her voice. In a tone as calm as she could manage she said, "Tell his lordship I will join him within the half-hour."

Still Simpkins lingered, his expression openly curious. Thinking of the dear friend who awaited her nearby, Catherine felt the stirring of some long-lost sense of her own position. "Well, man, why do you stand there gaping?" she demanded. "Were my orders unclear?" To her surprise, the butler's eyes fell and he made her a sketchy bow before scuttling from the room.

Once Simpkins had gone, Catherine exhaled a tense breath. Lord Ryde at Trenwich? It did not seem possible. Why had he come? Was he here to visit her in her exile, or did he think to make peace with her father? Surely he must realize the latter was impossible. As to the former, she had often imagined such a visit with the wistful longing one feels for the unattainable.

She looked up at the massive oak bookcases that lined the walls of this, her favorite room. They were filled with the only true companions she had known for some time. At least, since Emily had been sent away. But now there was a visitor waiting for her: a visitor with a familiar face and a genial spirit who had once cloaked her in the warmth of his good opinion.

She smiled, but the smile faded as her gaze veered from the bookcases to the large painting that hung on the red brocade wall at the end of the room. The auburn-haired young lord with the proud eyes and the determined chin looked down at her with an assessing air. That she would be found wanting was inevitable, though this particular portrait of her father had been painted several years before she was born.

Perhaps if she had looked more like a Denton he might have been more forbearing in his judgment of her, but except for the Denton hands and chin and an auburn tint to her hair when she was out in the sun, Catherine resembled her father only in the stubbornness of her temperament and in the skill with which she sat a horse. She looked down at the tiny, butterfly-shaped birthmark on the inside of her wrist. It was the Denton stamp, a symbol of belonging that went back generations, yet it had never worked its magic on her. Her father bore an identical mark, but it was too small a sign of their commonality to signify.

Another sudden draft caused her to shiver. She turned and saw that the small fire in the grate was nearly out. She should not be woolgathering. She had to speak with Mrs. Perkins about preparing Lord Ryde a room. Catherine crossed to the red velvet bellpull and gave it a tug. She was glad her stepmother was away for the evening. Tonight Catherine could show Lord Ryde the hospitality due his rank and place in her affections.

Mrs. Perkins grumbled loudly at being roused from her bed, but Catherine paid the sour-faced housekeeper no heed. She told Mrs. Perkins what was required for their guest and cut off the housekeeper's protests with a curt reminder that while the countess was absent, Catherine was mistress at Trenwich and expected her orders to be carried out.

Despite her brave words, however, Catherine felt more like a poor relation than daughter of the house as she descended the main staircase twenty minutes later. The azure silk dress she wore was her prettiest and newest London gown, but at that it was nearly three years old and hopelessly out of fashion. Since her failed come-out and banishment to Trenwich, Catherine had had difficulty persuading her stepmother to the necessity of new gowns, especially fashionable London gowns. The one she wore now had been purchased only so she could attend a cousin's engagement party.

Picking nervously at the gold locket she wore about her neck, Catherine wondered what Lord Ryde would think of the dress—and of her, after all this time. What negative comparisons would he make between the spinster of three-and-twenty and the naive girl of seventeen who had stumbled into him at Lady Henson's rout, her eyes blinded by tears?

Ryde paced the drawing room, raking a restless hand through his still damp hair. Where was the earl's lady? He had ridden at a breakneck pace for nearly thirty hours only to be left to cool his heels in a draughty room with a fire he would not have set his dog before. What had he done to deserve such treatment? Answered the summons of a sick man and rushed to his bedside without thought of the havoc it played with his own plans?

Yet it was not the thought of his disrupted plans that set Ryde pacing. It was the notion that the earl might even now lie dying while Ryde was forced to dally in this cursed room. He shook his head and crossed to the fireplace, stabbing at the poor-spirited embers with the poker. Blast! For all the good he was doing, he might as well be in London as here dancing attendance on Trenwich's countess.

London was where he had planned to be. At the age of twenty-four, after five long years of struggle, he was finally in a position to partake of the diversions society had to offer a gentleman. His last sister was safely married off, his estates were beginning to see a profit, and the large loan he had accepted from the earl to pay off his father's debts had finally been repaid—with interest. At last he was able to call his soul his own. At last he was free to enjoy the pleasures his friends at Oxford had all assumed him deeply knowledgeable of, being the son of a notorious rake. Yet, forced to leave Oxford at nineteen because of his father's debts, Ryde had never had the opportunity to steep himself in the dissipation his sire had excelled at. Now, though he had no intention of following in his father's mired footsteps, he was determined to claim some of London's enjoyments for his own.

Yes, everything had been ready for his trip to Town. He had been packed and ready to depart when the message from the earl had come, and he had hastily started north to Trenwich.

And for his reward was left to wait.

Devil take her, where was the woman? He had to admit, he was curious to meet the earl's wife. She was acclaimed to be quite a beauty, if rather an incorrigible flirt. He had never had the opportunity to make her acquaintance before now, for whenever the earl had come to visit, he had always come alone.

Five years ago, when Trenwich had offered Ryde the loan that had saved his family and name from disgrace, the earl had begun his visits to Ryde's estates under the guise of monitoring his progress in retrenching the family fortune. It had not taken Ryde long to realize, however, that the older man enjoyed his role of mentor and adviser, and he had not taken it amiss when the earl's visits became more frequent. Ryde had enjoyed the older man's company. Over time, he had come to love and revere the earl almost like a father. Actually, more than a father, for what had his own father ever done to deserve love and reverence?

At last one of the doors to the drawing room opened, and a tall young woman wearing a pretty blue gown entered. Ryde frowned. She was not at all what he had expected.

For one thing, she looked far too young. He had heard that the countess was nearly two decades the earl's junior, but still—Trenwich's heir was a boy of twelve. This woman looked barely into her twenties.

Also, she was no Incomparable. Her hair appeared in the flickering candlelight to be the same nondescript brown as his own, its unruliness controlled by a single ribbon quite inadequate for the job, though he had to admit the escaped wisp curling down her right cheek had a certain appeal. Her eyes were pretty enough, but it was too dim to make out their color, and her nose, while classical enough in form, was a trifle too long. Her mouth was too wide. Her lips ... now why were they parting in such a look of surprise?

"My lord — " she began and then stopped. She was staring at him. Confound it, what was she staring at? Her gaze finally turned away, but not before he had seen a look of profound disappointment. He felt himself tense. He remembered that look, had endured it times uncounted in the year following his father's uncharacteristically quiet death. But now? After all this time? Surely if she had known his father, she would have heard of his death from her husband?

"You look dismayed, my lady. Is something amiss?"

"Forgive me, sir. I fear I was expecting someone else. Our butler erred and informed me that the Marquess of Ryde had arrived."

"There is no mistake. I am Ryde."

"Impossible! I am acquainted with the marquess and you are not he."

"Madam," he replied stiffly, "I am not accustomed to having my word questioned. I am Lord Ryde. Ask your husband if you do not believe me!"

"My husband?" she repeated, her soft voice full of bewilderment. "Sir, I have no husband. I am not married."

He looked down at her finely shaped hands. It was true. She wore no wedding ring. "You are not Lady Trenwich?"

"No!" she replied with surprising vehemence.

"I rather think we must be playing out our own 'Comedy of Errors.' If you are not the earl's wife, then who are you?" Intent on an answer to his question, Ryde gazed directly into her eyes. For a moment he felt an odd jolt that left him feeling slightly breathless. Quickly, he looked away.

"I am his daughter, Lady Catherine Denton."

He had forgotten the earl had a daughter, only child of a previous marriage, perhaps because the earl never spoke of her.

"Sir," Lady Catherine continued, "the mystery of my identity is solved, but yours remains a puzzle. The Lord Ryde of my acquaintance is a man quite senior to you, with silver hair and eyes the color of a cloudless sky."

Ryde scowled. Was there a female in all England who was not to be numbered among his father's conquests? "From your description, I presume you refer to the previous marquess, my father."

"Previous? Do you mean to say — " Lady Catherine stopped, biting her lip. Her eyes, he noticed, glittered suspiciously.

"Yes, my father is dead, and has been nearly five years now." He knew his words were stark, but devil take the girl, what right did she have to mourn a man whose own son could not?

A tear rolled down her cheek, and he had to stifle the urge to reach out and brush it away. "Lady Catherine," he said in a gentler tone, "forgive me, but I have little patience for a discussion of things long past. What I care for now, what I must know is this: how fares the earl?"

"My father is gravely ill, sir," she said quietly.

"But he lives!" exclaimed Ryde in relief.

She nodded. "However, his physician doubts he will survive the week."

It was Ryde's turn to be pained by stark words. "Can nothing be done?"

Slowly she shook her head. "No, or so Sir Henry informs me."

"I must see him at once."

"Sir Henry?" Lady Catherine regarded him in surprise. "But he left hours ago."

"Not the physician, your father."

"Sir, my father is sleeping, the only respite he has from the constant pain of his illness. I will not have him deprived of that peace by you or any man."

"Of course, Lady Catherine. I mean the earl no harm. If he sleeps, I would not have him disturbed, but I must insist on seeing him first thing tomorrow, for he has summoned me himself and with great urgency." He withdrew a letter from his waistcoat pocket and handed it to her.

She read it through and then looked up perplexed. "The hand is unfamiliar to me, but the signature and seal are his."

Ryde did not like the lingering skepticism in her voice. "No doubt it was dictated. Is that so strange? Your father is hardly in a condition to be handling his own correspondence."

She shook her head. "You do not understand. My father discharged his secretary a month ago. Since then, I have been writing all his letters for him."

Ryde felt a growing impatience. "The letter was delivered by your father's solicitor—a Mr. Barrett. Perhaps he acted the part of secretary as well as messenger?"

"I suppose it is possible, but why should my father go to so much trouble to secretly summon you to his bedside?"

"As I do not yet know what he wishes to discuss with me, I cannot say, but perhaps it is a matter he prefers his daughter remain ignorant of."

Anger flared in her eyes, and her cheeks were washed by a wave of color Ryde would have thought pretty if it had not so clearly betokened her ire. For a moment he saw his own struggle to control his temper mirrored in Lady Catherine's tempestuous expression. Then suddenly her countenance lost all animation. "You are probably correct," she agreed in a weary, beaten voice.

His own anger drained away. Deuce take it, she positively drooped. If only he could think of something to say to cheer her, to make her smile. That generous mouth was not made for sadness.

She looked up at him. Something of his concern must have shown in his face, for her expression softened, and she favored him with a faint smile. "My apologies, Lord Ryde. You have come all this way out of concern for my father, and I have been less than hospitable to you in return."

He began to protest, but she stopped him, placing a warm, restraining hand on his arm. "No, sir, it is the truth. Forgive me, and be assured I will see to it that my father is informed of your presence as soon as he wakes in the morning. In the meantime, you must be tired after your journey. If you like, I will show you to the bedchamber that has been prepared for you."

"Thank you, Lady Catherine," Ryde replied, wondering why she did not leave it to the housekeeper to show him the way. Still, he was glad enough to have her as his guide. Gathering her skirts up with one hand and holding a candelabrum aloft in the other, she led the way up the main staircase and down a long, seemingly endless corridor. Following behind her, Ryde enjoyed the graceful sway of her walk. So the earl had a daughter. He wondered at her age, deciding she was, in all probability, the same age as his sister Jane. Strange that she wasn't yet married, when poor Jane, at twenty-three, was already a widow.

Lady Catherine finally stopped before a white door that looked identical to every other door they had passed. "Here it is," she announced. "The Rose Room."

Ryde gazed back down the corridor. "I assure you, Lady Catherine, I believe you, but pray enlighten me: how can you tell?"

To his great pleasure he heard her laugh, a low pleasant sound that made him smile. "Astonishing, is it not? I cannot think why they were all made to look so alike."

"To confound guests who overstay their welcome?" he suggested drily.

"An interesting hypothesis, but one rarely put to the test nowadays. We do not get many visitors." She paused and then added, "The countess generally prefers to do her entertaining in town."

He wondered at the bitterness of her tone. Hoping to restore a lighter mood, he said, "It is fortunate I do not make a habit of walking in my sleep. Once set forth, I might never find my way back again."

His gambit worked. She smiled. "Shall I leave a spool of thread with you to mark your way?" She opened the door to reveal a warm and well-lit chamber.

"I am flattered you see me in the role of Theseus, and I must say you make a charming Ariadne, but I cannot help wondering who is to be assigned the role of Minotaur."

The smile vanished.

"Lady Catherine?"

"I hope you will find the room to your liking, my lord. Please do not hesitate to ring if you want for anything."

"Have I said something to upset you?"

"No. I am tired, I think."

It was true she looked under some strain, which was hardly surprising under the circumstances. "Then I must not keep you. Goodnight."

"Goodnight, Lord Ryde. Sleep well."

He watched her retreating figure disappear down the hall, the light from her candelabrum radiating like a halo around her darkened silhouette, and he found himself wondering rather irritably just how well she had known his satyr of a father.

Chapter 2

Ryde rose late the next morning. He had slept well, thanks to the thoughtfulness of his hostess. He had entered his chamber the night before to find a fire blazing in the grate, a tray of cold roast and savory stew waiting on the table, and a hipbath filled with hot water in the corner. For a girl not yet wed, Lady Catherine knew how to see to a man's comforts.

He dressed quickly, for he was eager to descend and obtain news of the earl. But as he started to leave the room, he stopped short. What of the labyrinth ahead? He pondered ringing for a servant, until his gaze fell on a piece of paper lying on the floor. Ryde picked it up and unfolded it.

> *Dear Theseus,*
> *The spool of thread would not fit beneath the door,*
> *so here is a map to the breakfast parlor.*
> *Ariadne*

He scanned the carefully drawn diagram of the castle with a smile. She had indicated the breakfast parlor with a large X and a small sketch of a fried egg.

He found the room without misadventure and entered to find Lady Catherine sitting at the table near the window, her back to the door, sunlight shimmering on her hair. The sight of her wayward tresses, which were as inefficiently controlled as they had been the night before, charmed him. Her hair was not the dull brown he had imagined it, but a rich sparkling auburn.

For a moment, he wondered how it would feel to run his fingers through that warm silkiness. Then he drew close enough to see the sad, tense lines of her profile, and all his fear for the earl returned. The food on her plate sat untouched and seemingly forgotten as she gazed blindly ahead, so deep in thought she had not even noticed his entrance. "Lady Catherine?" he exclaimed with unintended harshness.

She turned, her sudden smile fading at his tone. "Good morning, Lord Ryde. I trust you slept well?"

"Very well, thank you, but what of your father? He is not — " Ryde stopped abruptly, wondering if all his address had fled with his composure. "His condition has not worsened?"

"No, he spent an unusually peaceful night. He is with the doctor now, but he knows of your arrival and is quite anxious to see you."

Lighthearted with relief, Ryde nodded and crossed to serve himself some breakfast. He suddenly felt quite hungry. *And why not?* On such a beautiful morning, surely miracles were possible? The earl might yet recover and the earl's daughter—Ryde looked across at Lady Catherine, bemused to realize he still did not know the exact color of her eyes—the earl's daughter might perhaps be coaxed to bestow a smile upon him once again.

He had just seated himself opposite the lady and determined that the elusive eye color was an unusual blue-green, when a rustle of skirts from the doorway announced that their *tête-à-tête* was at an end. Ryde turned to see who had entered the room. The small, beautiful woman who stood poised in the doorway had obviously been waiting for his attention, for now she glided forward, her golden looks displayed to advantage.

"What a pleasant surprise to find such a handsome gentleman seated in my breakfast parlor," she drawled in a low throaty voice. "Catherine, if you would be so kind as to make the introductions?"

There was a brief, awkward silence. Then Lady Catherine said, "Ma'am, this is the new Marquess of Ryde. He arrived last evening. Lord Ryde, allow me to introduce my stepmother, the Countess of Trenwich."

"Charmed to make your acquaintance, my lady."

With a slight inclination of her head, the countess indicated that he should escort her to the table. "I am sorry I was not here to greet you when you arrived, my lord," she said as she laid her arm on his. "But I paid a sympathy call yesterday upon one of our neighbors who is newly widowed, and I was trapped by the storm." She glanced up at Ryde from under her lashes as she waited for him to seat her in the chair next to his. "Needless to say, it was an inconvenient situation to find myself in, but I console myself with the fact that I was able to offer a fellow Christian needed comfort." An odd, stifled sound erupted from Lady Catherine, but the countess paid it no heed. "Not that I do not have my own burdens to bear, of course, with Trenwich being so gravely ill."

"Of course," he murmured, as he crossed to fill a plate for her. When he returned to the table, Lady Catherine was on her feet.

"I pray you will excuse me." Not waiting for an answer, she hurried from the room, leaving Ryde to stare after her.

"Forgive my stepdaughter's ramshackle manners, sir. She is no doubt impatient to be off to the stables."

"The stables?" he repeated in surprise. "I suppose she finds riding an antidote to melancholy?"

Something hardened in the countess's china blue eyes. "Melancholy? My stepdaughter does not grieve at her father's illness. The two are not close, and I suspect she cares little whether Trenwich lives or dies."

Ryde sucked in his breath, certain she misjudged the lady. He opened his mouth to say so, but the countess had already moved on.

"Enough about my stepdaughter, sir. You are a much more interesting topic. Pray tell me, what brings you to Trenwich at such a time?"

He told her of the earl's summons. When he had finished, she flashed him a considering look. "Sir, this is past strange!"

"Countess?"

"Forgive my plain speaking, but I do not comprehend. Why

should my husband look to you, of all people, to race to his bedside when he regarded your father, while he lived, with the greatest enmity?"

"Your husband knows I would do anything he asks of me, ma'am, for I owe him more than I can ever repay. As for his feelings toward my sire—well, your husband has great magnanimity of spirit. He does not hold the son accountable for the sins of the father."

"Forgive me again, but considering the gravity of the offense your father committed against this household, I find such magnanimity difficult to credit."

Ryde flushed. "To what offense do you refer? I know that in their youth the earl and my father were estranged over my father's dishonorable treatment of a lady. Is it to this that you allude?"

"I am unaware of the matter," she said with a sniff, "for it must have passed while I was yet a babe. No, the disgrace I refer to is of a much more recent and much more painful nature."

She seemed unwilling to say more, but Ryde could not leave it there. A sudden disastrous suspicion filled his mind. "You cannot mean to say—my father and *Lady Catherine?*"

The countess gave a tiny, distressed nod. "I am afraid so. It was remiss of me not to have suspected, but Catherine was just out and, I believed, innocent, and your father was more than a quarter century her senior and a married man. I was concerned, even so, to see them together at public functions, your father's reputation being what it was, but then Trenwich discovered them openly embracing in Lady Carsey's gardens ..." Her voice trailed off as she dabbed at her eyes with a small froth of white lace.

Beneath the table, Ryde's hands clenched into fists. Was he never to escape his father's dishonor? Seducing an innocent girl, and she the only daughter of the man he owed so much to. Ryde pressed his booted feet into the floor to resist the urge to leap from his chair and kick it across the room. And what of Lady Catherine? An image of her auburn hair, loose and free and cascading against his father's chest suddenly filled his mind, choking him.

The sound of a man clearing his throat recalled Ryde to his surroundings. Edward Barrett, the young solicitor who had delivered the earl's summons, stood in the doorway. "Forgive the intrusion, countess, Lord Ryde."

"It is no intrusion, sir," she assured him frostily, "though perhaps an unexpected surprise. I thought you had gone to London."

"That was my destination," Barrett replied calmly.

"Then to what happy circumstance do we owe the renewed pleasure of your company?"

"The earl instructed me to return, ma'am."

I am not the only one to have ridden hard, Ryde thought.

"To what purpose?" She glanced uneasily from lawyer to lord.

"I am afraid I am not at liberty to say, ma'am."

"I see." There was a long pause. "Well, no matter. Trenwich has little enough time left. It is only right, I suppose, to indulge his small whims."

"In that spirit, ma'am, I hope you will forgive me if I rob you of your breakfast companion." Barrett turned to address him. "Lord Ryde, if you will follow me? The earl wishes to see you now."

Feeling a sudden sense of trepidation, Ryde rose from the table and followed the lawyer from the room.

⁂

Horse and rider galloped across the frost-touched meadow. Faster and faster they flew, the illusion of a single entity with a single purpose streaking across the horizon. Then the rider pulled back, and the blurred vision resolved itself back into duality: horse and rider, slowing to a walk along a muddy road.

Useless. The single word echoed in Catherine's head. *Useless to run. Useless to flee.* The memories that had haunted her all night refused to be banished. They clung to her like burrs, and even racing on Midnight's strong back could not sweep away the hurt.

Lord Ryde was dead, and no one had thought to tell her. She stared angrily at the distant house. Lord Ryde was dead. How could such a simple statement hold such pain? And yet, how could it not? He had been her friend, and more than a friend. He had been like a father to her. She had known him less than a single season, and yet in that short time he had shown her more concern and affection than her own sire had in the fourteen years since her mother's death. She had never been quite sure what he had seen within her that merited such consideration, but she had found his good opinion balm for her soul.

This morning in the breakfast room with the new Lord Ryde, she had felt that warmth again, almost as if the caring spirit of the father had been passed to the son, though she could discern little resemblance between the tall, broad-shouldered lord and his blue-eyed father. Then the countess had appeared, and the spell had been broken. Hearing her stepmother cloak her tryst with the master of Hilliard House in the guise of Christian charity, Catherine had been reminded all too forcibly of another time and another place when the countess had twisted the truth to her own purpose and turned an innocent act into a scandal that had cost Catherine everything.

Following her discovery of Phillip in the arms of her stepmother, Catherine had repeatedly attempted to break with him without having to acknowledge her discovery or cut him directly. But Phillip was a determined suitor, and though Catherine did everything in her power to avoid him, at Lady Carsey's ball he had insisted on standing up with her for a dance.

At first, she declined. Then the countess teased her in front of her father, remarking archly that perhaps she preferred to dance with someone else? Catherine, wishing to stop her stepmother's tongue, finally agreed, and Phillip claimed her for a waltz.

Afterwards, he led her back to her family, but her father had left for the card room, and her stepmother suggested a walk in the garden would be just the thing to cool Catherine's flushed cheeks. Though Catherine demurred, the countess insisted there could be nothing improper in an affianced couple taking a stroll.

So Phillip guided her out to the solitude of the garden and with tender looks and whispered endearments he breached her defenses. They drifted to a darkened spot and he kissed her, and she, wanton that she was, enjoyed it and allowed him liberties—such liberties as still made her blush to think of. Then somehow she recovered sense enough to pull away and tax Phillip for an explanation of the embrace she had seen him sharing with her stepmother.

For a moment, he was struck dumb. Then he grew thoughtful, and emitting a rueful laugh assured her she had simply misconstrued the scene. He had not been kissing her stepmother, merely assisting her when the lady had grown faint from lack of air.

"Do you think me such a lackwit as to believe such a tale?"

He regarded her with a look of impatience. "What does it matter if perhaps I gave the countess a somewhat over-friendly embrace? It meant nothing. You are the woman I mean to marry."

She attempted to slip from his arms, but he drew her closer.

"I tell you, it does not signify," he snapped.

"It does to me."

"Catherine, please. You are acting like a child." He pinned her struggling arms and pressed his mouth to hers.

"No!" The word was lost against the pressure of his lips.

"Leave her be!" roared a voice out of the darkness. Suddenly Phillip was yanked backwards with a force that sent him sprawling. Lord Ryde's silver hair shone in the moonlight as he stepped forward to inquire if she was harmed. She shook her head, too overcome by shame at the situation to speak.

Phillip stumbled to his feet. "What the devil do you think you are about, sir?"

Lord Ryde ignored him entirely. "Here, child, tidy your clothes." He stooped to pick up her shawl, which had fallen away.

Phillip grabbed at the older man's arm. "I repeat, sir, what are you about? This woman is my fiancée, and I will not have her addressed in such a fashion by a gentleman of your reputation."

The marquess replied icily, "Sir, remove that hand from my sleeve, or I must perforce remove it for you."

Phillip removed the offending appendage from Lord Ryde's person and transferred it to Catherine's. "Come, let us go inside."

She demurred in a small voice, "No, I wish to remain here."

"Nonsense! I cannot leave you here alone—with *him!*"

"I am safer with him than with you. Please, will you not just go?"

"Of course not! Catherine, as my betrothed —"

"Phillip," she begged, fighting to hold off the emotion surging up her throat, "it will not do. As I have been trying to convince you for some time, I no longer wish to be your wife." Her voice wavered. "I fear we would not suit. Please, consider our engagement at an end."

Still he would not leave her, but foregoing further argument began to drag her toward the house. Lord Ryde seized his arm and twisted it behind his back. "Begone, you young fool! Or I'll teach you a lesson in manners you'll not soon forget." He propelled Phillip toward the house in an undignified lurch.

Phillip stumbled to a stop. "How dare you, sir!"

"Daring is easy," Lord Ryde drawled in a low and dangerous voice, "but perhaps you'd prefer grass before breakfast to settle the matter once and for all?"

She caught at his arm. "My lord, please! This is not worth the shedding of blood!" Seeing the marquess's expression, she added, "Consider the scandal."

The older man gave a grim sigh. "Yes, I suppose killing the fellow would put a damper on Jane's come-out."

"Are you withdrawing your challenge, sir?" Phillip demanded. "For if you are, I stand ready to offer one of my own."

"Phillip!" Catherine cried. "Leave it be!"

He turned a tense, dark face to her and demanded, "Is it *my* safety you fear for or *his*?" She gazed at him, searching for a way to explain to him—without goading him into further fury—that she could not bear harm to come to either of them. But he took her silence as reply.

"So your stepmother was right!" he exclaimed bitterly. "She said you'd turned cool to me because you had taken a lover, but I refused to credit it. More fool I!" He regarded her with a look of contempt. "Very well, I shall not deprive you of your paramour, though perhaps you would have been better served choosing one who hasn't already bedded half the *ton*." He turned and started back toward the house.

Lord Ryde swore under his breath and made as if to go after him, but Catherine, fearing further violence between the two, gripped his sleeve and begged him to forbear.

In the long years that followed, Catherine had often wondered how differently her life might have turned out if she had let the marquess stop Phillip. For then Phillip would not have returned to the ballroom to tell the countess of his rout. And the countess would not have sought out Catherine's father and told him that something was amiss in the garden. And her father would not have rushed outside to discover Lord Ryde cradling her in his arms while she wept against his shoulder like a babe.

Midnight let out a whinny of protest, and Catherine returned to the present, unclenching her hands, loosing the reins, and murmuring words of apology to her mount. It was useless to dwell on matters long past when nothing could alter the painful present. Five long years had gone by, and everything was changed.

Phillip had married.

Her stepmother no longer bothered to keep her dalliances a secret.

Her father had forgiven her and deigned to call her daughter again.

And Lord Ryde was dead.

Spurring Midnight to a gallop, Catherine raced to keep from remembering the last time she had seen him, when he had come to try one last time to convince her father of the truth despite the gossip surging through the *ton*.

The marquess had emerged from the tempestuous meeting looking drawn, tired, defeated. "I am sorry little one," he had apologized sorrowfully, "but your father refuses to believe me, and I fear he plans to send you from town at once." She had tried to convince him that all would be well, but he had only shaken his head. "I can scarcely bear having brought such trouble upon your head. Can you forgive me for landing you in such a predicament?" Shakily, she had assured him there was nothing to forgive, and seeing the anguish in his eyes she had taken the great liberty of kissing his cheek in farewell.

Catherine snapped the reins and Midnight wheeled to a stop. How thankful she was for that farewell gesture now. "Goodbye, my lord!" she whispered into the rustling stillness of the November morning, as the tears she could no longer keep in check began to spill down her face.

It was a moment worthy of the theater, Edward Barrett reflected, as he watched the two men at the far end of the earl's bedchamber.

A silence pregnant with drama hung heavy over the room as the thin, grey-faced lord lost among the pillows awaited a response from the astonished young peer seated near his bed.

Finally, the marquess found his voice. "Sir, you cannot be serious!"

"Of course I am serious, you young pup!" growled the earl. "Do you think I have strength left for jests?"

"But in God's name, why *me*?" Lord Ryde exclaimed.

"Why not you? You're the closest thing I have to a grown son."

"Surely it is a task for a woman? The countess or some aunt?"

The earl snorted, which led to a rather frightening coughing fit. At the end of it, he slumped, wheezing, against the coverlet. "Blast it, boy, I want it to be you. Can you not just trust I have my reasons? You've married off four sisters. What is so difficult about finding one more husband—for my daughter?"

"But sir, I really do not think I am the best choice ..." Ryde's voice trailed off. The earl, exhausted from coughing, had closed his eyes.

Ryde cast Barrett a desperate look. "You must help me make him see reason. It simply will not do!"

Barrett shook his head. "I fear he has set his mind to it and there is no shifting him."

Heaven knew Barrett had tried. The idea of the marquess playing matchmaker to Lady Catherine had seemed laughable until he had seen the look of stubborn determination on the earl's face. He had argued with Lord Trenwich, trying to convince him it was a plan fraught with danger. Ryde was too young: only four-and-twenty. He was too needy: though no pauper, his extensive holdings could all benefit from infusions of capital. His morals were uncertain: though of noble birth, his father had been a notorious womanizer and gambler. Finally, and most importantly, he was no relative, and therefore unhindered by any tie of blood.

"Speak bluntly, sir!" the earl had exclaimed. "You fear he'll woo her for himself!"

Barrett had nodded. "Excuse me for saying so, my lord, but if you place him in the role you propose, he would be a fool not to."

"Ah, but you see, I mean to stipulate it be a love match, and I'll have his word on it that any marriage he approves be just that."

"Surely you do not expect him to abide by such a promise when three-hundred thousand pounds are at stake?"

The earl had regarded him coldly. "Whatever you may think, I am sure of one thing absolutely. Ryde is a man of his word."

Barrett regarded this man-of-his-word from across the room. For Lady Catherine's sake, he hoped the earl was right.

The earl's eyes fluttered open, and Barrett heard him whisper, "Well, man, I need an answer. Will you do it?"

After hesitating a moment, Lord Ryde replied quietly, "Yes, sir. For your sake, I will."

Barrett shook his head. The die was cast.

※

Catherine was waiting in the hallway when the two men came out of her father's suite. Mr. Barrett smiled faintly at her, but Lord Ryde looked uncomfortable and would not meet her eye.

"Is my father quite exhausted, Mr. Barrett, or do you think he can bear another visitor?"

"If it is you, Lady Catherine, I believe he can. Though I fear our business has left him sadly fatigued."

She resisted the impulse to inquire the nature of that business, or what was contained in the well-worn portfolio the lawyer clutched to his breast. Instead, she said simply, "I understand, Mr. Barrett. I will keep my visit brief." Turning to enter her father's chamber, however, she was acutely aware Lord Ryde watched her still. Her hand went to her eyes. Drat it, were her recent tears so obvious?

Apparently so, for when she drew near to her father's bedside, he looked up at her and whispered, "Why, Catherine, have you been crying?"

She nodded.

"Why, my dear?"

She hesitated a moment, then said honestly, "I fear I am much grieved to learn of the late marquess's death."

Her words angered him. His fists clenched on the coverlet and two bright spots of color appeared in his grey cheeks. Then, as if remembering something that for a moment he had forgotten, he quieted and his expression softened. "My poor Cathy. All this time and you did not know."

"How could I, when there was no one to tell me?"

"Aye, I should have seen to it you were told, only ... " His voice trailed off and he looked up at her pleadingly. Seeing her expression, his eyes fell. "It is impossible for you to understand what it was like," he murmured gruffly. "My only daughter had been soiled—ruined by a married man, and that man my one enemy in all the world!"

For a moment the old bitterness and anger surged through her. Then she looked down at him lying there, so thin and fragile and sick, and the flame inside her died. She said mildly, "But there was no truth to it, sir."

In the faintest of whispers he replied, "I know."

The shock of his words left her legs weak. She took a step backwards and sank into a chair. "You say that? After all this time?"

His voice shook. "What can I tell you, child? I was a fool—a blind and angry fool. I did not think that my enemy would speak the truth, or that my wife would lie." He added bitterly, "I did not know her then for the trollop that she is."

"But you did know me, sir! Why were you so ready to believe me guilty?"

He would not meet her eyes.

Catherine slowly slipped the locket she wore over her head and opened the clasp to reveal a delicate miniature painting of a smiling young woman in old-fashioned dress whose features were strikingly similar to Catherine's own. "I resemble her strongly, do I not?"

He nodded mutely.

"Is that why you could not have faith in me?"

"Catherine!"

"Is that why you never wished me near?" Her voice trembled.

"My dear — "

Her heart was pounding, but she continued on, for if she did not speak now, she would never dare again. "Is her memory still so painful to you, Father? Did you hate her so very much?"

He gave a start and jerked himself upright, gasping. "Curse it, child, where did you come by such a notion? Your mother was dearer to me than my own soul!" His voice caught.

She stared at him in disbelief. "You loved her? But I thought you married Mama out of pity when she was jilted by another man."

It was the earl's turn to stare. "Who told you that?"

"Aunt Serena."

He sank back against the pillows, his expression grim. "Curse that sister of mine! Never did have a civil word to say about your mother." He closed his eyes wearily. "Even when Anabelle was at the end, dying of the fever, all Serena could think to say was: 'At least now, there will be no scandal.'" His fingers twisted in the coverlet. "I never forgave her that." He broke into a fit of coughing.

It suddenly struck her that her father was truly dying. A horrible ache filled her chest, and she reached out to cover the hand on the coverlet with her own. "Oh, Papa."

He gave her a weak smile and said wistfully, "Goodness, child, you haven't called me that in years. I hadn't realized how much I missed the sound of it." He ran one hand furtively across his eyes, and Catherine felt her own grow wet.

For a few minutes they sat in silence. Then she said quietly, "A scandal, sir? Was Aunt Serena telling the truth, then, when she said Mama abandoned us to run off with a lover?"

His eyes snapped open. "Miss! I'll not have you speak of your mother so!"

She stared down at the locket in her hands. "But I must know the truth. Did she?"

At first, he would not speak. When he finally did answer, it was a single sharp word that seemed torn from his flesh. "Yes."

The locket slipped from Catherine's slack fingers and clattered to the floor.

"Cathy — "

"Now I see why you did not wish me near to remind you of her," she said thickly.

"You know nothing," her father snapped. "Your mother was

a fine woman, and I'll not have you thinking wrong of her." He reached out and caught at her hand. "Yes, she ran from me and from this house, but her provocation was great. I had done her a great—an unforgivable—wrong, and she had come to learn of it from another." He paused for breath. "She was not gone long. Once her anger cooled, she realized the harm such a scandal would cause you, and she returned. Unfortunately, in her haste to undo any mischief, she continued on in a storm instead of putting up at a posting house. She took a chill. By the time she reached Trenwich she was delirious with fever." His voice faltered. "And I never had the opportunity to ask her forgiveness."

Catherine rose to bend over the bed and wrap her arms round her father's bony shoulders. "I am sure she forgave you, Papa," she said softly, "just as you have forgiven her."

"Thank you, child," he whispered.

She stooped to pick the locket off the floor, and placed it gently into his hand. "Shall I leave this with you awhile?" Her father nodded, his fingers closing tightly around it. Catherine leaned over and dropped a light kiss on his forehead. "Try to rest now."

He shook his head. With a trembling hand he brought the small painting close to his face and gazed at it. For a moment he smiled. Then his eyes closed, and his breath began to deepen.

She anxiously watched the rise and fall of the covers for a long time. The rhythm finally settled, and she was about to leave, when her father's eyes flicked open, and his hand reached out for hers. "As I look back on my life," he murmured, "it seems I have always most wronged those I loved best. But heaven help me, Cathy, this time I am determined to make amends as best I'm able."

"Please! You must not tire yourself."

"Don't fret, child. I'm at the end. But I can die easy now."

Catherine grew alarmed. "Papa!"

He roused himself to look at her, but his voice, when he spoke, was the weakest of whispers. "You are the veriest image of her, my dear."

His eyes closed and he sank back against the pillows, his mouth curved in a faint smile.

Chapter 3

Oh, dear. What a dismal gathering!"

The words, spoken in an undertone and meant for his ears only, were dangerously close to Ryde's own feelings, which is perhaps why he gave the young lady standing next to him such an irritated scowl. "Confound it, Jane, this is a funeral luncheon, not a dinner party. It is meant to be dismal!"

"In that case, it is succeeding admirably," replied his sister, Lady Jane Brawley. "And to think that if I had not had a letter from Letty describing your dramatic departure from Chase, and one from Georgiana Waverly with the sad news about the earl, I might have missed all this gloom." She glanced up at her brother, and added gently, "Not that I would have had you face this misery alone, Drew. I know how much regard you had for the earl, and what a loss his death must feel to you."

He flashed her a grateful look. "It was kind of Waverly to invite you to stay."

Jane chuckled. "Kind? Perhaps. But I suspect Georgiana hopes having me visit will lure you back into her orbit. She still carries a *tendre* for you."

"Nonsense!" he exclaimed. "I haven't seen the girl in ages. When last I clapped eyes on her she was still wet behind the ears."

"So were you, as I recall."

Ryde grimaced. "May I remind you, madam, that I am still one year your senior?"

"You may. To be truthful, Drew, I am grateful for the reminder. I have been feeling rather ancient lately."

Ryde gazed down at her in concern. Her unexpected arrival had been such a welcome surprise he had given no thought to how painful such an occasion must be to her in her recent bereavement. "Janey, I am sorry."

She shook her head. "Do not fret. I am managing, and anyway, it is only right I pay my respects. After all, the earl's loan to you after Papa died pulled the fat—or, more accurately, you—from the fire, and provided me with a dowry that allowed me to marry Bevin with my head held high."

Ryde stared at her. "How do you come to know that?"

Jane's gaze dropped, as did her voice. "When Papa first took ill, I overheard him telling Aunt Celia his pockets were terribly to let and your situation would be quite desperate if he died."

Ryde sucked in his breath.

"Please, Drew! I could not help hearing at first, and after a bit, well, I simply had to listen; things sounded so black."

Ryde was in no mood to explain to his sister that it was not her eavesdropping that disturbed him, but the knowledge that their father had told his sister Celia of his disastrous financial situation without bothering to inform Ryde, his son and heir.

"When you went to meet with Papa's man of business after the funeral," Jane continued, "I feared you would be dragged off to debtors' prison, and I went crying to Aunt Celia. She assured me you were in no danger. She reminded me that you were a peer, and at least safe from that indignity. Then she told me she had spoken with Lord Trenwich, and he intended to loan you the money to pay off Papa's debts."

"I do not understand! The earl was always at great pains to keep the entire matter a secret, even from his own family. Why should he tell *Aunt Celia* of his plans?"

"Who can say?" Jane said, an odd note in her voice. "I believe she knew the earl when he and Papa were still friends."

Ryde frowned but said nothing. Jane's disclosure gave him cause for speculation, but this was neither the time nor the place to pursue it. The earl's death had left him feeling bereft and oddly at sea. Memories of the dark days after his own father's death kept rippling through his thoughts, as if the emotion he had been unable to feel then was now bobbing to the surface like flotsam.

"Jane, I think we ought to present ourselves and our condolences to the countess." He turned toward the center of the room where Lady Trenwich, a sad vision in black lace, sat upon a large gilt-edged chair, one hand clasped to her throat. "No doubt these past days have been a sore trial to her."

"Have they?" His sister's gaze flicked over the swarm of gallant gentlemen pressing forward to lend the countess their comfort. "I wonder."

"How can you doubt it?" he exclaimed, surprised by the skepticism in her voice. "Heavens, Jane! You, of all people, should be sensible to the feelings of a lady newly widowed." His sister's face constricted slightly, and Ryde reached out to her in remorse. "My dear, forgive me! Too much time spent rusticating has left me a tactless clodhopper."

The appellation made her smile, and in relief Ryde squeezed her hand, causing the smile to change to a wince. "Tactless—and strong as an ox! Let go, Drew, before I call to Lady Catherine for rescue!"

"Lady Catherine?" he repeated stiffly, withdrawing his hand. "And why should you call upon that lady for assistance?"

She flashed him a teasing look. "As all day you have run from her company whenever she chanced near, I assume you must be in terror of the lady. Therefore, who better to act my champion?"

"If I have tended to avoid her, it is only because I find her lack of grief distasteful. Since her father's death she has not shed a single tear, nor voiced a single sigh." He turned to regard the subject of his critique, where she sat by herself, aloof and alone, on a settee. "I cannot know the reason for such unnatural lack of affection, Jane, but I fear it does nothing to endear the lady to me, nor give me a taste for her company."

His sister's expression sobered. "You judge her too harshly, Drew. It may not be her nature to wear her heart upon her sleeve."

Remembering Lady Catherine's dewy eyes and trembling lip at the news of his own father's death, he shook his head. "When her affection is engaged, she is transparent as glass. It is your good nature to think kindly of everyone, Jane, even strangers — "

"But she is no stranger to me! True, I have not seen her for five years now, but she had her come out the same year as I did and was a good friend to me when I was in sore need of one. Few ladies of the *ton* wished to associate with Wild Ryde's daughter, but Catherine made it a point to pay me calls, converse with me at parties, and encourage her beaux to dance with me. Eventually, people found me unremarkable." She paused to fix him with an intent look. "So you will excuse me, I trust, if I continue to think kindly of her."

He did not answer. He might have been moved by this testimonial, if an alternate motive for Lady Catherine's kindness had not been obvious. By helping Jane, Lady Catherine could hope to please their father. But Ryde could not explain the truth of the matter to his sister. Jane was, thank goodness, wholly ignorant of the relationship between Lady Catherine and their rakish sire.

"Anyway, I think you are wrong that she does not grieve," Jane said. "To me she appears quite melancholy. Perhaps we should speak with her first, to see how she fares through these dismal festivities." Before Ryde could protest, his arm was seized, and he was led across the room.

Catherine looked up and observed the approach of Lord Ryde and his sister with dismay. Jane's expression was kind, but what could his vastly disapproving lordship wish to say to her that he had not already shouted across the room with his scowls? She touched a hand to her throbbing temple, wondering how much longer this luncheon would last. Oh, for the privacy of her chamber and the ability to rid herself of the tears which seemed locked inside her.

But even if she could flee, it would not serve. The tears would still refuse to flow; presumably they had turned to stone within her. She grimaced. How dramatic she had become of late, how like a heroine in one of Mrs. Radcliffe's novels. And yet, not like a heroine at all. For what heroine worth the name could fail to pay tribute to a father's memory in the currency of tears? She swallowed with difficulty, her hand straying to the place where her locket should have hung. She must be an unnatural creature indeed to have stood the day's events dry-eyed when even the windows seemed to weep with mist.

A shadow fell across her lap and Catherine shivered; she looked up to find Lord Ryde staring down at her. She forced herself to meet his eyes. Their honey-brown depths had never regarded her so coldly. "Excuse this interruption, ma'am, but my sister was concerned that grief might be weighing too heavily on your spirits. Perhaps you can reassure her that *that* is not the case?"

There was such disdain in his look that she felt anger prick at her throat. "I am surprised, sir, you did not attempt to convince her of it yourself, since you are so certain it must be so."

"I have tried, ma'am, but unfortunately she will not take my word upon it."

His sister exclaimed in dismay, but Catherine replied coolly, "Indeed, sir? How strange. Pray tell me, what wrong have you done your dear sister to cause her to mistrust your assurances so?"

His lips went white with anger, and he said in a low, furious voice, "I will answer you, ma'am, if you, in turn, will explain to me what wrong your father ever did you, that you find it so difficult to display even the semblance of grief at his passing!"

Catherine winced as if struck and then rose, swaying, to her feet. "Excuse me, my lord, Lady Jane, but I feel in need of a little air."

Ryde felt a pang of remorse. Those strange eyes of hers, blue-green and as tumultuous as the sea, looked quite stricken as she gazed about rather blindly. Curse it! He had not intended to hurt her so. He watched as she made her way out of the room. A fine job he was making of fulfilling his promise to the earl. How was he to find a husband for the girl, when he could not exchange two words with her without losing his temper?

"Well that was prettily done!" Jane exclaimed, turning to face him after she had gone. "What shall we do now? Find you a dog so that you may kick it? Or perhaps a child so that you may steal its candy?"

"She is no child," he snapped, "and appears quite able to give as good as she is given."

His sister gave him a considering look. "True, I have seldom seen anyone put you so roundly in your place. But that does not excuse you. You were rude to her, and worse—cruel. For heaven's sake, Drew! Not everyone can display their grief decoratively when custom demands." Her gaze traveled pointedly toward the countess, who was embracing her son, the new earl, with a beautiful, but properly melancholy, smile.

"All right, Jane, I admit it. I was wrong to lose my temper. Indeed, I have greater reason to regret it than you can know, for I am to become Lady Catherine's trustee and shall need to have dealings with her for some time to come."

His sister stared at him in open-mouthed delight. "Oh, but Drew, that is wonderful news! I am so glad!"

"I wish I could share your enthusiasm, but I suspect I did wrong to accept the charge."

"Oh, no, you did quite right!" she assured him. "I am relieved. I was afraid the earl would leave it in the countess's hands."

"By my word, I would rather it were in her hands than mine! Four sisters or no, Jane, I hardly know where to begin."

She stared at him. "Nonsense! This should be as child's play compared to what you have managed since Papa died."

He smiled at this unexpected praise. "I suppose I did do a creditable job picking husbands for you all."

"Really, Drew! Bevin and I met at Almack's and managed quite well on our own, thank you very much. As for our sisters, they selected their estimable husbands without any assistance from you, though I am sure you would have been happy to offer your help if it had been needed."

"Well, if you credit me so little for their happiness, why do you suppose me so admirably suited to securing Lady Catherine's?"

"I think you admirably suited to protecting her inheritance. Isn't that what a trustee does?"

"But your mention of the countess, your relief that the matter was not to be left in her hands?"

She lowered her voice. "I know you will not approve my saying so, Drew, but I do not like the countess, nor do I trust her. I do not think she treats Catherine justly, and I was dismayed to think that Catherine might be dependent upon her for that which is rightfully hers."

Ryde frowned at these aspersions on the countess's character, but was too distracted to respond to them. "Then you did not mean — " He shook his head. "But why should you? It is a preposterous idea, and I was a fool to acquiesce to it."

"Acquiesce to what?"

"Before he died, the earl begged a boon of me which he refused to be dissuaded from and which I finally agreed to, against my better judgment."

"Something beyond acting as Lady Catherine's trustee?"

He nodded but felt no inclination to proceed. He regretted his promise to the earl. Indeed, he was beginning to think he would someday look back on it as the crowning folly of his life.

"Speak, sir, speak!" his sister cried impatiently. "Do not torment me with this silence! What was the boon?"

"I am to see to it that Lady Catherine marries, and I must ensure it is for love rather than the heaviness of her purse."

Mercifully, his sister remained cognizant enough of her surroundings and aware enough of the inappropriateness of the emotion that threatened to engulf her to clap a hand over her mouth, which reduced her mirthful roar to a muffled gurgling.

Ryde regarded her balefully. "It is not amusing, Jane!"

She nodded wordlessly, and then managed to choke out, "Of course not! A p-proper gentleman like yourself f-forced to play Cupid!" Her sky blue eyes danced with laughter. "Still, at least all those summer afternoons spent pursuing your childhood hobby shall not go to waste. Lady Catherine is fortunate indeed that you are such a fine hand with a b-bow!"

He was prevented from making a reply by the approach of Lady Crowe, the late earl's sister, and so contented himself with a scathing look and a promise to himself to deliver Jane a scold later. However, he had no further opportunity to speak with her alone, and all too soon, the luncheon guests began to make their goodbyes. Ryde had time only for a hurried farewell before Jane disappeared down the drive in the Waverly carriage.

He returned to the black-draped drawing room reluctantly. It was time for the will to be read, for the earl's dying wishes to be made known. Ryde gazed about the room. With a start he realized Lady Catherine was not present.

Barrett noted the fact as well and crossed to the countess and whispered something in her ear. With an expression of irritation she rose to her feet and rang for the butler, requesting him to find Lady Catherine and bring her to the drawing room at once.

The man was gone for some time. When he returned, he announced in a voice sufficiently loud to inform not only his mistress, but also the entire assemblage, that Lady Catherine had left the house to go riding. One would have assumed by the outcries that followed that the lady had committed an act of high treason or at least a small murder. Ryde was none too pleased with her himself, but he had to commend Barrett's courage in daring to suggest the reading of the will be postponed until she returned.

The countess rejected the suggestion out of hand and commanded the lawyer to begin. Barrett expressed his disapproval, but did as he was told, and Ryde listened as the dispassionate voice waded through a morass of legal jargon to arrive at the crucial information. The estate would, since entailed, pass wholly and intact to the earl's son and heir, so it was not of its disposition that the lawyer's audience waited so eagerly to learn, but of the distribution of the earl's large personal fortune.

Aside from a few small bequests to servants and relations, and a generous, though not extravagant, jointure for his widowed countess, the distribution of the earl's fortune was simple: half was to go to his son Carlton, Viscount Graves, and half to his beloved daughter Catherine. At this announcement, the countess gasped and turned to cast an angry and reproachful look at Ryde.

Barrett read on. Both inheritances were to be put in trust. He, Barrett, would serve as the young earl's trustee until the boy reached his majority. Lady Catherine's trustee was to be Ryde. He heard muttering and received a sharp, considering glance from Lady Crowe. The trust would continue until Lady Catherine married or reached the age of thirty. There was an additional condition set upon the trust; if Lady Catherine married while the trust was still in effect, the marriage had to be approved by her trustee. If the trustee did not give his approval, and if Lady Catherine married in spite of the ban, all monies would be forfeit, and her brother would inherit everything.

Barrett finished reading, and for a moment the room was ominously still. Then a cacophony of voices broke out. The countess muttered something about setting the fox to guard the chickens, while her brother, Mr. Daugherty, pettishly complained about the paltriness of her jointure. Lord and Lady Crowe grumbled at their poor treatment by the earl, and scowled at a distant cousin who had been more fortunate. Another cousin sidled up to Ryde and stated that he had been enamored of his cousin Catherine for some time and intended to ask for her hand after a suitable period of mourning had been observed.

Ryde did not bother to reply, but walked away feeling faintly disgusted. The earl had deserved better than this from his family. He had deserved better than this from his daughter. What kind of creature was Lady Catherine to go racketing round the neighborhood on the very day of her father's funeral?

"How long has it been raining?" inquired a voice at his shoulder. Ryde turned to find Barrett regarding him with a worried frown.

"Raining?" Ryde repeated, suddenly noticing the steady drumming sound that seemed to reverberate throughout the room. He went to the window and pulled back the curtain. Barrett joined him there, and both men gazed uneasily at the black sky, wind-whipped trees, and cascading torrents of rain.

"Surely she must be back by now?" Barrett said, as a flash of lightning burned briefly through the clouds.

A loud, groaning crack of thunder set the window to shuddering. "Of course, she must," replied Ryde, but he felt a wave of uneasiness. He let the curtain fall. "I shall go see."

To the dismay of both men, however, it was soon discovered that Lady Catherine had not yet returned from her ride. They were further alarmed to learn she had ventured out without a groom.

"We must go look for her," Ryde declared, a suggestion Barrett immediately seconded. The two men arrived at the stables just as a lone rider rode into the stable yard. "Where the devil have you been?"

Ryde demanded as he ran to the horse and caught Lady Catherine as she slid exhausted from the saddle.

Barrett seized the horse's reins and nodded his head toward several openly curious grooms. "Forgive me, my lord, but would it not be best to postpone such a discussion until we are out of the wet and behind closed doors? If you go ahead, I will follow quickly."

Ryde grimaced and set Lady Catherine on her feet, reducing his support of her person to a single proffered arm. Halfway to the house, however, she stumbled and nearly fell. Ryde, noting the coldness of her hands and the trembling of her limbs, picked her up and carried her the rest of the way.

He took her to the library, a chamber likely to be vacant since the only inmates of Trenwich who seemed to frequent it were Lady Catherine, Barrett, and himself. To his relief, his request to the countess that the library be made usable had been heeded, and a large fire burned in the grate. Selecting the closest chair, he lowered her into it. He removed Lady Catherine's sodden hat and cape and laid them before the fire, then retreated to stand by the mantel, imagining he could still feel the warmth of her in his arms.

"I am sorry, Lord Ryde, if I caused you and Mr. Barrett any concern by my absence," she said in a muffled voice.

He frowned, but could not call up the anger he had felt in the stable yard with her looking so repentant and pale. "All that matters is that you are returned safe," he replied gruffly.

Her eyes widened in surprise and Ryde saw how reddened they were. He realized it was not only the rain that had left her long, dark lashes spiked and glistening. "You have been weeping!"

She nodded faintly. "It is a great relief, I assure you. Well worth a drenching in the rain."

"Tears for your father?"

She did not answer, merely met his gaze steadily with her own, but the truth was in her eyes. Ryde felt something tighten in his chest. "I hope you can forgive me?"

"As I hope you and Mr. Barrett can forgive me for causing you to worry. I did not expect anyone to notice I had gone. I never would have ridden so far otherwise. As it was, I was only halfway home when the storm broke."

"How in the world did you expect your absence to be overlooked with everyone gathered for the reading of your father's will?"

"But that is to be tomorrow!"

He shook his head. "This afternoon."

Dismay showed in the sea-colored eyes. She turned away to stare into the fire. "I know what a poor opinion you have of me, sir, but I assure you that I never meant my ride to become widely known or to be interpreted as any disrespect to my father or his memory." Her long, tapering hands clenched against the wet fabric of her dress. "I left the house because I had need of fresh air and to be solitary awhile, but I never expected by doing so to elicit the least comment. I am used to going unnoticed, and I did not expect my absence to be of significance to anyone."

For the first time, Ryde considered the possibility that the earl's claims of having been a neglectful parent might have some basis in fact. *I did not expect my absence to be of significance to anyone.* Ryde ground his teeth at the matter-of-fact tone with which she had said the words. He thought of his own four sisters and his anger grew.

He strode to her chair and knelt down before it, so his face was only inches from her own. "Don't you realize your presence or absence should be of significance to someone? Don't you know someone should damn well care if you are out riding in a storm?"

For a moment she simply stared at him, her lips parted in surprise. Ryde found himself leaning toward those lips—so soft and pink— suddenly tempted to emphasize his point with a kiss.

"My lord, I presume Mr. Barrett has met with some delay?" The words were uttered in the softest of whispers, but they recalled him to his folly as forcefully as a shout. He drew back and rose quickly to his feet. "Lady Catherine, my apologies. I had no right to address you in such a manner."

She reached out and lightly touched his hand. The feel of her bare fingers oddly thrilled him. "Perhaps not, but I thank you for your concern. I can truly see you are your father's son."

Ryde felt a dawning smile freeze on his lips. What in Hades did she mean by that? He took a step backward, away from her touch, but not before he felt her shiver from the cold.

"I think you had best go change out of those wet garments," he said grimly, "before you take a chill."

She flashed him one long, searching look, then rose and left the room. Ryde watched her go, wondering bleakly if he would ever be free of his father's detestable legacy.

Chapter 4

Catherine had no idea what she had done to cause such a dramatic change in Lord Ryde's demeanor. One moment she almost thought he meant to kiss her; the next he was jerking away from her touch and regarding her with such a look of disdain she felt as if a door had just been slammed in her face.

She ascended the stairs quickly, eager for some privacy to consider the matter. When she entered her bedchamber, however, she found her stepmother staring out at the storm and her room as cold as ice, and at that, the room was a good deal warmer than her stepmother's expression as she turned to regard Catherine.

"So, you've finally returned. Wet, bedraggled, and looking like the highborn drab who bore you. Well, miss, what have you to say for yourself?"

Catherine was startled by the fury in her stepmother's voice. "I am sorry, ma'am, but I would never have left the house had I known my father's will was to be read today rather than tomorrow as you informed me."

An angry flush stained her stepmother's alabaster cheeks. "Yes, I am sure you would not have willingly cheated yourself of that pleasure."

"Pleasure?" repeated Catherine in surprise.

"Do not play the innocent with me. I know what hand you played in the unwelcome tidings of this day. I saw you insinuate yourself into your father's favor during his illness so that you might drive his affection from me. I know it was not filial devotion which motivated your many visits to his bedside, but rather greed and a determination to rob my son of what is rightfully his!"

"That is nonsense, ma'am! You know as well as I that Carlton is father's only heir. The estate is entailed. I could no more rob him of it than I could fly."

The blue eyes glittered. "Do not be coy. I speak not of your father's land but of his fortune, half of which you have snatched from your brother's pocket."

Catherine stared at her. "You must have misunderstood, ma'am. We will go down and speak with Mr. Barrett, and he will explain — "

"*Enough!* I have no more patience for your feigned ignorance."

"Then perhaps you should leave."

"Indeed, you treacherous little minx! I have no desire to remain in this cold, dreary room with you." Her stepmother swept by, black silk rustling, and added as she reached the door, "I came only to give you a warning."

Catherine regarded her steadily, though the cold of the room and the dampness of her dress was beginning to make her teeth chatter. "Very well. I am listening."

"Do not think you have won simply because you have triumphed in the first battle. I do not surrender so easily."

"Ma'am, this is hardly a war!"

Catherine would have said more, but something flashed and caught her eye, something that was clenched tightly in her stepmother's small, white hand. It looked like a key, but surely the countess did not intend...

Apparently she did, for before Catherine could utter a single word of protest, her stepmother had passed through the door and slammed it shut. In disbelief, Catherine heard the grating sound of a key turning in the lock. She ran to the door and rattled the knob. But it was true. She was locked in.

Ryde stared down into his glass, absently swirling the brandy and ignoring the rather heated discussion Mr. Daugherty and Lord Crowe were engaged in with Mr. Barrett about the perceived short-comings of Lord Trenwich's will.

The ladies had withdrawn almost an hour earlier. The other gentlemen were too immersed in their talk to note the passing of time. Ryde knew he ought to say something to remind them of the waiting women, but in truth he was quite content to remain where he was. He was not in a talkative mood, and the one woman he wished to speak to had not bothered to appear for dinner at all.

At first, Lady Catherine's failure to join them had been a relief, for Ryde was still uncomfortable about the scene that had passed between them in the library. However, as dinner progressed and no explanation was offered for her absence, he began to feel a glimmer of concern. Finally, he inquired of his hostess, "I hope Lady Catherine is not feeling indisposed this evening?"

Lady Trenwich smiled archly and raised one golden brow in surprise. "Indisposed, my lord? Hardly. Catherine has the constitution of a horse. I have never known her ill."

"And yet, she does not join us. Perhaps she is overset by the day's events?"

The rosebud mouth tightened into a brief grimace. "If you wish to know the truth, my lord, she is in her chamber sulking. I scolded her for her unseemly behavior this afternoon, and she flew into a rage, claiming that as she is now an heiress, she need not concern herself with anyone's opinion but her own. She threw a book at my head to chase me from the room, and then turned the key in the door to lock me out." She added with a small, weary shake of her head, "As far as I know, she remains there still."

For a moment, shocked silence ran the length of the table, and then conversation resumed. Ryde turned to reply to some comment of Lady Crowe's, but his thoughts were in a whirl. To think he had felt remorse over his harshness to the girl that afternoon.

After dinner, the ladies retired, and Mr. Daugherty and Lord Crowe began their harangue of Mr. Barrett. Ryde sat silent, for he was in no mood to discuss either the earl's will or the earl's judgment. He too greatly regretted both.

So he sipped his brandy and tried to focus his mind on the letter he needed to write his steward at Chase and not on the absent female whose conduct both infuriated and bewildered him. Yet despite his best efforts, she dominated his thoughts, and only when Lord Crowe and Mr. Daugherty rose and left the room was his attention successfully recalled to his surroundings.

He was just considering what polite excuse he could give that would enable him to retire to his room rather than join the ladies, when Barrett approached and said, "I confess to some concern about your charge, my lord."

"As well you should. Her behavior today has been abominable."

"Sir, I find it difficult to imagine Lady Catherine behaving in such a fashion to anyone, even her stepmother."

Ryde regarded him coldly. "Are you saying the countess is lying?"

"I merely advise you that I judge such behavior as she described to be highly out of character for Lady Catherine. She is a mature, intelligent young woman not given to tantrums."

"I see the lady has quite a champion in you, sir. A pity her father did not think to make you her trustee rather than me. You seem to have so much greater a taste for the role than I do."

"If you had no taste for it, my lord, I wish to heaven you had refused it. She deserves better than a half-hearted advocate."

Ryde felt his temper rising dangerously. "I assure you, sir," he snapped. "I will do my best by her."

"I am pleased to hear it, my lord."

Ryde set down his glass with a clatter. "Of all the impudence! Do not tell me you behaved so with the earl!"

"Frequently. It is the reason he engaged me. He knew he could trust me to speak the truth. Now, if you will excuse me, my lord. It is time to join the ladies." He turned and exited the room.

Ryde stared after him, wondering just what the truth was when it came to the baffling young lady who was now his responsibility.

❦

For perhaps the tenth time, Catherine twisted her arms up behind her and tried with numb fingers to undo another button of her riding habit. She had almost succeeded, when a wave of shivering caused her fingers to slip and lose their tenuous grip. With a cry of frustration she let her cramped arms fall to her sides. She would have to let them rest awhile before making another attempt. She collapsed into a chair, trying to ignore the cold discomfort of the wet wool upon her skin.

If only she had some heat. She gazed longingly at the grate imagining a large, cheerful fire burning there, but it was no use. The afternoon had darkened into dusk and dusk into twilight and twilight into the clear, cold darkness of a November evening, and still no one had come to light a fire, or help her from her clothes, or bring her something warm to drink. Repeated tugs at the bellpull had failed to bring anyone to her aid.

Feeling a sudden burst of anger, she was tempted to pound on the door and yell and scream until someone came and opened it, but the possibility that Lord Ryde might hear her made her hesitate. He thought poorly enough of her as it was. How could she explain such unseemly behavior without admitting to the humiliation of being locked in her room like a misbehaving child?

Grimly, she reached back behind her for the elusive buttons. She had managed to undo one more when there was a soft knock at the door and the sound of someone calling her name.

"Polly!" she cried out in relief. "Is that you?"

"Yes, my lady." The knob turned, but the door did not open. The maid began to rattle it.

"It is locked, Polly, and I do not have the key."

"Don't say someone's locked you in!" the maid exclaimed, sounding gratifyingly outraged.

"I am afraid so. Can you fetch a spare key to open the door?"

"Of course, my lady! I'll find one if I have to steal Mrs. Perkins's own ring to do it!"

Catherine sighed in relief and listened to the young maid's running footsteps fade into the distance. At first, she simply sat in her chair waiting for Polly to return. But as time passed and the maid did not return, Catherine resumed her efforts to undress herself. She finally managed to drag off her sodden riding habit and strip out of her wet shift. Slipping on a cold but dry flannel nightdress, Catherine climbed into her icy bed and curled up in a tight ball under the covers.

She must have fallen asleep, because she woke sometime later to find Polly crouched before the grate building a fire. "So you found a key after all," she murmured. Polly said something in reply, but Catherine was too groggy to puzzle out the words.

She slept fitfully the rest of the night and woke late the next day with a sore throat and the first warning tremors of a headache. She was abominably stiff and did not protest when Polly insisted on doing even the smallest things for her. Every muscle seemed to ache, and if it had not been for her eagerness to see Lord Ryde and speak with Mr. Barrett about her father's will she might well have crawled right back into bed.

But when Catherine finally made her way downstairs, she found that both Lord Ryde and Mr. Barrett were out. The two gentlemen had accompanied the countess and her brother and the new earl, Catherine's half-brother Carlton, to the neighboring estate of Waverly. Neither Simpkins nor Mrs. Perkins claimed to know at what time the party was expected to return.

Catherine kept her face impassive before the servants, but once they had gone she found herself startled by the intensity of her disappointment. Was she so desperate to speak with Mr. Barrett about her father's will that the delay of an afternoon could dismay her so? Or—she bit her lip nervously at the thought—was it just that she was so impatient to see Lord Ryde again that even the delay of a few hours seemed too great?

Before Catherine could ponder this dangerous question further, she heard raised voices in the hall. The door was thrown open and her uncle, Lord Crowe, stumped angrily into the room. "Ma'am, I warn you. I grow tired of the subject! We can return to town if you wish, but I will not spend another night beneath this roof!"

Her aunt followed close behind. "Sir, you cannot mean to leave my niece in the clutches of that fortune hunter?"

"Why should I care what becomes of the chit?" he demanded irritably. "She is no kin of mine."

Aunt Serena's voice rose. "She is to receive half of my brother's fortune. I would think that reason enough!"

Catherine, sitting in the darkest corner of the room, wished she could melt into her chair, but it was too late. Her aunt had seen her.

"So, miss," she exclaimed sharply, "hiding in the shadows? Eavesdropping? I suppose this is a sample of the conduct we can expect from you now that you are become an heiress?"

Catherine's face burned, but she replied evenly, "I do not know yet whether I am an heiress or not, Aunt. I have yet to speak with Mr. Barrett."

Aunt Serena sniffed. "That's as may be. I do not believe Trenwich was in his right senses when he drafted that will, for I cannot believe he would slight me in such a fashion."

"Why, did he leave you nothing, ma'am?"

"Nothing but a painting of his first wife!" grumbled Lord Crowe. "Though why he should do such a thing, I cannot imagine."

His wife's cheeks flushed red, and Catherine remembered her father's words about how much her Aunt Serena had disliked her mother. Catherine remarked drily, "Perhaps he did it in remembrance of Aunt Serena's strong feelings toward my mother, Uncle."

"Your mother?" he repeated, sounding confused.

"The lady in the picture," Catherine reminded him.

"Oh, of course. Don't suppose you want to keep the thing yourself? Can't think what we're to do with it. Passable-looking female, but she ain't blood. Can't very well hang her with the ancestors."

"No, I suppose not," Catherine agreed solemnly.

Aunt Serena was scowling dangerously. Her uncle, perhaps belatedly wondering if his comments had been less than tactful, said in a reluctant murmur, "Well, I suppose if you and the chit's mother were such bosom bows, we could hang the piece in some sitting room or other."

"Anabelle Stafford and I were never bosom bows!" his wife exclaimed vehemently. "Anabelle Stafford was a brazen nobody who tricked my brother into marriage after George St. John jilted her."

"Ma'am, may I remind you that you speak of my mother, *who is dead!*" Catherine exclaimed, her thoughts in turmoil. *George St. John—the late Marquess of Ryde.* Had her mother truly been jilted by the man Catherine had found so kind?

"I only speak the truth. Your mother was besotted with St. John, but he tired of her and eloped with Maria Stenby to Gretna Green."

Lord Crowe growled an embarrassed protest.

His wife paid him no heed and continued with grim relish. "Jilted, and fearing she would look a fool when the news became widely known, your mother determined to replace one bridegroom with another. She seduced my brother, and he was forced to make an offer for her."

"I do not believe you!" Catherine cried.

"Ah, but there are many that know the tale."

"Ma'am!" snapped Lord Crowe. "That is enough! I will not stand here while you slander your own family! Off with you now, and see to the packing. My mind is made up. We leave today."

Aunt Serena protested, but to no avail. Her husband dragged her off by the arm, leaving Catherine once again alone.

She felt strangely weak, and her cheeks still burned. She pressed her hands against them, but her hands, too, were hot, so she turned her head and pressed the side of her face against the cool leather of the chair.

Surely it could not be true.

Surely it was but another of Aunt Serena's lies.

Catherine tried to concentrate her thoughts. She tried to marshal the facts in her mother's favor. She tried to pursue a set of arguments that must prove her mother innocent. After all, her father had loved her. But her head ached, and her mind spun, and her thoughts seemed to twist and tangle like sticky threads in a spider's web.

Feeling more than a little dizzy, Catherine rose to her feet and slowly made her way upstairs. She was exhausted by the time she reached her room and collapsed on the bed fully clothed, which is how Polly found her an hour later.

❧

The air had grown surprisingly chill, and dark, lowering clouds threatened along the northern horizon, but neither of the two riders galloping along the road to Trenwich Castle spared much attention for the weather.

Edward Barrett did not, because he was too busy feeling relief at his escape from the company at Waverly. He had spent most of the afternoon feeling profoundly uncomfortable, his well-honed pride sensing every slight and snub. Only Lord Ryde and his sister had had the good manners not to treat him like a misplaced servant, and when Ryde had stated his intention to ride back to Trenwich early, Barrett had hastened to accompany him.

Lord Ryde did not, because he was too angry with his sister Jane. Despite the somber mood of the gathering at Waverly, he had found the outing a relief. Flirting a little with Georgiana Waverly and silently admiring Lady Trenwich—few women, he imagined, could look so lovely wearing black—Ryde had briefly been distracted from thoughts of the late earl and his unpredictable daughter. Then Jane had begun harping at him about Lady Catherine, wondering at her absence, berating him for his lack of concern, until finally he had felt obliged to offer to return early to Trenwich to check on her. *What a wild goose chase this will prove*, he thought irritably. *Odds are the lady is fine.*

Still, some prickling uncertainty, some contagion from Jane's worries, undermined the thought and caused him to urge his horse forward more quickly. It would be just as well to be sure.

They arrived at Trenwich slightly after four. Everything seemed calm, if a little quiet. Ryde informed the housekeeper that the countess, as well as her brother and the young earl, would be dining at Waverly. He then inquired when dinner at Trenwich would be served. The housekeeper grew flustered.

"It was my understanding from her ladyship that everyone would be dining elsewhere, my lord," Mrs. Perkins said. "Nothing's been prepared."

"What of Lady Catherine and Lord and Lady Crowe?"

"My lord and lady have gone, sir. They left more than two hours ago."

"And Lady Catherine?"

"I thought I would just send up a tray. It's what she prefers most days," she added defensively.

"I am afraid that will not answer, Mrs. Perkins. I trust your housekeeping is up to providing a cold collation in the dining room," he drew out his pocket watch, "one hour from now?"

"Certainly, my lord."

"And please be good enough to inform Lady Catherine that Mr. Barrett and I await the pleasure of her company at dinner."

"Yes, my lord."

Ryde and Barrett retired to their rooms to change. Standing before the mirror tying his cravat, Ryde reflected that it had been a wild goose chase, but he was not altogether sorry he had come back. At least now Lady Catherine would not be eating her dinner from a tray, and, truth be told, he was impatient to see her again. He wished to judge for himself whether she was truly the uncaring hoyden the countess described or the intelligent lady Barrett claimed her to be.

When he returned downstairs, he found Barrett already waiting. "The housekeeper was just here," Barrett informed him. "It seems Lady Catherine is not feeling well. She asks to be excused from dinner."

Under other circumstances, Ryde might have accepted the message with good grace. But he had abandoned a pleasant afternoon, had left Waverly early, expressly to see Lady Catherine, and he was not about to be put off by some made-up excuse. The inordinate disappointment he felt transmuted into anger. He strode to the bellpull and gave it a strong jerk.

Simpkins arrived to answer the summons. "Yes, my lord?"

"Please inform Lady Catherine that if she does not choose to dine with Mr. Barrett and myself downstairs, we shall partake of our meal in her chamber."

The butler's eyebrows rose a fraction, but he bowed mutely and left the room.

"Was that not a bit high-handed for a gentleman who is but a guest here?"

"Perhaps," Ryde admitted. "But I am tired of her ragamuffin ways. We are her guests, and she should be here to dine with us."

"Is it not possible that she truly is indisposed?"

Ryde made a dismissive sound. "This is the second night in a row she has not bothered to appear."

Simpkins returned to inform them that Lady Catherine would be joining them shortly. "You see," Ryde said grimly, "all she needed was a bit of prompting."

But minutes ticked by, and then a half-hour, and still Lady Catherine did not come. Finally, the heavy oak door opened and she stood in the doorway, wearing an ill-fitting black gown that served to emphasize the paleness of her skin. Her face, too, was pale, except for two bright spots of color on her cheeks. For a moment, Ryde wondered at such an obvious use of rouge.

"Mr. Barrett. Lord Ryde." The words came out a whisper.

The weakness of her voice and the realization that she seemed to be swaying caused both men to rush forward.

"I apologize ... for keeping you ... waiting," she managed to murmur, before collapsing in a heap at their feet.

Chapter 5

Ryde gathered the lady up and carried her to a sofa, cursing himself for his autocratic summons. She was not merely indisposed, she was ill—dangerously ill. The bright pink of her cheeks was from fever, not rouge; her skin was so hot she seemed to burn in his arms.

Barrett rang for assistance. Simpkins appeared promptly, but he fell back a step when Ryde turned to address him.

"What the devil are you about?" Ryde demanded.

"My lord?" the butler squeaked.

"Why, when I sent you to summon Lady Catherine, did you not see fit to inform me that she was ill with fever?"

Simpkins ran his tongue nervously across his lips. "I didn't know it was anything serious, my lord."

"Lady Catherine has just collapsed at our feet. Do you consider *that* serious enough for mention?" Ryde was sorely tempted to throttle someone, perhaps himself.

"I had my orders, didn't I?" Simpkins murmured defensively.

"Orders? What orders?"

"Her ladyship said we weren't to let Lady Catherine make any sort of a fuss while she was gone."

"Lady Catherine is a grown woman. She does not need to be watched and monitored like a wayward child!"

"That's as may be, my lord, but it is not my place to question instructions."

Ryde realized he was wasting time. There was no time for recriminations. He had to see to the lady's care. "The countess must be informed. Have a man sent to Waverly with the news that Lady Catherine is ill. Then send the housekeeper to me." Simpkins bowed and scurried from the room.

"Barrett, would you mind riding to summon the doctor yourself? There is no one else in this house I dare trust with the task."

Barrett readily agreed to go and departed. The housekeeper arrived soon after, looking frightened. Ryde crossed to the sofa and lifted Lady Catherine into his arms. "Mrs. Perkins, you will be so good as to guide me to Lady Catherine's chamber." Her eyes widened at his request, but she did as she was told.

It was a large room, but Ryde could tell little about it in the dark, except that it was inexcusably chill. He stared at the pathetic little fire burning weakly in the grate and swore.

"Do you mean to freeze the girl to death?"

The housekeeper began to sputter some reply, but he cut her off. "Enough! Make yourself of some use." He crossed to the bed and gently set Lady Catherine down. "I want three buckets of coal sent up immediately, and I want that fire stoked up to resemble something worthy of the name. Lady Catherine's abigail is to be sent to us, as well as some glasses, a carafe of wine, a jug of water, and as many clean blankets as can be found. Well, don't just stand there!"

"But, my lord!" Mrs. Perkins gasped. "I can hardly leave you here alone in Lady Catherine's bedchamber!"

"You can, and you shall. There is no time for such scruples. I mean to see her cared for and cared for properly. Now go!"

Mrs. Perkins expression grew stubborn. "I will not, my lord. The countess will have my head if I do."

"And I will have it if you do not," he growled.

She held her ground. "It is not proper."

"It is entirely proper," he lied. "By the late earl's will I am made Lady Catherine's trustee. In such a situation as this, I stand in *loco parentis*. In other words, I stand in place of her father. Surely you would not question a father's right to remain with a sick daughter?" Mrs. Perkins cast him a wary look, then with a shrug turned and left the room.

"You would make an excellent lawyer, my lord," came a weak murmur from the bed. "You have the knack of making nonsense sound quite logical."

"Ah, you are recovered!" Ryde exclaimed in relief.

She lifted her head slightly to gaze about her. "I cannot recall how I come to be here. Was I not down in the parlor with you and Mr. Barrett?"

"Yes, but upon entering the room you swooned."

Her mouth formed into a ghost of a smile. "How very dramatic of me. Perhaps it was the shock of viewing my new father."

Ryde grimaced in chagrin. "An exaggeration perhaps, but I could think of no other way to be rid of the woman. Your stepmother is not back yet, and I dare not leave your care to these fools."

"I am sorry to be so much trouble to you."

"Nonsense! You have nothing to apologize for." He looked away, wishing he could say as much. "How do you feel?"

"Exceedingly hot, and my head feels as if it were hovering somewhere quite apart from the rest of me."

"You have a fever, I fear. The doctor has been sent for. He should be here soon."

"Am I so very ill then?"

"Ill enough," he said as lightly as he could. He still seemed to feel her burning in his arms.

"Am I going to die?"

"No, of course not," he assured her, his voice calm. Yet somewhere in his chest he felt a sudden stab of fear.

She nodded gratefully and closed her eyes.

He stood by her bed and kept watch and tried not to notice how increasingly ragged her breathing sounded.

An army of footmen trooped in and out bearing buckets of coal, trays of food and drink, and baskets full of blankets. Mrs. Perkins arrived hard upon their heels accompanied by a teary-eyed girl named Polly who, Ryde was informed, did for Lady Catherine between performing her duties as second chambermaid.

Suppressing his anger at learning the earl's daughter was not even accorded her own maid, he instructed Mrs. Perkins in clipped tones to assist Polly in preparing Lady Catherine for bed. "She is to be dressed in the warmest flannel, and a hot brick is to be placed at her feet. Polly, do you have any experience with nursing?"

She nodded. "I've five younger brothers and sisters, my lord, and I've seen most of 'em through one sickness or another."

"Excellent. You shall remain with Lady Catherine through the night. I will return once she is comfortably settled to await the doctor's arrival."

"And I, my lord?" Mrs. Perkins inquired archly.

"You, madam, after you have performed the role of abigail, may retire below stairs and prepare for your mistress's return. I have had a surfeit of your company for one day." Ryde turned on his heel and left the room.

Restless, and with little appetite for the cold collation that waited untouched in the dining room, Ryde wandered to the library, poured himself a brandy, and began to pace up and down the room. Curse it, where was Barrett with the doctor? He strode over to the windows, drew back the drapes, and then swore in consternation. Clouds muted the moonlight, but there was enough light to see the air filled with a million swirling shadows and a swollen landscape blanketed by snow.

After allowing what he hoped was sufficient time for Lady Catherine to be got decently to bed, Ryde returned to her chamber to find her propped up on a pillow, asleep. She looked reassuringly peaceful, and he was pleased to see the room much improved. A well-stoked fire now blazed on the hearth and numerous candles had been lit to provide illumination. Perhaps things weren't as grave as he had convinced himself. She did not look so very ill. In fact, with her hair down and flowing about her shoulders and that soft lace at her throat ...

Suddenly the maid, Polly, approached, and one look at her face revived all his fears. "How is she?" he demanded.

"Not good, my lord. I fear she grows hotter by the minute."

"Have you given her anything to drink?"

"She won't take aught, though I tell her that she must. I pray the doctor comes soon."

"I fear the doctor may not come at all. It is snowing quite heavily. We shall have to see her through this as best we can."

"But what are we to do?"

"Is there anyone below stairs who knows something of remedies?"

Polly shook her head regretfully. "Old Sally was the one doctored us all, but she was sent away with the others."

"Sent away?"

"When the countess arrived after the earl got so sick, she sent for her own people in town and sent most of the regular staff off to his lordship's house in Kent."

"I see. Is that what became of Lady Catherine's maid?"

"Oh, no. Lady Catherine took care of Jenny herself. Jenny was sweet on a footman that was being sent away, and Lady Catherine gave her money so she and her Jack could marry and start an inn."

Ryde raised an eyebrow. "I see why the earl thought your lady might need her purse watched."

"Mayhap, sir, but below stairs we thought it was right handsome of her."

"And the earl?"

"His lordship were too ill to care, but her ladyship was furious. Said as how the money what was thrown away had to be made up somehow. So she gave Miss Lowery—that were Lady Catherine's governess—notice."

"Was not Lady Catherine past needing a governess?" Ryde inquired. "Perhaps, that was the reason the woman was let go."

Polly shook her head. "Beg pardon, my lord. Miss Lowery used to be governess, but when my lady came back from London, Miss

Lowery stayed on as companion. Good thing, too, my lord. Only company Lady Catherine had most of the time. The earl and the countess preferred being in Town." Polly sighed. "Was Miss Lowery always cared for my lady when she was poorly."

"Well, unfortunately, Miss Lowery is not here now," Ryde said. "I am. And I am going to need your help, Polly, to decide what is best to be done. I have little experience in the sick room, but fortunately you do, so together perhaps we can manage to do what needs to be done. Now, how do you advise we begin?"

Hesitantly at first, then with more confidence when she saw he was truly looking to her for guidance, Polly expressed her opinion that as the room was now warm enough that there was no fear of Lady Catherine catching chill, it might be best to remove the warm brick and heavy bedclothes from her bed. "She's already much too hot, my lord," Polly explained. "What we must try to do is cool her." Any doubts Ryde might have had about this advice vanished when the maid took his hand and pressed it against Lady Catherine's cheek. The velvet skin felt as if it were on fire.

Polly removed the bedclothes, leaving only a single sheet as cover. "Perhaps you can get her to drink something, my lord," the maid suggested as she filled a basin with water.

Ryde agreed to try. He poured a little watered-down wine into a glass and carried it to her bedside. "Lady Catherine," he called softly, gently shaking her shoulder to rouse her. Her eyes opened and she gazed up at him in bewilderment. "I want you to try to drink a little of this."

"Why?" It was barely a whisper.

"It will cool you."

"Yes... so hot."

"Here, let me help you." He raised her head with one arm and lifted the glass to her lips with the other. She took a few weak sips and then signaled with her eyes that she'd had enough.

"You really should try to drink a little more."

"Too tired... perhaps later." Her eyes closed again. Ryde lowered her head back down onto the pillows, and then abruptly stood up, striding to the window and staring out at the snow. He was beginning to wish he had never come to Trenwich.

First the earl, then his daughter. He pressed a clenched hand inside the other, and watched Polly's reflection in the glass as she bathed Lady Catherine's face, neck, and hands with a damp cloth. Had he come all this way just to see this girl die, too?

As the evening wore on, Ryde and Polly fell into a pattern. He would try at intervals to coax a few more drops of watered-down wine between Lady Catherine's increasingly parched lips. Then Polly would wring out the cloth soaking in the basin and bathe her face and hands. In the interim, both would simply sit by her bed and wait. As the long hours stretched by, they tried to take comfort in the fact that the fever did not rise higher, but they watched in vain for any sign it was ready to break.

Ryde was staring out at the falling snow, when he heard the sound of weeping. He turned to see Polly sunk to her knees by the bed, her face in her hands. He crossed to touch her shoulder, and she lifted her head.

"Forgive me, my lord," she said in a trembling voice, "but heaven help us! His lordship but a day in his grave, and now she has gone and killed his poor daughter."

Ryde's grip unthinkingly tightened on the maid's shoulder. "*She?* What the devil are you talking about?"

"Her ladyship. If she hadn't punished my lady so harshly, she would never have taken ill with the fever like this."

"How precisely did the countess punish Lady Catherine?"

Suddenly the small maid looked afraid. "I didn't mean to speak out of turn, my lord."

"I want an answer, Polly."

"But Mrs. Perkins will be that angry if she learns I said aught to you."

"I am waiting," he snapped in a tone that made it clear he would brook no further argument.

Polly hesitated a moment, then said in a voice that was barely above a whisper, "Yesterday, when Lady Catherine returned from her ride ... her ladyship locked her in her room."

"I think you have mistaken the matter, Polly. It was Lady Catherine who locked the door, not the countess."

His words seemed to alter the little maid's demeanor. In a stronger voice she said, "Beg pardon, my lord, but 'tis you are mistaken. Lady Catherine was locked in with no fire nor anyone to help her from her wet things."

"How do you know this?"

"She sent me to look for a key. I tried to take one off Mrs. Perkins's ring, only she caught me at it. Fair took off me head, she did, and warned me to stay away from Lady Catherine's room, or I'd have to answer to her ladyship.

"I went back to tell Lady Catherine, and there was the key in the lock—on the *outside*, my lord." The maid shook her head. "The room was cold as ice and there she was, poor lady, curled up like a kitten 'neath the covers. No wonder she went and caught her death — " The maid broke off, a stricken look on her face.

Ryde, unable to trust himself to speak, glanced down at Lady Catherine's flushed face, and then with a muffled oath, turned on his heel and resumed his vigil by the window.

Shortly before midnight the snow stopped, and an hour later Ryde finished stoking the fire to find Polly bent sideways in her chair, asleep. Spreading one of the comforters out in a corner of the room, he carried the sleeping maid over to the makeshift bed and covered her with a blanket.

Several more hours passed. Ryde studied Lady Catherine intently, wondering why it mattered so much to him whether she lived or died. He rose stiffly from his chair and stared down at the woman on the bed. Deuced take it, she wasn't beautiful. Not like her disturbing stepmother with the china blue eyes or even Georgiana Waverly, with whom he had been flirting so pleasantly just that afternoon. So why was it that those flushed cheeks, that soft, curling hair, those long-fingered hands so tightly clenched suddenly seemed so important to him—even precious?

She made a small sound. Ryde bent close. "Lady Catherine?"

She said something, but he could not make it out. He bent closer, his ear so near her mouth he could feel the flutter of her breath. "C-c-cold," she whispered. "S-so c-cold."

Then she began to shake.

Ryde covered her with comforters, but they did not help, so he lifted her up in his arms and carried her close to the fire, holding her tightly against him in an attempt to stop the violent trembling he feared would sap the last of her strength.

At first, the shivering which racked her body seemed just as strong, but after a while it began to diminish and eventually it subsided altogether. She gave a little sigh and fell back to sleep, her head nestled against his chest.

Unfortunately, sleep was the farthest thing from Ryde's mind. With the crisis past, he found himself acutely conscious of Lady Catherine's generously curved body pressed closely against his own. He tried not to delineate the curves in his mind, but it was impossible.

There were her full round breasts. There the sweet curve of her hips. There the soft bottom pressing against him far too temptingly. He began to disengage himself from the overly intimate embrace, but as he drew away, she cried out weakly.

"No! Don't go. Please, don't leave me."

Startled, he complied, drawing her close again and pressing his lips against her hair. "Do not fret," he whispered, "I am here."

She made a small, contented sound and nestled more closely against him. Feeling strangely elated, Ryde held her for some time like that, until Polly's uneven snores reminded him that it would not do for the little maid to see them thus. He carried Lady Catherine back to bed, tucked the covers up around her, and—unable to resist—traced one finger along her sweetly shaped lips.

"Phillip?" she murmured sleepily.

Ryde swore under his breath. *Blast him! Who the devil was Phillip?* He crossed to the dwindling fire and began stabbing it with the poker.

❦

Polly woke briefly and observed the marquess dutifully tending the grate. She cast a sleepy glance toward the bed. Lady Catherine seemed to be resting more easily; perhaps the fever had broken? Polly debated getting up, but decided against it, certain his lordship would rouse her if she were needed. Better to get some rest for the coming day. She closed her eyes.

She woke again at dawn and rose to find Lord Ryde asleep in his chair, which was pulled much closer to Lady Catherine's bed than it had been the night before. Padding softly so as not to wake the two sleepers, Polly slipped from the room to fetch coal for the fire and hot water for the basin.

The soft click of the latch roused Ryde from a dream he could not remember but was loathe to give up. As he struggled to wake, he realized he was in a decidedly odd position for slumber. He straightened his neck and winced. Devil take it, what was he doing sleeping in a chair? He looked down, and found the answer lying on the bed before him.

"Lady Catherine?" he called softly.

Her reaction startled him. She cried out softly and began to toss and turn amongst the covers. Without thinking Ryde reached out for her, drawing her into his arms. "*Shhh!* You must be still and save your strength."

For a moment, she quieted. Then she began to twist and push against him. "No!" she cried, "she is leaving! I must stop her!"

"Stop whom? Catherine, wake up!"

She paid him no heed. He tightened his hold on her, drawing her against his chest as he had the night before, but this time she did not lie docile in his arms. "I must run or I will lose her!" she sobbed. "Don't go! Mama, please stop! *Mama!*"

Ryde clamped her to him as tightly as he could, fearing she would do herself an injury. "No, sweetheart! Don't struggle so! It is only a dream!"

She stopped flailing and twisting, and opened eyes bright with unshed tears. She gazed up at him in confusion, and suddenly something in that look and in the feel of her pressed so intimately against him drove away all reason. He wanted to kiss her. Needed to kiss her with a desire so strong it made his chest ache. He began to dip his mouth to meet hers, when suddenly a trickle of moisture slid down her face onto his hand. Dear God, was she weeping? The thought was like a slap. He thrust her away from him, back onto the bed, yet when he raised his eyes to meet hers, he saw not tears but bewilderment.

"I do not understand ... Lord Ryde? Am I awake, or is this but another dream?"

Ryde stared at her for a moment, trying to gather the wits to speak. "You were having a nightmare," he managed finally. "I feared you might do yourself some mischief. You have been ill, feverish — "

He broke off, suddenly aware of the cool dampness of his clothes where she had been so warmly pressed against him. His gaze flew from her hair, matted wet against her face, to the moisture trickling slowly down the hollow of her throat, to her nightdress, which clung damply to her breasts. He reached a not altogether steady hand out to touch her forehead. It was cool and wet.

"There seems little to worry about now, however," he said huskily, as he withdrew his hand and turned away, "for it appears your fever has broken.

Chapter 6

What a pity black suits Catherine so ill," remarked the countess to her friend, Mrs. Bennington, in a loud whisper easily overheard by the young lady in question, though she sat at the far end of the room with Jane.

Mrs. Bennington whispered back on cue, "Yes, it makes her look quite washed-out and drab, poor dear. I fear she is not blessed with your lovely coloring, Maria." She made a gurgling sound that was supposed to be laughter, and patted Ryde on the arm. "I declare, sir. Have you ever seen a woman look more enchanting in her widow's weeds?"

Chagrined to remember that just ten days ago he had been of much the same opinion, Ryde replied drily, "No, ma'am. The countess is amazingly in looks for a woman so recently bereaved."

Mrs. Bennington smiled and nodded at this compliment to her friend, but the countess shot Ryde a sidelong glance, and a small, frowning line appeared between her brows. Pleased his shot had found its mark, Ryde focused his attention on Catherine, who, to his frustration, sat too far away for him to address a word to.

He had not seen her since the morning he had been chased from her bedside by the simultaneous arrival of Barrett with the doctor and the countess with her brother and son and Ryde's own sister, Jane. Ryde had waited impatiently in the hall until the doctor had pronounced Catherine safely out of danger, then had given in to the demands of the countess for a private interview to discuss his scandalous behavior toward her stepdaughter.

He entered the meeting with trepidation, for he was not sure he could hide his seething anger at the lady's dangerous mistreatment of her stepdaughter. Fortunately, he found that years of coping with his late mother's starts had trained him well. He was able to keep his temper and even apologized for the irregularity of his presence in Catherine's bedchamber, pointing out that her maid had been present throughout the night.

Still, the lady's too-blue eyes remained narrowed, as she demanded to know whether Ryde planned to take advantage of the situation to force Catherine into marriage—a marriage he would find so materially advantageous. Ryde assured her that he had no such intention, and suggested her energies could be better spent ensuring that word of the episode did not pass beyond the castle walls. To his surprise, she agreed. More surprising still, she began to treat him with a cordiality she had not shown him since the reading of the earl's will.

In the days that followed, Ryde was fully restored to the countess's good graces, her manner to him becoming not just cordial but warm. Indeed, the lady's behavior turned so friendly, Ryde grew wary of her company. He was determined to remain at Trenwich until Catherine was recovered and so dared not insult his hostess by denying her the gallantry her coquettish smiles and flirtatious conversation demanded, but he could tell by his sister's increasingly frequent looks of disapproval that his politeness was being interpreted as something far less honorable.

"My dear Ryde, you seem quite lost in thought," said the countess, recalling him to his surroundings. "Whatever can you be thinking of?"

He met her gaze. "I am thinking of the future, ma'am. And of the changes it will bring."

His answer did not please her. She turned to her friend. "Ann, would you join Catherine and Lady Jane for a moment? There is a matter I would like to discuss privately with the marquess."

Mrs. Bennington cast a surprised glance at her friend but rose and went to join the two younger ladies. Lady Trenwich's face assumed an expression of brave melancholy. She said in a soft, throaty undertone, "I wish to thank you, Ryde, for the comfort of your presence these past two weeks. I fear the burden of grief might have been too much for me, had I not had your strong arm to lean upon." She laid a small white hand upon his sleeve. "You will perhaps think me a poor creature, but I find myself quite at a loss without a man — " she glanced at him from beneath her lashes, "— to guide me. I hope you will consider remaining a while longer here at Trenwich to lend me your assistance?" She leaned toward him, and he could feel her breast pressing lightly against his arm.

For a moment, he was tempted to speak his mind to her, to tell her what he truly thought of her and of her behavior, but this was neither the time nor the place for such a scene as would ensue, especially with Catherine and his sister present. Instead, he drew decently back and said lightly, "You flatter me, ma'am, but I fear I must soon return home. My estates have only recently been brought back to order, and they require constant watching. I hope before I leave, however, to remove at least one burden from your shoulders." He stood up. "Now, if you will excuse me, countess, I shall invite Lady Catherine to a turn in the garden. The fresh air will do her good."

The carriage came to a lurching halt before a grey-colored house as poorly tended as its drive. Barrett descended the step and surveyed the scene before him with a rueful shake of the head.

Ah, well, he thought, *I've come this far.*

He strode to the door and gave it a loud rap with the knocker. After an age, a young, slatternly-looking maid opened the door and stared at him in open-mouthed surprise.

"My name is Edward Barrett," he informed her. "I have come to call upon Miss Emily Lowery, who I understand is employed here in the position of governess."

The girl neither spoke nor stirred, but continued to stand gaping at him. He held out a card to her. "Please take that to your mistress and tell her I desire a few words with her."

"Mistress t'aint in."

"Is Miss Lowery in?"

"She be up in nursery."

"Well then, can you please tell her I am here and wish to speak with her?"

The girl shrugged. "Yer can tell her yerself, if y'like. Straight up stairs and to yer left." She wandered away leaving Barrett to stare after her.

With a sigh he stepped inside, drew the door closed behind him, and started up the dusty staircase. Halfway up, he tripped over a misplaced toy horn and had to clutch at the banister to avoid toppling backwards. *How did I ever let his impetuous lordship persuade me to this foolhardy venture?*

He reached the next floor without further incident and turned left down a dim and dingy corridor. Loud whoops and hollers emanating from a room up ahead seemed to confirm he was moving in the right direction. By the time he reached what he took to be the nursery, the level of noise had grown quite alarming, and he opened the door wondering what he would find.

Whatever he had expected, it was not the sight that greeted him as he moved quietly forward into the room. A sweet-faced woman with short, nut-brown hair was batting blindly at the air as she moved hesitantly forward in the direction of three young boys who taunted her with malicious delight.

Suddenly one of the boys pushed a large footstool into her path, causing her to trip. Barrett rushed forward to catch her, treading upon something brittle as he did so. The sound of breaking glass and the boys' triumphant laughter made it clear what he had stepped upon.

To his great surprise, the lady in his arms muttered something decidedly unladylike under her breath and made a lunge in the direction of the laughter. His mouth curving into an unfamiliar smile, Barrett reached out again to catch her before she toppled onto her face.

He guided her to the safety of a chair, and then turned on the three young hooligans with a scowl that cut the laughter in their throats and a harangue that sent them scuttling from the room. After they had gone, he bent down to pick up the crushed remains of the lady's spectacles. He stood up again to find her peering myopically in his direction with the largest, most beautiful brown eyes he had ever seen.

He approached her and said apologetically, "Forgive me, Miss Lowery. I fear I have smashed them beyond repair."

The large brown eyes suddenly filled with tears.

He knelt down by her chair. "Please, Miss Lowery, do not cry!" He pulled out a handkerchief and placed it in her hand. "I promise you, I will have another pair made up for you as quickly as can be managed."

"But sir," she protested, her lower lip trembling. "It is not your responsibility."

"How can you say that when it is my clumsiness that has left you so bereft?"

She shook her head. "No. I am to blame. If I had better control of my pupils — "

"What, those toads! How can such an angelic lady be expected to deal with three such little devils?"

A flush of color washed her cheeks. "A telling question, sir, but there is a more pressing one I would wish settled first. Though it pains me to admit it, without my spectacles I cannot tell if we are known to each other or not. You have called me by name, but your voice is not familiar. Therefore I must ask a rude question: *who are you?*"

For a moment Barrett stared at her in surprise. Then feeling as if a fuse had suddenly been lit within him, he did something he had not done for a long time: he began to laugh. Perhaps because it had been so long, or perhaps because he was feeling strangely giddy, once begun, he could not stop, and he laughed until the tears squeezed from his eyes. When finally he quieted enough to look about, he cast a wary glance at his companion, fearful he had offended her beyond pardon by his strange outburst.

Her expression was indeed grave. He waited apprehensively for her to speak. She held out his handkerchief to him. "Here, sir. I return this to you. I think you have greater need of it than I."

Was it just his imagination, or were the corners of her mouth tipping toward a smile? "Forgive me, Miss Lowery. I do not quite know what came over me."

She shook her head. "There you go again, taunting me with my name," she chided softly. "It really is quite unfair of you since you insist on remaining anonymous."

Barrett sprang to his feet. "Then allow me to introduce myself to you, my dear Miss Lowery. I am Edward Barrett, at your service." He captured her outstretched hand and brought it to his lips.

Suddenly she became charmingly flustered. In a subdued voice, she asked him what business he had with her. Recalled to his mission, Barrett explained his connection to the Trenwich household and recounted the earl's death, Lady Catherine's illness, and—somewhat reluctantly—Lord Ryde's request that she return to Trenwich to serve as companion to her former pupil.

Her expressive face, over which a series of emotions had passed ranging from sorrow to indignation, now lit up brightly. "Of course! I will go to her at once."

"But Miss Lowery, consider!" exclaimed Barrett, startled by her hasty decision. "You will lose your position here, and I have no great confidence that your place at Trenwich will be a secure one."

"You are not arguing his lordship's case very well, Mr. Barrett."

"To be honest, at this moment, I could wish his lordship to the devil. He has no right to play about with your future this way. I confess I had misgivings before, but now that I have met you ... " He foundered helplessly to a stop.

She tipped her face up at him and smiled mischievously at his right earlobe. "I see. Now that you have met me you have decided that the toads and I deserve one another. And here I thought you were Lochinvar come to rescue me from my hideous fate."

He gazed at her with a mixture of pleasure and consternation. Then giving a small shrug of resignation, he swept her a deep bow. "My white horse is saddled and ready, my lady. When do we leave?"

An adorable dimple appeared at the corner of her mouth. "As soon as I can pack my trunk." She paused, and then added apologetically, "Though that may take considerable time without my spectacles."

He sighed. "Exit Lochinvar; enter Abigail. Very well. If you can manage to show me to your room, I will pack the thing for you."

Catherine fought a cowardly impulse to stare down at her hands and instead reluctantly looked up to meet Lord Ryde's searching glance. His expression was friendly and even full of concern, but what did it matter? She had not missed any of the nuances of his *tête-à-tête* with her stepmother. Even without Mrs. Bennington's coy comments, or Jane's disapproving looks, it was clear that Lord Ryde, like many a man before him, had succumbed to the countess's beauty. Catherine bit her lip, wishing desperately she were somewhere else, anywhere else, but sitting helpless beneath this gentleman's gaze.

"Lady Catherine," he said in that low, strong voice that seemed to resonate somewhere deep inside her, "it is unseasonably warm out and the day is quite lovely. May I persuade you to join me for a turn in the garden? I think you will find the fresh air quite restoring."

She could think of no way to decline his invitation without giving insult, so she went upstairs to don pelisse and muff and allowed herself to be led outdoors on Lord Ryde's arm.

The feel of the crisp air against her cheeks and the fresh, sweet smell of the dormant garden briefly distracted her from the tingling heat that ran from his arm into hers, and thence up into her chest. Drat the man! How could his mere touch wreak such havoc upon her? She drew a deep and somewhat unsteady breath. "Do you plan to remain much longer at Trenwich, my lord?"

She thought she saw him frown. "Not much longer, I think. Why? Are you so eager to be rid of me?"

"Really, sir, even if I were, I would hardly be rude enough to tell you so. No, I only wondered, because your sister told me that you were preparing to go to London when my father's summons arrived. I thought you perhaps wished to resume your interrupted plans."

She felt his hold on her arm suddenly tighten. "And I suppose when I have gone you will forget me completely?"

Catherine wished it were true. She tried not to think how bleak everything would become once he departed. But, she reminded herself, it would be no less painful if he stayed. He already appeared smitten with her stepmother, newly-widowed and clad in her black. How could she bear to stand by and see the countess win him completely, as she must given time?

For Catherine could not hope to compete with her. Her stepmother could charm the very birds from the trees. Heaven knew she had charmed every beau Catherine had managed to come by during her Season. Even Phillip. *Especially Phillip.* Catherine pushed the memory away, and suddenly realized that Lord Ryde had spoken and was awaiting an answer.

"I see I need not even leave," he snapped. "I am forgotten already."

"I beg your pardon, sir. I fear my thoughts wandered."

His expression changed. "Are you quite certain you have recovered from your illness? You look quite pale."

"I feel well all the same. Thank you." She wished to say more, to thank him for his care of her that first feverish night, but could not find the words. They walked on in silence.

"Are you much attached to this place?" he finally asked.

"Do you mean Trenwich?"

"Yes. Are you attached to your home here? Would it pain you to leave it?"

"I do not know. I have spent most of my life here. It is difficult to imagine living anywhere else."

"But surely you must have considered the possibility at one time or another?" he insisted. "For instance, when you marry you shall leave here. Do you think upon such a prospect with pleasure? Would you enjoy having a household of your own?"

A sudden startled hope took root inside her. "I suppose I would," she admitted.

He nodded, pleased, and flashed her a smile that caused her heart to pound. They walked on and soon came to a turn in the walk where a small bench stood sheltered beneath a yew tree. Lord Ryde motioned for Catherine to sit down, but, to her surprise, he remained standing and began to pace back and forth.

Catherine could not help thinking that he was acting precisely like the tongue-tied hero of the novel Jane had been reading to her during her long days of convalescence. That poor fellow had been struck almost dumb when he had attempted to propose to his pretty heroine. Somehow Catherine found it difficult to imagine Lord Ryde ever at a similar loss for words, but the possibility of a parallel left her feeling breathless.

"Lady Catherine."

She looked up, glad that the suspense was now to be ended, but one look at Lord Ryde's solemn expression sent her soaring hopes tumbling. This, surely, was not the face of a man preparing to propose marriage.

"Lady Catherine, you are aware that ownership of Trenwich and all its properties has now passed to your brother?"

Puzzled, she nodded.

"What you may not know, since, due to your illness, Mr. Barrett has had no opportunity to inform you of it, is that your father left half of his very considerable personal fortune to you, to be held in trust until you reach the age of thirty or until you marry someone of whom your trustee approves. If you marry without his approval, your inheritance reverts to your brother, the new earl."

So it was true. She *was* an heiress. It was difficult to comprehend. She pressed her hands against her cheeks and tried to take it in, but something in Lord Ryde's final words distracted her. A trustee? No one had told her of this. "And who is this trustee who is to have such a say over my life?" she demanded.

A faint flush tinged his cheeks. "I am."

Her breath caught. "You?"

"Yes. And as your trustee, and as a devoted friend of your father's, I feel it incumbent upon me to see that you are well-situated in your changed circumstances. You are an independent woman now, and need not remain in your stepmother's company. It is clear you and the countess do not rub along well together. I think it would be best if you remove from Trenwich and establish a household of your own.

"Mr. Barrett informs me that you own a property in Devon bequeathed to you by your mother. Rosington, it is called. I have made inquiries. The house, though in need of refurbishment, appears to be in good order, and the lands seem adequate to maintain you comfortably, if not in luxury. Of course, with your inheritance you can live in as lavish a manner as you choose, but at least if you marry against my wishes, you will not have to choose between your stepmother's company and penury."

He obviously meant it as a joke, and flashed her a smile to show it was such, but Catherine did not find it at all humorous. Noting her reaction, his own smile faded away, and he continued stiffly, "You will of course need a suitable chaperone to reside there with you, and to that end I have taken the liberty of sending for your former governess, Miss Lowery, to serve as your companion." He paused, waiting for her to respond.

She stared up at him, too agitated to speak.

"Well, Lady Catherine? What have you to say?"

She surged to her feet. "Say?" she exclaimed angrily. "What is there for me to say, sir? You inform me that I am an independent woman, then you proceed to rearrange my life to your own design without so much as a by your leave!"

Clearly taken aback by her reaction, Lord Ryde exclaimed tight-lipped, "What I have done, I have done for the best!"

"Whose best, I wonder, yours or mine? Once I am gone and my brother is returned to school, no doubt you will find it easier to climb into my father's bed?"

She regretted the egregious words immediately. A single glance at Lord Ryde's stunned, white face had drained away all her anger, leaving her feeling limp and miserable. How could she have said anything so dreadful? *And so untrue.* For she knew, deep in her heart, that he was an honorable man. Whatever his feelings for her stepmother, he would do nothing to dishonor her father's memory. If he did come to love the countess, he would wait for her year of mourning to be over and then marry her properly. She sank back down into her seat. "Please, forgive me, sir! I should never have spoken to you so."

Ryde stared down at Catherine's pale face and resisted the urge to seize her by the shoulders and shake her. Devil take the girl! What harm had he ever done her that she should regard him with such contempt? "If you were a man, I would call you out for speaking to me so."

She met his gaze squarely. "I am sorry I cannot offer you that satisfaction, sir. I know it is impossible for you to forgive my words, but I pray you will do your best to forget them. I only spoke so because I was overset — " She broke off and her gaze fled his face and fixed on the buttons of his coat. "I mistook your purpose in this interview, you see, and then there was the shock of learning I am to leave Trenwich."

"Mistook my purpose?"

Her cheeks flamed crimson. "I thought ... or rather, it seemed to me ... after all, you acted as if ... " She paused and took a deep breath. "The truth is, I thought you were about to propose."

The silence stretched between them for an eternity. "I assure you," he finally exclaimed, trying to convey his chagrin at having inadvertently misled her, "that was the very *last* thing I intended!" Only after the words were out did he realize how insulting they sounded.

Her mouth crumpled.

He suddenly wished he had succumbed to the strong impulse he had felt that feverish morning in her bedchamber. For if he had compromised her then, he would be honor bound now to ignore his scruples and his promise to the earl and ask her to marry him, and she would not be sitting there regarding him with such a look of hurt in her eyes. "Lady Catherine, please, I did not mean — "

"Of course you did not! You have made that plain enough. But what was I to think with all your allusions to marriage and leaving home and setting up households?"

"Forgive me. I should have realized my words were subject to another interpretation. It simply never occurred to me that you would mistake my purpose in such a way."

Her expression grew stormy. "Sir, I am not stupid. I know that in and of myself I am no matrimonial prize. But half my father's fortune may prove a considerable attraction to some men, I think."

He felt his own face heat. "First a seducer, now a fortune-hunter! I am flattered to learn what a high opinion you hold of my character, Lady Catherine!"

"Not of your character personally, sir. Only that of your sex." She stood and turned away, refusing to meet his eyes. "Now, if you will excuse me, my lord? I feel rather tired." Without waiting for a reply, she picked up her skirts and started for the house.

Ryde watched her go—too proud to call after her, though he felt a sharp sense of loss at her withdrawal. In no mood for the company of the others, he continued along the walk, from time to time picking up an innocent bit of gravel and hurling it at the shrubbery.

Suddenly he spied something glittering in the weak November sunshine. He pushed his gloved hand into a small hedge, withdrawing a large oval of gold from which sagged a twisted chain. A locket. How in the world had it come to land here, of all places?

Its outside was dented, as if at some time it had suffered the indignity of a footstep upon it. He removed a glove and slipped the latch. One of the small hinges was bent, but he managed to open it without too much difficulty. Inside was a miniature painting. The glass covering it was badly smashed, but he still recognized the face immediately. *Catherine.* The likeness was not perfect. The eyes were too placid a blue, the nose too small and pert, the lips too thin, and the hair—the artist had failed completely to capture the beautiful auburn glow of her hair, but it was Catherine, without a doubt. Ryde gazed up. It looked as if someone had chucked the thing from one of the upper windows. But how had it come to be discarded so cavalierly? And to whom did it belong in the first place?

No doubt some poor unfortunate you drove to fury with a single thrust of that determined chin of yours, he thought irritably. Yet despite his vexation, Ryde gazed down at the damaged glass a long time before gently snapping the locket shut, slipping it into his waistcoat pocket, and striding back toward the house.

Chapter 7

Lady Trenwich, her eyes narrowed in anger, gazed down from the window of her boudoir at the courtyard below. So, they were going. She hunted among the confusion of carriages, horses, and people for a single figure. At last she made him out, standing with his tall back to her by the new coach that had been purchased with money from her son's stolen inheritance. He was speaking with the lawyer Barrett. No doubt the two were plotting how best to steal the other half of her son's rightful fortune.

Suddenly Ryde turned in her direction. She gazed down at him and pressed one clenched hand against her stomach. He had made a fool of her, and she hated him for it, yet she could not look upon him without feeling a strong surge of desire that made her ache. She thought grimly back upon his pretty speeches and coaxing ways. To think that she, who had ruled so many hearts, had given her own away so easily. Why had she not seen that he was only using her to win the golden prize of her stepdaughter's hand?

He had duped her into accepting Catherine's removal to Rosington without protest, not bothering to inform her until a few days before their departure that his property of Farthingsgate actually bordered Rosington and that he and Catherine would now be neighbors. Still, she had not challenged him to his face until he had informed her of his plans to journey with Catherine into Devon. Then she had accused him of complicity, but he had affected innocence, protesting that it was his sister's notion, not his, to invite Catherine to Farthingsgate for a few weeks while Rosington was got in order.

She had been so besotted, she had believed him, and had even combined her forgiveness with an invitation to her bed. He had replied with a curt and disdainful refusal. Her face burned with the memory of his expression as he had slipped from her arms. She would make him pay for that look!

Her eyes refocused on the scene outside and she saw Ryde help Catherine into the new carriage. No doubt he thought he had his intended bride, and with her half the Trenwich fortune, clearly in his sights. The countess lifted the hand that had been clenched against her stomach and pressed it, fingers spread, against the cold pane of the window. Well, he would be well advised not to count his chickens too soon.

Her stepdaughter would be in mourning for six months.

And a great deal could happen in six months to disrupt even the smoothest ride to the altar.

❧

Smooth would hardly have been the word Catherine would have chosen to describe the deeply-rutted road they were traversing on this, the last leg of their journey to Devon and Lord Ryde's estate of Farthingsgate. The well-oiled springs of the new coach reduced the jouncing somewhat, but did not eliminate it. Catherine, who had insisted on taking her fair turn sitting with her back to the horses, was consequently feeling a bit the worse for wear.

She wondered if Lord Ryde, who sat next to her, was similarly afflicted. She stole a sideways glance at him, curious to catch his profile in repose. Since that unfortunate interview when she had accused him of having designs on her stepmother, he had treated her with distant courtesy, his reserve so pronounced it was as if he wore a mask of ice. Now, however, she was surprised to discover signs of tension around his mouth and a marked frown on his face as he gazed blindly at the space between Miss Lowery and his sister, Jane.

"Is something troubling you, sir?" she inquired softly.

For a moment, he seemed not to hear. Then he turned to regard her, his distracted expression that of a man who has uprooted his thoughts from some distant place. "I beg pardon, Lady Catherine. I was not attending. Did you ask something of me?"

Before she could reply, a sudden jolt of the carriage as it hit a deep hole in the road sent her spilling against his chest. For a moment, his arms enfolded her, and without thinking she pressed her face into the fine wool of his coat. Then she came to her senses and realized he was merely reaching out to help her right herself. Mortified, she pulled back, and he released her. She retreated to her corner, praying the afternoon's shadows would hide her flaming cheeks.

"You are unhurt?" he asked.

She assured him that she was, and to her relief he turned his attention to Jane and Emily, ascertaining that they, too, were unharmed. Emily made some comment about the road, and Jane took up the theme, and Catherine began to relax back against the soft leather squabs, confident Lord Ryde's attention was fixed elsewhere.

Yet when she cast a fugitive glance his way, she was disconcerted to find him gazing steadily back at her. "I fear this journey has become but another debit in my account with you," he remarked quietly. "I am sorry it has been so uncomfortable."

"Do you really think me so unjust as to hold you responsible for the state of the public roads?"

"Ah, but I am responsible for your being forced to traverse them and therefore for your resultant discomfort."

Their gazes met and locked. "Truly, I am not such an ungrateful wretch as that," she murmured. "Traveling in this carriage is like floating on air compared to what I am accustomed to." His eyebrows rose skeptically. "I am used to traveling, you see, on those rare occasions when I have had reason to travel, in an ancient laundau belonging to a great aunt of mine. The creaking used to drive me mad."

"Of the coach or of your aunt?"

She chuckled. "If you must know the truth, sir, both. Aunt Beryl possessed very creaky corsets."

Lord Ryde smiled for a moment, and then his expression grew solemn. "You seem determined to go easy with me."

She gazed at her gloved hands. "It only seems so, because I was too hard before, unfairly hard, I must own."

"Can it be that you have become reconciled to the notion of establishing your own household at Rosington?"

She looked up and met his gaze squarely. He deserved the truth. "More than reconciled. Since we departed Trenwich three days ago, I have felt a growing exhilaration at the prospect."

"It is generous of you to admit it."

"Not generous—just. I am greatly in your debt, you see, and not only for the change in my direction. I am gratified to have Miss Lowery restored to me as well." She cast a glance at Emily, who was deep in conversation with Jane.

He said drily, "I think Mr. Barrett may deserve more of the credit for that than I do." At the mention of the gentleman's name, Emily's head turned in their direction, and Jane, seeming to sense that she had lost the lady's attention, inquired of her brother if he had any notion how much further they had to go. The relaxed planes of his face suddenly tensed, and his frown returned. He glanced out the window. "The scenery is as unfamiliar to me as it is to you, Jane. I do not have the foggiest notion."

Curious, Catherine inquired, "Has the landscape changed so much since your last visit, sir?"

"Since my last visit to Farthingsgate occurred some fourteen years ago, I cannot recall whether it has or not."

Catherine stared at him in dismay. "*Fourteen years?* And you, Jane?"

"She's not set foot in the place since then, either."

"I will thank you to let me answer for myself, Drew," Jane replied, throwing a wary look in Catherine's direction. "Now my dear, please. Do not go flying up into the boughs."

"But look at all the trouble I have put you to!" Catherine exclaimed. "Opening up a house that has not been opened in years. Traveling all this way in the middle of winter. Burying yourself in the country when I am sure you would much rather be in Town. I knew it unlikely, but I had hoped that you had your own reasons for journeying to Devon, reasons that had nothing to do with me."

"But we do! Drew has seen to all his other properties, sorting things out, restoring them to order. A similar visit to Farthingsgate is long overdue. As for me, well, I am not quite ready to return to my house in London yet. Perhaps while you and Miss Lowery busy yourselves at Rosington, I shall try restoring the luster to our old home. It used to be quite lovely once, though perhaps I am recalling it through the rosy glow of childhood."

Catherine heard the wistful note in her friend's voice. "I am sure it is every bit as pretty as you remember it."

"Well, we shall see. In any case, I hope I have convinced you that Drew and I repair to Devon for purely selfish reasons."

Catherine noted the tight lines around Lord Ryde's mouth. "I fear that all you have convinced me of is that your kindness to me may provide you with some small benefit as well."

After an uneasy silence, Emily interjected softly, "Do you share your sister's fond memories of your childhood home, my lord?"

He turned to stare out the window of the coach. Catherine could not see his face, but she was startled by his bitter tone, "I wonder, ma'am. Did Adam have fond memories of Eden after he had been cast out from it?"

Emily seemed unsure as to how to reply to such a statement, so Catherine said quickly, "Sir, I hope you do not expect us to partake in a theological discussion while being jostled along such a road. Speaking for myself, my head feels so rattled I doubt I have wits enough left for a discussion of the weather."

He turned to look at her, and slowly the tense bitterness seeped from his face. For a moment they exchanged a glance that was as intimate as a touch. Then Jane said something to fill the silence, and Catherine reluctantly shifted her attention to answer her, and by the time she glanced back at Lord Ryde he was once more gazing grimly out the window.

❦

Ryde looked down at Farthingsgate's small housekeeper, Mrs. Jenner, as she reluctantly shook her head. "I fear I cannot, my lord. The room is locked and I have no key."

"Am I to understand," he exclaimed in disbelief, "that the key to the best guest chamber has been misplaced?"

The housekeeper drew herself up to her full height and said, "Not misplaced, my lord. The master kept that key himself. No one was allowed in the room, excepting the one girl he had in to clean, and she's been gone nearly five years."

"Well, and where is the key now?"

"I do not know, my lord. The master took it with him to town, and after his lordship died we heard naught of it, nor the room."

"Are you telling me the chamber has not been cleaned or aired since then?"

"We had no way to get in, my lord, and no instructions neither. When we received word the house was to be closed, well, we thought it best to leave well enough alone." Her voice dropped to a whisper, "There's something queer about that room, my lord."

"Nonsense!"

Her chin came up. "You may say so, my lord, but in nearly ten years service I never knew a single soul to sleep there, yet many have passed late at night and told of seeing a light within."

"Enough of this superstitious twaddle," he snapped. "I have tired guests who need rooms. I presume you have keys for the other bedchambers and that they are in some sort of order?" Mrs. Jenner gave a quick, tight nod. "Good. Then have Lady Catherine's things taken to the Red Room and her companion's to the Oak, and see to it that Lady Jane's luggage is carried to the master suite."

"And you, my lord? Will you be staying in his lordship's chambers?"

"No. Have my things placed in the Green Room."

"But your lordship! That room is far too small for the master of the house!"

Ryde shot her a quelling look.

Her mouth tightened into a small, disapproving line, but her head bobbed in a quick gesture of deference, and she soon bustled off to do as she was told.

༨ৎ

Emily Lowery was just preparing to retire to bed when she heard a knock at her door. Slipping on a wrap and her precious new spectacles, she went to answer it.

"Tsk, tsk," scolded her visitor in a teasing voice. "Opening your door without asking who is there? I could have been a lowly ruffian wishing to have my way with you."

"Hardly," Emily replied with a chuckle. "After all these years, I am quite capable of recognizing your knock when I hear it. Not to mention the way you pad along when you think you are being quiet. I have never met anyone with such a knack for treading on *all* the creaky boards."

Catherine grinned. "So much for my hopes of becoming a lady burglar."

"I would leave off attempting any elopements as well. You would have half the household following you down the stair."

Catherine's face sobered. "You need have no cares on that score. I am hardly the type of woman to inspire such desperate passions."

Struck by the wistfulness in her tone, Emily surveyed her critically. "I am not so certain. My brother was quite a man for the ladies, and he always insisted it was not the fashion plates that drove men to extremes."

Catherine's eyes widened in surprise.

"Have I shocked you?"

"You have a bit. I always thought you well ... innocent of such things."

"It was difficult to remain innocent of such things with my brother Roger about," Emily said drily. "But you are right. It is not a fit subject to be discussing so late at night."

Catherine laughed. "No, indeed, let us save it at least until breakfast."

"You have yet to tell me what you are doing up so late," Emily reminded her gently. "The old nightmare?"

"No. I was simply feeling a bit restless and could not sleep. I thought perhaps I would find you still awake."

"And so you did," Emily crossed to her traveling case and pulled out a well-worn deck of cards. "Since we are both awake and both in need of occupation, would you care to join me in a game of piquet?"

Catherine flashed her a grateful smile. "Oh, Emily, it *is* good to have you back."

Jane was also finding sleep elusive. She stared up into the darkness and tried to push memories of the house out of her thoughts. After all, it was all so long ago. It had been a happy house once, or, at least, it had seemed so to children who rarely saw their parents together. True, their mother spent most of her time in Town, and their father went for long, solitary rides and spent most evenings cloistered in his study. But for Jane, Andrew, and their three sisters, Farthingsgate had been an enchanted place full of joy and laughter. Then suddenly, in a single day, their paradise had been lost.

Jane closed her eyes, and as she did so the years slipped away. She was once again a frightened girl hiding behind the curtains in her father's bedchamber. Trapped. And forced to listen to truths she was never meant to hear.

Her father had taken a fall from his horse. He had been carried unconscious to the house and the doctor had predicted he would die. Terrified she might never see him again, Jane had slipped into her father's chamber and found him lying on the bed, his eyes closed, his face whiter than the sheets. Before she could think what to do, Jane had heard her mother's voice in the hall. Afraid of being caught in a trespass that seemed impossible to explain, Jane had slipped behind the draperies to hide.

Which is how she came to hear her mother's confession to a husband she thought already dead. But her father was alive and awake and heard every word, and in a weak, pain-wracked voice he had ordered his wife out of his house and out of his life. Thinking it would cause him to relent, her mother had threatened to take the children with her, but her father had said she was welcome to them, for they were born of a union he could only curse.

Jane turned over and pressed her face into the cool softness of her pillow. Andrew had never known, nor had her sisters, the reason for their sudden banishment from Farthingsgate, but she, nine years old and the apple of her father's eye, had been dragged into exile all too painfully aware of the truth.

⁂

Downstairs in the study, Ryde gazed moodily into the fire. The house was filled with a plague of memories. Everything around him was a reminder. Even the leather chair in which he sat served to recall the father he thought he had finally managed to forget. Not the rake and profligate, but the man who had taught him to ride and hunt, the parent with whom he had played chess and talked of books, the father he had loved and respected and believed could do no wrong.

Ryde sprang to his feet and began pacing up and down. How in heaven's name had he allowed Jane to persuade him to this folly? Why, at the moment when his life was finally put back in order, had he returned to this house, site of its first and greatest upheaval?

An unwelcome answer whispered in his mind. *You were not yet ready to be parted from Lady Catherine Denton, and this was the only way you could think of to remain near her.*

He paced faster. It was nonsense, of course. Beyond feeling a certain responsibility to see the girl comfortably settled in her new home, there were no ties binding him to her except those he had promised her father: to watch over her money and find her a husband when her six months of mourning were done.

Later that night, however, as Ryde tossed restlessly in his bed, he remembered his reaction in the carriage when she had been thrown so helplessly against him. For one long, warm moment he had not wanted to let her go. Which made him wonder. When the time came to turn her over to the care of the husband he had given his word to find her, what was it going to be like to see her step into another man's arms—forever?

Chapter 8

It is shaping up well, is it not?" Catherine said, as Jane gazed around in approval at Rosington's refurbished drawing room.

"Yes, I would hardly have recognized it," Jane affirmed. "That new green wallpaper is lovely and will look all the crack with the gold drapes you have ordered."

"I am glad you think so. Emily assured me it looks fine, but I feared she might simply be humoring me to encourage me to move on. There are so many decisions yet to be made, so much work yet to be done, you see."

"Yes, I do," replied Jane, glancing back toward the dilapidated hallway visible through the open doors.

Catherine tensed defensively. "It is a lovely house, Jane, truly! It simply requires work."

"A great deal of work," Jane said, flashing Catherine a smile that removed the sting from the words. "But it is going to be a jewel when you are finished with it. Indeed, you have already worked quite a miracle this past fortnight."

"I wanted you to see how far it has come along."

"Yes, though I am glad to know we will have your company at Farthingsgate for some time yet," Jane continued, oblivious to the direction Catherine had hoped to point the discussion, "Ryde and I would find it very dull at Farthingsgate without you and Miss Lowery."

Catherine was silent. While she believed Jane would miss them, she suspected Jane's brother would feel nothing upon their departure but deep relief. It was the reason she had wanted to show Jane how well the house was coming along in the first place.

"Speaking of miracles," Jane said. "Miss Lowery tells me you are making good progress airing out the bedchambers."

Catherine nodded. "And we have made plans for how they are to be refurbished. Would you care to come and give your opinion?"

"Of course," Jane replied. As they made their way upstairs, she added, "By the way, before I forget, a letter has arrived for Miss Lowery from London."

"For Emily? But who can it be from?"

"That is not difficult to deduce. After all, how many beaux does Miss Lowery have in London?"

Catherine gazed at her in bewilderment.

"It is from Mr. Barrett, of course!" Jane said with a grin.

"Mr. Barrett is hardly Emily's beau."

"Oh, no? Then why is he writing her letters?"

"I am sure he is merely being polite. Emily wrote to thank him for the new spectacles he procured for her before we left Trenwich. He is probably only replying to her note."

Jane remained unconvinced. "And why did he go to such lengths to obtain those spectacles for her so quickly, and all the way from London, no less?"

"He felt responsible for the loss of her previous pair."

Jane made a harrumphing sound. "Really, Catherine. Did you not notice the proprietary gleam in his eye when he delivered Miss Lowery up to the coach as we were leaving?" Catherine shook her head. She was not about to admit that she had been watching only one person that day. Jane continued, "And what of Miss Lowery? The mere mention of Mr. Barrett's name is enough to put a smile on her lips and to distract her completely from all common conversation."

"But they hardly know each other!"

"Long acquaintance is hardly a prerequisite to affection. Sometimes love bursts into one's life like a thunderbolt—without warning."

Something tightened painfully in Catherine's chest as she thought of a tall, brown-eyed thunderbolt who seemed, of late, to scowl every time she drew near. Feeling a surge of determination, she reached out and opened a door. "Here is the first bedchamber, Jane," she said, leading her friend into the dimly lit room. "Which reminds me of a matter I very much wish to discuss with you."

❧

Fighting down a sudden, irrational reluctance, Ryde fitted the key into the lock and twisted it hard until the creaky bolt slid free. Drawing a sharp breath, he turned the knob, pushed the door open, and entered the dim and dusty chamber.

The curtains were drawn tight. He made his way haltingly across the darkened room and snatched them open. A stream of mote-choked light poured in through clouded windows to reveal an unexceptional chamber, distinctive only in the staleness of its air and the thickness of its five-year accumulation of dust.

He reached down and tore cobwebs from his sleeves. Well, and what had he expected to find! A room haunted by ghosts? A cache of hidden treasure? The moldering bones of some long-dead corpse? He frowned ruefully. None of those really, despite Mrs. Jenner's dramatic pronouncements. No, what he had hoped to find was much more prosaic and infinitely more important to him: a clue as to the reason for his banishment from Farthingsgate all those years ago.

He looked about him with a sigh. Not that he'd had any real reason to believe he would find the answer here, except for the mystery that seemed to linger about the room, a mystery that seemed strangely to coincide with that banishment. Why had the room remained unoccupied for fourteen years, and why had his father been so assiduous in keeping it locked?

Ryde had written to his Aunt Celia asking for the key, and she had replied promptly with a small package containing both the key and a note expressing her pleasure that Farthingsgate was finally to be opened up again.

His disappointed gaze swept the room. There seemed little enlightenment to be found here, only an oppressive melancholy that made him eager to quit the place. He eyed the rumpled, unmade bed and the old, uncollected ashes in the grate. A candlestick stood on the table, the candle burned down to a nub. Next to it sat a dusty volume lying open as if its reader had set it down but for a moment intending to return. Ryde's throat tightened painfully at the thought. Then resolutely his gaze swept on, past an empty decanter and glass, to the mantel where a bouquet of long-dead roses drooped from a dust-coated crystal vase. His eyes rose briefly to the dimly visible portrait hanging above the desiccated roses, and his breath caught—then exploded in an oath.

He crossed the room for a better view, but there was no mistake. Dusty and cobwebbed though the painting was, it was obviously the original upon which the portrait in the smashed locket had been based. Ryde's jaw clenched. Upon learning the countess's true character, he had dismissed her stories about the relationship between Catherine and his father as simply vicious tattle. But now? With her portrait hanging in the best guest room at Farthingsgate?

He stared up at the painting, feeling his anger flare. So this was the reason his father had kept the room locked. Yet why hang the damn thing in plain sight, and then go to such pains to keep its presence a secret?

An answer sprang to mind that blunted his fury. His father hadn't seduced Catherine; he had been in love with her. So in love, he had spent his nights gazing at her portrait and his days keeping the fact a secret for the sake of her reputation. This romantic notion, though considerably at odds with the character he normally ascribed to his father, was infinitely more palatable to Ryde than the lurid possibilities that had burned his thoughts moments earlier, and he embraced it with great enthusiasm.

Which is perhaps why he wore such an expression of gentle melancholy as he dragged a dust-coated footstool over to the mantel, climbed up onto it, and carefully lifted the picture off the wall. Or why, as he draped a dingy velvet curtain over the painting and carried it off to the safety of the attics, he failed to notice the year jotted in tiny script below the artist's signature: 1786.

Two years before Catherine had even been born.

✢

Early the next morning Ryde strode into the breakfast parlor at Farthingsgate and found, to his surprise, that it was already occupied. His sister greeted him from the far end of the table, "Good morning, Andrew."

"Good morning, Jane." His gaze shifted from his sister to her companion. "Good morning, Lady Catherine. I trust you slept well?"

"Quite well, thank you," she replied politely, but the dark smudges beneath her thickly-lashed eyes belied her words. Ryde fought down a sudden urge to kiss the smudges away, and crossed instead to the sideboard to help himself to some breakfast.

He stabbed a slice of fried ham and shook it onto his plate. "Is it not rather early for you ladies to be up and about?"

"It is a bit," said Jane, "but we wished to speak with you, and as you are usually gone from the house by the time we rise and have lately not been returning even for dinner, I thought this perhaps our only opportunity to do so."

"I have had a great deal to keep me busy," he replied stiffly.

"Of course," Catherine agreed quickly. "That is precisely what I have been telling your sister. You have been burdened with guests for too long. Now that Rosington has been put back to order — "

"Catherine, it is still half to pieces!" Jane exclaimed. "Andrew, talk some sense into her. Convince her she must stay! The house is hardly fit to live in yet."

He set his plate down and regarded Catherine across the table. "It is, after all, her decision, Jane," he said quietly. "If she deems Rosington sufficiently restored, who am I to gainsay her?"

She nodded and rose. "Then it is decided. Miss Lowery and I will remove to Rosington today."

He frowned. Had he not learned his lesson well? Had he not resisted interfering, despite the temptation? Why then did she stand there with that strange, wounded look on her face?

She said goodbye to Jane and then suddenly was at his side. "Thank you for your hospitality, Lord Ryde, and for your many kindnesses since my father's death." She extended her hand to him.

He clasped it in his own and felt a sharp pang. "One would think you were journeying to the Antipodes," he remarked irritably, "instead of to a neighboring estate. Surely such formal leave-taking is unnecessary?"

Her cheeks flushed pink. "As you say," she said, snatching her hand from his grasp. "Then, if you will excuse me? I had best be off and see to our packing."

After she had gone, Jane turned on him. "Andrew, you are impossible! How can you let her go like that? Have you any idea what state that house is in? The bedrooms are damp, the fireplaces smoke, and much of the furniture is good for nothing but kindling!"

"If the place is such a shambles," he snapped, "then why is she so deuced eager to remove to it?"

"She thinks you are anxious to be rid of her."

Startled, he turned to face her. "And why should she think that?"

"Why indeed! You have only spent the past fortnight either avoiding her company or glowering at her! Drew, I know this house holds painful memories for you, and *that* is the reason you have been going around like a bear with a sore paw, but Catherine mistakenly believes she is the thorn you have been trying to worry out."

He shook his head. "I think it far more likely that she has grown tired of our company and wishes to remove to her new home so that she may escape it."

"What nonsense! Why Catherine adores — " Jane stopped abruptly, avoiding his eye, then continued haltingly, " — my company."

"No doubt that is true, but as you have already pointed out, I have hardly been the ideal host, and no doubt she has had a surfeit of mine." Ryde grimaced, disconcerted by the thought. "In any case, her departure leaves us free to accept the invitation I received yesterday from Maria to spend Christmas at Barnsworth. Letty and Crawford

will be there, as will Alex and the twins, and Godfrey, if Castlereagh
can spare him."

"I suppose we should go," Jane said reluctantly.

"You do not wish to spend Christmas with the family?"

"It is not that. It is only ... well, I had thought we would be
spending a quiet Christmas here at Farthingsgate, with Catherine
and Miss Lowery. It will not be much of a celebration for them alone
at Rosington."

Ryde, who still felt the warmth of Catherine's fingers tingling
against his palm, tried to push away the woebegone image Jane's
words conjured up in his mind. "With Lady Catherine in mourning,"
he said, trying to convince himself as much as Jane, "it is unlikely to
be much of a celebration in any case."

"I am in mourning as well, Drew. If we go to Barnsworth, I fear I
will be a damper on Maria's festivities."

Ryde crossed to her side and drew her hands in his. "Janey, what
nonsense," he chided softly. "Even in your weeds, you are the most
animated of us all. However, if it will make you happier, I will beg off
Maria's invitation, and we will remain here and celebrate by ourselves."

She looked up and searched his face. Finally, she said quietly, "No,
Drew. I think you have had enough of this house for a while. Write
Maria and tell her we are coming."

"Are you certain?" he asked, unable to hide his relief.

She nodded. "It will not be easy spending my first Christmas
without Bevin surrounded by three happily married sisters and their
devoted husbands, but I would rather face that than remain here and
see you haunted by memories of a different kind."

He squeezed her hands and their eyes met. "Very well then, it is
settled."

She nodded again, accepting his unspoken thanks.

Chapter 9

Christmas was a quiet and rather melancholy holiday at Rosington, but Catherine busied herself with the continuing refurbishment of the house. Thanks to Emily's cheerful company, she managed to maintain at least the outward semblance of contentment. Once the half-hearted festivities were over, however, it grew harder for her to pretend she did not sorely miss her friends from Farthingsgate.

Few of her new neighbors had yet come to visit, a fact that was beginning to weigh upon her. She had begun to wonder at the reason for it, when Emily fell ill and took to her bed. Catherine summoned the local physician, Mr. Elton, who quickly assured her that all Emily suffered from was a bad cold. Catherine took an instant liking to the doctor, youngest son of the local squire, for his dark eyes were intelligent, his manner was gentlemanly and kind, and he bore himself with the quiet confidence of a man certain of his abilities.

Mr. Elton was surprised to learn that so few members of the neighborhood had chosen to call upon her, but after a few moments of reflection he suggested that perhaps the neighborhood stood in awe of her. "An earl's daughter is quite a step up for us," he explained. "Lady Dent, the old baron's widow, has been the pinnacle of our local society for years now. It is possible people are waiting to see how she fares before venturing to call on you themselves."

"What of the late master of Farthingsgate?" Catherine asked. "Surely he ranked higher than either a baron or his lady?"

"The old marquess? I am afraid he died nearly five years ago, and before that—well, he kept very much to himself and did not socialize a great deal. To tell the truth, great hopes were raised when the new marquess sent word that Farthingsgate was to be opened up again at last. When you and your companion arrived with Lord Ryde and his sister to stay at Farthingsgate, it was quite the talk of the county! Every mother with an unmarried daughter began spinning dreams of dinner parties and balls and opportunities for the neighborhood to be enlivened with the presence of fashionable young gentlemen from Town." He gave a chuckle and shook his head. "Everyone was sorely disappointed when Lord Ryde departed again so soon. Do you know if he means to keep Farthingsgate open?"

Catherine shook her head. "I am afraid I do not know his plans."

"It is of no matter," Mr. Elton assured her. "*You* are staying, which is, of course, the much more important issue."

Catherine smiled at this gallantry. "You are very kind, Mr. Elton, though I fear your neighbors do not appear to agree with you—at least, to judge by our lack of callers."

He looked unsettled by this reminder, so Catherine turned the subject. "I am curious about the late marquess. Was he well liked in the neighborhood?"

"As I said, he kept very much to himself. Some thought him haughty, but my father always claimed it was grief, not pride, that made him so reclusive."

"Had he suffered some tragedy then?"

"None that I ever knew, but I gather—well, my father hinted that it was a matter involving a lady."

"What of his son, the present lord?" Catherine asked. "Do you know him? You two must be nearly of an age."

A smile lit the gentleman's face. "Actually, I am several years his senior, but yes, we played together as children. He was a spirited little fellow, always looking for mischief." Mr. Elton's eyes twinkled. "Of course, I must confess, I was often responsible for his finding it."

"Indeed!" she exclaimed, beguiled by this image of Lord Ryde as a young boy.

"Lady Catherine, would you consider it an impertinence if I asked how you and Lord Ryde became acquainted? Did you meet in Town?"

Catherine shook her head. "He is my trustee."

"I see," replied Mr. Elton, in a tone that made it clear he did not.

"He and my father were friends," she explained. "Since I am not married, my father thought there ought to be someone to manage my interests after his passing."

"Ah. Then he chose well. Andrew, I mean, Lord Ryde, always did have a good head on his shoulders, and there are not many men, let alone lads of nineteen, who can inherit an estate on the brink of ruin and still make something of it. I am sure he will do well by you."

"Do you mean to say his father left him in debt?"

Mr. Elton looked embarrassed. "Forgive me, I assumed you knew."

Slowly Catherine shook her head.

Mr. Elton continued reluctantly, "The old marquess tried for years to pay the debt down, but he died before he could redeem even half his notes. My father feared the family would be ruined, but somehow Andrew managed to keep things afloat."

Was this, Catherine wondered, why his memories of his father seemed so bitter?

Mr. Elton quickly turned the conversation to other topics, but Catherine's thoughts remained fixed on the masters of Farthingsgate, old and new, and when Mr. Elton rose to take his leave she was not sorry. The good doctor had given her much to think about.

Mr. Elton's judgment as to the severity of Emily's illness proved correct, and by the following day Catherine could find signs of improvement in her. Emily continued, however, weak as a kitten, and Catherine had little difficulty persuading her to remain in bed. Mr. Elton stopped in the following afternoon to check on his patient, and Catherine, tempted by another opportunity for conversation, invited the doctor to stay and partake of some refreshment. He politely declined the offer saying that he was on his way to visit a favorite aunt.

At first, Catherine was disappointed, but shortly after he departed a letter arrived from Jane. Holding it gingerly, like an especially precious gift, Catherine retreated to the study and, pulling her chair close to the fire, settled down to read it.

She had already had two letters from Jane: pleasant, amusing letters which had contained descriptions of Barnsworth, Jane's sisters, their families, and the yuletide activities that had kept them all busy. Her brother had been mentioned only once; in Jane's second letter she had told of coming upon him in the nursery one day playing with their two young nephews. As Jane had described it, Lord Ryde had been down on his hands and knees with both happily shrieking infants on his back shouting, "Get, horsey, get!"

"You cannot imagine how I laughed to see my usually sober and serious brother acting the role of my nephews' hack!" Jane had written in amusement. "He jumped up, red-faced, when he realized his performance had an audience, but as it was only me, he eventually gave in to the pleas of the twins and resumed his trotting about, which of course made them giggle with glee."

That letter had arrived shortly before Christmas, and Catherine had replied with an exaggeratedly cheerful description of the yuletide celebrations at Rosington. Since then three weeks had passed, and she had begun to wonder if her hastily added postscript asking when Jane and her brother planned to return to Farthingsgate had been a mistake. Now that she had Jane's reply she thought not. At least now she would know—one way or the other.

Jane began with an apology for her tardy response, explaining that, due to illness amongst the staff and her sister's twisted ankle, she had spent the past fortnight watching her sister's children—the very same twins who had so enjoyed turning their uncle into a horse. She went on to say that the party was about to disperse, and that she hoped to soon be returning with her brother to Farthingsgate. Catherine's spirits soared at this news and at Jane's closing words:

"My dear friend, I must say that I have missed your company, and I do not think I am the only one."

What had Jane meant? Was it possible Lord Ryde had missed her as well? Catherine stared into the fire. Perhaps, given time, he could come to feel some affection for her?

Slowly she shook her head. She must not set her sights so high. Friendship, that would be enough. To have him near to talk to and ask advice of and perhaps, on occasion, to argue with; surely that would be sufficient?

A small voice inside her cautioned it would not, but she was in no mood to listen. She wanted, at least for a little while, to be happy. Her happiness, however, did not last long. Glancing down at the envelope in her lap, she spied a small piece of paper that had fallen out unnoticed. It was a postscript from Jane, added as the letter was about to be posted. She was not returning to Farthingsgate after all. It had been discovered that her sister Maria was with child, and Maria's husband had begged Jane to stay and look after her sister during her confinement. Ryde had decided not to return to Farthingsgate without Jane, and instead was headed to Chase, his house in Sussex.

Catherine sat there contemplating the unwelcome news for some time. Finally, shaking herself to dispel the melancholy that for a dangerous moment had threatened to engulf her, Catherine rose to her feet and resolutely carried Jane's letter upstairs to share with Emily. Some wounds healed best when forced to the air.

The following afternoon, Catherine had unexpected visitors. She had been in a somber mood all day, but laughter, rude and wholly unacceptable laughter, threatened to bubble up her throat as she entered the drawing room and gazed upon her two callers for the first time.

The two ladies were so comically mismatched. One was tall and thin as a pole, the other short and round as a ball. The tall one was dressed in a simple though modish blue dress, the short one in an elaborately panniered pink gown at least twenty years out of date and more suitable for the assembly room at Almack's than for Rosington's green and gold drawing room. The hair of both ladies was white, but with the tall lady this was the work of nature, while with the short one it was the result of a liberal use of powder. The one commonality between both ladies was their plainness: one rather resembling a horse and the other a bulldog, and the bulldog was scowling at her fiercely.

Catherine bit her lip to keep from smiling and greeted the two ladies politely. The bulldog, who turned out to be the renowned Lady Dent, snapped irritably, "Well! You've kept us waiting here long enough. And without even a morsel to eat or drink."

"Now, Ada, is that any way to greet Anabelle's daughter?" chided her tall friend, Mrs. Howard.

Lady Dent's only reply was a loud harrumph.

Catherine, anxious to make peace, apologized for her tardy appearance and explained that she had needed to change, as she had not been dressed for company. Mrs. Howard smiled and assured her it was no matter, but Lady Dent remained unmoved until the timely arrival of Jenny with the tea tray. After her visitors had been properly served, Catherine inquired with some curiosity, "You mentioned my mother earlier, Mrs. Howard. Were you acquainted with her then?"

Mrs. Howard's blue eyes grew misty. "Oh yes, my dear. Ada and I both knew your mother from a girl."

"Then you must have known her well! What was she like?"

Mrs. Howard smiled, but it was Lady Dent who replied gruffly, "She was a sweet little thing, with a soft voice and a gentle nature. Too gentle perhaps. If she'd had more backbone, she might not have gone back — "

"Ada!"

Lady Dent flushed and stared down at her tea.

Mrs. Howard said softly, "You are very like her, you know. Taller of course, and your manner does not seem quite so pliant as Anabelle's used to be, but the resemblance *is* striking. Matthew told me it was so, but I never imagined ... "

"Matthew?"

"My nephew, Matthew Elton."

"The doctor? He is your nephew?"

"Yes. He visited me yesterday, which was a good thing. I knew Ada and I had been neglecting our duty to your mother by not calling, but it was not until Matthew pointed out that everyone else in the neighborhood was waiting upon our example that I realized just how negligent we had been. I hope you can forgive us, my dear."

"Of course, but might I ask why you were both so loath to make my acquaintance?"

"Not loath, my dear, merely reluctant. In my own case, I did not wish to stir up old memories. Your mother was quite dear to me, almost as dear as a daughter, and her death pained me sorely. I was afraid that if I saw you," her voice shook a little, and she took a deep breath, "that if I saw you, I might remember too much. As for Ada and her reasons — "

"They are of no consequence," Lady Dent interrupted hastily. "Sins of the father and all that. No judging a book by its cover. Can't blame the cart for the horse, and in any case it's all so many years ago anyway." Pausing to catch her breath after this rather incoherent statement, Lady Dent gazed at her apologetically, her slightly protuberant eyes full of some mute appeal.

Responding to that look, Catherine reached out and touched her hand. "It is of no importance," she said softly, and turned the conversation toward more comfortable topics. After a while, Lady Dent relaxed and even smiled, and as she and Catherine launched into a lengthy discussion of Lady Dent's beloved spaniel, Ajax. Catherine overheard Mrs. Howard muttering under her breath to herself: "Will wonders never cease! She has Ada eating out of her hand just like dear Anabelle used to!"

Chapter 10

Not until later, after her visitors had gone, did it occur to Catherine to wonder how Mr. Elton could know she and her mother resembled each other so closely. She had a chance to ask him about it two days later when he called to see how Emily was progressing.

Emily was seated in the drawing room near the fire, a warm shawl draped around her shoulders and a small rug over her lap. Mr. Elton greeted her with a satisfied nod. "I am pleased to see your recovery proceeding according to schedule, Miss Lowery."

"I must mend quickly, sir," Emily quipped, "else Catherine will have all the fun without me. Did you know your aunt and Lady Dent paid her a call several days ago while I was still abed?"

He nodded slightly and smiled. "Of course, Miss Lowery. I had the full report from Aunt Maria that very evening. By the way, Lady Catherine, I understand congratulations are in order."

"Congratulations?" Catherine repeated quizzically.

"On your conquest of Lady Dent. She was quite set against visiting you in the beginning, but now she is your greatest champion, aside from Aunt Maria, of course. I expect you'll be receiving any number of visitors in the coming days."

"It has already begun. The Branders and the Shorts called yesterday, and Mrs. Montague visited this morning. Everyone was quite cordial and friendly, though once or twice I did find Mrs. Brander staring at me in a rather disconcerting way."

"I would not worry about it. She was probably merely remarking the strong similarity you bear to your mother."

"Yes, your aunt mentioned that you noticed the resemblance yourself and commented upon it to her."

Mr. Elton grinned. "I wanted her to pay you a call and thought that might pique her interest."

"But how could you know that we were so similar?" Catherine asked. "My mother must have left Rosington while you were still an infant. You could not possibly remember her."

He shook his head. "Oh, I remember her," he said softly. "I was a boy of thirteen sent home from school with a cracked head. I was confined to my bed, and Aunt Maria came to look after me, my own mother having died several years earlier. While she was with us, your mother paid several calls upon her. During one such visit, she accompanied Aunt Maria up to my chamber to see how I was recovering.

"I did not remember your mother, though she assured me with a sweet smile that she had bobbed me on her knee when I was just a babe. I quite blushed at the thought, for I deemed her quite the grandest lady I had ever seen, and my vanity was sorely tried. However, sensing my discomfiture, she settled in a chair opposite and conversed with me for nearly an hour as if I were a man full grown." For a moment Mr. Elton was lost in the memory, then he recollected himself and looked up with a rueful smile. "So you see, I do know that you resemble her quite strongly."

"But I do not recall ever hearing that my mother visited this house after her marriage. When did this visit occur?"

Mr. Elton reflected. "Let me see. It would be fourteen years ago last September, I think."

Catherine suddenly felt faint. "Are you certain?"

"Yes, quite certain," he replied, regarding her with concern. "Lady Catherine, is something wrong? You look pale."

"It is an unfortunate coincidence, Mr. Elton, that is all," Emily explained. "I believe Catherine's mother passed away in the month of September."

His face registered genuine distress. "Forgive me. I am most sorry to hear it. How long has it been?"

It was Catherine who answered him. "Fourteen years."

❧

During the next few weeks, Catherine had little time to ponder the mystery of her mother's visit to Rosington. On the few days when the weather was fine, there were repairs to the roof to be supervised, and calls on neighbors to be returned, and trips to the village of Hamish to be made for fittings of the new gowns she and Miss Lowery had ordered from a seamstress named Mrs. Kent.

Other days, when the weather was not so fine, Catherine remained indoors. There were still many rooms that needed refurbishment, and when she wasn't busy with that work, there were meetings with Mr. Foley, Rosington's steward, to attend, for he had promised to teach her something of the workings of the estate.

Thus it was not until a dark, cold day in February that the matter of her mother's visit thrust its way back into Catherine's attention. She learned from her housekeeper, Mrs. Owen, that the family that had leased Rosington for so many years had actually been installed there when her mother had returned to the neighborhood. Perplexed and troubled, she worried at the matter for the rest of the day. The following morning she decided to pay a call upon Mrs. Howard to ask her about it.

She arrived at Rose Cottage, Mrs. Howard's small but appealing house, to find that the lady in question had gone out for a morning ride. "I shall await her return then," Catherine told Mrs. Howard's tiny housekeeper, Mrs. Kerr. Mrs. Kerr was as thin and angular as her mistress, but probably only half as tall. The flounce on her neatly pressed cap barely came up to Catherine's shoulder. Yet despite her petite stature, she radiated an authority that caused Catherine to add hesitantly, "That is, if my remaining will not be inconvenient?"

Mrs. Kerr replied primly, "Mrs. Howard's guests are always welcome," but a gleam of approval appeared in the moss-green eyes. "If you will follow me to the sitting room, my lady, I will have Doris bring you some chocolate."

She did not have long to wait. She was sipping the excellent chocolate brought to her by shy young Doris and gazing with interest at the faded but comfortable prettiness of the room when Mrs. Howard swept in like a sudden rather bracing gust of wind.

"My dear, how lovely of you to come visit!"

Catherine rose and smiled apologetically. "I know it is early, ma'am, but there is something I must ask you, and I fear I did not have the patience to wait until a more suitable hour."

"A more suitable hour? Nonsense!" Mrs. Howard exclaimed, gesturing for Catherine to sit again. "It is nearly eleven. I have already been out for my morning ride."

Catherine nodded. "So I see."

Mrs. Howard glanced down ruefully at her muddied riding habit. "I suppose I should go and change. Kerr will have my head if I get muck on the settee again."

Catherine choked slightly on her chocolate.

"Has that silly girl made it too hot?" Mrs. Howard exclaimed.

Afraid to speak, Catherine shook her head vigorously. Satisfied, her hostess excused herself and left the room.

By the time she returned, Catherine's uncertainty over how to proceed had banished all lightheartedness. When Mrs. Howard entered the rose-pink sitting room and inquired cheerfully what it was that she wished to ask her, Catherine felt her face grow hot.

"It is about my mother," she began uncomfortably. "About a stay in this neighborhood she made shortly before she died."

Mrs. Howard paled. "How do you come to know of that?"

"Mr. Elton mentioned a visit my mother paid him one day when she called to see you."

"I see," Mrs. Howard sighed, collapsing into a chair.

Catherine shook her head. "I do not think that you do. At the time of this visit, the Montgomery family was installed at Rosington, so where did my mother lodge?"

Mrs. Howard said weakly, "Some things are best left in the past, my dear."

"Fourteen years ago my mother and father had a falling out, and she fled from him—and from me. My aunt claims she ran off with a lover, but now I find she came here, to this neighborhood." She raised her eyes to meet Mrs. Howard's anxious gaze. "So you see, I must know, ma'am. Where and with whom did she stay?"

"At Farthingsgate," her hostess finally replied in a low voice.

"Farthingsgate?" Catherine exclaimed in surprise. "You mean with the late marquess and his wife?"

"His wife and the children had been bundled off to London the week before," Mrs. Howard said grimly.

Catherine stared at her in disbelief. "The marquess was her lover?"

"Heavens, child, why do you wish to speak of such things? It is not fitting. Your mother loved you, and returned to you at the cost of her life." Mrs. Howard's voice caught. "That is all you need know."

"I am not a schoolgirl, ma'am. I do not need to be shielded from the truth. I only wish to understand. Why would my mother take as her lover the man who had once jilted her?"

"You know of that, also?"

"Yes! Now please, answer my question."

"You wish to know why your mother fled your father's house and took refuge with Lord Ryde?"

Catherine nodded impatiently.

"For one simple but extremely foolish reason: she loved him." Mrs. Howard turned and gazed absently out the damp-clouded windows. "She always had, you know."

❦

"They knew each other as children," Mrs. Howard said, pausing to take a sip of her chocolate and leaning, as if for comfort, towards the fire.

"Ryde had a younger sister, Lady Celia. She and your mother were of an age and spent much time together. Ryde, despite his wild ways, was fond of his sister and allowed the two girls to follow him about, with the result that your mother was head over heels before she ever left the schoolroom.

"But Ryde had little use for schoolgirls. Wild as a boy, he grew into an even wilder young man, with a penchant for scandal and a thorough pursuit of the petticoat line. If it had not been for the title, he would have been barred from most decent houses, but those with marriageable daughters were reluctant to give up a chance at a marquess—even 'Wild Ryde.'

"Which is how he and your mother met again during her come out. He escorted his sister to a ball, and Lady Celia presented your mother to him and asked him if he remembered her friend, Anabelle. He did and apparently found her much improved, for he claimed two dances from her, and attended every rout, soirée, and ball where it was known your mother would be attending. A month later, much to the general astonishment of the *ton*, their engagement was announced.

"It was decided they should be married from Farthingsgate, and the necessary preparations were made. A party of friends and relatives were invited for the festivities, and the night before the wedding, a ball was held. Half the county came. Your mother seemed to be dancing on the very clouds that night, and as for Ryde—well, I would have sworn he was very much a man in love."

She broke off her narrative to stare moodily into the fire.

"But he jilted her," Catherine said.

Mrs. Howard nodded slowly. "The next morning it was discovered he was gone. He had eloped with Maria Stenby to Gretna Green."

Catherine shook her head. It was difficult to reconcile the kind and gallant man she had known with this tale of heartlessness and dishonor. "Poor mother! To be so humiliated."

For a moment grim anger burned in Mrs. Howard's normally mild eyes. "Yes. Fortunately your father stepped forward and announced that his friend was a fool, and that if Anabelle would have him, he would marry her himself."

"It is so hard to understand. Why would my mother leave my father to run to a man who had treated her so?"

"I do not know," Mrs. Howard admitted heavily. "We had several rather heated quarrels about that exact subject. The only thing

Anabelle would say was that Lord Ryde was not what I thought him, and that it was not he who had wronged her so grievously."

"I suppose her presence at Farthingsgate was widely known?"

"No, Lord Ryde still had some sense, even if Anabelle did not. His servants were a loyal, tight-lipped lot and he saw to it that Anabelle rarely left the house."

"But her visits to you —"

"He would have prevented those if he could. He had plans to take her to the Continent, away from prying eyes and tongues. Both Ada and I counseled against her going. The scandal would have made it difficult for either of them ever to return. Ada suggested Anabelle come live with her, while I," her voice faltered, "I urged her to return to her husband and child. I warned her that if she did as Ryde asked she would be parted from you forever."

The anguish in the older woman's voice caused Catherine to reach out and clasp her hand. "You could not know that she would take ill. In any case, it was her own choice."

Mrs. Howard shook her head slowly. "I fear my conscience will not let me off so lightly. You see, it was I who suggested Anabelle visit Matthew in the sickroom. He was an attractive child, with an endearing, affectionate nature that I hoped would stir her motherly instincts. Unfortunately, my stratagem worked with a vengeance, and she determined to return to you straight away, with the terrible consequences that ensued." She lifted her head, and Catherine saw that her eyes were full of tears.

Words and phrases of empty comfort rushed to Catherine's lips, but when she spoke an unexpected question burst out instead: "And what of Lord Ryde? How did he take the news of my mother's death?"

Mrs. Howard seemed to wince. "I was wrong to think he did not love her."

"He grieved?"

Mrs. Howard nodded sadly. "Like a man given a mortal wound."

Chapter 11

Look at that blackthorn tree, Alfred!" Catherine exclaimed in excitement. "It looks like Faeries have dusted it white with their magic. And listen. I think I hear a warbler. Oh, at last, spring has come!"

A reproving snort came from behind her. "'Tis still lacking a week 'til Lady Day, beg pardon, milady."

Catherine pressed her lips together in frustration. Her lugubrious groom, Alfred, begged her pardon with the annoying regularity of a clock, yet it never seemed to prevent him from offering his unasked-for corrections to any cheerful thing she might say. Her groom might be a boy of sixteen, but he had the crotchety outlook of a man of seventy, and just as much willingness to put his oar in when it was not wanted.

Catherine made no reply. Instead, she put Midnight to the gallop and rushed the rest of her morning ride. Emily came to inquire what was wrong, when several doors mysteriously slammed as Catherine made her way up to her bedchamber to change, but Catherine could not truly tell her. Though she would have liked to blame her ill humor on her troublesome groom, whom she would have long since sent packing but for the mother and four sisters he supported with his wages, she knew it was something else. She was restless—so restless that she feared that the delicate contentment she had been feeling of late was about to evaporate like mist in the sun.

As cold, dark February had melted into wild and windy March, the ladies at Rosington had settled into a comfortable routine. Catherine would rise early for a morning ride with Mrs. Howard. If the lady was indisposed—for Mrs. Howard, though an energetic soul, sometimes suffered from the rheumatism—she would ride with Mr. Elton. Emily, who had been thrown from a horse when quite young and who had consequently developed an aversion to equestrian pursuits, would join Catherine upon her return for breakfast, and then the two would separate to pursue the household duties each had apportioned to herself.

Catherine would seek out Foley and go over the accounts, or ride out with him to visit her tenants or inspect the estate. She was beginning to find, however, that he had less and less to teach her. Foley was an honest and able man, but he was trained in the old ways. He was both ignorant and skeptical of the new scientific farming methods she wished to pursue.

Emily, for her part, saw to the smooth running of the household. She would meet with Mrs. Owen to discuss housekeeping and menus and would sort through correspondence and set aside letters requiring Catherine's attention. Then, if needed, she would consult with Mr. Bridges, the builder overseeing the renovation and expansion of Rosington's library, for it was Emily who had drawn up the plans for the expansion, after many hours spent poring over pattern books and guides and especially the engravings of Works in Architecture by the Misters Adam.

So the days passed, and both ladies kept busy—enjoying the company of friends and treasuring their new independence. Catherine still missed Lord Ryde, but the sharp pain of his absence had abated to a dull ache that she managed to ignore most of the time, except perhaps at night.

Yet the sight of that beautiful tree and the promise of spring after so much winter had awakened all Catherine's old restlessness, and nothing seemed to quell it: not Emily's patient attempts to amuse her with talk of the library, nor the opportunity to sample Cook's new receipt for plum cake, nor even Mr. Elton's afternoon visit to see if Catherine wished to join him for a ride.

Catherine flashed him a look of reproach. "I suppose you are trying to make up for disappointing me this morning?" she demanded, her tone more brittle than she intended. "And well you should. Do you realize what a melancholy time I had with sour Alfred trotting along at my heels?"

"I can only imagine," he said with a smile. "Forgive me."

"Well, what was it this time? A pretty milkmaid with a twisted ankle?"

"Catherine!"

"Now, Emily," she snapped. "Do not pretend I have shocked you when you and Mr. Elton spend hours discussing the most gruesome details of his exceptional profession. Goodness, sometimes I feel quite faint just listening to the two of you."

Emily raised her eyebrows in admonishment. "A lady should have at least a passing knowledge of the healing arts. That does not necessitate, however, a discussion in mixed company of the misadventures of a hypothetical damsel's nether limbs." She then flashed Catherine a quick grin to show that she was teasing.

Emily's good humor finally caused Catherine to relax a little, but she noticed that Mr. Elton's smile did not reach his normally affable eyes. "Mr. Elton," she said, "you look quite grim. I hope no one in the neighborhood has been taken seriously ill."

Mr. Elton shook his head. "Not ill, injured. That fool Norris — "

"The gamekeeper at Farthingsgate," Catherine explained to Emily under her breath.

" — set out another of those damned—excuse me, ladies—accursed man traps and did not think to notify Bagshot, the steward, of it."

"Of course old Norris wouldn't," Catherine said. "Mr. Bagshot told him to leave off with such devices weeks ago. Oh, dear, has some poor poacher gone and got himself caught in the thing?"

"Not a poacher," Mr. Elton said, "Bagshot himself."

Catherine felt her stomach clench in dismay. She had developed a strong affection for Farthingsgate's rough but intelligent steward. "How badly is he hurt?"

"I fear his leg is quite mangled. He may lose it."

"Poor man!" Emily exclaimed.

"Is there nothing that can be done?" Catherine demanded.

Mr. Elton shrugged. "I have cleaned the wound as best I can and have set a maid to change the dressings regularly. The rest is up to time and God. We shall see."

Catherine was less than satisfied with this reply. Emily patted her arm. "Do not fret, my dear. I am sure Mr. Elton has done his best." Emily rose to her feet. "In the mean time, I will go speak with Cook. I am sure Mr. Bagshot could do with some nourishing broth and perhaps some fresh bread and butter."

Mr. Elton rose also. "Perhaps under the circumstances," he said, obviously puzzled by the strength of Catherine's concern, but willing to honor it, "you would prefer to forego our ride?"

"To the contrary," she replied. "I would very much enjoy your escort when I deliver that broth and bread to your patient."

Cook insisted on making up the broth fresh and warming the bread in the oven, so it was more than an hour later when Catherine and Mr. Elton, unaccompanied by the irksome Alfred, set off with their sickroom victuals. By the time they arrived at Mr. Bagshot's chalk and flint cottage, the daylight was fading to a mauve glow. Despite the approaching dusk, however, the windows of the neatly thatched house were dark and the moss green front door stood slightly ajar.

"Lady Catherine," Mr. Elton said, "I think we had best deliver your bounty quickly, and return straightaway to Rosington. It grows late, and it would hardly be fitting for us to arrive together unaccompanied after dark."

"Fiddle! No one will know but Emily, and fuss and scold though she might, she is sensible enough to realize nothing untoward would ever occur between us."

Catherine wondered at the pained look that flitted briefly across Mr. Elton's face before he slid from his saddle and helped her down from hers. After she had removed the well-tied crock of broth and the still-warm bread from her saddlebags, he relieved her of her burden and led the way toward the house. When repeated knocks on the front door brought no answer, he pushed it open and invited her to enter.

"I wonder where the maid can have gotten to," he said, as he led her through the dim front room to the kitchen. "I told her Bagshot was to be watched closely throughout the night."

"Perhaps she is with him now and did not hear us knock."

"Perhaps." He set down her gifts of food on the table. Then he led the way back to the staircase. "Bagshot's room is above. Please wait here while I go to see how he fares."

Reluctantly, Catherine nodded, though the gloom of the house was growing oppressive. She gripped the banister tightly as her companion disappeared up the narrow stairs. For several long moments she stood thus in the darkness. Then the weighty silence was broken by a loud exclamation.

"Lady Catherine! Please, come at once!"

She hurried up the stairs, feeling her way towards the top as the light grew dimmer and dimmer.

"In here!"

She turned toward a door that was ajar on her right, grateful for the faint glow that emanated from the narrow slit. She opened the door and by the light of a single candle could see Mr. Elton bent over the bed, struggling to pin down Mr. Bagshot's arms as the poor man flailed violently back and forth.

"He is delirious with fever," gasped Mr. Elton. "I fear he will do himself a mischief if we do not get him quieted down."

"What can I do to help?"

"Hurry downstairs and fetch my bag. I have some laudanum drops inside. Perhaps if we can get some down his throat we can render him unconscious."

Catherine rushed down the stairs and out the door, running to the doctor's horse and unbuckling the saddlebag with trembling fingers. She was poised to return to the house, when she heard the sound of distant hoofbeats. She turned and saw a rider approaching down the lane. Here was a chance to recruit a strong arm to assist Mr.

Elton. She waved at the man, and despite the faint light he must have seen her, for he slowed and turned off the lane towards the cottage.

Catherine called out to him as he drew near, a hazy silhouette against the deepening dusk. "Please, sir, you must hurry! There is an injured man inside who is delirious with fever. The doctor is with him, but — " She broke off as the rider came to a stop before her. It was Lord Ryde.

She heard his breath catch sharply as he recognized her. Her own breath seemed trapped by the pulse suddenly thundering in her throat. He swung out of his saddle and dropped to his feet in front of her.

"I was unaware you had returned," she said faintly.

"I only arrived a few hours ago," he said, scanning her face with an intensity that caused her own gaze to drop. "I was greeted by a weeping maid who insisted my steward is dying of a fit. I thought it unlikely, but decided to come and see for myself."

Catherine remembered the saddlebag in her hands. "He *is* very ill. The doctor is upstairs with him now, but we must hurry." She turned to go, but he caught at her arm.

"You have not yet explained your own presence here."

"There is no time. Please!"

He let her go. She hurried into the house, and, to her relief, he followed.

Jacob Bagshot was not a tall man, nor a large one, but he was wiry and strong, and despite his injured leg and burning fever it took the combined efforts of three people to keep him still enough for the doctor to force a dose of laudanum down his throat. Even after this had been accomplished, he would not stay still, but continued thrashing about as if he imagined himself the biblical Jacob wrestling the angel.

Ryde, fighting to keep Bagshot's legs from kicking free of his grasp, glanced up at Catherine's white face and tightly-set mouth as she valiantly struggled to hold the steward's left arm down by his side.

"Dammit, man," he swore, "how much longer until that drug of yours takes effect?"

The sandy-haired doctor, narrowly avoiding a cuffing, regained hold of Bagshot's right arm and assured Ryde breathlessly, "It should not be long now."

And it wasn't. Within a few minutes, Bagshot's struggles began to lessen, and after a few more minutes he grew quiet. Ryde released his hold and hurried to Catherine's side. "Here. Come, sit down." He led her to the room's one chair.

She sank down wearily. "Thank you."

"I hope you will forgive my language earlier. I fear the sight of you striving at such a task disturbed me."

"It needed to be done," she said lightly.

"Perhaps, but I could wish it had not involved you."

She did not reply to that, but instead addressed herself to the doctor. "Mr. Elton, the violence of the fever. It does not bode well for Mr. Bagshot's leg, does it?"

The physician, seemingly satisfied that his patient was resting comfortably, crossed to join them. "I fear not, though I have not given up hope completely. Now that he is quiet, I can change the dressings and take another look at the wound. It is possible it may still heal cleanly."

Ryde stared at the man and said coldly, "I see no reason to distress the lady with such details."

To his surprise, the reprimand did not silence the man's wayward tongue. Instead, the doctor regarded Ryde with a bellicose expression. "It was not my intention to distress her, only to inform her how matters stood."

"And I thank you for doing so, Mr. Elton," Catherine said hurriedly. "Lord Ryde, there really is no — "

"*Lord Ryde?*" exclaimed the doctor.

"That is my name."

The other man's expression changed, grew friendlier. He eyed Ryde up and down and finally said, "I should have known it was you. You always did have a knack for turning up when trouble was brewing. I am most grateful the old instinct was in force tonight.

I doubt Lady Catherine and I could have managed to dose the fellow alone."

"Lady Catherine should never have been here in the first place, and as for you—am I supposed to know you, sir?"

The diminutive doctor smiled. "You do not recognize me, eh? Well, I can hardly blame you. I did not recognize you either." He bent his head back to regard the top of Ryde's six-foot frame. "You have grown a bit since the days when Coal used to try to toss you into the pond."

"Coal?" Catherine asked.

"A black stallion owned by a neighbor of ours," Ryde replied absently, staring at the sandy-haired man before him. Yes, now that he actually looked, there *was* something familiar about the square-jawed face, the dark eyes, the slightly lopsided tilt of the grinning mouth. Could it be? What was it she had called the man? Mr. *Elton.*

He took a step forward. "*Matthew?*"

The other man nodded and held out his hand. Ryde seized it and shook it vigorously.

"It is good to see you again, my lord."

"For heaven's sake, Matt, lord me no lords! Ryde will do."

"As you like, my lord—Ryde, but are you certain you wish a mere physician to address you so informally?"

Ryde frowned. "I admit, I am confounded to find you about such work. It hardly befits your station."

Matthew flushed, and Catherine interjected, "Healing the sick is hardly an unworthy calling, sir."

"Perhaps not, but it is not the proper business of a gentleman." He flashed her a reproving look. "Or a lady."

"Gentleman or no," Matthew replied, "I am a youngest son and must earn my bread."

"But as a physician?"

Matthew squared his shoulders. "I consider it an honorable profession, even if others do not, and I happen to be good at it."

Ryde regarded him dubiously.

"In any case, I haven't the temperament for a clergyman."

"What about the army?" Ryde queried. "Surely your father could procure you a commission?"

"I am too short to make a decent soldier, and in any case, why is it more gentlemanly to break bodies than to mend them?"

Ryde could think of no easy reply, but he knew it to be true nonetheless. Still, Matthew had once been his closest friend, and he was loath to have the argument continue. "All right, truce. I would not have us come to blows over the matter." Ryde smiled. "Though I do seem to recall there being, when last we met, the small matter of a wrestling match."

Matthew Elton's taut face relaxed. "Oh, no, my lord Hercules! I have a living to make now. I cannot afford to be laid up in my bed like that poor steward of yours there. When I made that appointment with you, you were a considerably smaller fellow."

"All right, Matt, I will let you off that, but I must insist, at least, on a game of billiards. I have improved considerably since you trounced me so ignominiously in front of Cassie all those years ago."

"Have you now? Well, I would like to see that, but I fear it must wait for another evening. Tonight my entertainment shall be limited to an exacting scrutiny of poor Bagshot's leg and a snore in that chair so fetchingly occupied by Lady Catherine. That is, if you do not mind seeing the lady safely home?"

Catherine rose to her feet. "I can see myself safely home, thank you."

"I will be happy to escort the lady back to Rosington," Ryde replied, flashing her a quelling look. He turned to Matthew and said, "You will come by tomorrow and let me know how Bagshot fares?"

"I will," Matthew assured him. "Lady Catherine, goodnight. I am sorry that our outing ended in such a disconcerting way."

"You are hardly to blame for that, Mr. Elton. I am only glad I was able to be of some help."

"You were of the greatest assistance, my lady," he said with a gallant bow, "and when I partake of my dinner of bread and broth later, I will think of you most kindly."

"Yes, I suppose poor Mr. Bagshot is in no fit state to eat it, but surely you would prefer something more substantial? I can send Will over — ”

Feeling a rising irritation, Ryde interrupted. "*I* will see to it that Mr. Elton is properly fed. Now may we be going?"

She nodded stiffly, then made her goodbyes to his old childhood friend in such a warm tone that Ryde was provoked to demand, when they emerged from the house, just how well acquainted she was with Matthew Elton.

"He is a good friend."

"I see. And do you make it a practice to ride about the countryside, after dark—without even a groom to lend you countenance—with all your good friends, or is that a privilege reserved to him?"

"We did not intend to be gone so late."

"That, of course, makes everything right!"

They had reached the horses. She turned to him, and light from the rising moon illuminated her face so that he could see the temper flashing in her eyes. "Will you help me to mount, sir, or would that offend your finely honed notions of propriety too gravely?"

He lifted her up, and the feel of her in his arms did nothing to cool his irritation, but only fired it higher. How dare she treat him as if he were a prig railing over trifles! Did she not realize the impulses men were prone to—even honorable men like Matthew—when they found themselves alone with a woman in the moonlight?

His breath began to come more quickly. *Perhaps the problem was that she knew too well.* The thought, unbidden, taunted him as he gazed up at her. The moon was behind her now, so he could not see her face, but white light cascaded over her body highlighting every graceful line, every delectable curve. He suddenly regretted that she was safely on her horse, for he ached to indulge one of those dishonorable impulses right here, right now, right this very minute.

He swung himself up into his saddle, trying to push the notion away, but it would not go. After all, if the countess's tales about the lady and his father were true ...

His hands tightened convulsively on the reins, causing his stallion to rear slightly. He eased his grip and pulled alongside Catherine's mount. "Stay close," he instructed her tersely. "I will lead the way."

They made for Rosington. For some time the only sound breaking the silence between them was the monotonous cadence of the horses. Then Ryde shot a wary glance her way and inquired in a carefully neutral tone, "I presume Matthew—Mr. Elton—does not ordinarily ask you to accompany him on his sick calls?"

"No, he does not." She no longer sounded angry, but he could not make out her expression. Her head was bent forward, and the hood of her cloak masked her face in shadow.

"Then did he have some particular reason for asking you to accompany him on this one?"

"It was I who suggested the visit, not he. When I heard of Mr. Bagshot's accident, I wanted to bring the poor man some broth to eat, and I asked Mr. Elton to escort me."

"Indeed?"

"When we arrived we found him in the state which you saw. Mr. Elton asked me to fetch the saddlebag in which he carries his medicines, and I was doing as he asked when I saw you riding down the lane and hailed you." She paused and glanced briefly in his direction. "You know, I am not really the wild creature you think me. Sometimes I merely become impatient with the notion that it is more important to do what is proper than what is right."

"Are not the two equivalent?"

"No. For one is a matter of appearance, and the other substance. Someone may be regarded as entirely proper by society and yet do wrong as a matter of course. Likewise, a person's reputation may be quite ill, and yet he or she may behave with great gentility and kindness."

"Illusion or no," he said sharply, "one's reputation determines how one is treated by society, and therefore must be jealously guarded."

She replied in a low voice, "It is difficult to guard that which has already been stolen."

His pulse was suddenly beating hard in his throat. "Do we speak now of the appearance of virtue or of its substance?"

She checked her horse, and Ryde, too, drew to a halt. She pushed back her hood and turned slowly to regard him. Her face was white, her eyes dark and unfathomable, her lips parted in pained surprise. "What lies has my stepmother told you about me?"

Ryde suddenly wished himself anywhere but where he was. He was tempted to remain silent, but her steady gaze made it clear that was not an option. "She implied that you and my father...that he and you were...intimately acquainted."

She seemed to contract into herself. "I suppose I cannot wonder that you would believe such a tale of me. After all, you and I are relative strangers, and the countess can be—as I know to my cost—very persuasive. But did you not doubt it on your father's account?"

"Surely you know my father's reputation!" Ryde exclaimed. "I would credit almost any tale told of him, no matter how vile. No, if I doubt, it is on your account, not his. If you tell me the thing is false, I believe you."

"Very well," she said stiffly, turning away. "Nothing untoward ever occurred between your father and me."

He waited in silence—his heart thumping wildly—for her to say more, for her to explain just what her relationship with his father *had* been. But she remained as she was, head bent, profile in shadow, silently twisting the reins in her gloved hands.

Finally he said brusquely, "We had best continue on our way."

"Yes."

It was not until they had passed Rosington's gates that she spoke again. "Lord Ryde, hold a moment, please. There is something I wish to say to you before we arrive and are no longer alone."

He pulled up short and waited for her, suddenly unsure he wanted to hear what she had to say.

She, too, seemed reluctant. "Your father was very kind to me," she said at last.

Ryde frowned. "He often was kind to strangers. It was friends and family he treated ill."

"He always seemed most caring and considerate of your sister Jane," she countered.

"Lady Catherine, I have no desire to sit here and discuss my family relations while our horses grow cold. If you have a point to make, please make it. Otherwise, let us proceed. I have matters enough to attend to at home."

"Very well then. I was very fond of your father. In fact, in the short time I knew him I grew to love him almost as a daughter. I realize he had his faults. Indeed, I have recently learned my mother was among those he wronged. However, I cannot accept the black portrait you and many paint of him. The gentleman I knew had a warm heart and a gallant spirit, and I cannot help but think there must be some explanation for the wrong that is thought of him."

"There is but one explanation. My father was a blackguard, but a blackguard beloved of women. *I* cannot excuse him, however, and I would prefer to quit the subject at once."

"You may think ill of him, but he was very proud of you."

"I do not wish to discuss this any further!"

"He spoke of you often. He told me of your studies at Oxford, and of how he hoped to send you on your Grand Tour when the war with Napoleon was over."

"*Enough!*"

But she continued softly, "I believe he even cherished the hope he might perhaps accompany you."

He wanted to shake her. Instead he said coldly, "Do you think I care about his chatter or his daydreams when both were but the whimsy of a moment soon forgotten?"

"Can you truly be so bitter towards his memory?"

"When I was ten years old, he turned me, my sisters, and my mother out of his house, and when I was nineteen, he died and left me a mountain of debt that I have only now, after five long years of work, managed to escape. If I am bitter, I think I have cause."

"I am sorry."

"As am I. This discussion is at an end." Not waiting for an answer from her, he set off up the drive without a backward glance.

Chapter 12

Ryde called at Rosington the next morning. He had not really expected to find Catherine alone. Still he was disappointed to enter the drawing room to discover her flanked not only by her governess but by a small, round lady with powdered hair and the face of a bulldog.

"Lord Ryde, welcome! We were just taking tea. I trust you will join us?" It was not Catherine who uttered the polite words, but the governess, Miss Lowery.

His gaze turned toward his silent hostess. "I have no wish to intrude."

Her eyes widened slightly. "It is no intrusion, sir," she assured him. "Please, be seated."

He pulled forward an old carved armchair upholstered in Italian velvet that stood exiled in the corner. Placing it opposite the delicate Sheraton chairs upon which the ladies were seated, he sat down.

Miss Lowery made the necessary introductions. "Lord Ryde, may I introduce Lady Dent? Lady Dent, this is Lord Ryde."

Lady Dent acknowledged the introduction by raising one grizzled brow. "So, you are George's son."

Ryde, who had never before heard his father referred to by his Christian name, replied faintly, "Yes, ma'am."

"Hmmph. Knew him from a boy. Always was a wild one. I suppose you are cut from the same cloth?"

Before he could reply, Catherine said drily, "No need to fear, ma'am. *This* Lord Ryde is quite the paragon."

Stung by her mockery, his gaze locked with hers, but he kept his voice light, "I fear Lady Catherine's judgment is more generous than sound. I am merely an ordinary man with ordinary faults."

"That don't say much," harrumphed Lady Dent. "Ordinary men are scoundrels."

A footman picked this opportune moment to enter with more tea and cakes, and Catherine, chin quivering suspiciously, busied herself pouring him a cup of tea. To Ryde's great satisfaction, however, her expression sobered abruptly when he accepted it from her and their bare hands touched.

"Deuced funny time to come calling," Lady Dent quipped as she took an energetic bite out of the new slice of cake Miss Lowery had just handed her.

"Yes," agreed Ryde, taking a sip of his tea. "You and I must have the same independent turn of mind. I hope Lady Catherine does not find our eccentricity tiresome."

Lady Dent paused mid-chew.

Miss Lowery said diplomatically, "We enjoy our visitors whenever they choose to come, Lord Ryde."

Catherine added with a smile. "Besides when people come to call, we can enjoy Cook's fine tea and cakes, and now that I am safely on the shelf, I need no longer pretend to the appetite of a sparrow."

"On the shelf, indeed!" exclaimed Miss Lowery indignantly. "Really, Catherine, you are hardly at your last prayers. You are only three-and-twenty."

"Not to mention an earl's daughter and heiress to a considerable fortune," Ryde added with asperity.

"Won't have it long if she marries some bounder," warned Lady Dent. "Perhaps she should come live with me when her mourning is over. Keep the wolves at bay."

"Thank you, Ada, but I am quite safe here with Emily. Besides," she paused and flashed Ryde a challenging look from across the table, "if there are any wolves, I believe Papa has left me his lordship to play shepherd."

He grimaced. "I must search out my slingshot."

She cocked an eyebrow at him, "Do you really think it will be needed?"

"Though you are a rather formidable lamb, yes, my lady, I expect so. Especially when news of your inheritance becomes widely known."

Lady Dent looked a bit out of her depth. "What is all this talk of sheep and shepherds?" she demanded.

Miss Lowery rose to her feet and held out an arm to help Lady Dent to hers. "I shall explain it on our way to the library. I want to ask your opinion of some purple marble Mr. Bridges suggests for the new mantelpiece. I am having a great deal of trouble making a decision. You two will excuse us?"

Ryde acquiesced politely, pleased at the chance for a *tête-à-tête*. After the two ladies had gone, Catherine asked in a low voice tinged with chagrin, "Do you truly find me formidable, sir?"

He was startled into an honest answer, "I do, at times." Ryde saw her generous mouth crumple a little, and he cursed himself for a tactless fool.

"Strange," she said, her tone rueful, "I do not *feel* formidable. Most of the time I feel quite the opposite." She looked up. The expression in those remarkable eyes suddenly made him feel quite fierce. Such vulnerability had to be protected.

As did such innocence.

Yet the added thought held less conviction, despite the extraordinary conversation they had shared the night before when she had assured him her relationship with his father had been an innocent one, and he had promised to believe her. It was easier to pledge belief, he realized, than to truly feel it. Especially when there was still the portrait hung in the locked room at Farthingsgate to be explained.

"My lord?"

"Yes?" he replied abstractedly.

"Is something...wrong?"

He emerged from his reverie to find her gazing fixedly at his neckcloth, her cheeks quite pink. "Wrong?" he exclaimed sharply. "No, of course not. Why should anything be wrong?"

"You were staring at me ... strangely. I thought perhaps you were still angry about last night."

"No ... no. I fear I was woolgathering, that is all. Forgive me."

She seemed to relax. "Of course. Though I do think we should avoid any further allusion to sheep. For poor Lady Dent's sake." Her tone was grave, but her eyes twinkled.

Ryde felt his mouth twitch and his mood lighten. "Indeed. No doubt she already thinks me quite muttonheaded."

She laughed. "No one could think you that."

"I am glad. Why then does the lady scowl at me so fiercely?"

"Because you are a man."

"I am pleased to acknowledge the point, though I am at a loss to see why that fact alone should place me in Lady Dent's black books. Pray tell, what wrong has our sex done the woman that she stands ready to condemn us all out of hand?"

Catherine's expression turned serious. "I fear her husband, the baron, was not a pleasant representative of your gender. He drank to excess and beat his wife at the slightest provocation. When Lady Dent was *enceinte* with their first child he flew into a rage and knocked her down the main staircase. She lost the infant, and nearly died herself, and was told by the doctors that she would never again be able to bear children."

Ryde said heavily, "That explains a great deal. I perceive why she might regard gentlemen with disfavor."

"Actually, she is willing to tolerate single gentlemen. It is the whole notion of husbands she cannot abide. She believes them to be onerous and dispensable things."

"Thankfully, most ladies would disagree with her."

"Perhaps. Yet there is some reason to her view. Some ladies gain little and lose much when they marry."

"Do not be ridiculous!" he exclaimed, feeling inexplicably angry with her. "What is life for a woman if she does not marry and have children?"

"What is it for a man?"

"Now you are being completely nonsensical! For men there are affairs of the world to be pursued; for a woman there is only the home. What kind of home is it if it does not have a master?"

She did not answer.

Feeling a growing exasperation, Ryde demanded, "Surely *you* wish to be married?"

She met his gaze with a look so intent, he felt a strange jolt. "Do you?" she asked softly.

"Of course I will marry—eventually. I must provide myself with an heir."

She looked away. "Ah, but you see, I have no need for an heir, though now that I think upon it, I do wish for children. Perhaps a husband is necessary after all."

It seemed an absurd reply, and yet he sensed he had missed something—some subtle nuance that gave it meaning. Angry at feeling so out of his depth, he replied with unseemly bluntness. "I doubt your husband will appreciate being seen in the light of a prize stud."

Her cheeks flamed crimson, and he instantly regretted his coarse words, but she would not leave it there, but replied in a voice that was barely above a whisper: "Is not that the precise light in which you see your future wife?"

He stared at her, dumbfounded. This was plain-speaking indeed. "My lady, have you no notion of the limits of polite conversation?"

"Forgive me. I did not intend to be rude. I have been away from polite society for so long, I had forgotten its dislike for honest speech."

First a prig, now a hypocrite! Once again she had maneuvered him into the wrong simply for believing the rules of society counted for something. "At last I perceive the bond between you and my father," he snapped. "He, too, enjoyed flouting convention for its own sake."

"Please, let us avoid further discussion of the late marquess, for I have no wish to quarrel with you, and we never broach that subject without contention."

"It seems we never broach *any* subject without contention, Lady Catherine."

"And yet I wish that we might be friends." Her tone was wistful.

That brought him up short. "As do I. How do you propose we go about it?"

She extended a hand across the table to him. "We might make a pledge, my lord, to strive to be in all things amiable, no matter our inclination otherwise."

"Very well. Let us shake upon it." He clasped her hand, filled with a sense of the rightness of the moment. Her long, warm fingers rested appealingly against his palm. Her skin was like velvet. Her hand fit in his as perfectly as if it were formed to rest there.

Yes, they should strive to be cordial. After all, he was her trustee—no, more than a trustee, for thanks to the pledge he had made to her father, he was entrusted with protecting her happiness as well as her purse. His role was truly more like that of a brother.

His thoughts caught and tripped on the word. There was nothing brotherly in the tingling pleasure he felt in the touch of that soft hand, or in the desire he suddenly felt to run his fingers up her well-shaped arm and pull her closer, so he could smell her skin as well as the faint and rather intoxicating scent of lavender that wafted towards him across the table.

He released her hand abruptly and jerked to his feet, turning and crossing to the mantel. "Here I go nearly forgetting the reason for my visit. I come bearing news and a gift."

"What news?"

"Elton stopped by this morning to inform me that Bagshot is faring better. The fever has gone down, and the leg seems to be mending cleanly after all."

"Oh, I *am* glad!" she exclaimed, her face lighting up with relief. Ryde noted with interest the small dimple which accompanied her sudden smile. Fleetingly he wondered what it would be like to kiss that dimple. Then he pushed the thought away.

"Yes, I can see that you are." He was surprised by the strength of her reaction. The tidings, while admittedly satisfactory, hardly seemed to warrant such rejoicing. "I confess to some curiosity, Lady Catherine. Do you feel such concern for all your fellow creatures, or has my steward somehow earned a special place in your affections?"

"I have been attempting to learn how an estate ought to be run. My steward, Foley, is a fine fellow but quite behind the times. Your Mr. Bagshot, however, is quite knowledgeable and an excellent tutor. He has been very patient with me, and I like him very much."

"You amaze me, my lady."

"Because I consider your steward a capable man?"

"Because you burden yourself with such tedious matters. You need not trouble yourself with such things."

Her chin went up defiantly. "What is wrong with my learning how to manage my own land?"

"That is a role for a gentleman, not a lady. That is a role for your husband."

"But I have no husband."

"Then someone shall have to find you one."

Her blue-green eyes narrowed. "And who would presume to do such a thing?"

He said lightly, "Perhaps I shall try my hand at it."

She stared—first at him, then angrily down at her tea.

"It would be fairer to direct your anger at me rather than that poor, innocent china cup."

She looked up.

"Ah, that's better. I suppose you were contemplating it so fiercely, because you were imagining dashing its contents at my head?"

She stared at him for a long moment. Then she shook her head, and her mouth relaxed into a smile. He noted the reappearance of the dimple with pleasure. "I am not so undisciplined as that, sir. *That* would be a shocking waste of good Hyson."

He could not help it. He smiled back at her. "I am sorry that we quarreled."

"As am I."

"I shall strive in future to abide by our pact of amiability more stringently, and keep my ill humors in check."

"I fear that it is not only your ill humors that are to blame, sir," she replied. "I, too, have a quick temper. Perhaps it is unrealistic to pledge harmony, for I suspect we are likely to clash often, but perhaps we can pledge to be reconciled afterwards?"

Ryde's mind was suddenly filled with a much too warm image of how exactly he would like to be reconciled to her. "I am agreeable, if you are," he said, struggling to keep his tone light.

"I am."

"Good, then that is settled. And now, before I am distracted from my intent a second time, I wish to return something to you that I believe someone may be missing." He reached into the pocket of his waistcoat and removed a small, black velvet pouch. Crossing to where she sat, he placed it in her hands.

She flashed him a wondering look, then loosened the drawstrings and spilled out the contents of the bag into her palm. The gold locket glittered prettily. Old Jeffries had done a fine job; the dents were gone as if they had never been and the catch swung open easily to reveal the picture, under new glass, inside.

She looked up at him, her eyes suddenly bright with tears. "I thought it lost forever. Wherever did you find it?"

"At Trenwich, dropped into a hedge in the gardens. It was smashed and dented, so I sent it to London to be repaired."

"Oh, that was kind of you! Thank you! There are, of course, other portraits of my mother, but this one is by far the most dear to me. I am exceedingly grateful to have it restored to me."

Ryde swayed slightly, as his startled senses registered what she had said. "*Your mother!*"

"Yes. I suppose it is my favorite, because she looks so young and happy. It was painted during her first Season."

Ryde gazed down at the small portrait, feeling some inner tension, as of a watch spring wound too tight, suddenly spin free within him. "Was it a copy of a larger work?"

"I do not know," replied Catherine. "I have never seen the original if it was."

Ah, but I have, thought Ryde, happiness bubbling up within him like water from a long dormant spring. "You resemble your mother a great deal."

"Yes, though I am taller and not as pretty as she was."

He shook his head vehemently. "At the risk of another argument, I fear I must disagree with you on that point."

She gazed up at him, her cheeks charmingly flushed, her lips parted in surprise. He tried to focus on the somber grey of her gown, rather than the pale rose of her mouth, but—despite his best efforts—this time, the impulse to act was too strong to overcome. Without pausing to think of the consequences, he placed his hands on her shoulders, leaned down towards her face, and kissed her.

It was a light kiss at first—his mouth brushing hers with the faintest of touches, but her lips were warm and soft and intoxicatingly yielding, and each touch of those lips seemed to strip some of his control away. He pressed more hungrily, more insistently against those lips until they opened totally to him, and then he was inside, and her mouth was sweet enough to drown in. Soon her mouth was not enough. He buried his hands in her hair and his face against her neck, and still he did not have enough of her.

He sank to his knees and slid his arms completely around her, pulling her against him until he could feel the rise and fall of her breath against his chest. His mouth was in a frenzy now, determined to kiss every inch of her face and throat and the warm, velvet skin rising above the neck of her gown. He was dizzy with the need to touch her as well. His fingers trailed along her neck and shoulders and the sweet curve of her breasts.

Voices and the sound of approaching footsteps broke the spell.

Startled back to his senses, Ryde released Catherine and jerked backwards into the safety of his chair, grateful for the shield the table provided for his state of perturbation. He had no opportunity to apologize to her for his abominable behavior before the door opened, and Miss Lowery and Lady Dent entered the room. He thought he detected a flicker of speculation in Miss Lowery's dark eyes, but her face remained placid as she greeted them. She launched into a discussion of the renovations in the library, which mercifully deflected Lady Dent's attention from the curious proximity of his chair to Catherine's, as the baroness felt it necessary to respond to everything Miss Lowery said with a mutter and a sigh at the waste of so much good money on a chamber designed primarily for the use of men.

"Ma'am, do not tell me you think books to be the province only of gentlemen!" Miss Lowery exclaimed softly. "Why Catherine values her library much more highly than any gentleman I know. As for me, well, I visited the book room in my parents' house more frequently than ever my brother did. Indeed, as a girl, I spent many of my happiest times there."

Ryde looked across at the former governess and was reminded of his sister Jane. His other sisters had never been the bookish sort, but Jane had always loved to read. The two of them had spent many happy days as children in Farthingsgate's library, sprawled on the bearskin rug their grandfather had brought from Russia, or curled up in their father's old leather wing chair.

His throat tightened, but the memory refused to be banished. Yes, he and Jane had spent many happy afternoons in their father's library, and, if the truth be told, in their father's company. He had been tolerant of their interruptions. He had never objected to having his reading curtailed or his letter-writing postponed to answer a question, or to read a book aloud to them, or to lead them over to his treasured old globe and tell them about their grandfather's many travels as a diplomat.

He suddenly wondered if Catherine had spent similar times with her father when she was a girl. Had she trailed after that formidable gentleman in a pinafore and sausage curls dragging a book with pretty pictures that she longed for him to read? He smiled to himself at the image. But then he thought of the earl and imagination faltered. It was hard to picture the proud and haughty Earl of Trenwich toting a young daughter up upon his lap and reading to her or bobbing her upon his knee. The late earl had been a good man and a wonderful benefactor, but it was difficult to imagine him as an affectionate father.

Affectionate or not, Ryde reminded himself grimly, the earl had cared about his daughter's welfare and had entrusted him with its safekeeping. And how had he repaid that trust? By nearly seducing the girl in her own house.

Filled with a sense of shame, Ryde cast a covert glance at Catherine, but shame quickly turned to anger as he watched her politely listen to the other ladies' conversation looking as calm and composed as a statue. His jaw clenched as she took a ladylike sip of tea. Minutes before they had been clasped in a passionate embrace so all-consuming his head still reeled from it, his pulse still raced, but she sat there lifting her cup with a hand that did not tremble. For a moment, he was tempted to hurl the cup from her hand and make not just her hand, but her whole body tremble. Then she turned her head, and he saw her shining eyes, and he realized just how terrible a mistake he had made.

Damn his father's intemperate blood! He had acted out of desire and she had mistaken it for love.

What was he to do now?

He could simply marry her and be done with it. It was a cowardly notion, but a tempting one, for he was loath to have those shining eyes regard him with reproach. He had not thought to marry so young, but it was unlikely he would ever have a chance at a better match, and honor would be served.

For a moment, he relished the thought. She would make him a very fine wife, and the thought of sharing her bed filled him with excitement. Then his conscience pricked him. Would it truly be an honorable choice?

Catherine was still in black gloves. There had been no chance for her to be wooed or courted, as she most certainly would be once her mourning was over. She was a well-born heiress who could have her pick of the *ton* as a husband. Was it honorable for him to take her choice away simply because he resembled his sire too well to restrain his lustful impulses and behave as a gentleman should?

Bleakly, he thought of the countess, that great prevaricator. She had accused him long ago of wanting to seduce Catherine to secure the earl's legacy for himself. Was he to make a truth-teller of the woman? And she would not be alone. All the *ton* would think him a fortune hunter and Catherine a witless heiress unable to discern a true suitor from a conniver bent on forcing her hand. Where would the honor be in that?

Especially if Catherine, herself, began to believe it. His stomach churned. No, *that* he could not bear.

He had promised her father a love match, and a love match it would have to be. He had given his word, and Catherine deserved no less.

But until he found the right man for her, he would have to undo what he had done.

She cast a shy but sparkling smile his way. He resisted the temptation to smile back, and instead regarded her coldly, turning pointedly away to address Miss Lowery. The cut was quick and direct, but not so quick that he missed her look of pained surprise. That look seemed to wrench something loose inside of him, but he ignored the strange, hollow feeling and entered into a discussion of the weather with grim determination.

After sufficient time had passed, he rose to take his leave. Lady Dent seemed unaware that anything untoward had passed between him and her young friend, but Miss Lowery watched him go with a puzzled frown. As for Catherine, she flashed him one long, confused look, and then straightened her spine and regarded him with an expression of such frosty disdain that he was left teetering between a desire to drop to his knees and beg forgiveness and an even stronger desire to wrap her in his arms and win it from her.

Fortunately—or so he told himself—he managed to resist both impulses, and instead merely bowed and left the room. But she remained in his thoughts the rest of the day; and that night, as he tossed restlessly in his sleep, he dreamt he was on his knees before her, trailing kisses across her breasts.

This time, however, there were no footsteps to interrupt them, and as their passion grew he swept her up into his arms and carried her off to bed. He laid her down on the coverlet, and she held out her arms to him, beckoning to him, but as he bent over her to kiss her soft mouth, she called out another man's name.

He woke with a start and stared about him. The dream had been so real he expected to find her lying next to him. When he realized she was not there, he felt such a surge of frustration he seized his pillow and hurled it against the wall, where it exploded in a cloud of feathers.

He stared down at the white remnants of his pillow in dismay. *Another man's name.* Yes, that was the right of it. She was not destined for him. Yet, mourning or no mourning, she was ripe for a husband, and the sooner he found her one, the safer they both would be.

Chapter 13

To Catherine's great disappointment, Ryde's stay at Farthingsgate proved to be a brief one. He lingered only long enough to be assured his steward would recover and to send for a man from his Sussex estate to take over Bagshot's duties in the interim. Then he was off to London, presumably for the length of the Season.

He stopped at Rosington to make his goodbyes, and to give Catherine the direction of his man of business in Town, a Mr. Munroe. "You may send all your bills directly to him," he told her, "and he is authorized to advance you whatever cash you may need— within reason, of course."

Catherine was tempted to ask to whom she should address any unreasonable requests, but held her tongue, for she knew her ill humor stemmed not from the arrangements themselves, but from the fact that he was leaving and she would not even have the excuse of unpaid bills to justify a correspondence with him.

"We shall miss your company, my lord," Emily said, as Ryde bowed over her hand in farewell, "though I cannot blame you for choosing the gaiety of London over seclusion here amidst the cattle and the corn."

He straightened stiffly. "You make me sound the truant, Miss Lowery. Truth be told, I have spent the past five years amidst cattle and corn, and consider myself overdue for a change."

"I meant no reproach, my lord," Emily assured him with a smile. "I was merely envious, that is all."

Relaxing visibly, he smiled back, an action that transformed his face. He looked so much younger when he smiled, and so much more like his charismatic father. It seemed strange to recall, Catherine reflected, that when she had first met him she had only been able to see how he differed from his late sire. Now, she saw him for himself and was plagued by a desire to trace the outline of his shoulders, the shape of his mouth, the span of his well-shaped fingers with her hands.

"Farewell, Lady Catherine."

He had crossed to stand before her. She looked up and found herself caught in the gaze of his honey-brown eyes, and for a moment rational thought fled. Then she took a deep, steadying breath and gathered her wits sufficiently to speak. "Farewell, my lord. I hope your stay in Town will be a pleasant one."

"I shall be satisfied if it is a successful one," he countered, his smile vanishing and his expression turning bleak.

"You have business there?"

"Of a sort. I have a duty to perform that can best be attended to in London, I think."

"I see," said Catherine, struggling to keep her tone light. A duty to perform best attended to in Town? Was he off to find himself a wife—to provide that all-important heir? When she had asked him if he meant to marry, she had inferred from his tone that he meant to avoid the wedded state as long as possible, but perhaps she had mistaken his intent. She wondered what sort of lady he would choose. An image of her stepmother's porcelain features, beautiful but cold, rose up unbidden before her eyes. She wished she had the right to approve or disapprove his choice as he had the right to approve or disapprove hers, for then she might warn him to choose a loving heart over a beautiful face.

"Will you be returning to Farthingsgate this summer, my lord?" inquired Emily, picking up some embroidery work she had set aside.

"Yes, and when I do I hope to bring company with me. The neighborhood offers little diversion for you and Lady Catherine."

"Oh, do not be concerned for us, my lord," Emily assured him with a calm smile. "We are quite content. Mr. Elton keeps us amused and *au courant* with his visits, and Mrs. Howard is always going out of her way to introduce us to any visitors, especially any young gentlemen who might make *un beau parti* for Catherine."

Lord Ryde did not look pleased by this intelligence; in fact, he positively scowled. "Mrs. Howard is hardly a proper arbiter of who would and would not make a suitable husband for an earl's daughter, and even if she were, it is not fitting for her to play matchmaker while Lady Catherine is still in black gloves!"

"I would have thought you eager to see me married and no longer your responsibility," Catherine remarked in an undertone.

"I will, of course, be glad to see you wed to a gentleman of the proper rank and fortune," he replied tensely. "However, I greatly doubt such is to be found in Mrs. Howard's parlor!"

"Need I remind you that Mrs. Howard is my friend?" She resented his disdainful attitude, and she resented his assumption that she was not to be trusted to find a proper husband for herself, but most of all she resented the fact that despite her rank and fortune, it did not seem to occur to him that he might do worse than to offer for her himself. Especially after the way he had embraced her during that kiss—the earth-shaking, soul-shattering kiss—that they had shared in this very room two weeks ago. She looked up at his mouth and for a moment her whole body grew hot remembering how wonderful it had felt.

"I am sorry if I offended you," he said stiffly.

Catherine struggled to wrench her thoughts back to the current conversation. They had been discussing Mrs. Howard, hadn't they?

"I was under the mistaken impression you preferred honest speech to polite fiction," he added, when she made no reply.

He was throwing her own words back at her, but she still could not recall about what. She inclined her head helplessly. "*Touché*, my lord."

"No, Lady Catherine," he said in a gentler tone, "let us not continue to fence, for I take my leave of you and wish to do so on friendly terms."

He took her ungloved hand and bent to bestow a polite kiss upon it, but as his lips veered from her fingers to press softly against the sensitive skin on the back of her palm, Catherine was filled with an odd aching warmth. His lips lingered there for a ridiculously long time, causing her stomach to flutter, and when they finally withdrew, she was sorely tempted to beg him to bid her *adieu* in this same sweet fashion a second time.

As if reading her thoughts, he straightened abruptly and—avoiding her eyes—addressed Emily. "I had best be going. If either of you ladies should need for anything, contact Mr. Munroe. He will know where I am to be reached." Without waiting for a reply, he turned and strode from the room.

The chamber remained silent for a time after he left.

Emily tactfully concentrated on her stitching, while Catherine stared unseeing at the closed door, wishing she could undo the mischief his brief return had done to her heart. She had thought herself accustomed to his absence. Then he had galloped up out of the dark, and she had found herself more his captive than ever. She had thought herself acquainted with his character. Then he had revealed a capability for charm and good humor that belied the stern image she had used to solace herself on lonely evenings. She had thought herself assured of his disfavor. Then he had kissed her so passionately she had believed for one brief, perfect moment that he loved her.

She had thought herself fortified against wanting what she could not have. Now her defenses had crumbled, and he was leaving.

Did he comprehend what he had done to her? If he meant to stay such a short time, why, in heaven's name, had he bothered to return to Farthingsgate at all? He obviously cared little for the place and was in a hurry to be gone from it. The few weeks he had been in residence, he had spent most of his time at Rosington disturbing her peace. Yet each time he visited, he had all but ignored her. It made no sense!

"May I suggest a little needlework to settle your thoughts, my dear?" Emily suggested gently.

Embarrassed to have her upset so obvious, Catherine rose and crossed to the work table to extract one of the slippers she was embroidering as a gift for Lady Dent. Returning to her chair, she frowned down at a cluster of pansies, which fluttered in slightly uneven splendor above a small expanse of creme silk outlined in green and destined to be leaves. She certainly did not have Emily's way with a needle. Nor, she thought with a sigh, did she share Emily's laudable composure. Try though she might to emulate her friend's ladylike tranquility, she had yet to master the volatile Denton nature she had inherited from her father. Lord Ryde had awakened a restlessness in her she could not allay.

She threaded her needle and began to work, but her mind kept wandering, and so did her stitches.

"It is a pity Lord Ryde's stay could not have been a longer one," Emily said after a while. "The time flew by so quickly."

Catherine stabbed at her embroidery irritably. "If you wish my opinion, his lordship's stay was not too short, but too long—two weeks too long. I wish he had never come."

"You surprise me. I confess I rather enjoyed his visits. He can be quite charming when he chooses to be."

"I did not find him so, but then I suppose it is difficult to detect charm when one is constantly being frowned at."

Emily looked up from the pink rose she was stitching and said thoughtfully, "He was not frowning that first day he came to visit, when Lady Dent and I returned from the library."

Catherine felt her face warm. "No."

She tried to remember what his expression had been the following day, when he had come to call. He had sat there stolidly for over an hour saying nothing, until Emily had finally made up an excuse to leave them alone. Catherine had desperately hoped that he might repeat the embrace, or at least explain it, but he had just offered her a terse apology for his "abominable behavior." It had hurt to have him refer to their wonderful kiss in such a way, but it had hurt even more when he had asked her to please forget that it had ever happened.

She had been too proud to admit that such a thing was quite beyond her ability. That she would never forget it until the day she died. Instead, she pretended that it was of no importance, and for a few minutes, at least, she had the satisfaction of seeing him look quite as angry and distraught as she felt.

By the next day, however, he seemed to have done an excellent job forgetting that the episode had ever occurred, and Catherine was left to think of it as one does a vivid dream that becomes more and more engraved in memory, yet more and more unreal, the more it is recalled.

Emily broke into her reverie. "I do not believe Lord Ryde means to be unfriendly, my dear. I think he is simply uncomfortable with the role assigned to him by your late father."

Catherine jerked her needle through the cream silk with a force that caused it to pucker. "That he dislikes being my trustee, I have no doubt. It could hardly be otherwise, when he seems to find my company so distasteful."

Emily emitted a soft, disapproving cluck that reminded Catherine of their days in the schoolroom. "My dear, your logic leaves much to be desired. If Lord Ryde found your company distasteful, he would hardly have called so frequently to see you, now would he?"

"Since whenever he came he either ignored me or scolded me, I do not find that a very convincing argument."

"It is true that when the two of you are together you have a tendency to squabble, but in this case I do not consider that reliable evidence of dislike. On either side."

"Then why is he leaving again so soon?"

"I am sure he has his reasons, probably none of which has to do with you. It is hardly unusual for a gentleman to wish to visit Town, especially during the Season, and Lady Jane told me he was planning such a trip when your father sent for him in November."

"Do you think he is off to look for a wife?" Catherine inquired with a studied nonchalance that was belied by the accidental prick she gave herself with her needle.

"It is possible, but somehow I do not think so," Emily said, producing a plain linen handkerchief, which she wrapped gently around Catherine's finger.

"Not that it is of any moment to me whether he marries or not, of course."

"Truly? And here I thought you might prefer he remain a bachelor— at least a little while."

Catherine flushed. Emily had always warned her she had no skill for dissembling. "Are my feelings so very obvious?"

Emily patted her arm. "Only to someone who knows you as well as I do. You have actually been looking quite frosty all week."

"Then you do not think Lord Ryde — "

"Do not fret, my dear. I would wager his lordship is as convinced of your ill opinion as you are of his." There was a faintly amused note in her voice that Catherine found vexing.

"Really, Emily!" she exclaimed irritably. "I doubt you would find the matter so droll if it were Mr. Barrett galloping off and leaving us here to molder!" She had only meant to tease, but seeing her friend's face, her tone softened. "Forgive me, Emily. That was not very kind of me. Do you miss him very much?"

Emily, calm, imperturbable Emily, grew quite pink. "I do not know what you are referring to, Catherine."

"I refer to the rather attractive solicitor who led you out of slavery in Egypt—or rather, Yorkshire—and back to me, your affectionate pupil. Do you not care for the fellow?"

"Yes, though I know I should not. It is a nonsensical attachment, one I have tried to rid myself of without success."

"Why is it nonsensical?"

"A spinster of thirty mooning over a gentleman who is, I am sure, sought after by any number of young and attractive ladies?"

"Well I think him an exceedingly lucky fellow if he manages to secure your affections. You would make him an excellent wife."

"Thank you, my dear, but I think you are a bit prejudiced on my behalf."

"Then accept another's opinion. Only the other day I overheard the builder, Mr. Bridges, remarking to Mr. Elton what a fetching lass you were and that he envied the fellow who might spend his days gazing into your fine, soulful eyes."

The soulful eyes opened wide. "I cannot believe Mr. Bridges said any such thing! Why, he is a married man!"

"So Mr. Elton reminded him. Still, you must admit it was a pretty compliment, even if it did come from a round little man with eight children."

Emily tried not to smile, but a corner of her mouth twitched. "Fine, soulful eyes indeed. Makes me sound like a spaniel!"

"Many gentlemen adore spaniels."

"Catherine, that thoughtful expression of yours makes me uneasy. You are not getting one of your notions, are you?"

"Now Emily, really! What can I do with you here and Mr. Barrett far away in London?"

"I have no idea, but I have the uneasy feeling I may find out nonetheless."

❧

Lord Ryde's valet, Doddy, watched as his gentleman pulled on his white silk gloves, set his high-crowned beaver hat upon his head, and accepted his blackthorn cane with an abstracted air. He seemed little interested in how he looked in his new black dress coat and white satin knee breeches. He did not even glance in the mirror to admire the fine *Trone d'Amour* in which Doddy had tied his cravat.

Doddy was not offended, however. He was too pleased to see his gentleman finally dressed in a manner befitting his rank. It had taken some doing. After years of having to count every shilling, his lordship had been balky at the cost of outfitting himself with a first-class town wardrobe. But when Doddy had pointed out that the entire *ton* was waiting to see how the sixth Marquess of Ryde was faring in his attempts to restore the family fortunes, his lordship had been persuaded to make the requisite trips to Conduit Street and St. James's.

Doddy viewed the result with satisfaction. The exquisite tailoring of the black coat served to show off his lordship's broad shoulders and admirable height, and the gold-embroidered waistcoat, topaz stickpin, and antique gold watch fob added just the right touches of color to the black and white ensemble.

Emerging from his reverie, the marquess gave Doddy a wry look. "Well, you seem to be scrutinizing me hard enough. Will I do?"

Doddy draped his lordship's cloak about his shoulders and with a slight nod and a faint smile replied, "Yes, my lord."

"I am glad to hear it. My sister is most particular about her escorts, you know."

"I am sure Lady Charlotte will be quite satisfied, my lord."

His lordship raised a skeptical eyebrow. "Then you don't know Letty. Fashion is the very air she breathes, and she is terribly hard to please. Still, if I can scrape by her harsh judgment, I should be able to pass muster elsewhere."

Doddy said nothing, but he felt quite smug as he watched his master's elegantly clad back disappear down the hall.

❧

Despite his trepidation, when Ryde arrived at Crawford House in Park Lane, his sister surveyed him from head to toe in silence and then looked up, her green eyes wide and admiring.

"Heavens, Drew! When did you grow so devilish handsome?"

Startled a little by her reaction, he replied wryly, "Perhaps when I turned to Weston for my tailoring. What do you say, sister mine, do clothes make the man?"

"In your case they do," she said, giving him another disbelieving glance. "The ladies at Sally's ball are going to be most impressed."

"As are the gentlemen," he replied gallantly, though he suspected his comment would prove little more than the truth. His sister was looking disconcertingly pretty. "Indeed, I begin to wonder if George should not accompany us to fend the fellows off."

A shadow passed over his sister's face, and she flashed him a brittle smile. "I doubt George cares whether the gentlemen approve of me or not. He has other matters to occupy his thoughts."

Her bitter tone startled Ryde. Letty's marriage to the rich George Crawford had united an old name with new money but no one had mistaken it for a marriage of convenience. It was only too obvious that the two were rather ridiculously in love. Indeed, wagering on how long George could go without openly embracing his wife had become something of a running jest at family gatherings.

"Do not frown so, Drew. It is nothing worse than what happens to all married people eventually, I suppose." She slid an arm through his and said in a voice he would have thought cheerful if it had not contained that rather breathless catch she always got when she was upset, "We should be leaving soon. It is going to be an awful crush."

Ryde led his sister out to the carriage he had hired for his stay in town. She climbed inside without even seeming to note the worn state of the red leather seats or the complete lack of fashionable trim, and his concern deepened. He noted that their arrival at Lady Jersey's ball did not banish the small droop from her mouth or the suspicious glitter from her eyes.

Then a gentleman approached to ask Letty to dance. Ryde disliked the fellow on sight, for an air of dissolution clung to him as thickly as the sickly-sweet perfume he wore. Letty, however, seemed pleased to see him. She introduced him to Ryde with a large—if rather reckless—smile.

"Drew, allow me to introduce Mr. Ralph Daiches. Mr. Daiches, this is my brother, Lord Ryde."

Daiches flashed a smile that revealed too many white teeth. "No need for such formality, Charlotte. Your brother and I are old friends. The two of us were up together at Oxford."

Ryde, whose fists had clenched at such familiar use of his sister's name, stared at the man and realized with a shock that the latter part of his statement, at least, was true. This was Daiches, the dashing young buck everyone had longed to emulate. Handsome, rich, and royally arrogant, he had been the envy of every bumbling freshman drowning in his neckcloth. Yet here he stood, a dissipated dandy with ridiculously high collar points and red-rimmed eyes. For the first time, Ryde considered that his forced exile from Oxford might not have been a wholly bad thing.

Perhaps something of his thoughts appeared in his face, for Daiches suddenly colored and made a stiff bow. "Will you excuse us, Ryde? They are about to strike up a waltz, and I am eager to take the floor, for your sister is such a pretty armful."

Ryde almost called him out then and there. Then he saw the belligerent gleam in Daiches's pale blue eyes and the fear in Letty's chalk-white face and chided himself for a fool. He had not struggled five long years to restore the family name, only to plunge it into scandal because a slug like Daiches made him lose his temper. He was not his father, after all.

"I am afraid you will need to find yourself another partner, Daiches, for my sister is feeling too ill to dance."

"She looks well enough."

"Ah, but looks can be deceiving. It is such a sad crush in here, and what little air exists is so thick with scent —" Ryde paused significantly and regarded the other man, " — that I fear she is feeling quite faint. If you will excuse us? I think a restoring turn in the gardens will do her good."

There was nothing for Daiches to do but bow grimly and murmur that he hoped the lady would feel better soon.

Letty was not similarly constrained, however, and as soon as they reached a place in the gardens where they could not be overheard from the house, she turned on her brother and demanded fiercely, "How dare you humiliate me so!"

"Daiches treats you like his paramour, and you think it is *I* who have humiliated you? Heavens, Letty, I nearly called the man out. If it had been George standing there instead of me — "

"He would never have spoken so before George!" she exclaimed hotly, but despite her assured tone, she seemed to be trembling. "He was only trying to goad you, because you kept looking at him as if he were ... something quite foul."

"The fellow isn't actually a friend of yours, is he?"

Her chin came jutting out. "What if he is? I do not see that it is any affair of yours."

"For goodness' sake, Letty! Do you expect me to stand meekly by while you make mincemeat of your marriage?"

"It is my marriage," she retorted, her voice cracking, "and I will make of it what I will!"

A large tear, white with reflected moonlight, rolled down her cheek, but she kept her head held high. Ryde felt a sudden upwelling of tenderness and said in a much gentler voice, "There, there, mouseling, I am sure things cannot be as bleak as that."

"Yes, they can! George no longer holds me in affection."

"Nonsense! He was his usual besotted self at Christmas."

"Perhaps. But since our return to London he has been cold and aloof and spends little time in my company." Her voice caught. "I thought, perhaps, if I could make him jealous..."

Flirting with the likes of Daiches was hardly a rational or safe way to go about repairing a marriage, but Ryde refrained from saying so, for he suspected his sister now realized the fact as well as he. Instead, he said in his most bracing manner, "I suspect you are distraught over nothing, but do not fret. I will see if I can get to the root of the matter."

"But Drew — "

"Do not fear. I will be discreet. In the meantime, however, put the matter from your mind. I have a favor to ask of you."

"A favor?"

Ryde hesitated a moment. He had not intended to tell Letty his true reason for coming to Town. However, he needed something to keep her occupied and out of mischief until he had a chance to speak with Crawford, and he could think of nothing better than to enlist her aid in his efforts to find Catherine a husband.

He cleared his throat and began. "What I am about to tell you must remain entirely confidential." He noted with amusement that with those words he had suddenly gained his sister's complete attention. "Perhaps Jane has mentioned to you that when Trenwich died, he appointed me his daughter's trustee? Well, on his deathbed the earl entrusted me with another task ...."

The gentleman stared off into the distance, seemingly unaware of the dwindling voices or receding footsteps of the couple making their way back to Lady Jersey's ballroom. The young lady at his side, who had had plenty of time to repair her disordered clothing during their lengthy retreat behind the shrubbery, patted his arm and whispered, "They have gone, Phillip."

There was invitation in her tone, and in the way she pressed against him, but the gentleman did not respond. The coquettish smile turned to a pout, and it was suddenly apparent that the pretty young ingénue had more years in her dish than the kind moonlight had revealed.

She stamped her small foot, but the satin slipper she wore made little noise as it impacted the ground. "Phillip, really, this is outside of enough! Those two prattle on for an age, and when they finally leave you just stand there."

He turned abruptly. "Did you recognize their voices?"

She sniffed. "And what if I did? I am not an eavesdropper you know. I am not accustomed to listening to private conversations."

"It is rather late to be standing on your dignity, Louisa. You overheard that particular conversation, because you were cowering here in the shadows with your bodice undone. Now did you recognize the voices or not?"

She raised her hand to slap him, but he seized her arm and held it. "Well, Louisa?"

She glared at him a moment before capitulating. "The woman sounded like Lady Charlotte Crawford. I did not recognize the man's voice." The gentleman released the pressure on her arm and she pulled it away. "You are a beast, Phillip."

He did not answer. He turned away and stared in the direction of the house.

"Phillip, what is it? Why are you so interested? What did they say to turn you so … cold?" There was reproach in her tone but also a dawning curiosity.

He reached back and drew her to him, placating her with a kiss. The kiss was long and deep and led to a period of silence punctuated only by sighs and the rustle of silk. The lady asked no more questions, and the gentleman gave her his full attention, save for an occasional abstracted glance over her shoulder at the lantern-draped porch leading into the ballroom.

Later that evening, however, Mr. David Arthur was asked to point out Lady Charlotte Crawford to an old friend who wished to view the lady from afar. Mr. Arthur performed the requested identification but later remarked to his wife, "Do you not think it rather odd? I mean, Far hasn't a shy bone in his body, so why did he not wish to be introduced?"

Mr. Arthur's wife, who knew Mr. Arthur's friend, Phillip, Lord Farleigh, a great deal more intimately than her husband suspected, gave a tiny shrug of her lace-draped shoulders. "Perhaps he is planning his next seduction and wishes to be rid of Lady Charlotte's intimidating brother before he begins it."

Her words shocked him, but Mr. Arthur was even more shocked by her bitter tone. He knew Farleigh's reputation for seducing married women, but surely *Mary* was not to be numbered among Far's conquests?

"Oh, David," his wife snapped. "Do close your mouth, and go fetch me some punch."

Mr. Arthur clamped his lips together and stalked off in the direction of the punch bowl determined to find Farleigh and have it out with him.

Unfortunately for Mr. Arthur's peace of mind, however, he was not to have the chance. Lord Farleigh had already left the ball, departing almost immediately after Lady Charlotte Crawford had been pointed out to him.

Chapter 14

For several days after Ryde's departure, Catherine moped about, wrapping her melancholy about her like a cold but comforting blanket. Then one afternoon Mr. Elton called to request a favor.

He wished Catherine to pay a sickroom visit to Mr. Bagshot. The poor man seemed to be fretting endlessly over something, but would not tell Mr. Elton the cause. The steward had recovered amazingly, even miraculously, but the doctor feared the man's worrying would soon undermine all the gains he had made. Mr. Elton hoped a visit from Catherine would distract the steward from whatever it was that was cutting up his peace.

Despite her concern for Mr. Bagshot and her desire to accommodate Mr. Elton, Catherine was, at first, reluctant to go. She feared visiting Mr. Bagshot's chalk and flint cottage again would remind her of her first visit there, and of Ryde, and of the painful conversation they had shared upon returning from it. Ryde had claimed he believed her when she told him that she and his father had never been lovers. But had he really? Or did he believe her the trollop her stepmother painted her? Was *that* why he had kissed her and then been so cold to her? Did he think kissing her was of no significance?

The thought stung.

Mr. Elton pressed his point, and at last she agreed to visit Mr. Bagshot with Emily the next morning. When they finally entered Mr. Bagshot's room, however, and Catherine saw the steward's anxious face, she felt ashamed. She had been so wrapped up in her own misery, she had not taken Mr. Elton's concerns seriously. But the doctor was right. There were dark circles around Mr. Bagshot's eyes and tense lines near his mouth, and a mood of fretful restlessness all about his person that seemed unlikely to promote his health. Catherine, glad of Emily's always soothing presence, began to engage the steward in conversation.

Mr. Bagshot seemed cheered by their company, and Emily even managed to make him smile twice, but Catherine soon realized that a half-hour of lighthearted banter would not be enough to erase the lines of worry from Mr. Bagshot's face or to quiet the frustrated fidgeting of his still-healing body.

She returned the next day for another visit, this time alone, and after nearly an hour of careful coaxing managed to get Mr. Bagshot to confide in her that he was upset because he had learned Mr. Parker—the steward Lord Ryde had assigned temporarily to oversee Farthingsgate while Mr. Bagshot recovered from his injuries—planned to change the planting of the north and west fields. Poor Mr. Bagshot was certain Mr. Parker had no notion of what he was doing and would quickly drive the estate to ruin. Seeing how agitated the man was over the matter, she promised to have a word with "that know-nothing fellow." Only later, as she was returning home, did she pause to contemplate Ryde's reaction to what he would no doubt consider her unwarranted interference in his affairs.

The thought of his irritation made her smile.

She entered her meeting with the temporary steward in a cheerful frame of mind and quickly realized Bagshot's fears had been unwarranted. Mr. Parker was a reasonable man. When she mentioned, in a tactful way, some of Bagshot's objections to the plan for the new planting, Parker seemed to weigh the matter and modify his views. Catherine returned to Bagshot with Parker's revised plan and an explanation of his reasons for it, and Bagshot gave it his grudging approval.

In the days that followed, Catherine performed her duty as intermediary between Ryde's two stewards many times. For while both men were not nearly as far apart in their views as they believed, each was too proud of his position to negotiate directly with the other. In the process, she learned a great deal about diplomacy.

Perhaps, she thought wryly, *if my matchmaking effort for Emily proceeds well, and she leaves me to marry her lawyer, I should disguise myself as a gentleman and go offer my services at the Foreign Office.*

Unfortunately, as it turned out, her attempt at matchmaking did not start well. In fact, it began as a disaster.

Her idea had been to bring Mr. Barrett to Rosington. She assumed that once he and Emily were in the same house, nature would take its course. To that purpose, she had written to the lawyer and summoned him to Devon, saying she wished to consult him on a legal matter she purposely left unspecified. He replied with suspicious eagerness, assuring her he would come as quickly as he could arrange it. Catherine awaited his arrival with suppressed glee, making sure the new gowns she had ordered for Emily were all delivered before the appointed time.

Yet three days later, when her impatient ears heard the distant clatter of a carriage in the drive, she hurried to the front hall and beheld a scene of commotion that made her blood run cold. Mr. Elton stood in the doorway barking orders while two of her footmen carried a pale, crumpled-looking gentleman with a bloodied head toward the stairs. Feeling a lump of ice begin to form in her throat, Catherine realized the identity of the unfortunate. It was Mr. Barrett, whose post-chaise had overturned a mile south of Farthingsgate. Catherine was trying to think what to tell Emily, when Emily herself came out into the hall.

Catherine had known her friend harbored a *tendre* for the gentleman, but she was unprepared for the sight of Emily's stricken face when she spied Mr. Barrett, recognized him, and for a moment thought him dead. Catherine was filled with guilt, and promised God that if Mr. Barrett survived, she would do whatever she could to see her friend happy.

Mr. Barrett was installed in a chamber upstairs, and with Mr. Elton's careful ministrations did better than anyone could have hoped. Within three days he was even able to leave his bed and sit up and receive visitors. Emily did not wait for this milestone to attend him, however. She rushed to his bedside that very first night and would not leave his side until he was again conscious and Mr. Elton had assured her that he would make a complete recovery. Even then, she would not leave him long, but insisted on doing what she could to care for him. It was she who helped him raise his head so he could take his first drink of water, and it was on her arm that he first traveled the short distance to his chair.

Perhaps Catherine should have remonstrated with her friend as to the propriety of such devoted attention to a bachelor gentleman, but—as she was sure Ryde would be the first to assert—she was hardly a pattern card of decorum herself, and, in any case, she did not think it would signify once Emily and Mr. Barrett were wed, as she began to think they surely must be. Emily watched over Mr. Barrett with a fierceness quite out of keeping with her usual ladylike calm, and Mr. Barrett kept precise track of Emily's every movement, staring after her like a moonstruck calf whenever she was not in his immediate vicinity. The two were so wrapped up in each other, they did not require much attention from Catherine, which was just as well, for a few days after Mr. Barrett's accident, another guest arrived on Catherine's doorstep: her stepmother, the countess.

The lady informed her that she had been on her way to London when the whim had struck her to visit her stepdaughter at Rosington. Catherine was at a loss to understand why the countess—who harbored a dislike of her that verged on loathing—should wish to spend even a day beneath her roof, but she could think of no acceptable way to deny her stepmother her hospitality.

Ten long days passed without the dowager countess showing the least sign of shifting. Each day Lady Trenwich would sigh over how dull life at Rosington was and how meager and ill-bred the society, but despite her obvious discontent, she never mentioned a departure date. Catherine could think of no excuse to send her away. She began to fear that she would never be rid of her.

Then she conceived a plan.

Excited by her idea, Catherine hurried to call on Lady Dent to ask her friend for assistance. To Catherine's relief, that lady was only too happy to give it and suggested that Mrs. Howard would be pleased to help as well. With Lady Dent's agreement obtained, Catherine began her preparations. She was glad for the occupation, for it kept her busy and out of the countess's way most days. And even the nights improved, for Catherine could tolerate her stepmother's company quite well when she knew she would be escaping it soon.

Presently, all that remained was to dash off a quick letter to Jane and await Mr. Barrett's full return to health, a state Mr. Elton assured her would be achieved within a day or two. Catherine went about the house with a smile constantly tugging at her lips, for soon she would be free—not only of the countess, but perhaps of her longing for Lord Ryde's company as well.

After six long years of exile, she was going to London!

"Shall we leave him?"

Ryde looked down at the man slumped in a drunken stupor over his few remaining counters and slowly shook his head. "No, we had best see to it that he gets home in one piece." He turned and surveyed the dim and dangerous gambling hell that the Honorable Harry Marlow, the man face down on the table, had brought them to. This was not White's or Boodle's where a gentleman's servants could be discreetly summoned to cart a fellow home. No, if they did not see to it that Marlow was delivered to his apartments in St. James's Street, he might well not arrive at all. Ryde leaned over to pull one limp arm over his shoulders and staggered a bit. He had drunk a fraction of what Marlow had, but his head was swimming.

"Steady on," murmured his companion, Lord Farleigh, placing a steadying hand at Ryde's back. "Here, let me help you with him."

Between the two of them, they were able to drag Marlow out, none too soon judging by the looks that flashed their way as they went. Farleigh announced in a loud and nonchalant voice as they passed through the hell's dingy, low-hung doorway, "Oh, by the by, in case any of you dear gentlemen is contemplating following us, I ought to mention my carriage waits around the corner and my large friend here carries a rather sharp sword in his stick."

The looks grew darker, but the three men rising from their seats sank back down into them.

"A very good night to you all," Farleigh trilled pleasantly. Ryde, however, put all his concentration into not tumbling down the steps leading down to Jermyn Street and dragging Marlow and Farleigh with him. He felt unsteady and more than a little sick.

"I suppose that carriage of yours is as nonexistent as the sword in my walking stick?" Ryde inquired as they toiled down the dark, dank street.

"Actually, no. It exists. Indeed, here it comes now."

Ryde heard the rattle of wheels and the jingle of a harness with relief, but he dared not look round for fear his head would spin right off his neck. He had never been so bosky in his life. He left Farleigh and the driver to hoist Marlow into the coach, then turned away into the shadows to violently cast up his accounts. Farleigh waited discreetly for Ryde to be done, then handed him a handkerchief and assisted him up into the coach.

Ryde tried to apologize for his condition, but Farleigh cut his apologies short. "You're not drunk, old fellow, but drugged. It was obvious you were not going to do their work for them like fool Marlow did, so they slipped something into your wine. Once you were passed out as well, I could not possibly have gotten both of you out of there, and they would have been sure to retain at least one bird for the plucking."

Ryde gave Farleigh an appraising look. "So that is why you refused to taste a drop."

"Yes."

Ryde nodded approvingly and then winced at the fireworks that set off in his head. "Has anyone ever told you that you are a damned handy fellow to have around?"

Farleigh smiled his enigmatic smile. "On occasion."

❧

Ryde walked gingerly up the steps of his mansion in Grosvenor Square and stopped before the door. He did not knock, however, and Farleigh, watching from his carriage, assumed Ryde's head was too clouded for him to remember to do so. Farleigh realized his mistake, however, when Ryde, with a slightly unsteady hand, pulled a key from his pocket and inserted it in the lock. He opened the door quickly and, after making a listing but still elegant bow in Farleigh's direction, disappeared inside the house.

Farleigh watched the door close and shook his head. The sixth Marquess of Ryde continued to surprise him, and he found that unsettling. He had expected Ryde to be a younger, greener version of his profligate sire, but while the fellow gave the outward appearance of setting down the same wild path, there were subtler signs that gave Farleigh pause. To set out on a carouse and yet take a key so as not to wake the servants? It was not common behavior amongst the bloods of his acquaintance. And though Ryde had all evening acceded to every mad notion to spill from fool Marlow's mouth, it had not been with an air of enthusiasm or even pleasure, but with the air of one carrying out a necessary duty.

Farleigh had a suspicion as to what that necessary duty might be. He had observed Ryde, who at times could seem as green as a lad just down from school, eyeing the leading bucks of the *ton* with the cool, appraising air of a judge. He had noted how Ryde, while wishing to appear friendly and sociable to all, had inexorably winnowed his companions down to an elite few that consisted of the most eligible bachelors in England. He had sensed in Ryde, who acted the part of an ordinary young fribble come to Town for pleasure, the strength and calm assurance of a man with a clear goal in mind.

That his goal was to find a suitable husband for Lady Catherine Denton, daughter of the late Earl of Trenwich and the woman Farleigh had nearly married six years ago, Farleigh had known for some time, since the ball at Lady Jersey's when he had chanced to overhear a private conversation between Ryde and his sister. What he had not known, and could hardly have expected, was that the man would pursue the task with such personal attention and shrewd care.

No, Ryde was guarding Catherine well. He was weeding out suitors before they even knew they were in the running, for it was not yet common knowledge that she was an heiress or that Ryde was her trustee. That ignorance would not last long, however, now that Trenwich's widow had come to Town, for she seemed eager to set every fortune hunter within the sound of her voice upon her stepdaughter's scent.

Farleigh frowned. Damn the woman. She always had been a spiteful tart. Still, it might work to his advantage in the end. He had acquitted himself well this evening, and he sensed that he had cleared some unspoken hurdle with Ryde and was now safely in the race for Catherine's hand. If the news that she was an heiress became well known, Ryde might well close the field to newcomers, and Farleigh's position would be strengthened.

His clenched hand tapped restlessly against his mouth.

All he required was the opportunity to woo her, for this time he was determined to win her. And once he had won her—well, then he would take his revenge on her.

Revenge. For six long years of wanting her.

Farleigh raised his cane and tapped twice against the roof of the carriage. As it moved forward, he leaned back, closed his eyes, and began planning his seduction of Lady Catherine Denton.

Chapter 15

Ryde woke the following day feeling as if his mouth had been stuffed with uncombed wool and his head with the clapper of a bell that, with the slightest movement, seemed to clang painfully against his skull. For some time he remained as he was, sprawled across his bed in the artificial darkness of his curtain-drawn chamber, but at some point Doddy slipped into the room and placed a glass full of orange-brown liquid into Ryde's limp hand.

"Drink, my lord," Doddy murmured in a mercifully low voice, "it will ease the pounding in your head."

Ryde was in no condition to argue, and he obediently drank down the vile stuff in painful little sips. To his surprise, after a few minutes the ache in his head began to ease. As the pain receded, he began to be aware of a nauseating stench emanating… from himself.

"A bath, Doddy," he whispered hoarsely.

"At once, my lord," his valet replied in the same soft murmur. "The tub and hot water are waiting."

When Ryde emerged from his warm and restorative bath some twenty minutes later, he was beginning to feel a little more the thing. He had not, however, any patience for fashion, and donned a clean but worn shirt, his most comfortable pantaloons, and an old waistcoat that was cut unfashionably long. He forbore a cravat, preferring to leave his shirt open at the neck, and slipped his feet into a pair of Turkish slippers. Doddy attempted to render his hair presentable, but a few minutes of having his wet and tangled locks tugged at with a comb was enough to put Ryde entirely out of patience and to set his head to aching again. He curtly told Doddy to leave off and descended to his study.

Feeling grim and weary, Ryde crossed to the large oak desk that dominated the far end of the room and sat down. He pulled out a single sheet of paper from one of the drawers. On the paper, written in his large, sprawling hand, were two columns of names. Through a majority of the names, a single, black line had been struck. Ryde scanned the list and then picked up a pen and dipped it in the pot of his ink stand.

It had been common talk that the Honorable Harry Marlow was a drunkard, a gambler, and a fool, but Ryde had decided to see for himself whether the rumors were true. Last night he had found out that they were—and then some. It was clear Marlow would never make a suitable husband for Catherine. With a sigh of disgust that masked a deeper feeling of relief, Ryde crossed out Marlow's name.

The list, which had once boasted thirty names, had now dwindled to a mere four—no, five, Ryde corrected himself, for it was about time he added another name to the list that should, by rights, be written there. Farleigh was a widower, but he was considered extremely eligible, and he had proven himself to be a sober, intelligent, and capable fellow. He possessed a large fortune in his own right, and though not particularly handsome, many ladies—according to his sister Letty—found him attractive. Ryde had heard one or two rumors that Farleigh was a womanizer, but Ryde had seen no evidence of it in the time he had spent in his company, and, of late, that time had been considerable.

No, Farleigh seemed a good candidate, and yet Ryde hesitated. He had discussed his hesitation with his sister.

"Perhaps you fear Lord Farleigh would make *too* good a suitor," Letty had suggested with a sideways glance.

"Nonsense! What the devil have I been about these past five weeks, but trying to find her a good husband?"

Letty had shrugged her dainty shoulders. "I thought you were trying to find her someone to love."

"Of course," he had replied through tight lips.

"Well then, do you think Farleigh the sort of man your Catherine could become enamored of?"

"She is not *my* Catherine, and I don't think enamored is quite the word — "

"It is precisely the word, Drew! So far you have done an excellent job of sorting through the eligibles and eliminating the rascals, but the few gentlemen you have approved are a tame lot and hardly the sort to inspire a woman to any sort of passion."

"Catherine is a lady! Passion has nothing to do with it!"

"On the contrary, it has everything to do with it." Letty paused, her cheeks growing quite pink. "Believe me, Drew," she said in a lower voice, "if your Catherine is to fall in love, it will be with a gentleman who thrills her, not one who impresses her with his fine upstanding behavior."

He had icily requested a change of subject, and Letty—perhaps realizing she had gone too far—had complied with uncharacteristic docility. He had departed soon after, still angry, and it had been several days before he had been able to admit, even to himself, that Letty had been right about one thing. Farleigh seemed just the sort of man Catherine would probably admire: sophisticated, charming, urbane, and with an insouciant disregard for society and its opinions.

In other words, everything that Ryde was not.

He stared down at the paper in his hands and then wrote down Farleigh's name. That was the task he had set himself, was it not? To find Catherine a man she might care for. To find her a man she might love.

Angrily he blotted the ink. Perhaps Farleigh was that man.

He told himself that he hoped he was. If Farleigh wooed Catherine successfully and married her, then Ryde would at last be free to forget her and return to his life as it had been before. Only what if Letty was right? What if Catherine came to feel not only love for Farleigh, but passion? What if she came to burn for his touch and tremble for his kisses? Where would Ryde's satisfaction be then? Where even his composure? His hand tightened on the paper convulsively, and he crumpled it into a tight ball and sent it sailing across the room.

Perhaps Ellarby was a better choice after all. Or Jack Branston. Or Henry Capple. Or even that milksop Denby. At least the thought of her with one of them would not drive him mad.

"Excuse me, my lord."

Ryde looked up to find his butler, Harcourt, hovering apologetically in front of his desk. "Forgive the interruption, my lord, but a lady has called to see you. I informed her you were not home to visitors, but she refuses to leave. She says she has come too far to settle for the usual polite discourtesies."

"Polite discourtesies?" repeated Ryde, amused. "Was that truly the phrase she used?"

An affronted crease appeared between Harcourt's bushy eyebrows, but the rest of his egg-shaped face remained emotionless. "I quote the lady exactly, sir."

"Go on."

"She says she wishes to speak with you on a matter of some importance."

"Does she! And did she inform you what that matter was?"

"No, sir. She would only say that she doubted your man of business would consider it 'within reason.'"

Ryde suddenly went very still. "Did this mysterious lady offer a name?"

Harcourt nodded and was about to speak, when the door suddenly opened, and the lady herself appeared in the doorway. Ryde surged to his feet. For a moment, he was too startled to completely take in that it was really her, no longer in her mourning, but dressed in a reddish-brown gown the color of autumn leaves. Then the reality of her presence sank in, and he was grateful he had left off his neckcloth, for he suddenly found it difficult to catch his breath.

"Lady Catherine Denton, my lord," Harcourt announced unnecessarily, with a disapproving frown in the lady's direction as she folded back the veil that trailed so stylishly from her hat.

She did not seem to notice his butler's displeasure, however. Her attention was fixed on him. Ryde, sensing her scrutiny, strove to hide his tumultuous feelings, and the impulse he felt to pull her into his arms, snatch the fashionable hat from her head, and bury his face in that lovely, soft hair that seemed this afternoon to shine with the same autumnal glow as her gown.

He hoped she would speak, but she seemed to be waiting for him to break the silence. He groped for something calm and reasoned and polite to say, but nothing came. All too conscious of his disordered clothing and damp hair, and feeling a growing sense of injury that she had caught him so off guard, he adopted the frigid drawl and frosty expression of that most cold-blooded of Corinthians, Wintry Martin, and exclaimed in cool exasperation, "Do you plan to lurk in the doorway all day, madam, or would you care to sit down and explain what you are doing here?"

Catherine had braced herself for Ryde's disapproval, even anger, but not for the icy impatience she heard in his voice as he invited her to be seated and explain herself. For a moment, she was tempted to turn and flee, but instead she crossed to a chair and sat down. She had pushed her way into his study like the mannerless hoyden he thought her to be. Now she must sit and endure his annoyance until she had achieved what she had come for.

The butler bestowed another disapproving look upon her and turned to leave the room. Ryde, however, would not look at her at all. He sank back down into his large, leather chair and gazed off at some point behind her—no doubt a tear or ink spot in the carpet which he found less tedious than this unwanted guest.

She wished she could match his coolness. She wished she could school her features to look just so blank and bored, could will her voice to sound just so glacial and unfeeling. Unfortunately, it was quite beyond her powers to simulate indifference when her heart pounded and her pulse raced and her skin flushed warm at the glimpses she caught from beneath lowered lashes of Ryde's tousled hair, coatless shoulders, and open shirt.

He looked so raffish and romantic, so unlike his usual formal self, that she had to keep fighting the impulse to reach out and touch him to assure herself he was real. Her gaze kept slipping to his cravat, or rather to where his neckcloth should have been. Soft, curling hair peeked from beneath the open collar of his shirt, and she could see his pulse beating along the fine column of his throat.

There was a smooth, well-oiled thump. Catherine turned her head and realized with a start that the butler had not left the study's heavy oak door ajar, but had closed it shut behind him. She was suddenly acutely aware of how very masculine the chamber was. The darkness of the colors, the sprawling disorder of the furniture, the smell of leather and books and spirits and—she struggled to iden-tify another scent, faint but pleasing that brought back memories of childhood—ah, she remembered now: shaving paste. Her father had used a mixture that had smelled quite similar. Had Ryde been shaving? She cast another covert glance his way. He certainly had the look of having just come from his bath, despite the strange hour, for his hair still curled damply about his ears.

"Well, Lady Catherine? In case you have forgotten, I am awaiting an explanation. What are you doing here in London?"

Startled out of her reverie, Catherine replied more bluntly than she had intended, "I came to escape my stepmother."

His eyebrows rose. "Jane mentioned in her last letter that the countess had descended upon Rosington and showed no signs of leaving. Am I to understand that, unable to shift her, you decided to shift yourself?"

Catherine nodded. "Lady Dent has a house here in town. I explained the situation to her, and she very kindly invited me and Emily to join her and Mrs. Howard for their annual shopping expedition."

"And the countess?"

"She left Rosington shortly after we did."

"How long have you been in town then?"

Catherine hesitated. "Two weeks."

"*Two weeks!*" he exclaimed. "And you did not think to inform me of your arrival?"

"You did not leave me your direction."

"Yet you seem to have discovered it easily enough."

"Jane wrote and supplied it to me before we left Rosington."

"How very obliging of her. So you have known for the past fortnight where to find me, but did not think I merited even a note apprising me of your presence here in town?"

Catherine was not inclined to soothe his irritation, for his voice had warmed and his eyes, for the first time since she had arrived, sought hers. She could not read the emotion churning in their golden depths, but she was relieved to find any emotion there at all. She had begun to fear he had turned to ice. "I thought you would prefer not to be disturbed."

"Then why the devil have you turned up on my doorstep now? Defying all propriety, risking your reputation — "

"I wore a veil!"

" — outraging my servants," he continued inexorably, "invading my study — "

"I have come to ask for money!" she exclaimed, impatient to interrupt this catalog of her sins.

Despite his new impassivity of expression, she could clearly see that her answer did not please him. Well, what had he expected her to say? That she had missed him and had grown almost desperate for a glimpse of him? It was true, but it was not why she was here.

"In that case," he snapped in clipped tones, "I wonder you did not simply address your request to Mr. Munroe. He is quite capable of handling such matters. That is what I pay him for!"

"I would have done so, but I feared Mr. Munroe might not comply with a request for ten thousand pounds."

For a moment she feared he would choke. "*Ten thousand pounds!*" he shouted. "What the devil do you need ten thousand pounds for?"

She felt a wild temptation to say something outrageous, to say she needed it to buy ... what? A horse? A diamond? A lover? Instead, she told the truth. "I wish to arrange an independence for Emily so that she may marry Mr. Barrett and be happy."

She waited for that disapproving scowl she knew so well, but it did not appear. Instead his mouth, which had been stretched into a taut line a moment earlier, relaxed into a smile. "Has he gone and asked her then?"

She stared at him in astonishment. "Yes, shortly before we left Rosington. Only the silly goose refused him because he has two widowed sisters and a mother to support. She does not wish to be a burden to him, you see. So, I thought to solve the problem by providing her with — "

"Some money of her own."

"Yes." Catherine paused and then said with a hint of reproof, "You do not seem very surprised."

"Surprised about what?"

"About Mr. Barrett and Emily. You act as if you expected him to propose."

"I did, though not quite this soon."

"You cannot have known!" she said in disbelief.

He grinned at her. "How could I not? It was obvious from the first that they were taken with each other. Though I admit, I did not expect Barrett to make such short work of it. I had been planning to invite him to Farthingsgate this summer with the—with some other friends—so he could woo her properly. But clearly he needs no help from me. When is the happy day?"

"There is none! Have you not heard me? She has refused him!"

"A minor setback. I am sure you will manage to smooth the way of true love."

His amused, cynical tone irked her. "If it is within my power, I am determined to see them united."

"Of course. You make a habit of financing happy outcomes."

She glowered at him. "Emily's happiness is my uppermost concern."

He replied wryly, "As your bank balance, for the moment, is mine. Surely your purpose could be served as well by the payment to Miss Lowery of a yearly allowance of, say, five hundred pounds per annum? That would be sufficient for her to marry Mr. Barrett without worry, and yet allow you to make payments from your income instead of dipping into your principal."

"No. I wish her to have the money outright. Should something happen to me, I want her position to be secure."

Ryde frowned and snapped with considerable asperity, "You need not make it sound as if you had one foot in the grave."

"I have come close enough to dying to realize one cannot take such things for granted."

"Enough of such talk!" he exclaimed angrily.

"In any case," Catherine said, surprised by his vehemence. "I do not wish Emily to feel beholden to me. I thought there might be a way to disguise the source of the funds. Perhaps we could say it was a bequest from some forgotten relative?"

"We? What makes you think I mean to assist you in this folly? I am your trustee. I am supposed to protect your money, not help you to squander it."

"I am not squandering it. I am investing it in something—in some-one—very dear to me."

"Ten thousand pounds is an exceedingly large sum."

She assumed a thoughtful expression. "True. However, I dare say if I lost that much at the gaming tables, you would have no choice but to pay my markers."

He scowled at her—that old, familiar, beloved scowl. "You little minx! Are you attempting to blackmail me?"

"Of course not," she replied innocently. "Though I *was* thinking the other day how pleasurable it would be to sit down to a nice, friendly game of faro with Lady Chalmley and her friends."

Lady Chalmley's reputation for winning large sums by questionable means was well-known. Ryde gave a faint shrug and said with surprising mildness, "I see I am outmaneuvered. Very well, your governess shall receive her ten thousand pounds, and I shall contrive that she remain unaware of the true source of the funds."

Catherine stared at him in surprise, wary of this sudden acquiescence. "And what do you wish in return?"

"Merely the opportunity to show you around London and, now that your mourning is done with, to introduce you to a few acquaintances."

Chapter 16

If Ryde's offer to escort her about town gave Catherine hope that her trustee was not as indifferent to her as he appeared, she soon came to the conclusion that such hope was ill-founded. Ryde paid polite and even frequent visits to Lady Dent's house in Curzon Street. He showed Catherine, along with Emily, Lady Dent, and Mrs. Howard, around the sights of London. He saw to it, with the assistance of his sister Lady Charlotte Crawford, that Catherine and her friends were invited to most of the remaining social events of the dwindling Season.

Yet in all this, he treated Catherine with cool courtesy. He rarely sought her out, preferring the company of Emily or Mrs. Howard or even Lady Dent. Catherine might have been better able to bear Ryde's aloofness, if it had not been for the added insult of his matchmaking. Not satisfied with ignoring her, he began to arrange supposedly impromptu introductions to eligible gentlemen.

The first of these occurred when she expressed a desire to visit Montague House to view the Rosetta Stone. Ryde offered to accompany her there, and as Emily and the other ladies were unable to come due to a prior engagement, Catherine thought for once she would have Ryde to herself. At the last moment, however, he invited his sister and Lord Ellarby to join the outing. Ryde spent the entire trip deep in conversation with his sister, and Catherine was left to enjoy the afternoon with a stranger.

This subterfuge was repeated many times. She was introduced to the Honorable Jack Branston at a musicale, to Mr. Henry Capple at a picnic supper at Vauxhall Gardens, and to Lord Denby at a dinner party given by Lady Charlotte. And while Catherine was left to entertain the gentlemen foisted upon her, Ryde would saunter off and discuss music with Emily, or laugh at the fireworks with Mrs. Howard, or introduce Lady Dent to the Duke of Rutland so the two could exchange anecdotes on the breeding of hounds.

Three weeks came and went. Catherine grew more and more vexed with Ryde, and with the other inmates of 21 Curzon Street, who could not seem to grasp his perfidy. Emily thought him entertaining. Mrs. Howard found him amusing. Lady Dent considered him quite a considerate fellow—for a man. None seemed to find his behavior questionable. None seemed to notice his matchmaking.

Catherine was determined to tell him what she thought of his meddling, but she dared not speak until she knew Emily's independence was secured. Thus it was that the morning of the last major event of the Season, the Sunflower Ball, Catherine arrived back from her fitting at Madame Renée's with a carriage full of boxes and her stomach in knots. Tomorrow they would be closing up the house and returning to Devon. Tonight would be her last opportunity to speak with Ryde. And still the matter of Emily was not settled.

Catherine entered the hall, abstractedly untying the strings of her bonnet.

Suddenly a deep voice behind her said, "It would be better if you left the thing on." Too late she registered the click of the drawing room door. The gentleman had spoken so close to her ear, she had felt the warm tickle of his breath on her neck.

She whirled round and found her face only inches from his chest. She stepped back. "Ryde! Whatever are you doing here?"

For a moment, he seemed disinclined to speak and merely gazed down at her with an intensity that set the knots in her stomach to vibrating. Then he looked away and said casually, "I thought I might take you for a drive in the park."

She stared at him in surprise. "And what fine new gentleman shall I find waiting in your carriage if I agree to such an outing?"

"No one. Only myself. Does that disappoint you?"

"No, it pleases me—very much."

Something lit up in his face at her answer, something that at once gratified her and ignited some mischievous need to revenge herself on him for weeks of being ignored. "You see, sir," she continued, "if it is only you who is to be my companion, then I need not change my dress, and as I have spent the morning being poked and prodded in the name of fashion, I find that a great relief."

The warmth vanished from his eyes. "Anything to be of service, ma'am. Shall we be going?"

Catherine placed her hand on Ryde's stiffly proffered arm and wished she could think of something to say to lighten the mood between them. She could think of nothing, however, and the first portion of their drive was conducted in awkward silence.

After a time, however, even Ryde grew uncomfortable with the quiet. "I presume your visit to the *modiste* was in preparation for this evening's entertainment?" he inquired, glancing briefly in her direction before returning his attention to the horses.

"Yes," Catherine replied, glad to have the silence between them ended. "I had a final fitting of my new ball gown and collected the gowns I ordered for Emily, Lady Dent, and Mrs. Howard as well."

"I see."

Catherine eyed his profile warily. "I fear Madame Renée's bill will be quite exorbitant." She paused, waiting for him to say something. When he did not, she added, "If you wish to scold me, please do so now, for if the other ladies' gowns have turned out half as beautifully as mine, you will not find me repentant later."

Ryde frowned. "I hope you do not think me such a clutchfist as that," he said. "It is your money, after all, to do with what you will. In any case," he added in a softer voice, "it would be hypocritical of me to decry an expenditure I suspect I will enjoy as much as this one." He turned and regarded her. "I look forward to seeing you in your new gown, Catherine."

She felt her cheeks grow warm. "It is a pity you are not our escort this evening, sir, for then you would see it in its greatest glory, before it has been creased in a carriage, had its hem stepped on in a crush, or suffered the indignity of a splash of spilled punch or candle wax staining its beauty."

They had come to a quiet and secluded path. Ryde brought the horses to a stop. "I pray your gown will suffer none of those catastrophes," he said, his voice suddenly so low and deep it seemed to echo somewhere deep inside her, "but seeing it in its pristine state is not the greatest of my reasons for regretting that Ellarby will be escorting you to the ball tonight instead of myself."

"It is not?" she replied in a voice that came out a whisper.

He shook his head. "No." He lifted her hand and kissed each of her gloved fingers. Then he turned to stare moodily ahead. "Tell me, my lady," he said, allowing her hand to drop, but refusing to relinquish his hold of it, "what price do you put on honor?"

"Honor?" she repeated, unsure she had heard him correctly.

"Yes, honor. We gentlemen think it a virtue peculiar to our sex, yet I believe you ladies value it as well."

Catherine regarded him in surprise. "We do."

"Very well, then. As a lady of honor whose opinion *I* value more highly than any other, I would like your answer to a question."

She felt her throat grow tight. "I do believe, sir, that is the finest compliment you have ever paid me."

He turned to regard her, his eyes dark with some emotion. He reached up to touch her cheek with one gloved finger, then he dropped his hand and looked away. "The question, my dear Catherine, is this: is it ever acceptable to place happiness before honor?"

"I believe you know the answer to that before I give it, my lord. Honor must always come first."

Reluctantly he nodded. "Yes, but I thank you for reaffirming the point, for of late I have been sorely tempted to disregard it.

He abruptly released her hand and straightened in his seat, fixing his gaze straight ahead. "And now I had best be returning you to your friends, for no doubt they will be bursting to tell you of Miss Lowery's good fortune."

The horses began to move forward.

"Good fortune? Do you mean to tell me Emily has finally learned of her inheritance? When? Why did you not tell me?"

"The lawyer I hired for the task was about to inform her of it as we left. It is one of the reasons I spirited you away to the park. With that clear-as-glass countenance of yours, I knew you would be incapable of evincing suitable surprise otherwise."

"I beg your pardon!" Catherine exclaimed, sorely vexed, especially to learn what Ryde's true motive had been in taking her for a drive. "I am as capable of dissembling as the next lady!"

Ryde shook his head. "You are not, thanks be to heaven."

She could think of no suitably stinging rejoinder, so she gave a loud harrumph and settled into glowering silence. Ryde told her of his invitation to Mr. Barrett to attend the Sunflower Ball so he and Emily would have a chance to be together. After a time, her ingratitude struck her. "I should be thanking you for arranging everything so beautifully, instead of railing at you." She reached out and lightly touched his hand. "Forgive my grumbling. I am greatly in your debt."

His other hand came up to cover her own. "There is no debt," he replied brusquely. "Nor ever can be. I will always be at your service if you need me."

The tightness was back in Catherine's throat. "I am fortunate indeed," she said, "to have such a true friend."

When Catherine returned to 21 Curzon Street, the house was strangely quiet. She hurried to the drawing room, where she found Mrs. Howard pacing up and down, and Lady Dent darting worried glances up at the ceiling.

"Thank goodness you have come!" exclaimed Mrs. Howard.

"Is something amiss?" Catherine asked.

"No, not exactly. That is, we are not sure. It is Emily. She has had a bit of a shock. Oh, nothing to be worried about. No one has died, or rather, someone has, but it was months ago and she hardly knew him apparently. A distant uncle, I understand."

"Perhaps we should begin at the beginning?"

"Of course. Forgive me, my dear. I am a bit flustered. It was such an innocuous remark. I never meant to make her cry."

"Who was crying?" demanded Catherine confused. Surely she did not mean that Emily had been crying. Emily never cried.

"Don't blame the girl," snapped Lady Dent. "Comes into a bit of blunt, and you immediately suggest she leg-shackle herself to a man who will probably spend all her money and beat her in return."

"Really, Ada! All I said was that ten thousand pounds would allow her to make a fine match after Catherine marries."

"Catherine ain't marrying! She's too much sense for that!"

"Surely you do not expect her to go through life as a spinster? Why she has two or three suitors dangling after her already!"

"Those namby-pamby — "

"*Ladies, please!*" Catherine interrupted, startling the two women who had apparently forgotten she was present. Mrs. Howard flushed scarlet and Lady Dent sank further into her chair.

Catherine softened her tone. "Now let us return to the subject at hand. Am I to understand Emily has finally received notice of her inheritance?"

Mrs. Howard looked up in surprise. "You know of it?"

Catherine tried to shrug it off. "I heard rumor that a wealthy relative of hers had died and left her some money."

"Yes, an uncle. He died in March, but apparently it has taken some time to settle the estate and determine Emily's direction. The man's lawyer called this morning and requested an interview with her. They were closeted alone for nearly an hour, and after the gentleman left, Emily informed us her uncle had bequeathed her ten thousand pounds! That is when I made my unfortunate remark about her now having the means to marry."

"I see," said Catherine, not really seeing at all. Why had the reminder that she could now gratify her heart's desire reduced Emily to tears? "Perhaps she was undone by the shock of such good news," Catherine suggested uneasily. "I will go and speak with her."

Beginning to fear she had not fixed things quite as well as she thought she had, she started for the door. Seeing her friends' glum faces she added as cheerfully as she could, "I have brought you presents from Madame Renée. Why do you not go up and try them on? I would like to see how they look on you."

When Catherine arrived at Emily's chamber, she saw several of the boxes she had brought home with her stacked neatly outside Emily's room by one of the maids. Pressing her ear against the door, she could hear no sound of crying, so picking up the largest of the boxes, she took a deep breath and knocked. She thought she heard a muffled invitation to enter, so she pushed the door open and said brightly, "There you are. I have brought you a present."

Emily was curled up on the window seat. She turned at the sound of Catherine's voice but did not bother to dab at her tear-stained face with the handkerchief she clutched in her right hand. "I suppose you have heard the news?"

Catherine, after a moment's hesitation, put pretense aside and set the box down. "Yes," she answered gravely, "I have."

"No doubt you think I am behaving quite inexplicably, weeping when I should be rejoicing?"

"I am perplexed, but assume there is some reason behind it."

"No reason. Only regret."

"Surely you do not regret possessing ten thousand pounds?"

Emily shook her head. "No, *that* is like a dream come true."

"Then why are you weeping?"

"I have spent nearly half my life believing that if only my brother had granted me my fair share of our father's inheritance, I would have the life I wanted and be a happy woman. Today I realize I was wrong. I now possess twice the sum my father directed my brother to give me, and the one thing I want most in all the world can still never be mine."

"And what might that be?" Catherine demanded.

Emily hesitated and blushed. "Mr. Barrett's love."

Catherine was torn between a desire to laugh and an urge to shake her friend by the shoulders. Instead she said in the calmest voice she could muster, "You already have that! The poor man is besotted with you!"

Emily stared at her. "But... he cannot be!"

"Why not?"

"I am too old. I am a governess. I am not pretty."

"You are the same age as Mr. Barrett. Being a governess is a perfectly respectable occupation. And as for your not being pretty—for goodness' sake, Emily! Have you never looked in the glass?"

"Am I not plain? People have always treated me as if I were."

"You mean that silly family of yours!"

"Even when I left my family and became your governess, I was still ignored as only plain women are."

"I suppose it is possible that in those dull gowns you used to wear, and with your hair pulled back instead of cut short the way you have it now, and wearing those forbidding spectacles Mr. Barrett so fortunately crushed—well, I suppose it is possible some people might not have noticed how pretty you are."

"Do you think Mr. Barrett noticed?"

Catherine grinned. "Oh, yes! Sometimes at Rosington I would catch him regarding you as if you were a particularly tasty morsel, and he a man who had not eaten in weeks."

Emily's cheeks reddened further, but her expression did not brighten. Instead, new tears filled her eyes and spilled down her cheeks. "Oh, I have been such a fool! I never imagined he could truly care for me, else I would never have turned down his proposal."

Catherine stared at her in consternation. "But what about your lack of means? What about his mother and two widowed sisters? I thought you rejected him because you feared to be a burden to him."

Emily shook her head, looking miserable. "That was merely my noble excuse. You see, I feared he was proposing out of a sense of obligation, because I was so forward in my attentions to him during his convalescence. If I had known he truly loved me, I would have accepted him in a moment, even if I had to join him in my shift and steal the bread from his sisters' mouths!"

"A pity he did not think to mention so salient a fact during his proposal," Catherine remarked drily.

Emily rushed to her lover's defense. "It is not the way of men to put such sentiments into words. Especially at such a time."

Catherine was tempted to say it was at just such a time that clarity was vital, but she held her tongue. "Well, at least now you will not have to go to him in your shift. As a woman of means you can purchase a fine wedding dress and feed your in-laws cake."

"There can be no wedding without a groom, and as I have foolishly rejected mine, I'll have no use for either gown or cake."

"You shall simply have to persuade him to propose again."

"How? Since we have been in London he has not called once."

"Yes, you two are well matched. He is every bit as proud as you are." Seeing new tears begin to roll down her friend's cheeks, she added more gently, "Oh, Emily, do not despair. You will get your chance. Indeed, you shall see him tonight. I meant it as a surprise, but I will not have you crying any more. Ryde informed me of it while we were driving in the park. He has contrived for Mr. Barrett to attend the ball." Catherine allowed her voice to grow teasing, "Perhaps now you would care to see the delightful confection Madame Renée has created for you to wear tonight?"

Emily dabbed at her eyes with her handkerchief and nodded. Fifteen minutes later, as Emily stood before the long pier glass admiring Madame Renee's creation—a delicate white sarcenet gown trimmed with satin ribbon the same velvety brown as Emily's eyes and covered by a gold net overdress—her mouth fell open in awed delight. "Oh, Catherine! I feel like Cinderella!"

Catherine laughed. "Then we had best start getting you ready for the ball."

Miss Lowery was not the only one to benefit from Madame Renée's considerable talents that night. Mrs. Howard looked almost pretty in a rose-colored chemise robe over a cream white satin slip. Lady Dent was striking in a jonquil yellow evening dress with full melon sleeves and a regal quarter train. And the white Chinese silk gown Catherine wore was a deceptively simple masterpiece. The gored bodice was cut not in the usual fashion, but in a deep 'V', which at first glance gave the gown a modest and demure appearance. Filled out by Catherine's buxom figure, however, the dress, with its short Spanish sleeves and closely-draped skirt, became a striking tribute to the female form.

It was a tribute that did not go unappreciated by the gentlemen attending the Sunflower Ball, Ryde noted with irritation as he watched Ellarby escort the four ladies into the Argyle Rooms' Grand Saloon. Each of the ladies received their share of approving glances as they slowly made their way around the large, crimson-curtained room, but the glances directed at Catherine seemed to linger in a manner that made Ryde wish to land someone a facer.

The ladies finally found some unoccupied chairs amongst the chaperones. Ellarby took advantage of his role as escort and led Catherine away for the first set. Ryde, irked to have been deprived of her company so soon, approached Miss Lowery and requested the honor of leading her out onto the floor.

"You are looking very pretty this evening, Miss Lowery," Ryde said, as the steps of the country dance brought them together.

"Thank you, my lord, though I might take the compliment more seriously if your gaze were not fixed elsewhere."

Startled, Ryde's attention snapped back to his partner's face, but she was smiling up at him benignly.

"She looks quite lovely this evening, does she not?"

Ryde knew it was useless to pretend he did not know to whom she was referring, so he replied shortly, "Yes, she does."

The dance parted them, and when they next had chance to speak, Ryde firmly steered the conversation in another direction. "Miss Lowery, I understand you have had some salutary news."

"Oh, you speak of my inheritance. Yes, it was very kind of my uncle to remember me in such a way, though I am surprised by such consideration. I do not recall meeting him more than twice in my life. Still, I am most grateful. I have regretted being a burden to Catherine, and I am glad to now be able to pay my own way."

"I doubt Lady Catherine ever considered your maintenance a burden," he replied gravely. "You are more than a friend to her, you know. I think she sees you more as the sister she never had." Miss Lowery looked startled, but also pleased.

When the set was over, Ryde returned Miss Lowery to Mrs. Howard and Lady Dent, and she was soon asked to dance by an eager young man named Thornton. Ryde, meanwhile, was again deprived of an opportunity to dance with Catherine when she was claimed for the next set before Ellarby could even escort her back to her friends.

"If you continue to grind your teeth so, dear brother, you will have nothing left but stumps," advised his sister Letty in dulcet tones, as she slipped in next to him where he stood gazing fiercely at the dance floor.

"No one knows the meaning of courtesy any more," Ryde replied irritably, his attention fixed on one particular couple as they minced their way through the steps of a minuet.

Letty slanted an amused sideways glance at her brother. "Jack Branston cuts a fine figure, does he not?"

"Hmmph."

"You really are a rather expert matchmaker, my dear. He and Lady Catherine make a fine couple. They are much of a height, and his dark coloring contrasts well with her auburn hair and ivory skin." Ryde cast his sister a quelling look, but she continued, "He is rather a quiet fellow, but I hear she is just the type he favors: tall and buxom."

As if cooperating with Letty's teasing, the Honorable Jack Branston chose this moment to cast a surreptitiously admiring glance at Catherine's bosom. Ryde took an impulsive step forward, then recalled himself and came to a tense stop. Letty glanced down at his clenched hands and remarked gently, "Have you considered making a match with her yourself, Drew?"

"I promised her father a love match."

"You do not love her?" his sister asked in surprise.

He felt his face grow hot. How could he explain to his sister that what he felt for Catherine, what burned his blood as he watched her twirling round the dance floor in the arms of another man, was not love but lust?

Admittedly he had come to realize during the past few weeks that quite apart from the maddening physical attraction he felt for her, he cared about Catherine. He cared about her happiness, and he cared about her future, and he fretted at the thought that responsibility for both would soon be transferred to another.

He wanted to take care of her himself.

But surely that feeling, however strong, did not equate with love?

He realized his sister was still waiting for an answer. "Really, Letty, my sentiments are of no importance."

Letty raised a skeptical eyebrow. "Is that so?"

Ryde cleared his throat impatiently. "Lady Catherine's feelings are what signify. It is she who must choose."

"True, but how can she choose someone who has not even bothered to place himself in the running?"

He looked away and said in a low voice, "How can I, when I do not know my own intentions?"

Letty gave a startled choke of surprise, "Oh, Drew, you really are a dear! What are you worried about, that you will cause Lady Catherine to fall in love with you and then jilt her?"

"There is a family precedent," he said stiffly.

"Are you not being a bit presumptuous, my dear? I mean, I admit you have grown deucedly handsome, and you are developing a considerably more rakish reputation than I ever expected of you, but do you really think Lady Catherine will surrender her heart to you quite that easily?"

He stared at her. "Rakish reputation?"

She gave a tiny shrug. "Really, Drew, you cannot spend your nights carousing with the rowdiest bloods in London without expecting tongues to wag."

"Perhaps," he replied irritably, "but I can expect my sister not to listen to the tattle."

"Oh, Drew," Letty exclaimed, "do not frown so. Do you not know that a rakish reputation is to the ladies what nectar is to the bees? It can only do you good in your quest for Lady Catherine's heart."

"I desire no such assistance," Ryde snapped as the last notes of the minuet trembled to a close. "Still, you are right. Though she may be as impervious to my few charms as you suspect, it is time I put the matter to the test." So saying he turned and strode purposefully toward the couples leaving the floor.

Catherine made her closing curtsy and then rose and flashed a jubilant smile at her partner. It was her first London ball in six years, and she was enjoying herself tremendously.

Jack Branston smiled back and slipped her white-gloved arm through his with a possessiveness that seemed quite out of keeping with his usually placid nature. "You look quite shining," he exclaimed.

"I suppose that is because I am having such a wonderful time. I have not had the opportunity to dance in ever so long. I had quite forgotten how pleasurable it is."

"I suppose being just out of mourning, you have been deprived of a great number of the social pleasures you women rely upon."

"Actually, it has been a great deal longer than six months since I last danced the minuet, Mr. Branston. Closer to six years, I should think."

He regarded her with flattering amazement. "Unbelievable! Are the gentlemen of your acquaintance all blind, Lady Catherine?"

She laughed, gratified by his tone of disbelief. "That is very sweet of you, Mr. Branston, but gentlemen cannot dance with a lady who is not present. I have been hidden away in the country, you see, which is why I have such trouble remembering all my steps."

"Nonsense! You are an excellent partner. Why, you … you almost seem to float upon the air."

She flashed her dimple at him. He really was a dear. Not all that clever, and, though handsome, not very romantic, but he had a sweet nature, and there was something to be said for a man who gazed at one with such open admiration.

"Catherine!"

The painfully familiar voice jolted Catherine from her meditations. She turned to her right and saw the gentleman who had hailed her. For a moment she felt as if time had reversed itself, had flown backwards and she was once again a trembling girl of seventeen.

Then she regained control of herself and said in a voice of remarkable composure, "Why, Phillip, how lovely to see you again after all these years."

Chapter 17

Emily Lowery observed Lord Ryde's purposeful march with relief. Thank goodness! He was going to ask Catherine to dance, and the next dance was to be a waltz. Emily settled herself into an empty seat by Lady Dent and, hiding her hand in the folds of her dress, crossed her fingers. Perhaps his lordship was finally coming to his senses. She had almost begun to give up hope.

She watched as Lord Ryde drew near to where Catherine and Mr. Branston were making their way through the crush. Then she saw him abruptly stop. She nearly surged to her feet in frustration. Why did he tarry? Did he not realize some importunate gentleman might snap Catherine up before he reached her side?

Then Emily saw why he had checked his advance; he was already too late. Catherine was no longer in Mr. Branston's keeping. She was being led onto the floor by a dark-complexioned gentleman with broad shoulders and a strangely familiar face.

Emily struggled to put a name to the face, and then she remembered. Heavens, it was Lord Farleigh! An unladylike oath escaped her lips. Why must *he* show up at such a time?

The prune-faced matron on her right glared at her in outrage, and Lady Dent turned and exclaimed, "Goodness girl, what ails you?"

"Perhaps she is chagrined to find me standing here before her," suggested a deep, melodious voice above her.

Emily felt her face flame hot, but despite the hammering in her chest she managed to look up and reply in a voice that trembled only a little, "Why, Mr. Barrett, that is a rather nonsensical hypothesis. Have you come to tease me?"

His grey eyes regarded her gravely, "No, ma'am. To ask you to dance." He held out his hand to her, and she took it and rose to her feet.

Catherine saw Emily and Mr. Barrett twirl by, their faces lit with happiness, their movement about the floor as fluid and graceful as leaves spinning in a stream. She sighed.

"Is something wrong, my dear?" inquired her partner, who was holding her too close, his hand clamped possessively at her waist.

"It is nothing, Phillip. I was merely reflecting that I will soon have to be looking for a new companion, I think."

Her former fiancé's mouth quirked into that crooked, boyish grin that had once turned her knees to water. "You cut me to the quick, my dear. Here I am, transported above the firmament to have you back in my arms again, and all you can think of are your domestic arrangements?"

His charm was as facile as ever, yet it left her curiously unmoved. Catherine smiled in relief.

He drew her still closer. "Ah, that is better. I like to see you smile. You have a mouth made for laughter." He paused and then flashed her a look full of mischief. "For laughter, and for other things we gentlemen find even more pleasant."

"Phillip, behave yourself!" His charm could not move her, but his outrageousness could still make her laugh. Catherine fought down a chuckle.

"I cannot," he said with a grin. "Don't you remember? I never learned how."

"Sir, you have not changed."

His expression sobered. "Ah, but you have, my dear. You have."

Ryde saw Catherine's laughing face as she and Farleigh danced by and found he could not bear to watch the couple's spinning progress a moment longer. He turned away and went in search of stronger refreshment than was available at the punch tables. Thus he was on the other side of the room when the music stopped and Catherine and Farleigh, instead of heading back toward the chaperones, turned and disappeared through a small doorway.

"Damn!" Ryde swore under his breath as he made his way through the crush after them. The door led to a balcony that overlooked the street. Ryde found them there alone, standing in the darkness, and only the fact that they were at least two feet apart prevented him from planting his fist in Farleigh's face. "Lady Catherine."

She turned a startled face toward him.

He extended his hand to her. "I believe this is our dance."

"I think perhaps you had best excuse her, Ryde. She is feeling a bit faint. It is why I brought her out here for some air."

"When I want your advice, Farleigh, I will ask for it."

For a moment, Farleigh eyed him belligerently. Then he shrugged. "Very well." Turning to the lady he said, *"Adieu,* Catherine. Now that Ryde is here to escort you back to your friends, I suppose I had best go find the lady I was promised to for this set. May I call upon you tomorrow?"

"I fear I and my friends leave London tomorrow."

Farleigh blinked, but his smile never faltered. "A pity," he said lightly. "Still, I am sure we will meet again soon. Until then." He took her hand and kissed it, lingering over it for so long Ryde was tempted to snatch it from him. "Goodnight."

"Goodnight," replied Catherine, and to Ryde's consternation, he detected a sigh in her voice.

After Farleigh had gone, Ryde crossed to her and inquired stiffly, "Was he telling the truth? Are you feeling unwell?"

"I am, a little. Perhaps it is all the excitement. This has been an eventful day."

He fought down a sudden urge to smooth away the anxious lines around her mouth with a kiss. "I trust nothing went amiss with the announcement of Miss Lowery's inheritance?

"No, not in the end, and what little difficulty there was—well, it was not of your making. I am grateful to you for arranging everything so wonderfully. Emily is quite convinced the money came from her uncle."

Her gratitude pleased him, but the soft, faintly breathless timbre of her voice as she expressed that gratitude sent dangerous warmth radiating through his body. Feeling like a man caught unawares by drink, he clamped his mouth shut, afraid of what folly he might utter if he dared to speak.

Catherine, too, fell silent, and the quiet stretched between them until Ryde could bear it no longer. "If you are not feeling well, perhaps I should summon your carriage to take you home?"

"No, please! Emily would come with me, and she and Mr. Barrett have only had the one dance. There is nothing wrong with me really. I am a bit fatigued, that is all." Her voice trailed away, and Ryde noted the weary droop of her shoulders with a frown.

"Truly, sir, you need not be concerned. All I require is time to collect myself. The cool air is helping. I shall be fine soon."

"Very well," he said, wishing he had the right to sweep her up into his arms and carry her home to rest. "However, I think it would be best if we did not remain alone out here much longer."

"Why?" she said teasingly. "Do you fear I will do harm to your reputation?"

There were pearls twined in her hair, and light from the rising moon slanted across her throat and disappeared between her breasts. Ryde took a step backward and pressed his arms firmly to his side. "No," he replied thickly, "I fear I may ruin yours."

He heard her breath catch and saw her eyes open wide. For a moment he contemplated how much he wanted to kiss those eyes— the delicate lids, the feathery lashes, the piquantly arched brows. Then he remembered Farleigh's manner of address.

"Why did he call you 'Catherine'?"

She stared at him, uncomprehending.

"Farleigh, he called you by your given name. Is that not rather surprising familiarity for a man who has only known you the span of a single waltz?"

She sighed. "Phillip and I have known each other a great deal longer than that."

"*Phillip?*"

She turned and looked out at the moonlit street. "He was a beau of mine once. It was thought, briefly, that we might marry."

"I … see," said Ryde heavily, feeling rather as he had the time one of his prize mares had kicked him in the stomach.

"It never came to anything. I was sent home, and Phillip—Phillip married someone else."

The words stuck in his throat, but still he forced them out. "Did you love him?"

"What does that matter now?"

Ryde felt his heart hammering in his chest. "Did he not tell you? He is a widower and free to marry again. His wife died nearly four years ago."

"Why are you telling me this?"

"I repeat: *did you love him?*"

She turned abruptly to face him, her eyes glittering in the moonlight. "What concern is it of yours?"

The answer was obvious, and it struck him with a force every bit as powerful as his prize mare's well-shod foot. "This is what concern it is of mine," he said, pulling her to him and kissing her with all the pent up passion of his newly discovered love.

When he had kissed her before, at Rosington, he had felt as if he were melting. Now he felt as if he were on fire, and she were his only hope of being quenched. He reveled in the coolness of her: the cool softness of her lips against his mouth, the cool silkiness of her hair spilling past his cheek, the cool smoothness of her arms twining around his neck. His feverish hands slid over the cool, rustling curves of her gown, and he wished desperately he were more in control of himself.

He wanted to show her how much he cared for her, how much he treasured her, but his father's intemperate blood burned in his veins, and he could not keep his caresses in check. The kiss deepened until he was not just kissing her, he was invading her, his tongue wantonly bucking and plunging into the sweet wetness of her mouth with a desperation that frightened him. He needed her so very much.

All the hard-fought discipline he had clung to these past weeks was gone as if it had never been. All the frustrated desire he had ruthlessly suppressed was back, surging through him in relentless, unending waves. His hands were as intemperate as his mouth. They roamed wildly up and down her body, stroking every precious curve, caressing every exposed bit of skin. He wanted to claim her; he wanted to make her his in any way he could. He was teetering on the edge of total abandon.

Exerting the last bit of his will, he managed to tear his mouth away from her sweet lips, but it turned out to be an empty gesture, for he just began trailing kisses across her eyes, her cheeks, down her neck, following the moonlight as it disappeared between the perfect swell of her breasts.

She sighed—a long, trembling sigh that finally seemed to restore his reason. He drew back and looked anxiously into her face.

"Catherine? My dearest, I am sorry! Can you forgive me?"

She shook her head and opened her eyes and smiled tremulously at him. Then with a shy gentleness that caused his heart to begin drumming loudly in his chest, she reached up and pulled his face down and kissed his cheek and then his chin and then his mouth. He tried with all his might to remain still beneath the tantalizingly delicate pressure of her lips, but then—to his total wonder and delight—her tongue flicked diffidently against his mouth. The tentative gesture was repeated, and when his lips parted in response, her soft tongue slipped inside his mouth and began caressing it. For a moment, he went a little mad with the pleasure of it. Then the tiny part of his mind that was still functioning realized things had to stop. He had to stop them now—right now—or he truly would ruin her out on this cursed balcony. He gently pulled free and retreated a good three feet away from her.

Neither of them spoke. Ryde was grateful for the shadow he had moved into, for he did not want her to see his state of disorder. He tried to calm his labored breathing as well, for he was embarrassed to have her hear how truly out of control he was. She, however, was still illuminated in moonlight, and he stared at the rapid rise and fall of her chest in wonder. She was breathing just as hard as he. That pleased him, and, for a little while, he stood there watching her—feeling a small thrill of triumph. Then suddenly she made an abrupt movement toward him. "Ryde?" she whispered, her tone anguished. "Have I given you a disgust of me?"

He was so chagrined by her words, he rushed forward and put his arms around her. "No, of course not, my dear! How could you think it?" It felt dangerously good to hold her, and he realized he was playing with fire, but he felt too tender to abandon her a second time.

She looked up at him, her expression still anxious. "Was I being too forward?"

He shook his head. "No, my sweet. I was worried about my behavior, not yours." He pressed his cheek against her hair and added softly, "Your kisses pleased me greatly." He felt her relax in his arms.

To his considerable surprise, he had calmed enough that he was content to just hold her like that, and they stood quietly for a long time. Then suddenly he felt a tickling tug at his neckcloth. He looked down. Her long, beautiful fingers were busily trying to untie his cravat.

"You are sailing into dangerous waters, my dear."

She looked up at him mischievously. "I have been wanting to do this ever since that afternoon in your study." She finally managed to untie the thing, and he saw her push the white linen aside. Suddenly, he felt the gentle brush of her lips against his throat.

He groaned.

"Well, well. What have we here?" sneered a deep and not entirely sober voice to his right.

Ryde spun around, pushing Catherine behind him.

The intruder flashed him a mocking grin. "Where are your manners, Ryde? Are you not going to introduce me to the lady?"

"I think that would be unwise, Daiches. That nauseating scent you use might cause her to swoon."

"Sir, I would be a little less free with your insults, if I were you!" Daiches cried angrily. "You are in a rather tight coil."

"Am I?" inquired Ryde with surprising cheerfulness.

"You may pretend nonchalance, but I am quite aware of the identity of the lady cowering in your shadow."

"Is that so?"

"Yes. It will make an interesting piece of tittle-tattle, will it not? How Lady Catherine Denton was out on the balcony being seduced by her trustee?"

Ryde's smile faded. He would need to marry Catherine now—and quickly. He had already seen the necessity of it, and it pleased him. But what was he to do about this poisonous slug? He was not about to allow his darling's name to be dragged through the mud. He said with quiet menace, "You tell tales about my betrothed at your risk, Daiches." There was a small gasp behind him, but Ryde kept his attention focused forward.

The other man's eyes narrowed. "She said you would likely force the little heiress's hand." His mouth twisted maliciously, "Well, that still makes quite a tale, does it not?"

Ryde felt his temper flaring dangerously. He forced it under control, and said with silky politeness, "You know, Daiches, you are not looking at all well. Perhaps I had best see you home."

"I have no intention of leaving."

"Are you certain? It would be a pity if you endangered your health with too much conversation."

Daiches eyes widened, and his mouth went slack in alarm.

Ryde continued, "You know, too much indulgence can weaken a man. Thankfully, since my arrival in town, I have been able to maintain my own health through regular visits to Jackson's boxing saloon. Do you box, Daiches?"

The other man did not answer. Ryde allowed his gaze to drift lazily over Daiches's narrow shoulders, corseted stomach, and padded calves.

"It is an exhilarating activity," he continued, "though if one is too accomplished at it, one runs the risk of becoming a bit of a bruiser. It becomes so terribly tempting, you see, to settle even minor disagreements with one's fists, rather than with reason."

Despite the coolness of the evening, Daiches's face was shiny with sweat. "Now that I think on it, Ryde, you are right. I am not feeling at all well. If you will excuse me, I think I had best be leaving." He turned abruptly and disappeared from the balcony.

Ryde turned back to Catherine. "I had better follow him to make sure he behaves himself. You will be all right?"

Catherine nodded, looking subdued.

He tried to reassure her. "No worries, my dear. Things will work themselves out. I will call on you in the morning, and we will discuss everything." He hesitated a moment, wondering if he dared kiss her goodbye. He decided against it. Tomorrow, after he had declared himself properly, he could indulge in tasting those delectable lips again. For now, what she needed was time to recover from Daiches's embarrassing intrusion.

"Goodnight, sweetheart," he said gently.

"You are leaving?"

"Yes, but you must not concern yourself. I will see to it that all is made right."

He started to go. She called after him, "Sir, your neckcloth!"

He had forgotten. He stopped to retie it, his mouth quirking into a smile as he remembered how it had come to be untied. "Thank you for the reminder, my dear. My valet would have been most shocked if I had come home to him in such a state."

❧

In truth, Doddy was growing quite accustomed to shocks, or at least surprises, from his young master.

Since the deathbed summons that had sent his gentleman haring off without him eight months earlier, Doddy had noticed a change in his master, and since their arrival in town, the change had grown considerably more pronounced. Gone was the predictable country gentleman with the sober habits and placid routine. In his place was a lord of quicksilver moods and surprising starts who seemed at once younger and more mature.

Which is perhaps why Doddy maintained such aplomb when he entered Lord Ryde's bedchamber the next morning to find his master already up and bathed and pacing the room in his dressing gown while three footmen stood at attention receiving his instructions.

Lord Ryde addressed the first one: "I want roses, John, fine, large, red ones, as many as you can find, delivered to 21 Curzon Street as early as can be managed. Sam," he said, turning to the second footman, "I want you to run to the shop of Mr. Jeffries, the jeweler, in Bond Street. Tell him I would appreciate if it he would open his doors a half-hour early for me, as I wish to make an important purchase. And Thomas, you are to deliver this note to my sister, Lady Charlotte. There is no need to wait for a reply, but let her maid know that I will be calling for an answer in an hour."

The footmen filed out, and Lord Ryde turned and saw his valet.

"Ah, Doddy, there you are. Just in time. I am in a hurry to be dressed. I would have begun without you, but you are the expert in such matters. What does one wear to call upon one's future mother-in-law?"

Without blinking an eye, Doddy crossed calmly to his lordship's wardrobe and began picking out the proper clothes.

❧

Catherine was still in bed when Emily knocked softly at her door. "Are you awake, my dear? I am sorry to intrude so early, but there is something I must discuss with you."

"And I with you," Catherine replied, hurriedly sitting up. "I was only waiting until I thought the hour late enough to rouse you. I am in sore need of your advice."

Emily came and sat on the edge of the bed. "Your meeting with Lord Ryde on the balcony—it did not go well?"

"You know of it?"

Emily nodded. "I saw you leave with Lord Farleigh. I was debating whether to go after you myself, when I saw Lord Ryde follow you out. I considered you would be safe enough with him and thought no more about it until I saw Lord Farleigh dancing and realized you and Lord Ryde had not yet returned to the ballroom."

"Emily, I — "

"No, my dear, you owe me no explanation. Despite what Mr. Barrett thinks, I am content to let you find your own way in this."

"Oh, Emily! I fear I have made a terrible mess of things. Ryde is coming this morning to ask me to marry him, and I have no idea what answer I should give him."

Emily drew back to gaze at her in astonishment. "Heavens! You make my head spin! Here I thought I had come to explain Lord Ryde's behavior to you, and instead I need someone to explain yours to me. I thought you *wanted* to marry Lord Ryde!"

"I do! But he is only offering for me to protect my reputation. A man discovered us out on the balcony, you see.

"He saw Lord Ryde kissing you?"

"No, something far worse. He saw me kissing Ryde."

Emily laughed. "Kissing a gentleman is hardly a crime, my dear. If it were, half the ladies of the *ton* would be spending their days in the Tower."

"You do not think me fast?"

"No, my dear, only passionate. You always were, you know—about everything. It is one of your dearest qualities."

"I doubt Ryde would agree with you. My behavior has trapped him into a commitment he must regret."

"Am I to understand," Emily inquired archly, "that his lordship was merely standing there, innocently minding his own business, when you threw your arms about him and embraced him?"

"Of course not! He kissed me first; then I kissed him back."

Emily lifted one expressive brow.

"I take your point, but the result remains the same." Catherine was silent for a moment then said, "Emily, what did you mean when you said you had come to explain Ryde's behavior to me?"

Emily, looking suddenly uncomfortable, rose from the bed. She crossed to the curtains, and began drawing them open. "It is something Mr. Barrett confided in me last night."

"How selfish I am being! I have yet to ask your news. I saw you and Mr. Barrett dancing together. I had hoped he might take you in to supper, but I did not see him then or afterwards."

"I fear we had a quarrel. He left the ball early."

"A quarrel?" Catherine repeated in dismay. "What about?"

Emily did not answer at first, and when she did, she avoided Catherine's eyes. "Mr. Barrett brought up the subject of marriage again. He told me he harbored a deep affection for me, and I in turn assured him that I returned his regard." Emily paused. "He demanded we set a date to be wed, but I told him I was not ready to do so until I was more certain of your future."

"Emily, you didn't!"

"Catherine, I know what it is to be alone. I will not abandon you until I am sure you have someone to cherish and protect you as a husband would."

"I will not have you sacrificing your happiness for me! I can find another companion—Mrs. Howard or Lady Dent, perhaps."

Emily shook her head. "You need a husband, my dear, not another companion, which is what I told Mr. Barrett. I said I had hopes Lord Ryde and you might make a match of it."

"Surely you did not tell him of my feelings for Ryde!"

"Of course not. I merely indicated that I thought his lordship might be coming to feel some regard for you."

"But he doesn't."

"You did not see him look murder at any man who danced with you. Besides, you said yourself, he kissed you."

"I suspect he merely succumbed to an impulse most men experience when they find themselves alone with a woman in the dark. I could have been anyone. He would have done the same."

"You do not truly believe that?"

"I do not know what to believe. Most of the time he ignores me, and when he does pay me some attention, it is only to thrust some eligible gentleman under my nose like a dratted matchmaker!"

"My dear, there is an explanation. You see, last night when I suggested that Lord Ryde might marry you, Mr. Barrett grew

disturbed and told me that was not the idea at all. Then he told me
of the deathbed promise Lord Ryde made to your father."

"What promise?"

"To find you a husband."

Catherine stared at Emily. "You cannot be serious!"

Emily opened her hands in an affirming gesture. "Mr. Barrett
seemed to think Lord Ryde was hard at work at the task and expected
to secure you one by summer's end."

Catherine said faintly, "How very efficient of him."

"No, dear, you do not understand. His task was not only to find
you a husband, but to find you one who was not marrying you for
your fortune. No doubt he feared that if he courted you himself, it
would seem as if he were taking advantage of his position."

"You really think so, Emily?" Catherine asked, her voice skeptical,
though a budding sense of hope began to uncurl inside her.

"Yes I do, my dear. It may turn out that you have reason to be
grateful to the gentleman who intruded on you and his lordship last
night. For the threat of scandal may have given Lord Ryde exactly the
excuse he needs—to do what he has wanted to do for some time now."

Chapter 18

Ryde's first stop was the jeweler, where he purchased a ring that had caught his eye several weeks earlier. It was an unusual design, consisting of small, finely-cut sapphires encircled by sparkling pale green stones Ryde was informed were peridots.

"A symbol of marital happiness they're considered to be, my lord," Mr. Jeffries said with a wink as he placed it before Ryde. "Not as commonly sought after as emeralds, but they have their own unique beauty." *Like the lady I am buying it for*, Ryde thought.

Ryde waited with remarkable patience as the shopkeeper fussed and fretted over finding just the right box and then spent another ten minutes painstakingly wrapping it in paper and ribbon. When Ryde finally emerged from the shop, he glanced at his watch with a grimace, but the thought of the package nestled in his pocket restored him to good humor. He climbed into his curricle with a cheerful nod to Jeffries, who watched smilingly from the doorway.

In contrast to his stop in Bond Street, Ryde's visit to his sister's house was refreshingly brief, due in part to the fact his sister was still abed and sent her answer to his inquiry via a scrawled note of admirable brevity:

*Countess staying not at Trenwich House but
with brother in Portman Square. Am curious
what you are up to. Call on me this afternoon.
Letty.*

The butler in Portman Square was less than welcoming. "Mr. Daugherty is not home to callers this early in the morning, sir," he intoned frostily, preparing to close the door in Ryde's face.

Wondering if the Daughertys had a family predilection for rude servants, Ryde handed the man his card. "I am not here to see Mr. Daugherty, but rather his sister, Lady Trenwich, on a matter of some importance." The sour-faced butler grudgingly ushered Ryde inside and directed him to wait in a poorly-aired drawing room decorated rather gaudily in the Chinese style.

Lady Trenwich swept into the room fifteen minutes later in a black velvet gown that despite its mourning shade and high collar boasted a provocative panel of black lace over the lady's white bosom. Her blond hair was cut short and was covered by a sheer black veil that cascaded around her face and over her eyes and nose, leaving only her pale pink mouth visible. She seated herself on a scroll-shaped sofa upholstered in red-striped silk.

"Good morning, Ryde," she said, pushing back her veil to reveal those startlingly blue eyes.

"Good morning, countess."

"I have been expecting you."

"You have?"

She did not answer, but surveyed him intently from head to toe. Finally she said, "Do you think you might sit down, sir? As he seated himself in a chair opposite, she murmured, "I had forgotten how you tower over a woman."

"You said you were expecting me?"

"Ralph Daiches came round to see me last night."

"I see," Ryde said heavily. "Then you know why I am here."

The corner of her mouth twisted, but she did not speak. She regarded him silently, a strange expression on her face.

"Countess?"

"You are looking well, Ryde. Town life agrees with you."

"As to that, I have my doubts, but I thank you for the compliment. You fare well also, I trust."

"I do not fare well," she snapped, one hand clenched tightly in her lap. "I am alone—and lonely."

"Surely that is a common state for a woman newly widowed? With time I am sure your sorrow will ease."

Her voice lowered, almost to a whisper. "I speak not of grief, Ryde, but of need." She looked him full in the face, and he was shocked by the longing in her eyes. She said huskily, "I have missed you."

Immensely uncomfortable, Ryde rose to his feet and strode toward the fireplace. "I am sorry."

The countess rose and followed him. "Why do you ignore me? Do you not find me attractive?"

There was something almost plaintive in her voice. Ryde turned, but the expression on her face was one of challenge, not of supplication. She reached up, bent his head down to meet hers, and ran her tongue teasingly along his lips. "Does this not stir you?" she demanded in whisper. "Or this?" She took his hand and placed it on the black lace covering the swell of her breasts.

He withdrew his hand and stepped back. "I had thought I made myself clear at Trenwich, madam. I am not interested in what you offer."

Her eyes narrowed, and her pretty face grew hard. "No, of course. You are only interested in what my stepdaughter offers—a fortune of three hundred thousand pounds. Tell me, Ryde, while you were pawing her out on that balcony last night, did you sustain your ardor by thinking of all that gold?"

He seized her by the shoulders, and for one long, dangerous moment battled down his anger. When he was finally able to let her go, he took several steps backward and said grimly, "I think I had best take my leave, madam, for, woman or no, if you ever speak of Catherine like that again, I will not be responsible for my actions."

Apparently she took the threat seriously, for she retreated to the sofa and sat down. Adjusting her skirt, she said in a voice that despite its ladylike timbre carried clearly down the length of the long room, "Our business is not yet done."

Ryde watched her warily. "I do not think we can have anything more to say to each other."

"*Au contraire*, my dear Ryde. I think that we do. After all, you have come here to tell me you wish to marry my stepdaughter, have you not?"

Ryde felt a strange chill of foreboding. "You have yet to explain why Daiches should come running to you with his tales."

She shrugged. "I had asked him, as a friend, to keep an eye on you, as I suspected that sooner or later you would try—by fair means or foul—to persuade Catherine to marry you."

"Am I to gather you disapprove my suit?"

"Let us simply say I suggest you seriously reconsider your plan to marry my stepdaughter."

"Why?"

"Surely you do not wish to subject your family name to yet another scandal? What do you think will be said when it becomes known that you have betrayed the trust my late husband placed in you and seduced his daughter to win her fortune?"

"If Daiches breathes one word of what transpired last night, I shall tear him limb from limb."

The blue eyes regarded Ryde contemptuously. "Your bullying tactics may silence him—he was ever a weakling—but how do you propose to silence *me*?"

"You would drag your own daughter's name through the mud?"

"Stepdaughter! And lest you forget, it was you, not I, who seduced her on a public balcony to coerce her into marriage."

"I would never coerce Catherine into anything! If you and Daiches would but keep silent, her choice would be free. I — " he paused, loath to speak his heart before a woman who obviously cared so little for her stepdaughter's happiness, but it had to be said. "I love Catherine, and I hope that in time she may come to love me. I would not ask her to marry me otherwise."

The blue eyes glittered. "Do not gammon me with such nonsense! You love that ape leader? Why even when she was a girl, her beaux were more interested in pursuing me than in wooing her!"

"*That is enough*, madam!"

"You love her gold, Ryde, not her."

"I care nothing for Catherine's fortune."

"Then will you return it to my son when you marry?"

"I cannot. The money is Catherine's. I will not deprive her of it."

Her mouth curled in derision. "I thought as much. You are as lacking in honor as your father before you, and so the world shall know."

"We will leave my father out of this discussion! We speak of Catherine and of her future."

"No, we speak of the fortune you and that lawyer robbed my son of! I tell you, Ryde, I will not let you marry Catherine and reap the reward for your larceny. If you will not cry off, I will see to it that Catherine will not have you."

Ryde felt a tiny flicker of fear. "How do you propose to do that?"

"Catherine is as stubbornly proud as her father. No matter how desperate she is for a husband, she will not marry a man she despises."

"And why should Catherine despise me?" The coldness in his chest was growing.

"If I learn she is to marry you," the countess replied, "I will be forced to warn her of your true character. For her own good, I will have to confess to her that you are my lover; indeed, that you have been my lover since the day her father was laid in his grave."

"*She will not believe you!*" Even as he said the words, however, Ryde feared he was wrong. Had not Catherine accused him of this very thing when he had first suggested she leave Trenwich? It was all too possible, even probable, that Catherine would find the countess's story a confirmation of her own worst suspicions.

The woman's pale eyebrows rose, and she flashed him a bellicose smile. "Is it not fortunate that your manner to me while we were still at Trenwich was so warm! I cursed you at the time for your dissimulation, but now I may have to thank you, for it will give the tale so much greater credence in Catherine's eyes."

Ryde felt so cold now, his heart seemed incapable of finding its rhythm. Surely Catherine would know she was lying? Catherine knew the countess, knew her true character, knew the deceit she was capable of.

Yet *he* had known the countess's true character, and still he had believed the calumny she had told him about Catherine and his father.

Perhaps if he had more time—time to convince Catherine how deeply he loved her, time to make her fall in love with him—there would be a chance. But there was no time left. He came to a grim decision.

"And if I do not ask Catherine to be my wife?"

Lady Trenwich gave a small shrug. "Then I shall have no cause to invent past indiscretions."

"And the events of last night? You will keep silent? You will ensure that Catherine's name is not sullied by that slug Daiches?"

"Why should I wish to make scandal for my own daughter?"

He felt his fingers curl. "Really, ma'am, you give new meaning to the word hypocrite."

"I do not care what you call me, Ryde, as long as we understand each other. I trust my position is clear?"

"As crystal," he replied bleakly.

When Catherine had finished dressing, she descended to find Emily busily directing the closing up of the house. "Can I be of some help?" she asked.

"I would welcome the assistance, but first perhaps you should look in the drawing room. There was a delivery for you earlier."

Spurred by Emily's teasing look, Catherine hurried down the hall. She found the drawing room full of roses—large, red, velvety roses that filled the air with scent. Were they from Ryde? The thought made her tingle, and she went from bouquet to bouquet seeking a card, a note, some indication of who had sent them. But there was nothing. She returned to the dining room. "Oh, Emily, it is like a garden in there, but there is no card! How am I to know who they are from?"

Emily raised an amused eyebrow. "With all your many beaux, I suppose it is difficult to pin down."

"Do not tease me. I want to believe they are from Ryde, but I find it hard to credit. Surely there was some message?"

"According to Mrs. Taylor, the roses were delivered by a footman, but you know Mrs. Taylor's trouble with colors. She thought his livery familiar, but could not place it. She asked the fellow if there was a message to go with the blooms. He shook his head and said it would arrive later."

Catherine sighed with frustration that she had not been there to greet the footman herself, but realized all the wishing in the world would not solve the mystery for her. She busied herself assisting Emily and waited for Ryde to appear.

He arrived shortly before noon. Catherine led him to the drawing room in the hopes he would settle the matter of the roses once and for all, but after one long, indecipherable glance at the red bouquets as he entered, he ignored them entirely. Emily quickly excused herself saying she had to supervise the loading of the carriages, and Catherine and Ryde were left alone.

"How does the morning find you?" he inquired in a cool, polite tone that caused Catherine's heart to sink.

"I am fine, though a bit fatigued." She took a place on the sofa, and motioned for him to do likewise. "Will you sit down, my lord?"

He ignored the motion of her hand, and seated himself on a chair situated a good ten feet away. "So," he asked abruptly, "you are leaving London today?"

She bit her lip. "Yes."

"I will be leaving Town myself soon."

Catherine began to wonder if she had simply dreamed the interlude on the balcony the night before. "Will you be summering at Farthingsgate?"

There was a grim note of defiance in his voice as he replied, "That is my plan."

"That will please your neighbors. You were sorely missed when you left so abruptly in the spring."

He turned and gazed at her, his expression suddenly intent. "Devil take the neighbors! Did *you* miss me?"

Looking into his eyes she was unable to prevaricate. "Yes."

She thought she saw a flash of triumph cross his face as he rose and came to stand before her. He asked in a deeper voice, "And will you be pleased to have me near when I return?"

She would not look at him, but she could feel him standing there, his presence as palpable as a fire roaring in the hearth. Her body, against her will, grew warm. "Sir, about last night—"

"You need not trouble yourself about it," he assured in clipped tones. "Daiches has been persuaded to keep quiet. As for other tongues— well, I will see that they, too, remain silent."

"Other tongues?"

"Last night, Daiches visited your stepmother and informed her of what he had seen."

She looked up. "Why should he do that?"

He looked tense and angry. "It is of no importance. What matters is that I have spoken to her, and she has agreed there will be no scandal." He paused and added heavily, "You may proceed as if last night never occurred."

She tensed. "Then what you said to Mr. Daiches about our being betrothed—"

For a long moment he was silent. Then he said tightly, "I am sorry. I had to silence his prattling tongue."

"And what occurred between us last night—it meant nothing?"

He gazed at her, some strong emotion working at his mouth. Then he looked away. "I was wrong to behave as I did. I hope you can forgive me."

She felt a sudden ache in her chest. "I am not sure that I can."

He looked back abruptly at that, and she continued in a rush, before her pride could rise up to stop her. "Has it not occurred to you that perhaps I was pleased to have you kiss me? That perhaps I have hoped and longed for you to do so ever since that afternoon at Rosington? That perhaps I kissed you in return because I care for you?"

He stood there staring down at her, and she was tempted to turn and hide her face against the cushions like a shamed child. Why had she let her tongue run on so? She had mortified them both. She fixed her gaze on his well-polished boots. Soon they would turn and stride from the room, and she would be released from this disconcerting torture. Of course, once he was gone, it was unlikely she would see him again. His embarrassment over her extraordinary avowal would no doubt cause him to avoid her.

She was just contemplating the bleakness of such a future, when the gleaming Hessians she had been staring at disappeared from view, displaced by two well-muscled legs clad in cream-colored kerseymere. She dragged her gaze up from those finely-shaped limbs to his face— now that he knelt before her it was almost level with her own—and she was startled by his look of tender affection.

He took her hands in his and held them in a fierce grip. "My brave, reckless darling! Do you not know the danger of placing your heart in a gentleman's keeping?"

She tried to look away but couldn't. His gaze held her as tightly as his fingers did. With a sigh, she said shakily, "You are right. Give it back to me, and I shall strive to forget last night ever happened."

"And if I do not wish to give it back?"

"You must! You clearly have no use for it yourself!"

He reached out and touched her cheek. "Are you so certain?" In a deeper voice he added, "I have no wish to forget last night."

She found herself with eyes closed, leaning toward him as a flower leans toward the sun. She forced her eyes open and focused on what he had left unsaid. "But you have no wish to marry me."

He did not answer.

"I see. You enjoy kissing me and embracing me, but neither the threat of scandal nor your promise to my father is sufficient inducement to take me as your wife!"

"Catherine, please! The situation is complicated. My promise to your father — "

"Was to find me a husband. I know. I must admit, you have done an admirable job in selecting suitable candidates for the position. I find Lord Ellarby and Mr. Branston, in particular, most agreeable. Perhaps if you invite them to Farthingsgate this summer, I may be able to bring one or both up to scratch by summer's end, and thus release you from your obligation."

His grip on her hand tightened. "You would marry someone else, when you care for me?"

"Perhaps I have mistaken my feelings," she snapped, tears pricking at her eyes. "Perhaps I imagined you a different man than you really are. I thought you like your father—sharing his warm spirit and loving heart, but it seems all you really share is his propensity for playing the rake."

She felt his grip convulse on her wrist, and as he surged to his feet she was lifted off the sofa with him. He gazed down at her, his golden eyes blazing. "If that is the role you assign me, ma'am, then I had best do my utmost to live up to it." He circled her with his arms, pulled her fast against the length of his body, and kissed her.

At first the kiss was all about anger. His mouth was fierce. The hard arms holding her so tightly were unyielding. His whole body seemed to vibrate with his fury. But she was his equal in acrimony. Her body was rigid with her determination to show her disdain. Her arms were locked tightly at her sides. Her mouth was clamped shut against his onslaught.

Yet she had not reckoned on how susceptible she had become to his touch.

His lips pressed hard against her mouth, and she fought against the thrill of her mouth so weighted down by his. He worried at her lips, trying to force them apart, and her stomach filled with warmth as he sucked and licked and nibbled on them until she wanted to cry out with delight. Still, she managed to hold the line until his hot tongue flicked caressingly along the separation between her lips over and over and over again until she gasped. The moment her mouth opened, his tongue thrust its way inside, and she felt his arms tighten around her in triumph.

For a moment, she felt defeated. Then without thought, she began responding to his incursion with a foray of her own. She opened her mouth still wider, inviting him in, and when his tongue settled more comfortably inside her mouth, she began twining her own tongue around it—round and round—until she felt his tongue begin to quiver and his mouth tremble and his whole body begin to shudder. Now it was she who felt triumphant.

Her victory was short-lived, however. His mouth grew tender, his lips caressing. His hands slid up to softly stroke her hair. She began to struggle to remember her anger, let alone recall its source. He began to nuzzle her cheek and whisper endearments into her ear, and she found it difficult to remember anything except how much she needed him.

Now it was her mouth seeking his, and this time when they kissed, there was no anger at all—only aching sweetness. Her hands crept up to twine around his neck, and she clung against the press of his body. She felt almost dizzy with the notion that she was no longer entirely separate from him, for the pleasure of his embrace had eliminated her sense of where she stopped and he began.

That joyous sense of union did not last, however. A restless sense of separation began to gnaw at her. The warmth of his hard body pressed against her sent waves of longing through her. His strong arms had pulled her so tightly to him that there was not an inch of her that was not touching him somewhere, but still she did not feel close enough to him. She wanted him closer—needed him closer in a way she did not understand but made her ache. Her arms around his neck tightened, and she tried to push herself still more closely against him, desperate for a connection she had no idea how to achieve.

Suddenly he was wrenching his mouth free and pushing her away, his breath coming in loud, ragged gasps. *"Forgive me!"* The words emerged part entreaty, part groan.

She felt like groaning herself. Bereft of his warmth, robbed of his touch, she felt her whole body yearning for something that she sensed had been snatched out of her grasp. She wanted to be back in his arms, longed for it with an intensity that brought tears to her eyes.

He was staring at her, his golden eyes quite dark, an expression on his face that only seemed to fire her longing higher. Suddenly, she feared he knew exactly how intense her need for him was. The thought was so mortifying, she lashed out at him without thought. "Congratulations, sir, on your performance," she said haltingly, striving to fill up her heaving lungs. "You act the role of seducer most convincingly."

She heard him suck in his breath at her words. He looked as startled as if she had struck him.

"Unfortunately, I do not wish a lover," she continued. "I wish a husband." She paused to catch another breath.

He opened his mouth to speak, but she shook her head, cutting him off.

"Though you may think me one of those fashionable ladies who weds only to take a lover, I will not be unfaithful when I marry, I promise you, no matter how disordering your kisses may prove."

His cheeks went quite red. He shook his head and in a low, angry voice demanded, "Why are you always so quick to believe the worst of me, Catherine? Why cannot you accord me *any* of that reservation of judgment you bestow so easily upon my father?"

She could think of no answer to give, except the obvious and inexpressible one that she loved him. Soon, however, it did not matter whether she had an answer or not, for with a stiff bow, Ryde excused himself and left the room.

Chapter 19

Catherine looked up from the account books to stare abstractedly out the window of the refurbished study at Rosington. The strong summer sunshine that sparkled outside did nothing to warm her, though it poured through the glass and spilled over her desk like molten gold. What did sunlight or even summer matter, when one's life stretched before one as cold and empty as figures in a ledger? She took a deep breath. Heavens, how she dreaded the meeting to come.

As she gazed unseeing out the window, a movement in the distance caught her attention. A single rider, a gentleman, was coming down the road from Farthingsgate and turning down the drive. For a moment, as it always did under such circumstances, Catherine's heart began to pound. Then she recognized the man. It was only Jack Branston coming to pay a call. She watched him approach down the drive, and for a moment she allowed herself to pretend he was another man, a man whose face she could conjure up in perfect detail merely by closing her eyes ...

Her wistful imaginings were suddenly interrupted by the knock she had been expecting at her study door. Catherine turned and called out an invitation to enter with a voice that sounded steady and normal, though her throat was suddenly as dry as the paper in her blotter.

Emily stood in the doorway, looking faintly uncertain. "Mrs. Owen said you wished to see me?"

Catherine nodded, understanding her friend's skepticism. Since their return from town six weeks earlier, she had spent very little time in Emily's company.

In part, this was because Catherine was rarely home. Her stepmother had followed them from town and now lounged about Rosington like a malevolent house cat. Determined to escape the countess's company, Catherine spent a great deal of time either riding about the estate or participating in outings with Ryde's many house guests at Farthingsgate.

In part, this was because Catherine was avoiding Emily in order to make her see reason. The time for sacrifice was over. The time for her friend to begin crafting her own life had arrived. But first Catherine had to convince Emily that change was needed. To that end, she had summoned Emily to the study today so that they might play out the final act in a necessary, if painful, charade.

Catherine motioned for Emily to be seated in a chair opposite her desk. For a moment, as she did so, Catherine could only look at her. Then she cleared the large lump that had settled in her throat and forced a smile to her lips.

"I am glad you have come, Emily. It seems we have had little time to talk to each other of late."

A wistful look passed over Emily's face. "You have been busy. As have I."

"Yes. With all the amusing diversion Ryde has provided us with his house full of guests, it is not surprising we have had little time for each other's company."

Emily regarded her with anxious eyes. "Yet I could wish you did not find some of the company quite so entertaining."

Catherine tensed. "To what precisely do you refer, Emily?"

"I refer to your behavior towards several of Lord Ryde's guests." Emily paused, and then added in a lower voice. "My dear, you have never been a coquette. Your disposition is too modest and your heart too tender to purposely set out to capture an affection for which you have no use. But of late I have watched uneasily as you have set about not one, but two flirtations with gentlemen who seem all too likely to take the matter seriously. And what of Lord Farleigh? His attentions grow more marked by the day. He spends more time here at Rosington than he does at the home of the aunt he is supposedly visiting."

"You need have no worries about Phillip!" exclaimed Catherine with a bitter laugh. "His heart is quite safe. If he seeks anything, it is my fortune, not me."

"Perhaps. But the same cannot be said of Lord Ellarby or Mr. Branston. Their affections seem genuinely engaged. Do you mean to have one of them, or are you simply toying with them to make Lord Ryde jealous?"

Catherine flushed and replied stiffly. "Jack Branston and Lord Ellarby are entertaining themselves with harmless flirtations, as am I. As for Ryde — "

"Yes, what about that much-tried gentleman?" demanded Emily. "Do you take joy in seeing him consumed by jealousy?"

"Consumed by jealousy!" Catherine exclaimed with a snort. "Yes, so consumed that when Mrs. Herront and her oh-so-pretty daughter decide to return to London, he jumps at the chance to abandon his guests and escort them there!"

Emily continued the argument for some minutes, but Catherine was finally able to turn the conversation in a different direction.

"Emily, have you heard from Mr. Barrett lately?"

Her friend's cheeks grew pink. "No."

"That is a pity," Catherine remarked. "Are you sorry now that you refused him for my sake?"

Emily's eyes grew suspiciously bright. "I did what I thought was right at the time."

"And no doubt you would sacrifice yourself again for me if the occasion arose?"

"It will not arise," Emily replied, her voice bleak.

Catherine nodded. "No, there aren't many gentlemen who would ask a lady twice to marry them, let alone a third time. Still, it is a pity. You see, I have been thinking. Now that my stepmother has settled herself here and seems intent on remaining for the foreseeable future, I really have no need of an additional companion. And now that you have some money of your own, you no longer require my charity to keep a roof over your head."

Emily winced at the harsh words. "I have no wish to be a burden to you."

Beneath the cover of her desk, Catherine clenched her hands so tightly her nails dug into the flesh of her palms. "Oh, you are no burden," she replied in as blithe a tone as she could manage, "but we don't appear to rub together as well as we once did, so perhaps it is time you thought about finding a home of your own."

"Very well, Catherine, if that is what you wish." Emily's voice was the merest of whispers.

"I think it would be best for both of us," Catherine lied.

With tears now overflowing and slipping down her cheeks, Emily nodded and, head held high, she rose and exited the room with the dignity of a queen.

Catherine sat there a moment and watched her go. Then she dropped her head into her hands. She remained like that for some time, until the butler, Hodge, knocked on the door. Catherine wiped at her eyes, and bade him enter. Not by a flicker of his expression did he betray that he realized she had been weeping.

"Forgive me, my lady, but Mr. Branston is downstairs. Shall I inform him you are not receiving callers?"

Reluctantly, Catherine shook her head. "No, tell Mr. Branston I will be down in twenty minutes. And have Cook prepare a picnic luncheon for two. I feel the need for some fresh air and hope to persuade Mr. Branston to join me."

"Very good, my lady." He turned to leave.

"Wait, Hodge. There is one more thing. Do you recall the visitor I mentioned earlier this week?"

"Yes, my lady."

"I expect him today. When he arrives, I would like you to do the following ...."

❦

Emily was sitting on the edge of her bed, staring into the fire, a folded chemise forgotten on her lap, when Mrs. Owen knocked on the door. "Oh, dear," said the housekeeper, as she entered the room, "so it's true." Her eyes fixed on the half-filled portmanteau which lay open on the bed. "It's sorely missed, you'll be, Miss Lowery, and that's the Lord's truth."

"Thank you, Mrs. Owen," Emily said, maintaining a fragile grip on her composure, "but was there something you wanted?"

"Oh, sorry, miss. 'Fraid my wits are wandering. It's just that Lady Catherine left word with Hodge that you weren't to leave without picking out a few books from the library to take with you."

Emily felt her throat grow tight. She had returned to her room determined to gather her things and prepare for her departure from Rosington, but she had not imagined that her former pupil would expect her to depart this very day.

"Where is Lady Catherine?" Emily asked.

"She and Mr. Branston have gone for a picnic," Mrs. Owen replied, avoiding Emily's eyes. She paused for a moment, and then added, "I'm that sorry, miss, to bother you like this, but Hodge was wondering if you wouldn't mind picking out your books now, so he'll have time to find a proper box to put them in."

"I will be down directly," Emily said, willing her voice to remain steady. Mrs. Owen nodded in understanding and departed. After she had gone, Emily crossed to her dressing stand, poured water in the basin, and splashed water on her dazed face. How had she and Catherine ever come to such a pass?

Emily had known ever since that last morning in Curzon Street, when Catherine had emerged so pale and silent from her interview with Lord Ryde, that something had changed between Catherine and herself. It was not until they had returned to Rosington, however, that she had sensed the invisible wall her former pupil had erected between them.

At first, she had assumed the change in Catherine was temporary, a result of her unhappiness at having refused Lord Ryde's proposal.

That Catherine had refused him was plain enough. One glance at Lord Ryde's taut face and stormy expression as he swept from the house had been sufficient to discern it. Yet why Catherine had done so was a mystery, for Catherine refused to speak of the matter, or of anything else during the journey back to Rosington.

Once home, Emily hoped Catherine would be more forthcoming, but she continued her silence. Emily, used to Catherine's confidences and just beginning to grow accustomed to having someone to confide in herself, concealed her hurt and waited for the aloofness to pass. But it did not pass. Catherine grew even more withdrawn and spent her days riding about the estate, inspecting, supervising, rarely speaking of anything but drainage or crop rotations or repairs to the farms she wanted finished before the fall. Emily saw little of her, for Catherine rarely sat to breakfast and took to taking dinner on a tray in her study. Alone with her regrets, Emily spent her days managing the house and her nights curled up in the library sketching plans for the home she would probably never have.

Then two weeks after their return to Rosington, Lord Ryde returned to Farthingsgate, bringing a large party of friends from London and his sister, Lady Charlotte, to act as his hostess.

At first, Catherine seemed reluctant to have anything to do with the Farthingsgate party. Then Lady Charlotte paid a call on them and persuaded Catherine to accept an invitation to dinner. Emily noted with interest that Catherine, despite her reluctance to accept the invitation and her protestations that she did so only out of courtesy to Lady Charlotte, took great pains with her toilette and wore one of her as-yet-unworn new dresses, a flowing gown of Indian muslin printed with a swirling pattern of blue and green reminiscent of the sea.

Lord Ryde also seemed anxious to make a good impression. As soon as their carriage pulled up to Farthingsgate's steps, he hurried out to meet them, opening the door himself and helping them from the coach with a smile. It was a rather dazzling smile, full of warmth and greeting, and Emily was pleased to see that for once the powerful charm his lordship exuded almost unconsciously toward others was directed full force at her recalcitrant pupil.

Catherine's defenses seemed to melt. The tightness in her face eased, the wary line of her mouth relaxed, and her cheeks, which had been pale, became suffused with color. For the first time since they had returned from London, she seemed animated, and Emily began to hope a match between the two might still be possible.

Then Lord Ryde led them inside, and something went terribly wrong. Two of the other guests, Lord Ellarby and Mr. Jack Branston, were pointed out to Catherine, and suddenly her expression changed. For a moment, her eyes were filled with a look of hurt and disappointment. Then she cast one stormy glance at Lord Ryde and sailed forward to the two men with a determined smile.

Catherine had spent the rest of the evening flirting with every gentleman present but her host. Emily had watched anxiously as Lord Ryde had concealed his anger behind a facade of icy politeness, for that only seemed to drive Catherine to behave even more outrageously. In desperation, Emily had finally pled a headache to force a return home.

As she made her way down to the library, Emily reflected that things had only grown worse as the weeks dragged by. Catherine's flirtatiousness with Lord Ryde's guests had been matched only by her coldness to Lord Ryde—and to Emily. As for her former suitor, Emily had not heard anything from Mr. Barrett since their last angry parting in London.

Emily opened the library door wondering which books she could possibly choose to make up for so much loss, and nearly stumbled when she saw the gentleman standing there, regarding her with that familiar, grave look.

"It is good to see you again, Emily," he said softly.

She concentrated on keeping her tone light. "It is good to see you, too, Mr. Barrett. Though I must admit, I am surprised to find you here."

"Lady Catherine did not inform you that I was coming?"

Emily shook her head, as if the failure were a matter of indifference to her, but inwardly she longed to stamp her feet. Oh, how could Catherine neglect to tell her such a thing? Why, if he had arrived but a day later, she might already have been gone!

"Strange," he said, as he reached into the pocket of his coat. "Still, I see no reason my mission should be kept a secret. I have come to bring her a letter from her father. He instructed it be delivered at least ten weeks after her mourning was ended." He pulled the letter out and showed it to her. "Hodge informs me Lady Catherine is not in, but I thought perhaps you might give it to her."

"Oh. I see." She tried to hide her disappointment, but could not.

He took a step forward. "Emily?"

She resisted the temptation to open her arms to him and instead held out her hand. "Yes, Edward, I will take it."

He surrendered the letter to her, but instead of retreating he stepped closer. "Emily, delivering that letter is only half the reason I am here."

Against her will, she looked up and met his gaze. "And what is the other half?"

"This," he said simply, crossing the short distance that remained between them and folding her to him. "Oh, Emily," he murmured with a sigh. "I tried to stay away, truly I did. I thought that if I did not see you, the waiting would grow easier, but it did not. Finally, I could not bear it anymore. I knew the time was drawing near to deliver this letter to Lady Catherine, and I made up my mind to see you, regardless of the consequences."

"The consequences?"

He drew back to look at her and his well-modulated voice grew ragged. "You have no idea how sorely you tempt me, my dear. I must be expiating any number of sins in this wait to make you my wife."

"You mean you still wish to marry me?" Emily exclaimed. "But I thought after our quarrel … I did not hear from you for so long … I feared you had changed your mind!"

He gave a rueful smile and slowly shook his head. "How could I? There is no one else for me." He reached up and gently removed her eyeglasses. "From the moment I walked into that nursery and saw you blindly battling those three wretched charges of yours, I was lost." He folded her glasses with care and slipped them into his coat. "There, I have missed seeing those beautiful eyes of yours as they were that first day."

She pressed the palms of her hands against the rough nap of his coat, striving to prove to herself this exquisite moment was real. "Edward, we need not wait."

"What my love?" he murmured distractedly, brushing his lips along first one eyebrow and then the other.

"We need not wait to be married after all."

Suddenly she had his full attention. "No?" Hope battled with skepticism in his voice. "What of your charge?"

She looked away. "I was wrong! Catherine has no need of me. Indeed, she seems most anxious to be rid of me. We had a rather unpleasant interview just this morning, and she wishes me to depart from Rosington as soon as possible."

"Indeed?" he said. "I find that surprising news."

"I thought you would find it pleasing news."

"Oh, I do. Only, I cannot help but wonder what has caused this rift between two such devoted friends."

Emily felt tears prick at her eyes. "Does it matter?"

His tone gentled, and his arm tightened around her. "No. All that matters is that we can be wed. How does tomorrow sound?"

"Edward!"

"No, I suppose you are right. That is not very practical. There is still our trip back to London to consider, and then we must wait a few days for our families to arrive. Very well then, what do you say to a week from today?"

"A week from today?" Emily repeated weakly.

"Yes, I know. It seems an abysmally long time to me also, but I think I can manage to hold out if you can."

"But we cannot possibly be married in a week. There are still the banns to be read."

He drew out a piece of paper from his waistcoat pocket and waved it before her face.

"Oh, Edward, what is it? Without my spectacles I cannot make it out."

He grinned, or at least, the wavering line of his mouth looked like it was grinning. "That, my myopic darling, is a special license which I have been carrying about in my pocket since the evening of the

Sunflower Ball." His tone softened. "Now, where were we? Ah, yes." He knelt down before her and took her hand. "Miss Emily Lowery, will you do me the great honor of becoming my wife a week from today at, say, nine o'clock?"

She felt as if the warm summer sun had suddenly appeared in the library to shine down upon her. "Yes, my dear Edward, of course I will. Yes!"

He rose and drew her to him for an exultant kiss, and as they reveled in the happiness of the moment, neither heard the rustling skirts that whispered from the doorway or noticed that the letter Emily had been holding to give Catherine had slipped from her fingers and fluttered gently to the floor.

Chapter 20

By Jove, Ryde, I'd forgotten how lovely summer in the country can be!"

Ryde cast a sideways glance at his companion, who was jouncing along on his mount, an idiotic look of happiness plastered across his perspiring face. "Or how hot!" snapped Ryde irritably. "Really, Crawford, must you look so cheerful?"

"But I am cheerful," replied his brother-in-law. "More cheerful than I've been in months, thanks to you! To think that soon I will be reunited with my darling Letty —"

"Please, Crawford, spare me your ecstasies. I would never have fetched you from London if I had known I was going to have to endure these endless paeans."

"Sorry. I suppose it is difficult for you to understand the desperation love can drive a man to."

Ryde's hands tightened on his reins. "Crawford, we are less than five miles from Farthingsgate. Perhaps I should leave you to find your own way?"

"Very well, you have made your point. I will turn the subject. Only, before I do, I must say how grateful I am to you."

Ryde grimaced. "You need not be."

"But if not for you, Letty and I would still be apart."

"Crawford, you and Letty *are* still apart. You have not yet seen her. We have not yet arrived."

"What does that matter now that I know she still loves me!"

"Why you imagined she had ever stopped I cannot understand."

"But Marie told me —"

"Marie? Ah, yes, Letty's friend, Lady Howlett."

Crawford nodded. "When Letty and I returned to town in January, Marie warned me that if I kept living entirely in Letty's pocket, sooner or later she was going to stop loving me. Well, I was determined *that* was not going to happen, so I began spending more time away from home and leaving Letty to go more places by herself. But it did not help. Letty grew distant, and I began to suspect she had taken a lover. I nearly called the fellow out, but Marie warned me that that would just drive Letty yet further away. I tell you, Ryde, I was nearing my wit's end! You cannot imagine what hell it is to imagine the woman you love in another man's arms!"

Oh, can't I, thought Ryde grimly. "This fellow you almost called out, his name was not Daiches by any chance?"

Crawford's face grew fierce. "Letty spoke to you of him?"

"Do not fear. She only flirted with him to make you jealous. There was never anything between them. You can be sure of it."

Crawford's relief was almost comical to see. Almost, but not quite, for Ryde understood the pain that lay behind it. For a moment he would have liked to have boxed his sister's ears; then he remembered she was not entirely at fault. "This Lady Howlett—she is the attractive brunette I have seen hanging on your arm whenever Letty is not about?"

Crawford nodded. "Marie is very kind. She knows how miserable I am going anywhere without Letty, so she frequently offers to accompany me to raise my spirits."

"Has it ever occurred to you, Crawford, that perhaps being kind is not what Lady Howlett has in mind?"

His brother-in-law turned in surprise.

Ryde elaborated. "First, she tells you Letty is growing tired of you. Then she convinces you the only way to win Letty back is to ignore her. Finally, after Letty—and half the *ton*—are convinced *you* are the one having an affair, Lady Howlett appropriates you at social functions whenever Letty is not around."

"But Marie is Letty's dearest friend!"

"Stealing a friend's husband is not unheard of."

Crawford looked stunned. After a long pause, he said, "You must think me the veriest fool."

"It does not matter what I think," Ryde replied tactfully. "It is what Letty thinks that matters."

This seemed to cheer Crawford somewhat, but not enough for him to resume his chatter. To Ryde's relief, they traveled the next few miles in silence. Then the tranquility was broken when Crawford suddenly pointed toward a meadow on their right.

"I say, Ryde, look at that!"

Ryde turned to scan the area irritably. "What? I see nothing but a couple sharing a picnic."

"Exactly! Is that not the very epitome of summer and romance? Oh, how I wish I could hurry this beast along! I am so desperate to see Letty and tell her what a fool I have been. Perhaps if she forgives me, that might be us tomorrow!"

Ryde did not answer. There was something increasingly familiar about the lady picnicker, about the auburn hair that blew loose and free about her face, unfettered by the bonnet hanging unused down her back. She was laughing, and the gentleman seated on the large plaid throw rug next to her was watching her with an intentness that set the hairs on the back of Ryde's neck bristling. He searched in vain for sign of a chaperone. Confound it! Not even a footman or groom hovered nearby to maintain a semblance of propriety. The man on the rug took the lady's hand. She stopped laughing. He leaned forward to kiss her.

Ryde set off at a gallop.

Faintly he heard Crawford calling after him, but all his attention was focused on the couple ahead—and on their embrace.

It did not last long. The couple, hearing the beating hooves, quickly drew apart. Ryde arrived just in time to see Jack Branston's startled look turn to embarrassment and Catherine's to … he could not be sure what.

Furious, he slid from the saddle keeping his eyes fixed on her face. "Forgive the interruption, my lady, but I was passing by and could not help but notice you seem to have misplaced something."

"Ryde, I know how this looks — "

"I will deal with you later, Branston. For the moment, I am speaking to Lady Catherine."

She tilted her chin up at that angle he knew so well, and said softly, "What is it you believe I have misplaced, my lord?"

"Chaperone, maid, footman, groom—take your pick."

"There was a groom," interjected Branston. "I am afraid I sent him back to fetch us some more lemonade. See here, Ryde, if you will only let me speak with you in private, I am sure this whole matter can be settled to your satisfaction."

Ryde felt his stomach clench at the other man's words. Had Branston stolen a march on him and proposed to Catherine while he was away in London? Crawford picked this moment to come galloping up. "Ryde, what the devil has gotten into you? Demme, the way you galloped away, you looked like a bloody Hussar riding into battle!"

Crawford's gaze belatedly drifted past Ryde to take in the couple standing behind him. "Oh, dear! Forgive my language, ma'am. Didn't see you standing there. Sorry Ryde interrupted your picnic, but I am sure he had a good reason for haring off like that, for he is a steady fellow as a rule and not prone to — "

"Crawford!" Ryde roared. "For all that's holy, if you feel any gratitude to me at all, be still!"

His brother-in-law promptly fell silent, and Ryde made the necessary introductions. To his surprise, Catherine's hostility seemed to falter a bit at the news that the newcomer was Letty's husband. She flashed Ryde a curious look and then held her hand up to the man on the horse. "It is good to meet you, Mr. Crawford. I am glad you have finally arrived. Your wife has been missing you quite terribly, you know."

Crawford, who a moment earlier had worn the baleful expression of a hound unfairly chastised by its master, broke out into a beaming smile and seized Catherine's hand and began to shake it.

"Crawford, please! Lady Catherine's arm is not a pump handle."

"Forgive me," he said, releasing her hand and grinning down apologetically. "I fear I am not fit for anything until I see my Letty again. Which reminds me, Ryde, do you think we might be getting on?"

Ryde grimaced. "Branston, would you please escort my eager brother-in-law back to Farthingsgate?"

Branston frowned. "What about Lady Catherine?"

"I think, under the circumstances, I shall be the one to escort her back to Rosington." Seeing the other man about to protest, Ryde added, "Do not fear, Jack. We shall have the interview you crave when I return."

With this assurance, he reluctantly acquiesced. Ryde waited until Branston and his brother-in-law had ridden safely out of sight before turning to face Catherine.

She nodded in the direction the two men had ridden off. "Is that why you went dashing off to London?"

"To retrieve Crawford? Yes, it was one of the reasons."

"Because your sister was unhappy?"

He did not answer. His trip to London had been prompted partially out of concern for Letty, but mostly out of a selfish desire to escape the daily torture of watching Catherine flirt with Ellarby and Branston while she remained as cool as an iceberg to him. Still, good had come out of his flying visit to the capital, and not just for his sister and her lovesick husband. If all went as planned, he would soon have the means to silence the countess and declare himself to Catherine once and for all.

He went to fetch her horse and inquired with feigned indifference, "I trust nothing of importance has transpired while I was away?"

"That depends."

He cupped his hands together and helped her to mount. "On what?"

"On what you consider important."

He glanced up at her and then swung himself up onto his own mount. "I think you know very well what I consider important."

"I thought I did. I begin to wonder."

"Shall we cease these games? There is only one thing I wish to know.

Has Branston asked you to marry him or not?"

It seemed like an eternity before she answered, "No."

"But he intends to?"

"I do not know. It is possible I suppose."

"Very coolly spoken," he commented drily, though he felt almost giddy with relief at her tone. "I take it, then, that poor Jack's sentiments are not returned?"

The line of her jaw tightened. "What business is it of yours whether they are or not?"

"Besides the obvious fact that I must approve any match you make?" he inquired sweetly.

She glowered at him and then, apparently unable to come up with a sufficiently withering reply, turned her horse in the direction of the road and set off at a gallop. Ryde followed, his hopes strangely buoyed by the knowledge that he could still make her angry.

❧

The Countess of Trenwich peered impatiently from behind the half-closed door of the sitting room at the library opposite. When would those two be finished with their billing and cooing and be gone? She was anxious to retrieve the letter she had seen the impertinent Miss Lowery let slip to the floor.

As with other things of which she had been kept disgracefully ignorant, the countess had not known of the letter's existence before this hour. Now that she did, however, she was determined to discover its contents. Perhaps the information would prove of some use.

Suddenly footsteps were audible across the hall. The countess drew back as Barrett and the governess appeared in the doorway. His arm was about her waist; her head was resting on his shoulder. The countess grimaced at the spectacle they made as they turned out of the library and started down the hall. She quickly crossed the hallway and slipped into the library. Closing the door behind her, she turned the key in the lock.

At first she feared the two had recalled the letter and claimed it before leaving, for she could not find it anywhere on the floor near the place she had seen it fall. Then she thought to check beneath a small revolving bookcase, and there it was, lying in a small nest of dust.

Picking it up gingerly with two fingers, the countess gave the letter a shake. Then she crossed to the small desk in the corner and picked up a letter knife. She broke the wax seal and unfolded the thin but finely laid paper, covered from top to bottom with her husband's shaky scrawl.

> *My dearest Catherine,*
> *I write this to you with the knowledge that after you have read it, you may revile me for the rest of your days. Confession is good for the soul, however, and I never had the opportunity to do penance to your mother for the wrong I did her. I have also wronged you by believing the lies told to me by that baggage who calls herself my wife.*

For a moment the countess was sorely tempted to tear the thing in two. Then sense prevailed and she continued reading.

> *Therefore, I feel I owe you an account of what really passed between your mother and me. You see, I won her hand from the man who was once my dearest friend through a foul deception that injured your mother's honor.*

A look of intent interest appeared on the countess's face.

> *I fear it all began the night of the ball celebrating your mother's engagement to my friend George, whom you knew as 5th Marquess of Ryde....*

It was some time before the countess finally looked up from the letter, an amazed expression upon her face. The devil! What a plan! Yet it had worked! And if it could work once, it might do so again.

She stared at the fire, a look of calculation playing over the fine muscles of her face. Yes. Perhaps. It would be risky to arrange, but it might be just the thing to win back her son's fortune once and for all. Still, it would require a confederate. She thought for a moment and then nodded. *Farleigh.*

Of course, for the plan to work, it was imperative the truth about her husband's deception never be known. She looked down at the letter, and her hand closed around it and crumpled it into a tight ball. No, no one must know about the past, else someone might wonder just how closely history was repeating itself. She crossed to the fire and tossed the letter in. She waited patiently until there was nothing left but ashes and then turned and left the room.

The door of one of Farthingsgate's smaller and more remote sitting rooms closed softly behind Jack Branston, and Catherine was left alone with her thoughts.

Her first reflection was that she should never have accepted Ryde's invitation to dine at Farthingsgate. She had known what would happen if Jack contrived a moment alone with her, but Ryde had ensured her compliance. He had declared the dinner a celebration of Emily's engagement and had secured the happy couple's attendance before ever speaking a word to her. Since Emily and Mr. Barrett were departing in the morning for London, Catherine had been left with no choice but to accept.

So she had come, and after dinner Jack had insisted they speak in private. Giving in to the inevitable, Catherine had reluctantly followed him to this lonely room, listened to his declaration, and rejected his proposal of marriage.

She pressed her cheek into the soft velvet of the chair.

Jack had been too gallant to reprove her for her decision, but she had seen the surprise and hurt on his face and been ashamed. This playing with hearts was neither a kind nor noble game. Until this moment she had been too busy trying to make Ryde jealous to care, but now she was forced to see the harm she had done, and she was filled with remorse. She closed her eyes, but a tear still squeezed through her lids and trickled down her cheek.

No doubt Emily would feel vindicated, and Ryde—well no doubt he would express himself at length on her folly. Still, she had to undo what harm she could. At the first opportunity she would speak to Ellarby and deter him from even considering a proposal. She had no wish to cost another man his pride.

That she had cost Jack more than his pride still bewildered her. She was not the sort of woman, she had thought, to cause any man heartache, and yet the look in Jack's eyes when she had refused him had made her feel terribly guilty and regret that she could not love him.

She heard the door to the sitting room open behind her. Thinking Jack had returned, Catherine rose to her feet, but it was not Jack Branston who stood in the doorway, but Ryde.

"So, this is where you have been hiding." Despite his light tone, he glanced tensely about the room. "Where is Branston?"

"Gone."

His eyes sought hers. "You have refused him?"

"Yes."

His whole body seemed to sag.

"I am sorry if I have disappointed you."

"Disappointed me?"

"By rejecting your approved suitor. I fear your other attempt at matchmaking will fail as well. As much as I admire Lord Ellarby, I cannot bring myself to marry him simply to suit you."

"To suit me?"

"You are beginning to resemble a parrot, my lord."

He crossed to her side in three long strides and grasped her by the shoulders. "Let us have one thing clear between us, Catherine. I have no wish to see you married to Ellarby, or to Branston, or to any other man save one."

His intensity startled her. "Then why did you invite them?"

"When we parted in London — " He paused, the muscles in his jaw tightening until his cheeks looked quite hollow. "You informed me that you admired Branston and Ellarby very much. I decided that if I was to honor your wishes and keep my promise to your father, I had to allow you an opportunity to choose one of them for your husband, if you wished it."

"I see."

"No, you don't," he snapped, "but as I am not yet free to explain it to you, perhaps we should be getting back to the others. My sister Jane has arrived unexpectedly and is most desirous of seeing you. No doubt she will be anxious for all the details surrounding Miss Lowery's engagement."

Catherine wanted to know what it was he was not free to explain to her, but when he led her out into the hall, they encountered the young Misses Hartley, and all opportunity for private conversation was lost.

They found the company in the drawing room in cheerful spirits, though Mr. Branston was noticeably absent. She had to wait some time before she had an opportunity to speak with Jane alone, but when she did she was rewarded by a warm smile.

"Catherine! It is good to see you again."

"And you, Jane. It is especially pleasing to see you out of your mourning. I hope all is well with your sister, Maria?"

Jane smiled, but Catherine was surprised to note that Jane's smile did not reach her eyes. "Yes. She is delivered of a beautiful baby girl, and both mother and child are doing well."

"That is good news, indeed! By the way, your arrival is excellently timed. Now that your brother has fetched Lady Charlotte's husband to her, I suspect he will need someone else to act his hostess."

Jane turned to regard her sister, who was basking in the warmth of her husband's glances. "Yes, you are right. Usually, when they behave so at family gatherings, we shoo them off to dote on each other in private. At least they are not the only lovebirds here. I was happy to hear of Miss Lowery's engagement to Mr. Barrett. He tells me she accepted him only today."

"Yes, they were waiting for me with the news when I returned this afternoon." Recalling that meeting, Catherine looked away. She had accomplished what she had set out to do, but it was hard paying the price for her success. Emily, her governess, her friend, the woman who was dearer to her than any sister, had informed her of her impending marriage with the polite civility of a stranger.

"I understand the wedding is to take place in London?"

"Yes," Catherine replied, "a week hence. Mr. Barrett has procured a special license, and they leave tomorrow for London."

"Surely you go with her to be present at the ceremony?"

Catherine felt a tightness in her throat. "She has not asked me." Seeing Jane frown, she added, "I believe they mean to have a small wedding. Only members of the immediate family."

She would have said more, but at that moment they were joined by Lord Ellarby. Jane excused herself to make the rounds of her brother's guests, and Catherine took advantage of Jane's departure to lead Ellarby to a quiet corner and inform him that as much as she enjoyed his company, she did not think they would suit.

Apparently her expression was somber enough to convince him, for he debated with her only a few minutes, and at that pursued the argument so half-heartedly that only one pair of eyes turned to gaze in their direction. Unfortunately, that one pair belonged to Ryde, and as Ellarby turned and walked away, Catherine was forced to endure Ryde's look of satisfaction.

It required little exaggeration for Catherine to inform Emily a short time later that she suffered a headache and wished to go home. Emily, who had avoided her company most of the evening, became instantly solicitous and agreed at once to return with her to Rosington. Mr. Barrett offered to accompany them, but Emily declined the offer, for which Catherine was grateful. She had had enough of the company of men for one evening.

Catherine did not sleep well that night.

In a single day she had given up her dearest friend and the only two men in the world who seemed inclined to marry her. As she pondered the future that stretched before her, it seemed even more bleak and lonely than what she had envisioned those first dark days after her father's death. For then she had been accustomed to doing without affection or companionship, but now the thought of living without either drove her nearly to despair.

She woke early the next morning in, if not a more cheerful mood, at least a more determined one. Too restless to remain abed, she descended to the stables for a morning ride.

"No, not the sidesaddle," she snapped. "That one."

"But, my lady, you cannot be meaning to ride astride!" exclaimed Alfred in a shocked voice.

Catherine did not reply. She merely fixed him with a look that sent him scuttling to obey. When he began saddling a second horse she informed him that he need not bother.

"I mean to ride alone today."

Loath to challenge her a second time, her groom led Midnight to the mounting block, limiting his protest to a single dubious glance at Catherine's skirts. So as not to embarrass him, she left the billowing hem of her habit dangling low until she was well out of view of the stables. Then she hitched it up to her knees and set off, a feeling of exhilaration surging through her like a tonic. As she raced across one of her favorite meadows, she reveled in the sensation of the wind whipping against her stockinged legs. It had been years since she had ridden astride, and she had nearly forgotten the intoxicating pleasure of it.

"Which is probably why the gentlemen keep us from it," she murmured wryly to her mount. There was no answer from Midnight beyond the rhythmic beat of her hooves against the ground, but Catherine was content with that. It was a companionable cadence.

Perhaps it was a hypnotic one as well, for she did not notice the horse and rider waiting at the top of Parknam Hill until she had almost galloped into them. Startled, she pulled up hard. "Phillip!" she cried out breathlessly. "I did not see you there!"

Lord Farleigh, who had stood his ground with amazing aplomb, loosened his hold on his reins and raised one reproachful eyebrow. "You cut me to the quick, my dear. Here I have been told by not one but both the Misses Hartley what a fine figure I cut astride this new bay of mine, and yet you find the sight so unimpressive you nearly run me down."

"Oh, really, Phillip! My wits were wandering, that is all. Why did you not call out a warning?"

"I suspect I was a bit distracted myself." He let his glance slide meaningfully down to her stockinged legs.

Her face grew warm. She quickly pushed her skirts down to a more decorous position. "I thought it early enough no one would see me."

"You do this often?"

"Ride astride? No, more's the pity."

"You enjoy it then?"

She replied defiantly, "I do."

He nodded. "Yes, straddling one's mount yields a sensation at once more secure and more thrilling than being perched genteelly to one side." His tone was bland, but his eyes, she had forgotten what a rich blue they were, twinkled mischievously.

To her irritation, she felt herself blushing. He always had enjoyed twitting her with his double meanings. Well, two could play at that. She replied silkily, "Yes, you are quite right, Phillip. Riding astride is a pleasure to be keenly savored." She flashed him a bright and, she hoped, knowing smile. "Of course, one must be careful in one's selection of mount." She looked down casually and adjusted her left glove. "Fortunately, my judgment in such matters has improved with the years."

His mouth fell open slightly and his dark cheeks suffused with color. "And just how many mounts have you had, Catherine?"

"Hmmm, let me think." She paused and wrinkled her brow as if deep in thought. "There is Midnight, and my new bay gelding Ajax, and back at Trenwich I used to ride Cinder, and a feisty little mare inappropriately named Buttercup — "

"*Those are horses!*"

She gazed at him innocently. "Excuse me, Phillip, but is that not what we were discussing?"

His mouth twisted in irritation, and then relaxed into a rueful grin. "I suppose I deserve that."

"You do."

"Still, it was quite a shock you gave me."

"I consider it only fair, considering how much you used to enjoy shocking me when we were courting."

"Did I?"

"Suffice it to say I recall spending a great deal of time in your company either rendered speechless or pink down to my toes. "

A strange expression passed over his face and he said softly, "You cannot blame a man. You look very fetching that way."

"Speechless?"

He shook his head. "Pink down to your toes." He drew his horse next to hers.

"Phillip, I think I had best be getting back."

"Wait, Catherine—please! It is early yet. Phoebus has barely begun his ride. Can you not stay and talk a while? These past few weeks I have hardly had a moment to speak with you alone."

"I am sorry. I must go. Emily is leaving this morning with Mr. Barrett for London, and I must return to see her off."

"But you have plenty of time. All week, in fact."

"What are you talking about?"

"You left early last night."

"What if I did? What has that to do with anything?"

"Nothing," Phillip replied calmly, "only after you left, our host— who for some reason was in unusually good spirits—offered Barrett the use of Farthingsgate's chapel for the wedding."

"Ryde did what?"

"He also offered to put up Barrett's family and your governess's brother, and he is going to have a ball the night before the wedding. So you see, there is no need for you to rush back now. You will have all week to say your goodbyes. Come," he said, sliding from his saddle and tethering his mount to a nearby tree, "walk with me a while, and enjoy the lovely morning." He reached up to help her dismount, but she drew away.

He looked up at her. "You are still angry with me."

She answered him truthfully. "Yes."

"I do not blame you. In truth, I am still angry with myself. I made a terrible error. An error I have had ample time to regret."

"It was all a long time ago, Phillip. It does not matter now."

"I am not so sure." He reached up and covered her hand with his. "After all, I am a single man again, Catherine, and you are still unmarried."

"I hope you are not proposing, for I have no intention of having you. I know the only thing you are after is my fortune."

For a brief second his hand tightened on hers, and then, before she realized what he was about, he had pulled her from the saddle and into his arms. She slowly slid to the ground until she found herself staring directly into his vivid blue eyes. "You had no fortune six years ago when I asked you to be my wife."

She was pressed so tightly against him, she could feel the rise and fall of his chest. "No fortune. Only a beautiful stepmother you wanted in your bed."

"Catherine, please!" His voice was pleading. "I was young and stupid! I did not realize what I was risking."

She felt her implacability slipping away. She said weakly, "You cannot risk what you do not possess."

"But I did possess your love—once." He murmured the words caressingly into her ear.

"Perhaps ..."

"And I mean to again." His lips brushed her hair. He said in a deeper voice, "Catherine, my dear, I have missed you." Suddenly, he leaned forward and kissed her. It was a surprisingly passionate kiss.

He had caught her by surprise. She pulled her mouth free. "Phillip, no!"

He released her and stepped back, head bowed. "Forgive me, my dear." There was such sorrow in his voice that Catherine found herself seizing his hand and squeezing it.

"Never mind, Phillip, it is forgotten already."

"I would almost wish that you could not forget so easily." He sighed and then gazed into her eyes. "Is it too much to ask that we might be friends again, at least?"

Catherine bit off the comment that they had not been friends before and instead merely nodded. She suspected that she might stand in need of a friend during the coming week.

Chapter 21

With a feeling of immense relief and considerable exultation, Ryde strode into Farthingsgate's brightly-lit ballroom and scanned the crowd of revelers. He could not immediately find the face he sought, so he crossed to one of the evening's guests of honor.

Barrett turned and greeted him with a wide smile. "My lord, will you join me in a toast?" Barrett's eyes sought out a figure twirling gracefully about the room as he handed Ryde a glass of champagne. "To the most wonderful woman in the world."

"Yes, and to her lovely governess as well," Ryde agreed with a grin, downing the contents of his glass. "By the way, do you happen to know where she has disappeared to?"

Barrett's eyes twinkled. "Who, the lovely governess?"

Ryde laughed. "Lady Catherine. I have something rather important to discuss with her."

"When last I saw her, she was dancing with Mr. Elton."

Ryde thanked Barrett and moved on. After much fruitless searching, he finally discovered his old friend out on one of the balconies. "Matthew! What the devil are you doing out here?"

Elton did not turn around. "Go away."

"Is something wrong? You sound foxed."

"That is because I am foxed. Indeed, I am so foxed that if you do not leave immediately, I'll be tempted to land you a facer."

"Matthew, what on Earth!"

Elton whirled to face him, his expression furious. "How can you just stand by and let that Casanova make up to her like that? Farleigh has already broken her heart once, betraying her with her stepmother. Are you going to stand by and let him do it again?"

Ryde stared at him in surprise. Farleigh and the countess? So that was why Catherine had broken with him all those years ago. But what did Matthew mean about its happening again? Did she still love Farleigh? Ryde felt his mouth suddenly go dry with fear. And here he had foolishly assumed the danger gone with Branston and Ellarby.

Matthew's eyes narrowed. "So you do care after all."

Ryde nodded numbly.

"Then why the hell haven't you done anything about it? If I were in your shoes, I would have asked her to marry me long ago!"

Ryde said tightly, "I dared not do so before tonight."

"Why not?" Matthew demanded.

"The countess threatened to tell Catherine that she and I were lovers if I did."

Matthew's fist came up, and Ryde seized his arm.

"Hold, Matthew, it is not true! That is the damnable part of it! It is not true, but I feared Catherine might believe it was."

Matthew was still scowling at him fiercely. "You said 'before tonight.' Has something changed?"

"Yes!" Ryde made no attempt to hide the savage triumph he felt. "I have beaten her at her own game."

"What the devil do you mean?"

"As soon as the countess set down her edict, I knew I had to find a way around her. I suspected she was the type of woman who had secrets; I determined to find one dirty enough and dangerous enough to silence her tongue. While I was in London last week, one of the men I hired to investigate the matter came across something worth pursuing, and today I finally received proof."

"Proof of what?"

"Proof that the man the countess presents to the world as her brother is—in fact—her husband, and was so even before she married the earl."

Matthew's eyes grew wide. "Good God, Ryde! That would make the countess a bigamist and the new earl a bastard! Surely you do not mean to expose Catherine to such a scandal?"

Ryde's expression turned steely. "Of course not! But the countess does not know that. She thinks all I care about is Catherine's money, and mistakenly believes I would let her suffer any sort of notoriety to get it."

"And what of the succession?"

Ryde shrugged. "Fortunately, the boy's resemblance to his father is obvious. Bastard or no, Trenwich's blood clearly runs through the boy's veins. And he is Catherine's brother. Better he should inherit the earl's titles and lands than some obscure relation."

Matthew's expression had sobered. He said in a tone that sounded almost wistful. "So now you and Lady Catherine can marry?"

If she will have me, Ryde thought grimly. "Where is she, Matthew?"

Matthew shook his head. "I do not know. I last saw her some twenty minutes ago, when Farleigh came to claim her for the waltz."

The countess stepped back into the shadows and waited for the couple closeted alone together in the room opposite to emerge.

She had noticed the pair leaving the ballroom when she had emerged from her disastrous interview with Ryde, and had followed them almost without thought, her mind still reeling with the ultimatum Ryde had given her. Leave Rosington, then England within the week, or face exposure as a bigamist. Damn the man. He had her, and she would have to do as he said. But before she went, she would exact her revenge.

Farleigh had led her stepdaughter to this empty room, so presumably he meant to propose. The countess doubted he would be successful, but she would wait and see. If he was, she would depart secure in the knowledge that Ryde had been robbed of his final triumph. If he wasn't, well ... she reached into her reticule, felt for the small bottle inside, and stroked it like a talisman.

Damn you, Ryde! I have lost, but I will see to it that you, too, lose. You will not marry your heiress, and you will not see a penny of my boy's money, that I vow! I was determined on it before, but now—now that you have brought my very world crumbling about my ears—I will do whatever I must to stop you!

She clutched the little bottle tightly. *Whatever I must.*

Farleigh gazed in perplexity at the woman sitting before the fire. Light from the flames played upon her features, highlighting the downswept lashes, the shadowed cheeks, the full, kissable lips. He had brought her to this room to seduce her, but now after weeks of sham wooing he found it was he, and not she, who had been seduced.

What a fool he'd been! For years he had assumed that all that was needed to extinguish the flame burning inside him was an opportunity to possess Catherine for a single night, to bed her and bury his humiliation in her shame. Now he realized his mistake. It would not satisfy him to bed her once, twice, a thousand times. He wanted her to be his. He crossed to her chair and knelt before her.

"Catherine, will you marry me?"

She stared at him—her eyes wide, her expression unfathomable.

"I assure you. I care nothing for your money. It is you alone I want."

"Oh, Phillip!" she cried. Then to his dismay she burst into tears.

Farleigh had always detested female vapors, but he had grown skillful in dealing with them during his marriage. He produced a handkerchief and waited for the sobs to subside to mere sniffles.

"Forgive me," she said, dabbing at her eyes.

"Shhh. There's nothing to forgive."

"Oh, but there is!" she protested.

"No." He gently pressed a finger to her lips and then replaced the finger with his mouth. At first she struggled against the kiss, but then she quieted, and allowed him to show her how much he wanted her and needed her.

Somewhere nearby Farleigh thought he heard the sound of a door opening, but he was too immersed in what he was about to pay attention. Then someone seized him from behind and hurled him backwards. He landed against a settee, a light Sheraton creation that crumpled to pieces about him, and he stumbled to his feet to find his host looking bloody murder at him.

Suddenly, Farleigh felt rather murderous himself. Ryde might have the advantage of height, but Farleigh suspected the marquess was not as cognizant of the niceties of brawling as he was, and so it proved, for as he swung his joined hands down at Ryde's neck, the other man did nothing to guard against the knee driving upward toward his stomach.

"*Stop it*, the both of you!" Catherine cried as she rushed between them. Ryde straightened painfully and Farleigh wiped at his bloodied lip. "To think you call yourselves gentlemen!"

"I will be happy to name my seconds," Ryde murmured grimly.

"As will I," retorted Farleigh.

"No! Phillip, swear to me you will not!"

Farleigh considered the matter. He was not anxious to risk his skin, but he was also loath to be made to look either a coward or a fool. "He assaulted me, my dear."

"He mistook the situation. That is all. Please!"

"Very well, if that is what you wish. I will not fight him."

"And you, Lord Ryde?" she pleaded. "You will agree also?"

"I will not. He was pawing you—unforgivably, and in my house!"

"He was kissing me, and I was kissing him back. I apologize that it was in your house, but that is hardly an excuse for bloodshed."

Ryde's lips went an angry white. "Very well, I swear."

Catherine suddenly seemed to buckle and, to Farleigh's great frustration, it was Ryde who caught her and carried her to the sofa. Ryde crossed to the sideboard to pour her a small glass of brandy.

Farleigh joined him there and said in a low voice, "Thank you, Ryde, but I will see to my fiancée now—without your help."

The glass dropped to the floor and smashed to pieces. "Your what?" Ryde whispered.

"My fiancée," Farleigh repeated. "I have asked Catherine to marry me and she was in the process of giving me her answer when you burst in upon us so precipitately."

Ryde cast a bleak look in Catherine's direction. "I see."

"Then you will understand if I ask you to leave," Farleigh said. "Your presence here at such a time is a bit *de trop*."

Ryde's lips curled back in a grim smile. "As Catherine's trustee and the man entrusted by her late father with the task of approving or disapproving her choice of husband, I think you will understand if I ask *you* to leave. Catherine and I have much to discuss." Farleigh was about to protest, when Ryde added, "Need I remind you? It is *my* house, and if I rule against you, it is *your* loss of three hundred thousand pounds."

Farleigh, shocked by the size of her fortune, clamped his mouth shut. He was willing to take Catherine without the money, but if he had a chance to get her and it, he would be a fool not to take it. "Very well, Ryde. I will await Catherine in the ballroom."

He bowed and left the room and was imagining the sort of life he and Catherine could live with three hundred thousand pounds, when a hand snaked out and seized his arm.

"This way!" commanded the countess. "You and I must talk."

The silence in the room after Phillip left was crushing and, to Catherine, filled with reproach. What must Ryde think of her after seeing Phillip take such liberties? She tried to summon the courage to look up and meet his eyes, but all courage had deserted her, and with a small sigh she buried her face in her hands.

How could she explain to the man standing so silently by the sideboard that she had acquiesced to Phillip's kiss out of a sense of pity and guilt at having toyed with yet another man's heart? That she had not thought Phillip to have a heart capable of being touched—at least by her—was no excuse. He had asked her to marry him, and she had let him kiss her, because she was too much of a coward to tell him she did not want him.

She felt a hand touch her hair. "Catherine, you and I must talk." Ryde's voice did not sound angry, only strangely hollow.

She lifted her head. He was standing directly before her, his face haggard, his golden eyes so dark they looked muddy brown. She gestured for him to take a seat next to her on the sofa, and he did so wearily.

"I apologize, my lord, for disgracing myself in your home."

"Please, Catherine, keep your mockery to yourself. I have no strength left for fencing. Farleigh informs me he has asked you to marry him."

Hurt that he could not credit her sincerity in apologizing, she replied tersely, "Yes."

"You might have told me the wind sat in that quarter," he murmured in reproach. "You might have warned me."

"Warned you?"

His expression grew bitter. "Or does it gratify you to hold a man's heart in your hands and then break it in two?"

"Of course not!" she cried, thinking of all the years she had dreamt of revenging herself on Phillip. Now she had her revenge, and she did not want it. "Please, you must believe me. I never meant this to happen." Once more her eyes filled with tears. She bit her lip, willing them not to fall, but one overflowed and began rolling down her cheek.

Ryde brushed it away with his finger. "Did you know," he observed irrelevantly, "that when you weep, your eyes turn as green as a cat's?"

The tenderness in his voice undid her, and the tears began to spill silently down her cheeks like rain.

He gazed down at her for a moment, then gathered her up in his arms and squeezed her so tightly to him that her face was blotted dry against his exquisite black evening coat. "Catherine, my dearest, forgive me. I had no right to reproach you. You cannot help where your heart leads you."

Bewildered, but glorying in the feeling of his arms around her, she nuzzled deeper into the folds of his coat, enjoying his warmth and the soothing rise and fall of his chest. She would have liked to remain so all night, but all too soon he pushed her away. "I forget myself. You are engaged to another."

"What?"

"Farleigh. You are to be his wife."

Suddenly, understanding dawned, and with it, a burgeoning hope. "Actually, I have not yet given him my answer, for I knew I must first confer with you, and see if you approve my choice."

"Approve your choice?" he choked. "You go too far!"

"Then you disapprove it?" she inquired calmly.

The muscles along his jaw trembled dangerously. "I can neither approve or disapprove it. I am not a disinterested party."

"But what of your promise to my father? Is it not your responsibility to pass judgment on any suitor for my hand?"

"Very well," he agreed through clenched teeth. "I have already ascertained that Farleigh has no need to wed you for your inheritance, so that leaves only the matter of whether this is a love match. Do you believe Farleigh loves you?"

Catherine reflected on the matter. A week ago, she would have dismissed it as impossible. But Jack Branston had convinced her that one man, at least, could love her, and so now she found it easier to believe a second could. "I think so. In his way."

Ryde's face grew taut. "And you, do you love him?"

"No."

"Then I can see no reason—what did you say?"

"I do not love him."

"I do not understand! Why the devil were you letting him kiss you like that if…"

"If I had no intention of marrying him? Because I did love him once, and I felt sorry for hurting him."

"But you do not love him now?"

"No."

"Why?" His look was searching. "Because you are still bitter that he betrayed you with the countess?"

She shook her head. "Because I am in love with someone else, though this someone else shows little sign of loving me in return."

The color came flooding back into Ryde's cheeks, and seizing her in his arms he lifted her off the sofa and whirled her around. "Good, God! I do not love you! I adore you!"

She eyed him skeptically. "Then prove it."

He grinned. "Very well, my doubting Thomas, here you are." He sank down upon one knee, seized her hands in his, and intoned in the most sober accents, "My dearest Catherine, will you do me the great honor of joining your life to mine and becoming my wife?"

"Oh, do get up! I don't want you claiming some day that I forced you to it."

"I will not get up. I am waiting for my answer. As to being forced to propose, I will ignore the slur that sets upon my manhood and merely comment that I was on my way to find you to do precisely this, when I was distracted by finding you in a particularly provoking embrace with another man."

"Oh, Ryde, *truly*?"

He grimaced. "Oh, ye of little faith! Ask Elton if you do not believe me. He was the one who frightened me out of my wits with the news you had gone off with Farleigh."

She threw her arms around his shoulders and hugged him. "Oh, Ryde, I am so happy."

"As I will be when you have given me my answer, and I can get up off this knee!"

Catherine gazed into his now quite golden eyes and felt a sudden spark of mischief. "Oh, by all means get up now! And let me straighten your cravat, for it has gone sadly crooked."

They both stood, and he allowed her to fuss over him, and when she was done he leaned forward and kissed her softly on the lips. It was a sweet kiss and, she found, a strangely satisfying one, and when they parted she reached up and touched his cheek. "Thank you," she said softly. Then she withdrew her hand and started for the door. Ryde gazed after her, looking rather dazed, and it was not until she was almost gone that she heard him call out:

"But you have not yet given me my answer!"

With a grin, Catherine pulled the door shut and hurried down the hall.

Catherine was searching the ballroom for Phillip when Edward Barrett slipped his arm through hers and said in a teasing voice, "I have a bone to pick with you, my lady."

Relieved to have the unpleasant task of speaking to Phillip postponed, Catherine replied cheerfully, "Now, sir, do not claim I have done you some wrong, for you are one of the few gentlemen at this assembly who actually owes me a debt of thanks."

His expression sobered. "I am well aware of that, Lady Catherine, and believe me, I am grateful to you beyond words, but I fear this ruse of yours has gone on long enough."

"I fear I do not understand you, Mr. Barrett."

"I think you can call me Edward now, my lady, and I think that you do understand me. You may have fooled Emily with all this nonsense about your not wishing her about anymore, but you have not fooled me. Forgive the familiarity, but I know you too well to believe you capable of such fickleness."

"Emily has known me a great deal longer than you have, Edward, and she believes it of me." Catherine was unable to keep the bitterness out of her voice.

"Emily was too upset by the rift she perceived between us to think clearly. I suspect she feared that if I did not value her enough to remain constant, then perhaps you did not either."

"But you did remain constant!"

"As did you, though in an underhanded and thoroughly Machiavellian way I suspect poor Emily believes you quite incapable of." He raised his brows in mock reproof.

"Now, now, sir. I managed to get her to stop being a ninny and accept you, didn't I?"

"That you did, my lady, and for that I am eternally in your debt. But poor Emily is so melancholy over the supposed loss of your friendship that I think it is time you told her the truth."

"I meant to do so after you two were safely wed."

"You will forgive me, Lady Catherine, but tomorrow, when I stand with Emily in the church, and later when I—excuse my bluntness— truly make her my wife, I do not want any lingering despondency about this matter to mar her happiness."

Catherine felt her cheeks reddening. "I understand, Edward. I will speak with her at once."

"Thank you!" he exclaimed. She looked up to find him almost as red-cheeked as she. "I apologize again, my lady. I fear Lord Ryde would have my head if he knew I had spoken to you so, but Emily has been so distracted that I have grown a bit desperate."

"It is all right. Emily's happiness is the important thing."

"I knew you would understand." His expression turned grave. "There is another matter, I fear, that has been weighing on both of us. "Do you recall that when I wrote to tell you I was coming, I mentioned a commission from your father?" Catherine nodded. "Well, the commission was to deliver a letter to you that he wrote shortly before he died and which he directed be delivered ten weeks after your mourning was completed."

"Where is the letter?"

Barrett bowed his head. "That is the problem. It is missing. In the midst of our happiness I fear it was misplaced. Emily has searched high and low for it, but without success. We both feel deep regret at its disappearance, but I hope you will hold me, and not Emily, culpable for its loss?"

She felt a pang of disappointment so profound her knees shook. A letter from her father. What might it have said? That he loved her? That he was sorry for all the years he had avoided her? She would never know. She forced herself to smile. "Do not fret, Edward. We shall just have to trust it was nothing too important."

Chapter 22

atherine had finished her explanations to Emily and was receiving a warm embrace from that lady, when she spotted Phillip approaching and suggested it was time Emily danced with her intended. Edward Barrett seconded the notion and led Emily away.

Catherine managed a credible smile as Phillip joined her with a stiff bow. "I had begun to think you had forgotten me," he said.

"I am sorry, Phillip. I meant to come to you at once, but I needed to settle a small matter with Emily and Mr. Barrett first."

"It is no matter. The important thing is that now I can have your answer. Catherine, will you be my wife?"

He so obviously expected her to say "yes," she feared what he might do when she said "no." "Perhaps we could move to a more private place to discuss this, Phillip?"

He nodded and took her arm. She started a little at his touch, for his whole body seemed drawn taut as a bow, but his manner was calm and courteous as he led her out to one of the balconies. He waited until they were safely ensconced in the balmy night's shadows, and then asked, "Well, Catherine?"

She spoke in a rush. "I am sorry, Phillip. My answer is no. I cannot marry you, for I am to marry someone else."

She could not see his expression clearly, for her eyes had not yet accustomed to the darkness, but she sensed his anger.

"Phillip?"

For a moment, there was only the sound of harsh breathing. Then Phillip said in a voice that was somehow frightening in its calm, "I suppose this someone else is Ryde?"

"Yes."

"So it was the money after all. She said it would be."

"The money?"

"Can you not see?" he exclaimed. "Ryde wants your fortune for himself. Why do you think he drives away all other suitors? Not because he loves you, but because that profligate father of his bankrupted the title, and he needs to marry an heiress."

"Phillip, if Ryde had been after my money, he could have had it—and me—anytime these past few months."

"Perhaps he has merely been biding his time."

"Perhaps," she allowed impatiently. "I am willing to take that risk."

"Then I cannot persuade you to marry me instead?"

"No."

"And here I thought you loved me."

"I did once." She reached up and touched his cheek. "I suspect there is a part of me that always shall. But I have made my choice, and now I ask that you abide by it."

She sought to withdraw her hand, but he caught it and held it tightly. "It is difficult to lose you twice, my dear."

They stared at each other in the darkness.

Suddenly Ryde called from the door to the balcony. "Catherine? Are you there?"

Relief flooded through her at the sound of his voice. She whispered under her breath, "Phillip, please, my hand!" He released it, and she called out loudly, "Ryde, I am here!"

Ryde made his way toward them. A smile lit his face as he saw her but changed to a frown when he noticed Phillip. Catherine, hearing the musicians strike up their instruments, quickly said, "Ah, sir, no doubt you have come to claim me for our waltz?"

Ryde seemed reluctant to take his cue. He said coolly, "I would not wish to interrupt your *tête-à-tête*."

"You are not interrupting. Phillip and I have just finished."

Phillip gave her a long and indecipherable look. "Have we? Yes, I suppose we have—for now."

"In that case, you will excuse us, Farleigh?" Ryde held out his arm, and Catherine laid her own upon it gratefully.

"Of course," he said. "Catherine, would it be too much to hope I may still be allowed to escort you into supper?"

Catherine flashed Ryde an uneasy glance from beneath her lashes. Surely he would understand she owed Phillip that much? "Of course not, Phillip. I will expect you."

❧

Ryde did not understand Catherine's decision to allow Farleigh to lead her into supper. He led her wordlessly back into the ballroom, his earlier happiness evaporating like mist.

Was she already having second thoughts about accepting his proposal? But he was forgetting. She had not yet given him an answer, not officially, and there she had been in the darkness, alone with Farleigh. His jaw clenched and unclenched. He should never have given her his promise not to shoot the fellow.

"My lord, don't you think we would look less conspicuous here on the dance floor if we were actually dancing?"

Her tone was teasing, but the expression in her blue-green eyes was faintly hurt. He pushed a few jealous demons back into their box and took her in his arms. "I do have a first name, you know," he said irritably, as he tightened his hand at her waist and began twirling her about the room.

"Do you?" she murmured.

"Yes, and it is not 'my lord.' It is Andrew, and I would enjoy hearing you use it."

"Yes, Andrew," she said, her voice meek.

He gazed at her suspiciously, but her expression was innocent as she stared dreamily at his cravat. They danced like this for some time, until curiosity got the better of him. "My dear, far be it from me to be jealous of my own neckcloth, but what can you be thinking to cause you to moon at that poor piece of linen so?"

She blushed, and even her creamy shoulders went pink. "Forgive me. I was simply reflecting on how strange it is that this is the first time you and I have ever danced together."

"Odd, isn't it?" he agreed softly. "When holding you like this seems as familiar and natural to me as breathing."

Her blue-green eyes widened in surprise. "You feel it, too?"

The weight on his heart suddenly lifted, and pulling her more tightly to him, he grinned. "I do."

They spent the rest of the dance in contented silence. Once or twice Ryde was tempted to ask for an answer to his proposal, but in the end he decided to wait, not wishing to risk the magic of the moment simply because he was impatient. He trusted that he knew what Catherine's answer would be when she gave it, especially when he glimpsed Farleigh's tight-lipped expression as they danced by.

All too soon the dance ended, and Ryde was forced to yield Catherine to other partners. Not himself in a mood to dance with anyone else, he circulated amongst his guests. Encountering his sister Jane, he complimented her on the success of the ball.

"But it is your affair, Drew."

"I merely supplied the blunt. You are the one who did all the work. Truly, Jane, I appreciate the miracle you have wrought. Why, I gave you less than a week to prepare, and you have managed a ball that shall be the talk of the county for months to come."

Jane laughed, pleased. "Heady praise indeed, brother."

"You deserve it. I only hope you will not mind repeating the favor when I require it for myself."

"A wedding ball? Oh, Drew, are you to be to married?"

"Keep your voice down! The lady has not accepted me yet."

Jane made a dismissive sound. "She will. She would be a fool not to. You will make a wonderful husband."

He grinned at her. "Perhaps you would care to share that opinion? I am not sure my beloved is aware of the fact." He turned and gazed at the lady in question.

"Catherine? It is she you mean to wed?" He nodded. "Oh, Drew! I am so glad! When we were together here last winter it was so obvious she thought the world of you."

"Obvious to you, perhaps. Why did you not tell me?"

"I thought you would discover the truth sooner or later."

He was tempted to shake her. Instead he made her a small bow. They continued their circuit of the room. They had not gone far when Jane caught Ryde's sleeve and murmured, "I say, Drew, look at that." Ryde turned. Lady Trenwich and Farleigh were standing in a far corner, their backs to the room, deep in conversation. "How strange," Jane remarked.

Ryde said stiffly, "I understand they are old . . . friends."

"Perhaps. Yet every time the countess has approached Lord Farleigh this past week he has been as cold as ice to her. What do you think they can be discussing so intently now?"

Ryde felt a strange shiver of apprehension. "I do not know." He turned to seek out Catherine in the crowd. She was dancing a country dance with an elderly squire. As if sensing his scrutiny, she turned and flashed Ryde a dazzling smile. He smiled back and slowly let out the breath he had not realized he had been holding.

He did not think of Farleigh again, until it was time to go into supper, and the man approached to escort Catherine in. Ryde escorted Jane and was grateful when his sister diplomatically did not inquire why Catherine was taking supper with another man.

Ryde's eyes, however, strayed frequently to the table where Catherine sat. He tensed as Farleigh brought her a too-full glass of wine, and when he saw him rise to refill her glass for yet a third time, he almost rose to stop him. Fortunately, a warning glance from Jane reminded him not to act the fool.

Then a minor crisis erupted at their table when one of the gentlemen nearly choked on a chicken bone. By the time the crisis was over, Ryde turned to check on Catherine, and to his dismay found that both her seat and Farleigh's were empty. He looked over at where the countess had been seated. She, too, was gone.

With a sense of foreboding, Ryde rose to his feet. He was about to make for the door, when Farleigh reentered the room. Ryde crossed to intercept him. "I would appreciate a word with you in private."

"Of course," Farleigh drawled in reply. He turned and followed Ryde from the room.

When they were outside and beyond anyone's hearing, Ryde rounded on the man and demanded fiercely, "Well, where is she?"

Farleigh raised an eyebrow at his vehemence. "By 'she' I presume you refer to Catherine?"

"You know that I do!" Ryde's voice clearly conveyed the violence he would do this man if he did not get an answer soon. "What have you done with her?"

"I? Done with her? Nothing, I assure you. She is suffering from a slight indisposition, that is all. I escorted her from the dining room and gave her over to her stepmother's keeping. The countess is putting her to bed."

"A slight indisposition?" Ryde exclaimed, disbelief vying with fear. "Is she ill? Should a doctor be summoned?"

"Goodness, no. All she needs is rest."

"All the same, I will send my sister up to see how she fares."

"I would not do that if I were you." Farleigh's voice was suddenly sharp. "Catherine is in no mood for company."

Ryde was in no mood for advice, especially from Farleigh. "Lady Catherine and my sister, Jane, are old friends," he replied coldly. "I am certain she will not object to such a visit."

"You are wrong, Ryde. I do not believe she would care to have anyone, especially your sister, see her foxed."

"*Foxed*!" Ryde exploded.

"Exceedingly so. Indeed, quite three sheets to the wind."

"And whose fault is that?" Ryde demanded angrily. "I knew I should have stopped your constantly refilling her glass!"

"I suspect Catherine had a considerable amount to drink before we ever went in to supper," Farleigh retorted, "and in any case, it was she who kept asking me to bring her more wine."

"I do not believe you."

Farleigh shrugged. "It is Catherine's way to occasionally overindulge when she is upset about something or confused. We both know that may well describe her frame of mind tonight."

Ryde felt himself color, and Farleigh gave a grim smile.

"Now, if you will excuse me, Ryde, I would like to finish my supper." He turned on his heel and left.

Ryde bleakly watched him go, wishing he had insisted on an answer to his proposal after all.

It took two strong footmen to get Catherine quickly and discreetly up the stairs and down the long hallway to the pretty rose bedchamber she had been given for the night. Once the two men had deposited her onto the bed, the countess shooed them out with an imperious command to say nothing. Then she turned to Catherine's startled maid, Polly, and curtly told her, too, to leave.

"But, my lady, is my mistress sick?"

"She is drunk," snapped the countess coldly.

There was a shocked pause, and then the maid said, "Shall I see to her clothes?"

"No, she is to be left as she is to reflect on her disgusting behavior. Out with you now. You can sleep up in the attics with the other maids tonight." Fortunately, the little maid gave her no more trouble, but instead quietly left the room. Alone at last, the countess crossed to the bed and peered anxiously at her stepdaughter's inert form. Curse it, the girl was almost too still. Surely she had not overdone the dose Farleigh had slipped into the girl's wine? For a moment, the countess felt a stab of fear; then she saw the faint rise and fall of Catherine's chest. Her knees nearly gave way in relief. The image of a hangman's gallows receded into the shadows, and she stumbled to a chair to compose herself. Really, she should be calm. The plan was proceeding beautifully.

She remained in the chair for some minutes, and by the time she rose, the image of Ryde consigning her to a life of exile had fixed her resolve once more to an icy determination. Crossing to the bed, she removed Catherine's gown and corset and shift, not worrying about the buttons and tapes she occasionally tore free, for the more ravaged Catherine's clothing looked come morning, the better.

She undid the pins in Catherine's hair and pulled her hair loose about her shoulders. Then, using all her strength, she maneuvered her naked stepdaughter onto her side into a huddled pose with her back to the door. She pulled the coverlet up and cast one last, satisfied glance upon her handiwork. Then she left the room, locking the door behind her.

Farleigh sat rigidly in his chair, wishing his eyes had not adjusted to the darkness. For then he would not be able to see the torn clothes scattered so dramatically at the foot of the bed, or the bare outflung arm that seemed to reproach him with its innocence, or the huddled silhouette of the sleeping girl he was waiting, like a Judas, to betray.

He sat there for some time, his self-loathing increasing with each passing minute. How had he let himself be persuaded to such a devilish scheme? But he knew the answer. Rising to his feet, he strode over to the bed and looked down at Catherine's sleeping form. His gaze flicked over her cascading hair, ivory shoulders, and sweetly sloping arm. He ran a finger lightly up that arm, past her shoulder, tracing the curve of her neck, and running up to touch her half-parted lips. She was destined to be his.

If he had to act the knave to keep her, he would.

Ryde waited impatiently to see the last of his guests off. After Farleigh's disclosure, the remainder of the evening had dragged interminably, and now all he could think of was resolving the nagging uneasiness he felt that Catherine might be suffering something worse than too much wine.

He saw off the last coach, bid the last of his houseguests goodnight, and waited impatiently in his study for the last voices to disappear and the last doors to slam shut. When finally the house was quiet, he went upstairs. Finding the hall empty, he made his way to Catherine's room and paused before the door. Afraid a knock would be too easily overheard by some inquiring busybody, he instead twisted the knob and softly called Catherine's name.

But the door was locked, and when he risked knocking a few times there was no answer. Disappointed and more than a little concerned, Ryde retreated to his own chamber.

He was too restless to sleep. He remained dressed in his shirt and breeches and paced anxiously up and down his room, wondering how long he must wait before he tried to rouse Catherine again. Suddenly, he heard several soft knocks followed by some loud pounding. When he crossed to open his door, he found his sister Jane and the countess standing there.

Jane, white-faced and in her dressing gown, spoke first. "Drew, it is Catherine. The countess thinks she may be ill — "

"Dying, more like! I heard the most terrible moans and sighs coming from her chamber!"

Ryde tried to push past the two women, but Jane caught his arm. "Wait, Drew, the door is locked. We cannot get in. The countess has already tried. We need Mrs. Jenner's key."

Wordlessly he nodded, strode to the bellpull, and gave it a vicious tug. Doddy appeared in the doorway. "Yes, my lord?"

"Lady Catherine is ill and locked in her room. Please fetch Mrs. Jenner's key and bring it to us with all dispatch. We will be waiting for you outside her chamber."

Doddy did not pause to reply, merely bowed and sped off at a surprisingly undignified trot. Ryde paused to light a candle with a hand that shook and led the way for the ladies down the hall.

When they reached Catherine's chamber, there were no moans or sighs, only dead silence. Ryde, uncaring now if he was heard, knocked loudly and called out her name. There was no answer. He tried the door, but it was still locked. Growing desperate, he pounded on the door again. Other doors began to open.

"Is something amiss?"

"Is the house alight?"

"What is all this ruckus?"

"It is nothing," Jane assured everyone calmly. "One of our guests has taken ill, nothing more. Please, return to your beds."

One by one the doors closed and the hall fell back into silence. Ryde paced anxiously back and forth, telling himself that all was well, that Catherine was fine, that once he had her safely in his arms he would never let her out of his sight again.

Doddy came panting down the hall towards them. Ryde seized the key out of the man's outstretched hand and thrust it into the lock with such force he could hear the key on the other side clatter to the floor. Ryde wrenched the door open, snatched up the candle, and started inside, but the sight that greeted his eyes stopped him dead in his tracks.

Farleigh was standing next to Catherine's bed calmly pulling a shirt on over his bare chest, while Catherine, her naked back turned to the door, cowered into her pillow in shame.

For a long moment, Ryde could not breathe. Then anger surged up his throat, choking him. Dropping the candle to the floor, he started for Farleigh in a blind charge. The splash of cold water against his back and Jane's voice calling his name brought him back to his senses to find his fingers gripped around Farleigh's throat. Dazed, he let his hands drop to his sides.

Farleigh rubbed his neck gingerly and, taking a few wary steps backward, suggested hoarsely, "Well, Ryde, now that you have gotten that out of your system, perhaps we might step out into the hall and leave poor Catherine a modicum of privacy?"

Ryde ignored him. He stared at the still figure on the bed, willing her to turn and look at him and say something—anything—that would turn this madness into sanity. He called her name, but she did not turn or speak or even acknowledge his existence, and something broke apart inside him. Feeling suddenly numb, he turned and left the room.

Farleigh and Jane followed, and then came the countess, who firmly shut the door behind them. "Perhaps we can go somewhere more private than the hallway?" she suggested.

Ryde reluctantly led the way back to his bedchamber. As the group filed in behind him, he closed the door and then turned to face Farleigh. Ryde's earlier rage was gone, swept away by the numbness that seemed to be invading his very soul. In an almost matter-of-fact voice he said, "You are fortunate, sir, that I gave my word earlier this evening not to call you out, for it would tempt me very much to kill you."

Farleigh absently rubbed at his neck, but said nothing.

"Really, Ryde," said the countess, shaking her head and looking faintly amused, "Now that your head has cooled, surely you can see there is no need for violence. While it is indeed unfortunate the silly chit could not wait until her wedding night, there is no lasting harm done. After all, she and Phillip are engaged to be married."

"Engaged?" repeated Ryde, finally stung back into feeling. "Impossible! I saw his face after Catherine gave him his answer."

"Yes, she did say no to me, at first," Farleigh admitted. "But then she thought better of it. After she went upstairs she had a footman deliver me a note saying she had changed her mind and was desperate to see me." He paused, and then added, "She sent me her key."

Ryde's hands clenched at his sides. "So you took advantage of an intoxicated girl?"

Farleigh shrugged. "I was so pleased she had reconsidered, I did not wish to wait. "

Ryde almost charged Farleigh a second time but stopped himself and pointed to the door. "Get out!"

Farleigh's cavalier manner suddenly vanished, and his expression turned grave. "You need not worry, Ryde. I will do right by her. I will leave for London in the morning to obtain a special license so that we may be wed quickly."

Ryde, feeling intolerably weary, nodded. To his surprise, Farleigh made him a low bow before leaving the room.

"Perhaps I should be leaving as well," said the countess, lifting her skirts and starting for the door. "I shall spend the rest of the night in Catherine's room to insure there are no other — " she raised one finely shaped brow in amusement, " — *mishaps* until morning, then I shall return to Rosington and pack my things as per our agreement. That is, of course, unless you wish me to remain at Rosington until the little minx is safely wed to Phillip?" She met Ryde's gaze directly, and the look of malevolent triumph in her eyes made his breath catch in his throat.

"There is no need," he said bleakly. "I am sure you have done quite enough already."

"Yes, actually I believe I have," she said with a contented smile. She opened the door. "Tell me, Ryde, how does it feel to have your golden dream crumble before your eyes?"

He did not reply, and she gave a low, mocking laugh. "Goodbye, Ryde. Remember me in the years to come."

After the countess had gone, Jane began to hover about him like an anxious puppy—eager, no doubt, to dispense comfort he was in no mood to accept.

"Go to bed, Jane," he snapped curtly.

"But Drew, we must talk."

"I am in no mood for talk. I wish to be alone."

"Drew, I know you are agitated — "

"Agitated! I nearly throttled a man with my bare hands! I probably would have, too, if you had not thrown that basin of water at me."

"Actually, I threw it at the candle, which looked about to set the rug alight. Still, I am glad if it was a help to you, dearest."

He shrugged grimly. "Yes, I suppose it is just as well I left the wretch alive to make an honest woman of her."

"Andrew!"

Her shocked tone rankled. "I repeat, Jane. Go to bed."

"But I really must speak with you. There is something decidedly odd about all this. It is so eerily like —"

"*Enough!*" he cried, feeling his control unravel. He crossed to the door and opened it for her. "I do not wish to discuss this anymore."

"But what of you and Lady Catherine?"

He felt his face go rigid. "I can think of no way to avoid seeing her tomorrow at Barrett's wedding. After that, I hope never to behold her again."

"But Drew — "

"*No!*" His tone was steely.

With bowed head, Jane stepped out into the hall. She turned as if to say one last thing to him, but he could bear no more. He slammed the door shut in her face.

He turned and started toward his dressing room, but the sight of his own bed conjured up the image of another. He staggered as if struck, and he realized the numbness was gone. It had deserted him like an outgoing tide. Anger, loss, and pain rushed in to fill the void, but it was love that left him trembling. Feeling like a marionette whose strings had just been cut, Ryde sank to his knees, pressed his face against the cool wood of the floor, and, for the first time since he was a boy of ten, began to cry.

Chapter 23

She was dancing in a garden. She could not see her partner's face, but she could feel his warm arms around her as they danced their way up to the moon. Then the moon exploded in a great flash of light, which sent her tumbling, falling face first into a bed of flowers and inhaling the scent... of vinegar and sulphur.

Catherine coughed and spluttered and opened her eyes to find the room full of sunshine. The countess was leaning over her, holding a vinaigrette to Catherine's nose and a glass to her lips.

"Drink, you wretched girl!" her stepmother commanded, tipping the glass forward. Catherine took a few sips and almost choked.

"What is it?" she gasped.

"Something to sober you up, you brandy-faced baggage. I depart for Rosington in a few minutes, but I cannot leave with you still snoring, and all the evidence of your disgraceful conduct scattered about the room for your maid to see."

Catherine reached up to brace her throbbing head. "I do not understand," she whispered.

The countess curled her lip. "Do you mean to say you were so intoxicated last night you do not remember your wanton behavior?"

"My *what?*" Catherine repeated feebly, for the first time realizing that she was sitting in the large, soft bed quite naked. Suddenly frightened, she pulled the covers up over her shoulders.

"You do not remember inviting your fiancé to this chamber?"

Catherine mutely shook her head and flinched at the pain.

"Or allowing him to tear the clothes from your body?" The countess gestured toward Catherine's discarded gown and shift. "Or inviting him into your bed?"

"No," Catherine cried hoarsely, feeling herself in another dream. "Of course I do not remember it. It never occurred."

The countess said nothing. She simply raised her eyebrows in such a look of incredulity that Catherine felt a surge of panic. Surely if she had behaved so, she would remember—something.

"You play the innocent quite convincingly, my dear. But you forget: I saw you and Phillip *en flagrant délit.*"

If before she had been in a dream, now she was in a nightmare. "Phillip!" she cried raggedly. "I thought you said my fiancé!"

"Do you mean to say that Phillip, the man I saw half-naked in your room last night, is *not* your fiancé?"

"No!" It burst from Catherine's lips like a sob. "It is Lord Ryde I mean to marry!"

"Well, that hardly seems likely now, does it?" the countess remarked archly. "Most men frown upon marrying a woman who has had another man to her bed, and based on Ryde's reaction last night, I do not think he is an exception."

"He was here?"

"Both Ryde and his sister were with me when I entered the room last night. I roused them thinking you were ill, you see, for I heard such shocking moans and sighs coming from behind your door." The countess's eyes glittered with malicious amusement.

Catherine, numb with shame, stared at her stepmother in disbelief. "You are actually enjoying this, aren't you?"

The countess shrugged. "Let us say, I am not surprised."

Catherine gripped the covers tightly with both hands. "You say you are returning to Rosington. If so, madam, you had best have your bags packed at once, for I want you out of my house today."

The countess reddened. "You are hardly in a position to give me orders, my girl!"

"I am not your girl, thank God! My mother was a woman of flesh and blood, not a soulless harpy supping on the misery of others."

"How dare you!"

"I dare, because it is the truth."

"I warn you, Catherine — "

"Your threats are meaningless, madam," Catherine interrupted. "There is nothing you can do to me that would be worse than what I have apparently already done to myself. Now will you go, or must I summon Polly to throw you out?"

"I am going," snapped the countess. "I trust that you have enough sense of the honor due your late father and your brother not to further disgrace your name. Very well. Your lover has gone this morning to London to seek a special license. I expect before the week is out to receive news that the two of you are wed."

❦

Any lingering hopes Catherine had that the countess was lying died when she found the torn buttons on her ball gown and saw the startled look on Polly's face as she slipped into the room and found her awake. Catherine looked at the cot in the corner. "Polly, why did you not sleep here last night?"

The girl avoided her eyes. "The countess thought it would be better if I slept with the other girls upstairs, my lady."

"Why?"

Polly colored faintly. "Don't know, my lady. I suspect she was angry because you was a bit bosky when you came up last night."

Catherine flinched, but inquired with determination, "Polly, how do you know that I was, er ... a bit bosky?"

The girl's color deepened. "Must I say, ma'am?"

"Yes, Polly, I need to know."

Polly gave her one anguished look and then burst out unhappily, "I'm sorry, my lady, but t'was that obvious! It needed two footmen to carry you to bed!"

Catherine sank into a chair while Polly bustled about quietly preparing a bath for her. Suddenly there was a knock at the door. Catherine braced herself for Ryde, but it was only Emily, brimming with energy and wearing a smile that kept slipping up to her ears.

"My dear," she exclaimed, as she hurried into the room. "I only have a moment, but I wanted to make sure you were feeling better."

"Better?"

"I grew worried when you left supper so abruptly last night, though Lord Ryde assured me it was only a slight indisposition."

Catherine swallowed hard. She did not remember leaving supper abruptly. She did not remember leaving supper at all.

Emily frowned. "Catherine, was he mistaken? Is it more serious? You look exceedingly pale and drawn."

Catherine struggled to regain some composure. "Am I that out of looks?" she said archly. "Perhaps I should be the one wearing the veil."

Emily flashed her an exasperated look. "Now, Catherine, you know that is not what I meant at all! I was simply concerned — "

"But there is nothing to be concerned about, Emily. Last night's indisposition was ... of no moment, really. All that matters is that today is your wedding day and that you are happy."

"Well, if you are sure, I suppose I had best be getting back. Lady Jane has lent me her maid, and I am to have my hair dressed by the famous Monsieur Cyrano." Emily gave Catherine an impish grin. "Edward had best be careful. I could grow quite accustomed to such pampering." She started for the door and then stopped. "Catherine, you are telling me the truth? You are feeling all right?

Catherine forced herself to smile. "I am fine."

Emily did not look entirely convinced, but she returned to where Catherine sat and squeezed her hand and kissed her cheek. "I am relieved to hear it, my dear, for I am so nervous, I will need you next to me in church to keep me propped upright!"

After Emily had gone, Catherine took her bath, let Polly dress her, and sat passively under the ministrations of Monsieur Cyrano, fearing any moment that Ryde would burst into the room and demand an explanation she would be quite unable to give.

But Ryde did not come, and by the time Catherine descended to join the rest of the wedding party on the short walk to the chapel, her nerves were stretched to the breaking point. The idea of facing Ryde in private had frightened her, but now she realized that such a confrontation would have been far preferable to meeting him as she was about to now—in a crowd of people before whom they both would have to act as if nothing were wrong.

She moved forward into the milling throng. Pasting a smile upon her face, she greeted the Barretts—mother and daughters. She shook hands with Emily's brother and flinched slightly at the leer he bestowed upon her until she realized it was purely reflex. She greeted Lady Dent and Mrs. Howard.

Matthew Elton stood at the periphery of the gathering, and Catherine started toward him in relief, but stopped abruptly when the smiling bridegroom and Ryde joined him. She would have turned to retreat, but suddenly all three men looked in her direction, and she was forced to move forward and greet them.

"Good morning, Edward. Mr. Elton. Lord Ryde."

"Good morning to you, Lady Catherine," Edward Barrett replied cheerfully. "It is a lovely one, is it not?"

Catherine assented politely, but the groom's two companions, who clearly did not share his enthusiasm for the day, remained silent. He resumed questioning the two gentlemen about sights worth visiting in the Lake District, where he and Emily were taking their honeymoon trip, and Catherine took advantage of their conversation to sneak a surreptitious look at Ryde.

He, unlike herself, was showing to great advantage this morning. Wistfully she regarded his green kerseymere coat, gold waistcoat, and close-fitting buff pantaloons. He looked so handsome this morning, so stately. Not a hair on his well-brushed head was out of place. Not a fold in his beautiful white cravat was askew. His watch chain looped in a perfect arc. His boots gleamed with a perfect shine. Only a few haggard lines about his eyes and mouth hinted that all was not as it should be.

Suddenly, Catherine realized that Edward Barrett was gazing at her expectantly. "Forgive me, Edward. Did you say something?"

His eyebrows rose in amusement. "I merely asked whether you had seen Emily this morning," he repeated amiably.

"I have, and she is fine, and in good spirits, and will look quite breathtaking once Monsieur Cyrano allows her to descend."

He grinned. "I am all anticipation. Now, if you all will excuse me, I had best go see to my mother and sisters."

"There goes a happy man," commented Mr. Elton, in a tone that caused Catherine to stare at him in surprise. Seeing her look, he colored, bowed, and excused himself as well.

She gazed after him in bewilderment. Had Matthew somehow learned of her disgrace? Feeling tears prick at her eyes, she bit her lip and turned back—to find Ryde staring at her.

He quickly looked away, but not before Catherine had seen the look in his eyes. Swaying a bit, as if from a blow, she reached out and pressed her hand against the wall for support. "My lord, I know it is impossible for you to forgive my conduct of last night, but I — "

She might have spared her breath, for with a strangled oath Ryde had already turned and stridden off, leaving her to address the empty air.

❧

Ryde listened to Emily Lowery vowing to love, honor, and obey and found his gaze straying, as it had frequently throughout the marriage ceremony, to the woman with the downcast eyes standing next to Emily, holding her bouquet.

When he had first seen Catherine that morning, as she had come down the staircase looking as regal as a bride herself in an elegant mint green gown, Ryde had been shocked at how little she seemed changed from the sweet, innocent girl he had danced with the night before. Then she had joined Elton, Barrett, and himself, and he had gotten a closer view of her face. He had seen the pallor of her skin, the dark smudges under her eyes, the tight lines around her mouth, and he had felt a pang of concern for her that had made him furious with himself—and with her.

She had caught his look of fury and had stumbled back against the wall as if he had struck her, and for a moment he had actually been tempted to take her in his arms and beg forgiveness. Fortunately, he had come to his senses in time to recognize it for the ruse it was and had turned and walked away.

But here she was again, looking repentant and unhappy, and despite everything: despite the memory of her behavior last night, despite the discovery that she was a drunkard and a wanton, despite the knowledge that she loved another man, Ryde found a part of him still cared for her, a part of him still wanted her whether she had taken another man to her bed or not.

It was a part of him he wished he could tear out with his bare hands.

The ceremony ended, and the bride and groom kissed and were wished happy, and Ryde was forced to take Catherine's arm and follow the happy couple down the aisle and out of the chapel.

They emerged outside into the bright, morning sunshine, and for a moment she looked up at him. Her blue-green eyes were filled with tears, and they glistened like the gemstones in the ring he could feel even now pressing against his chest. Seizing her hand, he dragged her away from the crowd of well-wishers and back to the solitude of the chapel. "I find I cannot leave without asking after all."

"Asking what?" Her voice was a whisper.

"One simple question. Why?"

She did not answer, just stared up at him, the tears slipping from her eyes and rolling down her cheeks.

"If you wanted him that badly," Ryde demanded thickly, "why did you not just tell me and be done with it? Why did you invite him to your room and throw your passion for him in my face?"

"I did not ... I do not ... Oh, Andrew! I am so sorry!"

She began to shake, and not quite knowing what he was doing he put his arms around her and held her. They remained like that for some time, until the sudden vivid image of her naked in Farleigh's arms filled his mind, and he pushed her violently away.

She did not protest, merely pressed her fist to her mouth like a child trying not to cry out during a beating. It tore at his heart, but he knew, if he gave in to her now, he would be lost. He had to get away.

He had to rid himself of all association and memory of her.

Untying his neckcloth, he unbuttoned his shirt, removed the chain from about his neck, and seizing Catherine's hand poured the chain and the ring that hung from it into her palm. "There," he said savagely. "Consider that an early wedding gift for when you marry Farleigh."

"But I do not wish — " She broke off, shaking her head. She stared down at the ring, her tears slipping down and glittering on the stones. He gazed at her bent head, and was caught when she looked up at him. "Sapphire and peridots," she said in a voice that trembled. "An unusual combination."

For a moment, he was tempted. Tempted to trade pride, principle, and honor for a pair of glistening blue-green pools filled with remorse. *But she loves another.* The words echoed in his head like an alarm. He fixed his resolve. "They reminded me of your eyes," he snapped, as he turned and started for the door.

"Andrew, wait!"

He kept going.

She ran after him, seizing his sleeve. "But how long have you had this?"

He pulled away, turning his back on her. "I purchased it the morning after the Sunflower Ball."

He heard her gasp, but kept moving. He burst from the chapel like a drowning man escaping the sea, and ignoring his guests, headed blindly for the house.

Chapter 24

"What do you mean, he has gone?" Jane exclaimed in disbelief. "I have a room full of guests waiting for him to make a toast to the happy couple!"

"I am sorry, my lady. His lordship had his curricle brought round and departed nearly a half-hour ago."

"But where was he destined?"

"I fear his lordship did not see fit to inform me, ma'am," Jenner proclaimed in an aggrieved voice. "Perhaps Mr. Doddy may be of some assistance." But when they trooped upstairs, her brother's valet knew no more than the butler and was horrified to learn his master had departed for regions unknown without so much as a change of shirt or linen.

Jane returned downstairs, angry with Andrew for his rude disappearance, and angry with herself for her cowardice. She had meant to speak to him earlier today about Catherine and the events of the previous night, but he had looked so formidable, so steely and remote, she had hesitated to raise the obviously tender subject. She had persuaded herself it would be better to wait until after the wedding festivities were over and the guests were gone. But now here was her brother gone before the guests, in an act so unlike his normal, sober self she still did not quite believe it.

Of course, it had not precisely been like Andrew's normal, sober self to rush a man and nearly throttle him to death with his bare hands either. She approached the double doors to the dining room, where the wedding breakfast was being served, and stopped.

No, obviously Andrew's feelings for Catherine ran deep, far deeper than Jane would have thought possible for her reserved and proper brother. Which made it all the more regrettable that she had not told him of her suspicions when she had had the chance.

She sighed. Well, there was nothing for it now but to make the necessary excuses to her brother's guests and await his return. Taking a deep breath, she threw back her shoulders, fixed a smile upon her face, and reached down to grasp the well-polished door handles. Throwing open the doors she said in a bright and cheerful voice, "Forgive me, everyone. I come bearing Ryde's apologies. I fear he has been called away quite suddenly."

Catherine was not surprised by the news of Ryde's departure and managed to keep her composure and at least an outward semblance of calm during Jane's announcement and the ensuing flurry of speculation as to Ryde's real reason for leaving.

To Catherine's relief, no one hazarded any connection between Ryde's hasty departure and herself, but later, as the bride and groom prepared to depart on their wedding journey, Emily took Catherine aside and inquired anxiously, "My dear, Lord Ryde's departure—I would not wish to leave you, if there is anything amiss."

Catherine faltered. How tempting to pour out her heartache to her dear friend, as she had so often in the past. "Oh, Emily, I — " She stopped. She was forgetting. Emily had a greater claim on her affections now. She took her friend's hands in hers and squeezed them. "I am going to miss you."

"But Catherine — "

She shook her head. "No, Emily. From now on I must look after myself. You have a fine husband now, and soon, no doubt, you will have a house full of children."

"And you?"

Catherine felt a sudden tightness in her throat. "Perhaps, next time we meet, I shall be wed as well."

For a moment, their eyes locked, and Catherine sensed Emily saw all too much. Then she sighed and embraced Catherine fiercely. "God keep you, my dear."

After the newlyweds departed, the wedding breakfast wound to a close. Catherine managed to slip away and summon her carriage while Jane was trapped in conversation with Emily's voluble brother. Polly had already packed her things, so she departed for Rosington without even telling Jane goodbye. Catherine felt guilty treating her friend so shabbily, but found she did not have the courage to face Jane after the events of the night before.

When Catherine arrived at Rosington, she found to her relief that the countess was already gone from the house. Giving orders that she was not to be disturbed, Catherine retreated to her room. Finally alone with her grief, she threw herself on her bed and awaited the storm that had been building inside her all day.

But the storm would not come. The tears would not fall. Instead of being swept into a tempest of sensibility, she found herself sinking into a numb sort of lethargy where there was neither pain, nor its opposite, only dazed awareness.

She remained like that for three days. First Polly, then Mrs. Owen, and finally Matthew Elton came to knock at her door to beg her to eat. But she was not hungry, and it was only when Matthew Elton threatened to force the door that she consented to allow Polly in from time to time with tea and biscuits.

Then on the fifth day Mrs. Owen brought news that Phillip had returned and was waiting downstairs to see her.

Realizing she could no longer ignore a future she had, after all, created for herself, Catherine asked Mrs. Owen to send Polly up to help make her presentable. Polly did her best, but despite her efforts, when Catherine regarded herself in the mirror after Polly had gone, she grimaced and wondered what Phillip would think of his choice now.

And what of my choice, the one I cannot even remember making? Biting hard on her lip to force the thought away, Catherine crossed to a small box on her dresser and drew out the chain and ring she had spent the past five days trying to forget. With a sudden feeling of desperation, she ran to the window. But though she poised her arm to hurl it out, she could not bring herself to do it. Instead, with a sigh, she slipped it around her neck and tucked the ring into the hidden recesses of her bodice.

When she entered the drawing room, Phillip came forward to meet her. As he drew close, he frowned. "Heavens, my dear, you look as if you had not slept a wink last night."

"That is because I did not."

He paled. "Then you had best come sit down."

He led her to the gold striped settee. She sat down, but he remained standing. She wished he would speak, but instead he paced back and forth before her. Finally she could watch him no more, and closed her eyes in weariness. The footsteps stopped. She opened her eyes to find him gazing down at her, expectantly. "Well?" he said softly, but the softness had an edge to it.

"Well what?"

"How long must I wait?"

"For what, Phillip?"

"For the recriminations. The bitter speech of rebuke. When are you going to berate me as you have every right to do?"

"What would be the point?" she said heavily. "It was my mistake, Phillip, not yours. I invited you to my bed, and I cannot complain if you accepted the invitation."

His mouth quirked tensely. "Is that how you remember it?"

She swallowed hard, as if trying to swallow away the humiliation. "No. In truth, I drank so much wine that evening I have no memory of anything that passed between us."

He said, a strange note in his voice, "Then shall I fill in the gaps of your tattered recollection?"

"*No!*"

His blue eyes narrowed. "Does the thought of us together fill you with such repugnance then?"

For the first time, she felt a spark of anger. "It certainly does not fill me with pride! Dear heaven, Phillip! I have betrayed not only the honor of my name but the one person I cared most about in all the world."

His lips tightened into a thin white line, and he reached stiffly into his coat to pull out a folded piece of paper. He smoothed it out on his gloved hand, and then dropped it in her lap. "There. What I went to London for."

It was the special license. She gazed at it unwillingly. It looked so official, with her name and Phillip's carefully spelled out, and a five-pound stamp affixed to show the proper fee had been paid. She said, her mouth suddenly dry, "I suppose now we may be wed at any time?"

"Yes. That is," he added acerbically, "if you are willing to take a man who wants you and is willing to fight for you over one who abandons you at the first sign of trouble."

"That is unfair!" she cried.

"Is it?"

"You cannot expect Ryde to want me after … "

"After another man has had you?" he supplied harshly. "Why not? If our positions were reversed, I would not have given you up so easily."

"Hah! Six years ago, when you thought Ryde's father was my lover, you could not wash your hands of me fast enough. Why you married barely a month after we parted!"

"*Because you would not have me.*" He spat out the words through clenched teeth.

She stared at him in disbelief.

"It is true," he said, turning away and crossing to the window. "I never really believed you and the old goat were lovers."

"But that night at Lady Carsey's! You said — "

"I had just come to realize how much I wanted you, only to be told you would not have me. I was angry, and my pride was hurt, and when old Ryde tossed me aside like a misbehaving cully, I said the first thing that came into my mind. Believe me, once my head had cleared, I realized what nonsense it was."

She pressed her hands to her cheeks. "Did it never occur to you to wonder what harm your heedless accusation caused me?"

Phillip turned from the window and came to sit next to her on the settee. Taking her hands in his he said, "My dear, I am sorry! Still, what does any of that matter now? We have the license; we can be married tomorrow if you will but agree to it. Let me take you away. Let me make you happy! Please, Catherine, let me prove myself to you. I want to show you that I will make you a good husband. I want to show you that you were destined to be my wife."

Catherine felt no sense of destiny, but neither could she see any reason to delay the inevitable. "All right, Phillip," she said wearily. "If that is what you wish. Let us be wed."

Jane rose before the sun the next morning, and by eight o'clock she had worn a tread in the carpet of the morning room with her pacing. What was she to do? According to the note Mrs. Howard had sent her the previous evening via a groom, Catherine was to marry Lord Farleigh in the village church this morning at nine o'clock. That was less than an hour from now, and still Matthew Elton had not returned with her exasperating brother.

Perhaps he had been unable to track Andrew down? It was a possibility she considered reluctantly, for Matthew had given her his word that he would find her brother and bring him back to Farthingsgate with all due speed, and when Matthew promised a thing it usually got done. Even as children, he had had that air of competence and assurance that had sent them all running to him with their troubles. So when Matthew had shown up on her doorstep three days earlier demanding to speak with her, Jane had eagerly invited him in, and had poured out all her suspicions and concerns to him trusting that, with his help, all would be set right.

Now, however, there was hardly any time left, and things were still horribly wrong. Jane toyed with the notion of putting a stop to the wedding herself, but on what grounds?

If only Matthew and her brother would come.

Suddenly Jane heard the clatter of horses and the sound of voices in the drive. She ran to the door of the morning room and out into the hall. She reached the foyer just in time to see a startled Jenner dart backwards to avoid the swing of the front door as it burst open when a bedraggled giant rushed in.

The giant, whom Jane belatedly recognized as her brother, came to a complete stop at the sight of her, and his look of frantic concern quickly metamorphosed into a scowl of such icy ferocity Jane actually felt her knees wobble beneath her. Still, as he started to turn on the man that had followed him quietly through the door, she managed to cry out, "No, Andrew! There is no time! Come with me, and I will explain."

Perhaps it was the urgency in her voice, or perhaps it was the curious gaze of nearly a half-dozen servants, but whatever the reason, her brother turned and followed her without a word back to the morning room. Matthew Elton came, too, and when her brother made as if to shut the door in his face, Matthew thrust out his arm like a battering ram and said stiffly, "No, Ryde. I have a few things to say to you myself."

"Wherever did you find him?" Jane whispered to Matthew, after he closed the door and crossed to stand beside her in a gesture of solidarity.

"In the townhouse in London," he replied, in a voice quite loud enough for her glowering brother, who stood staring out the window, to hear. "He had not bothered to have the knocker rehung, and he had told the servants he wanted no visitors, so it took some doing to discover he was actually inside, ensconced in his study, drowning himself in port."

Her brother spun around from the window and advanced on them. "Elton, I will thank you to keep your nose out of my business! As for you, Jane, I would appreciate an explanation as to why you sent this fellow after me in the first place. Do you know the wretch had the nerve to tell me that you'd had a serious accident and were lying at death's door?"

Jane felt her cheeks heat. "Forgive me, Andrew. I fear the lie was my idea. I did not know how else to get you back here."

"And why the devil should I want to be back here?" he demanded tensely.

Jane referred to the small watch hanging from a chain about her neck. "Because in a little more than three quarters of an hour," she said baldly, "Catherine plans to wed Lord Farleigh."

Andrew paled, but said, "And what is that to me?"

Matthew Elton muttered something under his breath, and Jane replied acerbically, "As a week ago you informed me that you wished to marry her yourself, I thought you might want to stop it from happening."

Her brother flashed her a warning look. "The lady has made her choice. We must all now abide by it."

Jane wished she were tall enough to box her obstinate brother's ears. "Drew, I am not sure Catherine *did* choose. I think it possible someone chose for her."

"What the devil are you talking about?"

"I do not believe Catherine invited Lord Farleigh to her room that night, and I do not think — "

"Jane, be still!" her brother growled. "Have you no better sense than to trumpet her indiscretion before the world!"

"I am not the world, sir," Matthew interjected, "and I already know the tale. *No!* Before you start railing at your sister again, you should know that I insisted she confide in me as Lady Catherine's physician."

Ryde advanced on Matthew. "*Physician!*" he exclaimed. "What need has she of a physician? Is she ill?"

"I was summoned to Rosington three days ago by the housekeeper, Mrs. Owen, for fear she soon would be, for she was locked in her room refusing both food and drink. After much coaxing, I managed to convince her to allow a maid in from time to time with refreshment. Then I came here to learn what was preying on her mind. After considerable prodding, Lady Jane told me what transpired the night before Barrett's wedding. She also told me of her suspicion that the entire matter was staged to make it seem Lady Catherine was guilty of something she was not. I found her arguments compelling, so I agreed to find you and bring you back here to sort the matter out."

"You might have saved yourself the trouble," Ryde snapped, "for my sister's suspicion is nonsense. Nothing was staged. Farleigh was there in her bedchamber scurrying to clothe himself. Catherine was there in the bed naked. It does not take a scholar to put those pieces together and form the truth."

Jane opened her mouth to protest, but Matthew flashed her a look and discreetly held up a staying hand.

"Your sister tells me," he said mildly, "that when you were in Lady Catherine's bedchamber, she had her back to you, and you could not see her face."

"What of it?" her brother replied harshly. "It was her form. It was her hair. That was no impostor, I assure you."

"I did not mean to imply it was. But Lady Jane has told me that the entire time you were in her chamber, Lady Catherine neither turned nor moved nor shifted from her original position, even when you called out her name. Is that true?"

Her brother's face was a tense mask. "Yes."

"And does that not strike you as odd?"

Drew's mouth twisted. "No doubt she was ashamed."

"Perhaps. Or perhaps she was unconscious."

"Are you mad?"

Jane interjected, "I spoke to Catherine's maid the following morning, Drew. At first, the girl was reluctant to speak, but eventually she admitted that it took two footmen to get Catherine to her chamber, and when they deposited her on the bed she was quite dead to the world."

Her brother made a strangled sound. "So? She drank too much wine and became drunk. That does not excuse her behavior."

Matthew shook his head. "No one saw Lady Catherine take more than three glasses of wine at supper. That is not enough to floor even the weakest head."

Ryde turned away and said thickly, "Then she was already drunk when she went in to supper."

"No, Lady Catherine was quite sober," Matthew countered.

"As if you were in any condition to determine such a thing," Ryde snapped dismissively.

Jane's surprised gaze flew from her brother to Matthew, but Matthew flashed her a reassuring look and replied coolly, "I may have had too much to drink earlier in the evening, Ryde, but our discussion out on the balcony quickly sobered me up. I did not touch a drop the rest of the evening, and I was entirely clear-headed when I had the honor of being Lady Catherine's last dance partner before the meal. She was smiling, happy, and—despite darting covert glances at you every time we made a turn in the figure—entirely too graceful a dancer to be anything but entirely sober."

Her brother made no reply, but the hollow shadows in his cheeks deepened as Matthew mentioned Catherine stealing glances at him.

Matthew's tone gentled as he said, "So, friend, we are left with a riddle. How did the lady come to be in such a stupor when she was carried to her bed?"

Andrew's gaze flicked from Matthew to Jane. His expression shifted from derision to a sort of wary anguish. "Confound it! I do not know. Please enlighten me."

Jane felt a sudden glimmer of hope. Her brother was beginning to take them seriously. "She was drugged," she said. "We suspect with laudanum or something very like it."

❦

The room was suddenly very still. Ryde stared down at the back of a chair he had not even realized he was gripping. The idea was ridiculous, of course. But what if it were true? He remembered his own experience in the gambling hell Marlow had taken them to. It had been Farleigh who had informed him that he had been drugged. It had been Farleigh who had taken Catherine her wine. If she truly had not known what she was doing…

Ryde forced the tempting thought away.

"Even if she *were* drugged," he said heavily, "that does not explain everything." He drew a ragged breath. "When we burst into her room, she cowered under the covers while Farleigh pulled on his shirt. She was clear-headed enough to cover herself, and she was awake enough to feel ashamed."

"Was she?" Matthew Elton demanded. "Think, Ryde, what you actually saw. A woman stripped of her clothes, covered by a blanket, propped on her side. But she never moved. How do you know she was awake?"

Ryde felt his heart begin to pound. Could it be? For perhaps the hundredth time the scene in Catherine's bedchamber played out in his mind, but this time he did not fight the memory, but instead explored it painfully and carefully. When he was done, his eyes opened wide. *By God, it was possible!* He tightened his grip on the chair to keep from swaying.

Slowly he turned toward his sister. "If you are right, Jane, how did Farleigh get into her room?"

Jane's expression was grim. "I do not know for certain, but Matthew saw Farleigh and the countess speaking outside the ballroom shortly before the other guests departed."

"And I could swear I saw her slip something to him," Matthew added, "though I fear I was too far away to see what it was."

Farleigh and the countess.

He and Jane had seen the two speaking intently together shortly before supper, and the countess had disappeared from the table at the same time Catherine had. It had been the countess who had accompanied Catherine upstairs, and the countess who had raised the alarm that had caused Ryde to enter Catherine's bedchamber. It had even been the countess who had assured him that it was Phillip Catherine intended to marry. He thought of the malice in her eyes as she had bid him farewell. What had she said to him? *Remember me in the years to come.*

Ryde's hands clenched into fists. "What a fool I have been. Of course! This is her revenge on me for driving her from the country."

"What?" exclaimed his sister.

"I will explain later." Ryde shook his head in disbelief. "How did I not see it?"

"It was a well-crafted scheme," said Matthew.

Jane nodded. "Indeed, it was! I would never have suspected the truth myself if it had not been so like — " Her voice suddenly trailed off.

"So like what?" Ryde demanded.

"Matthew, would you please excuse Ryde and me for a moment?"

He flashed her a look of curiosity, but nodded gravely and left the room.

"Well, Jane?" Ryde prompted when they were alone. "So like what?"

Jane said reluctantly, "So like the scheme our mother and Lord Trenwich perpetrated on our father twenty-five years ago."

Ryde gaped at her. "You cannot be serious!"

"I fear I am. Father was engaged to Catherine's mother, but Mama was determined to have him for herself."

Ryde thought of his late mother, and of how she had never been able to gracefully accept that there was anything she could not have. Still, remembering her all-consuming bitterness toward their late sire, it was strange to think there had been a time when she had thought she could not do without *him*.

Jane continued her tale. "Mama convinced Lord Trenwich to drug Catherine's mother's wine and arranged for our father to come upon Lord Trenwich in her mother's bedchamber—precisely as you found Farleigh in Catherine's. Father was so furious, he eloped with Mama that very night."

Ryde thought of the misery of the past week and tried to imagine it stretched over years. He shuddered. *Poor Father.* "Jane, how do you come to know all this?"

She colored faintly. "I overheard Mama confess the entire tale to him the day Papa fell from his horse." She hesitated and then added, "That is why we were sent from Farthingsgate."

He was silent, absorbing the news. Then he looked up at her. "You must not blame him, Jane. I suspect I might have done the same in his place."

"I forgave him long ago, Drew."

Ryde flinched, wishing he could say the same. "Curse it, why did you not tell me the truth sooner?"

She avoided his eyes. "It was not a pretty secret. It weakened my affection for Mama in a rather shattering way. I thought it better to spare you that. Later, when you might have borne the knowledge of her complicity more easily, I was reluctant to tell you because of your affection for Lord Trenwich."

Ryde said bitterly, "And to think I once thought him such a superior gentleman to our own poor sire. I wonder now why he gave me that loan."

"I do not know for sure, but I think Aunt Celia may have threatened to expose his part in the plot if he did not. When father was sick, I think he told her the whole tale."

Ryde bowed his head. "So even that was a lie."

Jane shook her head. She crossed to him, and put a comforting hand on his arm. "Not entirely, Drew. Look how much interest the earl took in you, how much he helped you! Aunt Celia may have gotten him started, but eventually I think it was his own conscience that led him to do what he did for you."

Ryde made a dismissive sound.

"No, Drew. The earl *did* care about you," Jane insisted. "I think, at the end, he must have thought of you almost like a son."

His sister was trying to comfort him, but he was done with false comfort. "That is preposterous."

"Is it? Why else would he have gone to such lengths to make amends to you?"

Ryde snorted, "Such lengths? You mean loaning me a very small bit of his very large fortune; a loan that I repaid—with interest?"

"No, I mean entrusting you with something far more dear to him: *Catherine*. He put her future in your hands. Perhaps he did so, because he hoped the two of you might make a match of it. After all, Catherine is very like her mother."

"Am I to take it, then, that you think I am like our father?"

Jane took a step back and surveyed his rumpled clothes and unshaven face with a critical eye. "I never used to think so, but I begin to wonder."

Suddenly, his heart felt lighter. "There was a time I would have taken insult at the comparison, Jane, but now I find it does not sting." He paused, and then shook his head. "Yet there is one parallel I cannot bear to have repeated. I do not wish to spend my entire life mourning a lost love, as our father did. Do you think Catherine will still have me?"

"There is only one way to know, Drew. You must ask her. Only," Jane paused to consult her watch, "you had best hurry! Before she marries the wrong man!"

Chapter 25

Catherine looked about the empty church and felt the knot in her stomach tighten miserably. Well, wasn't this precisely what she had wanted? An empty church with only the minister and Phillip's two cousins to bear witness to a marriage she regretted before it even began? Still, the reality was more oppressive than she could have imagined, and as Phillip escorted her down the short aisle to where Reverend Whitcomb stood waiting at the chancel, she wanted desperately to break free and run away.

Only there was no place to run to. Ryde was gone, and so was Emily, the one person she might have trusted not to abandon her. And if she did not marry, and it turned out that her wanton lapse had resulted in a baby—well, she refused to give her child that sort of birthright.

They neared the communion rail. Phillip came to a stop before the waiting cleric, and Catherine, her heart drumming in her chest, stumbled to a halt beside him. Elizabeth and Caroline Montague, in their cheerful pink and yellow gowns, took their place on Catherine's left, and Reverend Whitcomb, an encouraging smile wreathing his aged cheeks, opened his book, adjusted his spectacles on the end of his nose, and began the service.

Catherine listened numbly to a description of the intent of matrimony and clamped her teeth together tightly when the clergyman inquired if either knew of any impediment why they might not lawfully be joined together in matrimony. Not expecting a reply, Reverend Whitcomb paused only long enough to catch a needed breath, and then continued solemnly, "Wilt thou Phillip Edward Henry take this woman for thy wedded wife?"

"He will not!" declared a peremptory voice behind them.

Reverend Whitcomb's eyes widened like an owl's and the Misses Montague began to titter nervously. Catherine spun around. Ryde, looking unkempt and decidedly bellicose, stood in the doorway. His gaze met hers, then flicked away and fastened on Phillip.

"Are you drunk, sir?" Phillip demanded. "How dare you interrupt my wedding in this fashion?"

"I dare, sir, because I am this lady's trustee and you have not obtained my permission to wed her."

"Your permission is not needed. The lady is of age and can wed whom she chooses. Now if you will excuse us?" Phillip turned back toward the astonished cleric and snapped, "Proceed."

"I will excuse you, sir, if you, in turn, will join me outside so that I may discuss a matter of some urgency with you."

"Go to the devil."

"Lord Farleigh!" Reverend Whitcomb exclaimed reprovingly. "Need I remind you that you stand in the house of God?"

Phillip's jaw ground sideways in anger. He turned and started down the aisle. "Very well, Ryde. If I cannot be rid of you one way, I will manage it another."

The two men disappeared out the church door.

Catherine stood there, staring after them, fixed to the spot as if she had been turned to stone. Then slowly the ominous import of Phillip's words sank in, and her limbs returned to flesh and blood. With a gasp, she started for the door, but a restraining arm shot out and held her. "No, my child, this is not a matter for you. Let the gentlemen settle it by themselves."

She struggled to pull free. "You do not comprehend. They mean to fight because of me. I must stop them!"

But now the Montague sisters had hold of her other arm. "No, Lady Catherine, you must not!" cried Elizabeth.

"Think how it would look if you interfered!" chimed Caroline.

"You need not worry for Phillip," Elizabeth assured her.

"Yes, he is an excellent shot, if it comes to that."

Catherine, who wasn't worried in the least about Phillip, wrenched one arm loose from the sisters' grasp and the other loose from the Reverend's, and ran out of the church. Emerging out into the bright sunlight, she blinked for a moment, then scanned the yard for the two men. At first she saw neither, then looking to her left at a nearby field, she spied a bent figure leaning sideways, as if ready to topple over. It was Ryde. Dear God, was that blood on his face?

She ran without thought, and was ready to catapult over the low stone wall that separated the field from the church grounds, when her nearness provided a more complete view of the scene. Ryde was not about to drop from a mortal wound, but was leaning over to give his hand to Phillip, who lay sprawled on the ground.

Feeling a fool, she stumbled to a halt. Why had she not heeded the advice of the others and remained in the sanctuary? It was too late now; the men had seen her.

Phillip rose unsteadily to his feet and came toward her. His face was pale, and a bruise was forming above his left eye, but he walked toward her like a man going into battle. Passing through a gate to her right, he came up to her and said in a low, urgent voice, "Catherine, will you seat yourself on this wall? There is something I must tell you." She did as he asked, and he began to speak.

When he had done, she realized she was gripping the edge of the wall so fiercely the jagged stones had torn through the lace of her gloves and cut her palms. Folding her bleeding hands in her lap, she said quietly, "How could you do such a thing to me, Phillip? The countess I understand, for she hates me and would do anything to hurt me. But you? What wrong have I ever done you that you should use me so cruelly?"

His blue eyes locked with hers. "What wrong?" he repeated bleakly. "Only the greatest wrong a woman ever did me. You made me love you." He lifted one hand as if to touch her, but let it fall back down to his side. "Goodbye, Catherine."

He turned abruptly and started back toward the church. Catherine watched him go and saw him speak to the Reverend Whitcomb and his two cousins, who were peering out the church door. The cleric disappeared into the sanctuary, and Elizabeth and Caroline Montague followed Phillip to his carriage and clambered inside with all speed. Before climbing in himself, Phillip glanced one last time in Catherine's direction and sketched a farewell salute. Without thinking, she raised her hand in reply. The bitter set of his shoulders relaxed a little, and he made her a deep bow before stepping inside the carriage and barking an order to the driver that sent the carriage rattling off down the lane.

"You almost look sad to see the scoundrel go."

Ryde's voice startled her out of her reverie. Focused on the carriage, Catherine had not heard the gate swing open a second time, nor heard him approach. "I pity him, that is all."

"And what of me? Am I not deserving of pity?"

She looked up at him. His coat was ripped, his lip was cut, and there was a smear of blood drying along his cheek. Yet despite all of that, he looked exceedingly well pleased with himself.

"Not a whit."

"Hardhearted woman."

"I am," she said grimly. "So you had best go back whence you came and leave me be."

"I dare not. If I but turn my head for an instant, some other suitor will appear from nowhere to demand your hand."

"Please, Ryde, I am in no mood for jests."

His expression sobered. "Then I shall be serious. I have no intention of stirring from your side."

She felt herself begin to tremble, but she pressed her hands into her lap. "You have no duty which compels you to remain here. You have stopped my wedding. You have convinced Phillip to tell me the truth. You have done your good deed. You can go."

He did not seem to be listening. His gaze was fixed on her hands.

Leaning forward, he gently lifted them from her lap and turned them palms up. His breath caught in an oath.

"How did this happen?"

Catherine tried to snatch them away, but he held them firmly. "It is nothing," she insisted. "I pressed them too hard against the stone, that is all."

Ryde's gaze flicked from the tattered lace of her gloves to the rough edge of the wall. "No doubt when Farleigh was telling you his tale?"

She nodded.

"I should have wrung his neck while I had the chance," Ryde muttered as he gently removed one torn glove. "And my own, as well, while I was at it." He peeled off the other. "I was so angry and immersed in my own misery, I refused to acknowledge that you, too, were suffering. When I think of the pain you have endured this past week..."

"It does not matter. It is over now."

Slowly he shook his head. "These poor hands make a liar of you, my dear. The hurt must run deep." He bent his head and brushed his lips softly against her scraped palms, and a shiver ran through her that eased the sting. "The question is," he murmured, sliding his lips down to caress the tiny butterfly-shaped mark on the inside of her wrist, "can you forgive me?"

She drew her hands away. "There is nothing to forgive."

"Isn't there?" he demanded, moving closer. "I fell easily into the countess's trap. I believed Farleigh's lies. I railed at you and deserted you, and just when you thought you had finally rid yourself of my irritating presence, I appear out of the blue to send the man you mean to marry packing."

How was she to respond? It was true. All of it. She felt thoroughly aggrieved at Ryde's treatment of her, yet she felt she had no right to be. "I can hardly blame you for believing a lie which I believed myself," she said stiffly. "As for Phillip —"

"Yes, what about that fellow?" Ryde interrupted. "Despite his confession, I sense a lingering fondness in you for the rascal."

Catherine stared at him in disbelief. She was furious with Phillip. She was furious with Ryde. She was furious with herself. She was just ... *furious.* All the hurt and pain of the last week seemed curled up inside her like malignant smoke she could not exhale.

Seeing her expression, the color drained from Ryde's face. "*Is* it too late? Did I do wrong thrusting myself back into your life? Would you have preferred ignorance and his ring on your finger to being left behind here—with me?"

Could he so misjudge her still? "If there is one lesson I have learned this week," she snapped, "it is the folly of dwelling on what might have been. All that matters is what is."

His golden eyes darkened. "Is that your way of telling me that you no longer love me?"

Anger left her mute.

Ryde fell back a step and said tightly, "Forgive me for my untoward interference." He bowed to her and then turned and strode off in the direction of the church.

Catherine jumped down from her perch on the wall. "Ryde, wait! Where are you going?"

He did not answer her.

Catherine tried to follow him, but his long legs carried him with a swiftness she could not match, and in her agitation, she let go of her hold on her skirt. Her shoe caught in the hem, and she tripped, falling to the ground. Oblivious to her plight, Ryde continued on past the church, towards the far yard where his curricle stood waiting. *Dear heaven,* Catherine thought, *he is leaving!* In her bitterness, she had driven him away. Suddenly panicked at her folly, Catherine regained her feet.

He had already alighted and was turning the carriage around.

Realizing she could not hope to catch him before he set his greys to the trot, Catherine veered sharply to her left and began running to intercept him as he advanced down the lane. Desperation gave her feet wings, and she ran faster than she had ever run before. As she saw Ryde's curricle turn the bend and approach, she said a silent prayer and ran out into the lane directly in its path.

With a fearful oath, Ryde yanked at the reins. The curricle veered wildly to the right and the startled horses came to a shuddering stop. For a long moment, Ryde stood there, still as a statue, staring down at her. Then he catapulted from the carriage, seized her by the shoulders, and shook her until her teeth rattled.

"*Of all the cork-brained, addle-pated, bird-witted —*"

"I couldn't let you leave —"

" *— sapskulled, mutton-headed fools!*" His arms slid down to her waist, and with an exasperated sigh he pulled her to him.

" —at least, not like that!"

"Dammit, Cat," he muttered angrily into her hair, "don't you realize my horses could have ground you to a pudding?"

Catherine rubbed her cheek against his coat and nestled contentedly into his decidedly bedraggled neckcloth. "Yes," she replied softly, "but I knew your ability with the ribbons, and I trusted you to stop them in time."

He shivered, and his arms tightened convulsively around her. "It was unforgivably foolish—and totally unnecessary. I wasn't leaving. I was bringing my curricle round to fetch you. I didn't want you to have to walk in your exhausted state."

She stared up into his face, her misery gone, sudden tears pricking at her eyes. "Oh, Andrew! You were?"

"Of course. Did I not tell you so before? Like it or not you are stuck with me." He grimaced. "Like a limpet clinging to your toe. So you had best — " He broke off suddenly and peered down into her face. "You called me Andrew."

"It is your name, is it not?"

He regarded her warily. "Yes, but how do you come to be using it?"

"Is it not the custom for a wife to call her husband by his Christian name?"

"*Husband?* But you do not love me anymore."

"Now who is being mutton-headed?"

"But you said ..."

"I did *not* say. I just failed to correct you when you did." She reached up and lightly touched his cheek. "I was angry that after all that has passed between us you could still doubt my feelings, but I was being unfair—and overly proud." She paused and swallowed hard. "So if you wish it, I will say it: Andrew, I love you." She added with a shaky laugh,

"If I did not, do you think I would be going about with this around my neck?" She reached into her bodice and withdrew the chain with his ring.

He looked from the ring to her face and then crushed her to him with a fierceness that would have made her cry out if she had not feared to be let go. "Then shall we be wed, my sweet darling?"

Pushing against his chest so she could find sufficient breath to answer, Catherine said, "That depends."

He glared down at her. "On what?"

"On whether my trustee approves. He is a high stickler, you see, and quite difficult to please."

"Is he now?"

"Oh, yes. He has chased away any number of suitors; he even came to blows with one who tried to marry me under false pretenses."

"Sounds like a formidable fellow."

"He is. A terrible man to cross. Therefore, be warned. He is determined to see me married to a man I can love — "

He squeezed her. "Thankfully, I think we have satisfied that criterion."

" — and who loves me in return."

He gazed down into her eyes. "That test was passed long ago."

"Was it?" she asked softly.

"Yes."

"When?"

"Hmmm, let me see. I suspect it was that very first night, when you mistook me for my father." He reached up and gently removed her bonnet. "There was this curl, you see," he drew the pins from her hair, sending it spilling down over her shoulders. "It had escaped its ribbon and was bobbing fetchingly near your face," he pressed a kiss against her hair and then softly nuzzled her ear. "I was quite taken with that curl, and I was sorely tempted to kiss it," his lips brushed along her cheek, "but, foolishly, I refrained." His mouth came to a stop a breath's distance from her own. "Yet if I had been a wiser man, I would have realized that from that moment I was lost," his mouth descended to hers, "irretrievably."

Chapter 26

Despite Catherine's pleading, Ryde refused to be married by special license, but instead insisted on the banns being read and a notice of their engagement being published in *The Times*.

Catherine was sorely vexed by her intended's lack of haste, for she herself was quite mad with impatience, and it rankled to think he might not be as eager for their union as she was. She could not, however, persuade anyone else to share her sense of grievance.

Jane pronounced an engagement of four weeks perfectly reasonable, and suggested with a laugh that Catherine savor the chance to be properly wooed. Emily wrote to say she was grateful for Ryde's deliberation, for it provided her and Edward an opportunity to be present at the ceremony. Mrs. Howard praised Ryde for disdaining marriage by special license, for undue haste in such matters could give rise to unfortunate gossip. Lady Dent chided Catherine for wishing to marry at all, when she could live so much more happily as a single lady. And Matthew Elton expressed no opinion at all, for he so studiously avoided Catherine's company that she had no opportunity to ask him what he thought.

So Catherine resigned herself to waiting, and at first—much to her surprise—she found it surprisingly tolerable. Jane had been right.

It was pleasant to be wooed. Indeed, it was more than pleasant—it was thrilling—for the man courting her was Ryde. He brought her flowers and invited her on picnics, flashed her admiring glances and stole surreptitious kisses, doted on her and fussed over her and occasionally whispered to her in a voice so full of desire it set her body tingling.

However, as time passed, and the weeks until their wedding dwindled down to days, Catherine noticed a growing coolness in Ryde's demeanor. His kisses grew less frequent, his embraces less ardent, his usual ease in her company disappeared, and he would go to almost any length to avoid situations where they might contrive to be alone together.

By the eve of the wedding, Catherine had grown so anxious, she followed him as he rode out to a meeting with his steward Jacob Bagshot. She waited until the two men had parted company; then she hailed him. Ryde turned and flashed her a startled smile and exclaimed on the coincidence of their meeting thus. Catherine assured him it was no coincidence and told him she was anxious to speak with him. Frowning, he quickly dismounted and reached up to help her from her horse.

"Tell me!" he exclaimed, seizing her by the waist and swinging her from the saddle. "What is wrong?" He set her on the ground, but did not immediately release his grip on her. "You said you wished to speak with me. Please do so, before the demons of my imagination provide their own explanation for that look upon your face. "

With him holding her so tightly and looking so concerned, her doubts began to evaporate. "Forgive me, it is nothing!" she said hastily. "I cannot imagine now why I was so afraid."

"Afraid?" he said sharply. "What the devil have you to be afraid of?"

"Nothing. I realize that now."

"Catherine!"

"Very well. I was afraid you had changed your mind and no longer wished to marry me."

He stared at her.

"You need not look at me as if I had lost my wits. You have been so cold and remote lately, I thought you were having second thoughts."

He made an uneasy motion, but said with surprising vehemence. "My dear, there is nothing in the world I want more than to be your husband."

She relaxed a little, but could not help asking, "Then why have you been so distant?"

He looked away. " Can you not merely accept that my feelings are unchanged? By tomorrow this time we shall be man and wife, and you will have no further cause for concern."

She might have been reassured by his words, had his tone not been so grim. Puzzled and in need of reassurance, she reached up and kissed him.

He abruptly stepped backwards. "Forgive me, my dear," he said in a low voice, "but I should be getting back to entertain my guests, as should you. After all, the Barretts have just arrived and are doubtless eager for your company."

He cupped his hands to assist her to mount. She gained her saddle and then gazed down at him in stony silence until he flushed and turned to his own horse. "It grows late," he remarked as he gathered up the reins. "I think perhaps I had best ride with you part of the way."

"Do not trouble yourself," she replied, turning her horse abruptly and galloping away.

That same day, a month-old edition of *The Times* was delivered into the hands of a young Italian diplomat in Florence. The young man, whose name was Antonio, was well pleased to acquire the dog-eared newspaper, for that evening he was to visit his new mistress, an English noblewoman residing with her brother in a villa outside the city. Though recently arrived in Florence, she seemed eager for news of home, and he thought the newspaper, along with the expensive box of chocolates sitting on his desk, would serve as an excellent token of his esteem and would, he hoped, earn him a pleasant evening in her bed.

Later, he was to remember such thoughts with bitter amusement and wish he had thrown the damned newspaper in the fire.

The evening began propitiously enough. His mistress greeted him at the door and announced that, as her brother was gone from the house, they could forego the usual formalities and retire at once to her boudoir. Antonio happily agreed, and when they arrived in that seductively furnished chamber, he presented her with the newspaper and the chocolates. She tossed the chocolates down with a negligent thump, but snatched up the newspaper and, much to his chagrin, settled herself on a chaise longue as if meaning to read it at once.

He attempted to distract her with kisses and caresses, but the chaise longue was too narrow to accommodate two, and when he tried to lift her to carry her to the bed, she batted his arms away impatiently. With a sigh of frustration, Antonio crossed to the small table that was already set with their supper. He was just filling his plate with a few slices of roast venison, when he heard a cry behind him followed by a string of oaths that strained even his broad knowledge of colloquial English.

"*Cara mia!*" he exclaimed in alarm. "Whatever is the matter?"

She did not answer, but jumped to her feet and began tearing the newspaper to shreds. "Damn you, Ryde!" she shouted. "Damn you! Damn you! Damn you!"

"You have had some upsetting news?" the diplomatic Antonio inquired warily.

Her head reared back, and for a moment she reminded him of an angry donkey. "You idiot!" she spat, seizing his chocolates and hurling them at his head. "Of course I have had bad news! I have just read that the man who drove me from England is to marry my stepdaughter!"

She began pacing back and forth muttering angrily under her breath. "All that money wasted on Daiches!" She seized a vase full of flowers and flung it against the wall. "All those weeks spent buried in the country!" She seized a gauzy curtain hanging from the bed and ripped it in two. "All the risks I took that last night—and for what?" She picked up the knife Antonio had been using to carve the meat and plunged it into a large melon, splitting it in two. She turned toward Antonio as if expecting an answer, but Antonio, fearing that his beautiful but tempestuous mistress might choose him as the next object to vent her rage upon, ducked toward the door and bid her a hasty goodnight.

The day of her wedding, Catherine rose early, and both Polly and Emily helped her to dress. Her wedding gown was made of white satin trimmed with ribbons made of pale pink love silk, and her headdress was a white satin garland from which a veil of Belgian lace cascaded down her back. The garland was beaded with pearls that glistened like drops of foam against her hair, which shone a particularly fiery auburn in the warm sunlight that graced the day.

Catherine could see in the face of her friend and her maid that she looked well, but it was not until she walked down the aisle of the church on her young brother Carlton's arm and saw Ryde's stunned expression that she dared accept the evidence of her own glass that today, at least, she was beautiful.

She passed through most of the ceremony in a state not unlike a dream, for though at the time she seemed quite aware of all that transpired, afterwards she could recall it only through a haze. The one moment of crystal clarity came when it was suggested the groom salute the bride, and Ryde bent to lightly touch his lips to hers. For the briefest of moments, the kiss deepened to something more passionate, then Ryde abruptly lifted his head and, seizing her arm, propelled her from the church.

The wedding breakfast was another pleasant haze, and then the time arrived for them to go. Catherine performed the surprisingly poignant business of saying goodbye, and then Ryde led her outside to where the carriages stood waiting. Family and friends gathered round to see them off, and when her brother—who had been acting so resentful and surly of late—suddenly dashed up to bestow a farewell kiss upon her cheek, she felt her smile tremble and slip from her face.

Ryde took her arm to help her into the carriage. "Suffering regrets already?" he murmured, in a tone meant to be teasing, but which instead was highly charged.

"It is difficult to leave everyone, that is all."

He leaned over to tuck a rug about her. "It is only for a month, and anyway—" he paused, and reached out to touch her cheek, "you do have me."

She closed her eyes to savor that touch, but from outside the carriage came a few loud cries of farewell, and one rather boisterous toast to the wedding night to come, and suddenly the touch was withdrawn. Catherine opened her eyes to find Ryde settled on the seat opposite, staring grimly out the window.

The carriage started up, and Catherine, upset that her new husband had not chosen to sit beside her, turned to gaze rather blindly out the other window. It would be at least four hours before they reached the inn where she and her new husband would spend their wedding night. She cast a surreptitious glance at him. If possible, his expression had grown even more grim. With a shiver, Catherine pulled the rug more tightly about her and closed her eyes. Four hours. She wasn't sure if she was sorry it was so long—or relieved.

Catherine did not recall falling asleep. So when she woke to find a silver button pressed against her cheek and her husband's arm tightly cradling her against his chest, she was surprised and more than a little pleased. For some time she remained where she was, feigning sleep so that she could enjoy the warmth of his embrace. She finally raised her head and cautiously peered up into his face. "Hello, sleepyhead," he said softly.

"Hello." They regarded each other in silence, then Catherine turned and gazed out the window at the dimming afternoon light. "Have I been asleep long?"

"Hours."

A horn sounded in the distance. She gazed enquiringly at Ryde. "That will be the mail coach," he informed her. "We have trailed it for miles. No doubt it arrives at our own destination: The White Boar."

She smiled up at him. "At last!"

Something flickered in his eyes. "I had not realized you were so eager to arrive," he said flatly, withdrawing his arm.

Stung by his sudden coolness, Catherine pulled away. "And I had not realized that you were so reluctant to do so."

He made no answer, beyond a tightening of the jaw that formed angry hollows in his cheeks. A thick silence settled between them that remained unbroken until they arrived at the inn. As they entered the hostelry, Ryde inquired stiffly if she preferred to sup downstairs in the private parlor he had bespoken or in their rooms. Catherine, her throat tight, replied that it was of no consequence to her one way or the other, and without another glance in his direction, she followed the landlady upstairs.

The room was large and warm and looked quite cozy. Polly soon appeared, followed by Doddy and their trunks. Doddy had the foot-men set her trunk down by the large oak wardrobe in the corner, but directed Ryde's to be delivered next door. Catherine, dismayed to realize that her new husband did not intend to share her room on their wedding night, crossed to a chair after the men had left, and buried her face in her hands.

"My lady? Are you feeling poorly?"

Catherine quickly raised her head and assured Polly that she was fine, only weary from the journey.

"Perhaps you'd feel better if you changed into a fresh gown?"

Catherine stared down at her now dusty wedding dress, and felt tears prick at the back of her throat. "Yes, I suppose I ought to remove this before it is ruined for good." Her voice caught. "Polly, pick something out for me, for I vow I am in no state to choose something myself."

Polly, perhaps sensing something more seriously amiss than a case of travel-sickness, nodded somberly and after much consideration set out a soft, amaranth-colored silk. She helped Catherine from her wedding dress and was just doing up the buttons on the silk gown when there was a peremptory knock at the door, and Ryde entered.

"Leave us," he demanded.

Polly, after one brief, apologetic glance at Catherine, made a quick curtsy and scurried from the room.

He had changed into fresh clothes himself, and his brown hair was neatly brushed and shone in the candlelight. "As you did not specify a preference, my dear, I have determined that we shall dine downstairs. I have asked Doddy to summon us when our meal is ready. As I expect that to be any time, perhaps you had best finish dressing yourself."

"That may prove a bit difficult as you have seen fit to dismiss my maid. I cannot reach the buttons by myself."

Ryde frowned and then crossed to stand behind her. "Allow me." His fingers moved swiftly and impersonally to perform the task, but he caught a bit of her hair in the top button, and as he moved to disentangle it, his fingers brushed across her back.

She trembled at his touch, and he gave an odd little sigh and then bent to press his lips where his fingers had been a moment earlier. "My darling Cat," he whispered, "I—"

There was a discrete knock at the door and then Doddy called out distinctly, "Excuse me, my lord, but you wished to be informed when dinner was served."

Ryde swore under his breath and then called out between gritted-teeth, "Yes! Yes! We will be right there!"

Dinner was a subdued affair. Catherine had little appetite and neither, apparently, did Ryde. The presence of Doddy, who hovered nearby to serve them, robbed the meal of any intimacy. Catherine kept hoping that her husband would excuse the fellow so that they might converse in private, but Ryde seemed more intent on his wine than on conversation, and it was Catherine who finally excused herself and retreated upstairs to her chamber.

Polly was waiting anxiously for her and helped her from her dress and into a chaste white nightgown embroidered with lace. It was no doubt a fitting outfit for a bride on her wedding night, but Catherine could not help but wish she had something a bit more alluring with which to greet her reluctant groom.

Polly turned down the bed and then discreetly left the room, and Catherine slipped between the covers to await Ryde's arrival. As the minutes ticked by, her fears that he might not be coming increased. Against her will, her thoughts kept turning to the other women he must have known. No doubt, she thought, gnawing at her lip, they were beautiful women, experienced and desirable and expert in the ways of love. How was she to compete with such women? Perhaps that was the problem. Perhaps he knew that she could not, and had been dreading this moment precisely because he feared she would disappoint him.

The thought made her ache. She pressed her face into her pillow and waited, knowing he would not come. But eventually the door opened, and he entered the room. He was still fully dressed.

She had left only one candle burning, and it was on the table next to the bed, so she could not clearly make out his face, but she could sense his hesitation and feel him gazing at her intently. He removed his coat and laid it over the back of a chair, then sat down and took off his boots. She watched, feeling a growing sense of anxiety and then excitement as he slowly unbuttoned his waistcoat and set it on his coat. He drew closer and stopped, drew closer still and then retreated to a chair pulled up before the fire. Catherine watched his silent form for some time. Then unable to bear the uncertainty any longer, she climbed from the bed and moved to stand before him.

"Andrew, please," she entreated in a voice that shook. "I know I may not measure well against the other women you have known, but I do love you, and I promise to do my best not to disappoint you." She reached out to touch his shoulder, and she heard his breath catch. Then he seized her hand and pressed it to his lips.

"You do not understand, my darling Cat," he whispered into her fingers. "The difficulty is wanting you too much, not too little." Reluctantly he looked up at her, and she found herself staring into eyes so full of longing and desire her breath caught in her throat. "What I fear," he said, his voice sounding fierce, "is not disappointment, but to disappoint. You see, my sweet innocent, I've little more knowledge of what lies ahead of us than you do."

For a moment she could only stare at him in surprise. Then relief and exultation swept through her, and in a rush of boldness she settled herself upon his lap. "That is prodigiously fine news, sir."

He gazed at her in astonishment, his arms creeping up to hold her tight. "You find it so?" He kissed her hair, and then lifted it up and kissed the back of her neck. She shivered.

"Indeed, yes," she replied, her voice not entirely steady. She untied his neckcloth and pulled it loose. "I am most pleased to find you are—so to speak—uncharted territory." She tugged his shirt off over his head and ran her fingers wonderingly down the curling hairs at the base of his throat and down his chest. He gave a small gasp.

"Am I now?" His voice was so deep now it sent heat pooling into her belly. "And what precisely do you plan to do with me then?" Slowly—tentatively—his hands slipped beneath her nightgown and slid along her bare legs.

"I would think that obvious," she replied breathlessly, running her hands over his broad shoulders and strong arms and down the muscles of his back. "I have often thought I would like to be a lady explorer." She bent down and began pressing kisses against his warm, hard chest. "Like Lady Hester Stanhope perhaps."

"Have you, my heart?" The hands on her legs moved higher, caressing her. She shuddered with pleasure, and a sound escaped her lips that caused her cheeks to burn in embarrassment. He flashed her a triumphant grin. "Do I take it, then, that you plan to explore *me*?"

She swallowed hard. "I do." She began unbuttoning his breeches with trembling fingers.

His grin faded. He suddenly yanked her nightgown over her head and tossed it aside, then slid a strong arm beneath her bare bottom and lifted her up, carrying her to the bed. As he laid her down, the light from the candle danced over the planes of his face and high-lighted the fine muscles in his shoulders and arms and chest. He gazed down at her with eyes that glittered gold.

"And what riches of Araby do you expect to find, my love?" He undid the last of the buttons and slid his breeches and small clothes off in one determined motion.

She stared up at him. The sight of his naked body suddenly made it difficult for her to catch her breath. "The only treasure I shall ever need," she replied softly, opening her arms to him in invitation.

"My darling little adventurer," he murmured as he bent over her, covering her with his body and lowering his mouth to hers for a kiss.

Catherine woke with a start, mortified to realize she had fallen asleep. Andrew still held her tightly in his arms. Fortunately, her face was pressed against his chest. She hoped he did not know she had nodded off. She did not want him to think she did not treasure what had just passed between them.

It had been so wonderful.

She had not expected it to be so fine. A secret part of her had hoped it would be as enjoyable as his kisses, but she had heard enough whispered mutterings and disparaging jokes about the marriage bed that she had thought the most she could truly aspire to was pleasing him and not being too uncomfortable. She had never dreamed that he could please *her* to such an extraordinary extent. She had never imagined that his kisses could be just a tantalizing prelude to a much greater joy.

But she began to fret. Had she possibly pleased him as much as he had pleased her? He was so very still. Had he fallen asleep as well? Or was he lying there contemplating his disappointment? She wished he would say something, but even his breathing was quiet and uncommunicative. She felt the warm rise and fall of his chest and longed to know that she had made him happy. But as the silence stretched on and on, she became more and more convinced that she had not.

Slowly, warily, she lifted her head, anxious to see his face. His gaze was fixed on her and his expression was grave. Her heart sank. "Andrew?" she whispered.

"Yes, Catherine." His deep voice was quiet and subdued.

Her whole body tensed. She reached up and touched his cheek. "Perhaps next time will be better?"

His demeanor changed completely, and she realized her mistake. What she had taken for gravity had actually been a sort of contented calm. Now his contentment was gone—as was his calm. He radiated consternation and distress. "Damnation! I *did* hurt you! I feared that I had. Forgive me! I did not mean to be so uncontrolled." His tight hold on her fell away.

She scrambled up so that her face was right next to his. "No, Andrew! You did not hurt me—or, at least, the pain was very brief, and it was completely forgotten in the pleasure that followed."

He regarded her with a tense frown. "But in the end I did not please you."

"You pleased me greatly!"

"Then why the devil did you say what you did?"

She hesitated. It was painful to put her doubts into words, but she had to make him understand. "It is still difficult for me to believe that I am your wife. That you love me. That my place is here, in your arms. Our lovemaking was magical for me, but I feared... I feared that it could not possibly be as wonderful for you. I thought I had disappointed you, and I wanted you to give me a second chance."

"A second chance, eh?" he growled in her ear. "And do you know what the first time was for me, wife?"

She shook her head mutely.

"It was not wonderful or magical." His voice was fierce.

She felt tears prick the back of her throat.

"It was perfect."

Startled, Catherine pushed herself away so she could see his face. "Truly, Andrew?"

He nodded and ran one hand caressingly down her hip. "So perfect, you have not only spoiled me for other women," his hand slipped back and possessively cupped her bottom, "I fear you have also awakened an appetite in me that may prove as prodigious as my rakish sire's." He grinned at her. "I hope you are prepared."

Heart suddenly light, she grinned back at him. "Do you doubt my fortitude, husband?"

His grin transformed into a smile so tender and warm, Catherine felt all her old loneliness and self-doubt shimmer and disappear like a desert mirage. "No, only your readiness for departure." He kissed her, and with startling quickness her body responded in anticipation. When he finally lifted his mouth away, he said huskily, "I am eager to set off on another adventure with you."

"I am ready whenever you are, sir," she declared breathlessly.

He gave a low chuckle and took her hand and kissed it. Then he guided it downwards. "As you can tell, beloved wife, I am already more than ready." He slid down next to her and his hands began stroking her lovingly, while his mouth began bestowing caresses with even more industry than his fingers.

Catherine gasped.

He peeked up at her. The grin was back, but this time it contained an expression of boyish mischief she had never before seen on his face. "You know, my sweet, I have ever been a fast learner. Let us see if I can improve on 'magical.'"

Sometime during the night, Ryde woke to the sound of rain drumming against the roof. For a moment he could not think where he was. Then Catherine stirred in his arms, and memory came rushing back in a happy flood.

You are mine now, my love.

He gazed down at her, relishing the feel of her bare back against his chest. She had flung one arm outside the covers, and he carefully tucked it back in, for the room had grown exceedingly chill.

He had been afraid he would disappoint her with his lack of experience, but instead she had taken his breath away with the pleasure of their mutual discovery. Even now he could not contemplate the wonder of their adventures without his pulse beginning to race. The first time he had been inside her had been perfect—so perfect he was glad he had not squandered the experience on a lesser woman, for the exquisite memory was now engraved on his heart.

The second time had been less perfect but more satisfying, for he had progressed beyond pure instinct and had begun the pleasurable business of learning Catherine's body. He had also been able to be more controlled, more gentle and caressing, and his reward had been incontrovertible proof that her pleasure was the equal of his own. He grinned to himself. That had given him a great sense of pride.

She stirred again. Now it was a creamy shoulder escaping from the covers. He kissed it, savoring her sweet smell and the silky softness of her skin against his lips. Yet as he went to tuck her in a second time, he could feel her shivering from the cold. He was suddenly poignantly reminded of the time she had been so ill, and he had watched over her through the night. He bent down and kissed her forehead, then slipped carefully out of bed and crossed to the fire. He stoked it with fresh wood, and when it had revived sufficiently, he returned to the bed and gathered Catherine up in the coverlet.

He laid her down before the fire's blazing warmth and climbed beneath the coverlet with her—spooning her back, but keeping his body at an angle to avoid any contact below the waist, for the sight of her had already had its effect on him, and he was determined to let the poor woman sleep, no matter what frustration it cost him.

But Catherine had other ideas. She snuggled up right against him, her curvaceous bottom issuing a difficult-to-resist invitation. She murmured drowsily, "Poor husband, you have taken cold. I shall have to heat you up."

He groaned. "Delectable wife," he warned sternly, "I suggest you desist, for if you keep that up, we shall soon be setting off to do some more exploring."

Suddenly her eyes opened wide, and she flashed him an impish grin. "I should hope so, husband! I have a great deal of catching up to do if I am to rival Lady Hester!"

Flossie Daniels, the White Boar's youngest chambermaid, had been up all night with a toothache, and was consequently not at her best when she began her morning duties. As was customary, she began her rounds with the rooms vacated by guests departing on the early morning coaches. Unfortunately, Flossie had listened with only half-an-ear when Mrs. Hodges had enumerated which rooms those were, and so she entered what she thought to be the unoccupied room of the departed Mr. Ezekiel Kent only to find it the very much occupied bedchamber of the Marchioness of Ryde.

Daring not even to breathe, Flossie backed toward the door praying with a fervency hitherto unknown in her young life that the couple on the floor would not wake. Fortunately, they did not, and

Flossie was able to escape undetected. Later she reflected with awe on her experience, and a certain amount of satisfaction, for certainly she had never had such a story to share with her friend Betty before.

"And you'll never believe how I found them," she exclaimed dramatically to Betty later that morning as the two stood, their arms full of linen, in the doorway of the now empty room. "They was lying there afore the fire—curled up like a couple of spoons — with only the quilt to hide their nakedness!"

Betty's eyes opened wide in amazement. "But she seemed such a nice lady. Her clothes were ever so grand!"

Flossie narrowed her eyes and nodded sagely. "Too grand, no doubt! I wager she's not even his wife, just one of them actresses Mr. Hodges is always whispering about!"

A surprisingly similar discussion was going on downstairs in the breakfast parlor between two elderly ladies Ryde had noticed earlier as he and Catherine had sipped their coffee in preparation for departure. He had dismissed the ladies from his mind until now, when having returned inside for one last word with the landlord, he heard the less-than-euphonious voice of the lady he had christened Mrs. Trout utter a pronouncement that stayed his step and caused him to pause in the doorway to listen.

"He has turned out just like his father I fear," said Mrs. Trout with grim satisfaction.

"Do you think so?" the woman he had christened Lady Spindle replied sadly. "And I thought he seemed such a pleasant fellow."

Mrs. Trout made a harrumphing sound. "Did you see the expression on his face? Like a cat who has just lapped cream. It was disgusting!"

"Well, if she is his wife — "

"Wife? Ladybird, more like!"

"But I do seem to recall reading somewhere about upcoming nuptials."

"Don't be a fool, Clarissa! When have you ever known a *wife* to look at a husband so!"

Lady Spindle considered the question earnestly. "Her own or someone else's?"

Ryde did not linger to hear Mrs. Trout's reply, but—fighting to suppress the laughter bubbling up his throat—strode down the hallway and out into the yard. There he burst out with a loud guffaw that caused his new marchioness to poke her head out the window of their carriage in alarm.

"Darling, I thought a volcano was erupting!"

"No, ma'am, merely your husband." Wiping the tears from his eyes, he crossed to the carriage, threw open the door, gathered his wife to him, and kissed her soundly.

After he had finished, Catherine said a bit breathlessly, "That was very pleasant, my dear, but what, pray tell, was the occasion?"

"My wife looking at me as only a ladybird would," he said with a grin. Then he sobered and added, "Sweetheart, promise me you will never stop."

She smiled at him—her blue-green eyes sparkling. "I promise."

Sometime later, as the carriage jogged along the road to London, Ryde inquired cheerfully, "My dear, I know I am most happily disposed this morning, and I do feel as if I am grinning far too much, but do I really resemble a cat who has just lapped cream?"

Catherine regarded him critically. "Yes, now that you mention it, you do rather."

"Hmmm. And do you object to that?"

"Not really. I am rather fond of cats, you know."

"Are you now?" he said with a laugh. "Well, in that case, come here, my lady explorer!"

There was a long and extremely satisfying interlude, then he leaned forward and whispered into his beloved's ear.

Catherine exclaimed in a voice full of mirth, "But, dearest! *In a carriage?*"

"Intrepid wife, do not tell me you are frightened of a few new vistas?"

Her only response was a series of delighted giggles.

Coming in March 2014

Reputation

A sequel to Legacy

Chapter 1

Devon, January 6, 1813

He is quite a devilish rake and actually kidnapped a poor girl—or was it two?"

Jane had been deep in a brown study and had heard little of her sister's whispered commentary on the gentlefolk entering Farthingsgate's candlelit ballroom. Now she looked around, startled.

"Who — " she began to ask. But there was no one to address her question to, for Letty had moved off to speak with Squire Elton and his family. As her sister looked back over her shoulder and flashed Jane a reproving look, Jane sighed. No doubt Letty was punishing her for not paying proper heed to her gossip, but it was also irritatingly certain that her sister knew exactly the effect she had achieved by making such a dramatic pronouncement and then moving on.

Jane scanned the latest arrivals searching for the gentleman in question. She could not, at first, find any man under fifty in the group, let alone one who looked as if he could be the Lothario of Letty's description. Then her gaze traveled farther into the ballroom, and she saw an unfamiliar gentleman dancing with her sister-in-law, Catherine. He was tall, though not as tall as Ryde, Jane's giant of a brother. His profile was handsome enough, but not anything out of the common way. His hair—though it glinted golden in the candlelight—was a bit shaggy compared to the precise cut Bevin, her late husband, had always insisted upon. His clothes were neat, but not ostentatious, and he danced with the tight, controlled grace of a military man.

Could this be Letty's rake? While the gentleman was perhaps attractive enough to endanger a few maiden hearts, neither his manner nor his behavior seemed in any way remarkable. Of course, Jane was perhaps not the best judge of how remarkable or unremarkable a rake would appear. Her late father, known to the *ton* by the unfortunate sobriquet "Wild Ryde," had never seemed either as wild or as terrible as his reputation made him out to be.

Letty picked this moment to gaze back and note Jane's scrutiny of the stranger. She gave a slow and deliberate nod, and then had the impudence to wink. Jane's lips tightened in irritation. Letty thought her tittle-tattle a fine joke, but behind every amusing *on-dit* there was a real person whose error or folly or heartache was being trumpeted to all the world. Sometimes people deserved such treatment. Often they did not.

Jane's high-mindedness did not last long, however. Curiosity—and the appeal of further distraction from her own melancholy thoughts—got the better of her, and she turned back to observe the mysterious gentleman and Catherine proceed down the line of dancers. The music was jaunty, and the dancers seemed in good spirits, especially Catherine, who was celebrating her first Christmas as mistress of Farthingsgate. Her dance partner looked grave, almost wary, but when Catherine bestowed one of her sunny smiles upon him, his mouth almost relaxed into a small grin.

The figure had reached the point where the gentlemen circled the ladies. The mysterious gentleman circled Catherine, and Jane had a clear view of his superfine-clad back. Her breath caught. Now *that*, she had to admit, *was* remarkable. His dark blue coat was expertly tailored to show off impossibly broad shoulders tapering down to a slim waist and powerful hips. For a moment, Jane pictured the contrast with Bevin's slight form, and—she could not help it—she imagined what this stranger's back would look like out of its coat.

Jane was quite lost in contemplating this imagined sight, when the thought of how disloyal such imaginings were washed over her. It did not matter that she now knew her late husband deserved no such loyalty. She felt her cheeks heat with shame.

Perhaps God, too, disapproved of her thoughts, for at that very moment the mysterious gentleman made another turn in the figure and looked straight at her. She had not noticed, during her study of the man, just how close the dance was bringing him. Now he stood a mere arm's length from her.

His face, close-up, was more handsome than it had appeared at a distance, despite the small scars above his right eyebrow and near his mouth, and his eyes were alight with an intelligence that made her acutely self-conscious about her indecent scrutiny. The heat in her cheeks spread across her whole face. The gentleman inclined his head slightly and flashed her a warm smile that contained just a hint of speculation. Heaven help her! Did he guess what she had been thinking? Mortified to think he might, she turned away.

"Jane!"

Adopting what she hoped would pass as a neutral expression, Jane turned toward her brother, who had come up behind her. "Yes, Ryde?"

He frowned down at her. "Well, what have I done?"

"Pardon?"

"What have I done to place me in your black books? You only call me 'Ryde' when you are angry with me."

"Do not be ridiculous. I was merely being polite. We are in public. Why should I not call you by your title?"

"Because you ain't Maria to stand on ceremony. I begin to think Catherine is right to fret about you. Are you enjoying the Twelfth Night festivities?"

"Of course. Dinner was lovely, the shawl you and Catherine gave me is beautiful, and the ball," she paused and made a small gesture with her hand, "is obviously a great success."

"Then why aren't you dancing?"

"Because no gentleman has yet asked me!" she replied acerbically, her tone sharper than she intended. Seeing her brother's startled look of chagrin, she added more gently: "There are few gentlemen willing to dance, Drew, and I would not deprive the young ladies of the neighborhood any of their gallants. They have matches to make. I do not."

"My dear, you have been out of your black for nearly six months now. I know you still grieve, but — "

"Do I?" she replied bitterly.

"*Janie?*"

This time her brother's startled look irritated rather than soothed her raw feelings, but this was hardly the time or place to speak of her hurt, especially when its cause was so depressingly hackneyed. Eager to divert her own thoughts almost as much as her brother's questions, Jane made a gesture toward her sister-in-law, "Why are you not dancing with your lady wife?"

He gave her a searching look. Then he accepted the change of subject with a slight lift of his shoulders. "Maria has decreed that I cannot monopolize the hostess. I am to be allowed two waltzes and a minuet. That is all." As he said the words, his gaze strayed toward Catherine, a smile tugging at his lips.

The affection in that look gave Jane a pang of envy. "You do not seem to mind overmuch. Are you not in the least bit worried that she is currently standing up with a gentleman Letty has pronounced a 'devilish rake?'"

He laughed. It was a deep contented sound full of complacence. "Do not be nonsensical, Jane."

"You used to worry about such things!"

"I used to be a fool who had no notion of the true state of my beloved's heart. I hope I am wiser now."

Jane was silent. What was she doing? Of course, her brother had nothing to fear. Catherine loved Andrew with an intensity that was obvious to anyone who caught even a glimpse of them together. As for Andrew . . . her besotted brother could not even speak his wife's name without grinning like a mooncalf. Jane reached out and seized both his hands in hers. "Oh, Drew, forgive me! I am being an idiot—a sad, bitter, cynical idiot. Please ignore me."

"Janie, what the devil is wrong? You must tell me what is weighing on your spirits so heavily! Catherine warned me that something was amiss, but I—blast! They are headed this way. Our talk will have to wait, but talk we shall. Understood, sister mine?"

Jane gave a reluctant nod.

Her brother turned to greet his wife as the mysterious gentleman escorted her back to him.

The gentleman made his bow. "Thank you, Lady Ryde, for a most pleasant dance."

Catherine smiled. "Mr. Winston, you know my husband the marquess."

Her brother inclined his head, and the gentleman nodded. "Lord Ryde."

Catherine continued, "And this is my husband's dear sister, Lady Jane Brawley."

The gentleman turned to meet Jane's gaze. "A pleasure, Lady Jane," he murmured dutifully, though she could detect no pleasure in his tone. It was as stiff as his suddenly rigid spine.

"Jane, allow me to introduce Mr. Anthony Winston. Mr. Winston is our newest neighbor. He has rented Rosington until Michaelmas."

"Welcome to the neighborhood, Mr. Winston," Jane murmured in return.

Catherine, seemingly insensible to the tension in the air, continued cheerfully, "Mr. Winston, I am sure Jane would enjoy standing up for a dance with you as much as I did."

Something tightened still further in Mr. Winston's handsome countenance, but he bowed and said politely, "Lady Jane, if you would do me the honor?"

Dancing with this suddenly fierce-looking stranger was the last thing Jane wanted to do, but rake or not, she could not humiliate him by refusing him after Catherine had basically ordered the man to dance with her.

"Of course, sir," she replied, taking the arm he extended to her.

Only when they were out on the floor did she realize the next dance was to be a waltz. As Mr. Winston took her gloved hand in his and placed his other warm hand at her waist, it suddenly occurred to her that she had never waltzed with anyone besides Bevin. The thought was enough to send her into a panic.

The music started, and he began twirling her in graceful circles across the floor. Her agitation slowly subsided, or rather transmuted into something less frantic but more painful: longing. He was a lovely dancer, and she enjoyed the feel of his strong arms around her and the sensation of being held so close to his broad chest. Unfortunately, his nearness felt so very good, it served to underscore how lonely she was feeling. The lilting rhythm of the music at once soothed her and made her want to weep. It was Twelfth Night, she was dancing with a stranger, and nothing was right with the world. She wanted to be loved and cherished as her sisters were, as Catherine was, as she had once thought herself to be.

Suddenly Mr. Winston drew her closer and leaned near enough to speak into her ear. "Lady Jane, your dislike of my company is obvious, but could you please attempt the semblance of cordiality or at least glance my way on occasion so that the entire neighborhood does not believe I have offered you some unforgivable insult?"

Abashed, Jane looked up directly into his green eyes. For a moment she saw a tumult of emotion in them. Then all went still, like a becalmed sea, and she could make out nothing but a normal gentleman's irritation at being ignored.

Jane wavered. It would be easy to lie. What could it possibly matter to this gentleman with the opaque eyes why she had treated him with such incivility? Yet she was suddenly certain that it did matter to him. *Intensely.* And, somehow, the fact that he did care made it impossible for her not to offer him the truth.

"Sir, forgive me," she said quietly. "It is not your company that pains me, but my own bleak thoughts. I am a widow, you see, and this is the first time I have danced with a gentleman since my mourning was over."

She paused, expecting him to offer her the usual polite sympathy for her true, if incomplete, statement. But he did not. Instead, he watched her face intently—his hand on her waist tightening as they continued their spinning progress—and waited for her to continue.

When the silence had drawn out beyond what she could bear, Jane reluctantly added, "The truth is, sir, that I do enjoy dancing with you. Indeed, I think I enjoy it more than I ever enjoyed dancing with anyone, even my late husband." She paused, searching for moisture in her suddenly dry mouth. The intentness of his gaze as he watched her was having an odd effect on her, making her strangely breathless.

"But you see, you are reputed to be a rake, and I am a lady whose heart has been broken, and dancing with you is quite wonderful, but also quite terrible, because it reminds me of what I have lost and what I will never have." She finished in a rush, stupefied by her disastrous candor to this handsome stranger. Lord in heaven, what was wrong with her!

She could not imagine what he must think of her after this extraordinary avowal, but though she longed to run off and hide in a corner, she forced herself to keep her head high as they whirled through the last measures of the waltz.

His green eyes were no longer opaque, but dark and full of feeling. "You do not balk at your fences, do you, Lady Jane?" he said with surprising gentleness.

She regarded him for a long moment in silence. "No. I merely have a terrible tendency to rush them." She bit her lip. "Mr. Winston, I do beg you will forget my nonsense?"

The music had come to a stop, but still he stood there, holding her in his arms. "And if I do not wish to?"

"Sir, the dance has ended."

"Has it?"

"Yes, and in another moment we will become the focus of attention."

"And are you a lady who cares so much what people think?" The sudden intensity of his tone sent shivers across her skin.

She looked up into his eyes one last time. She wanted to deny it, to deny anything to remain in his arms a few moments longer. But she was Wild Ryde's daughter, and she knew too well the price to be paid for flouting society's opinion. "I fear I am," she said in a whisper.

"Very well, my lady," he said, his voice suddenly emptied of all the feeling that had thrilled her moments earlier, "I will return you to your brother."

Mr. Anthony Winston joined the throng headed for the dining room to partake of Twelfth Night cake. He was grateful not to have to take another turn around the ballroom, ignoring the covert glances thrown his way by the clumps of whispering ladies who watched him as he walked. He was even more grateful for the temporary suspension of the dancing, for he was in no mood to stand up with anyone. His thoughts were still focused on Lady Jane Brawley.

Even if that had not been the case, it was unlikely he would have found another lady willing to grant him the honor of a dance. Tales about him had clearly burned through the room with the speed and efficiency of a wildfire. Every chaperone in the place was watching him as if he were a fox among the chickens. He had but to begin to walk in the direction of a maiden lady and her mother or aunt or sister would hurry the girl to some other part of the room, out of his way.

It was not surprising really. Indeed, he was used to it. It was the reason that in London he never danced with or even approached any lady who was not either married or a widow. But it was worrying that it was already happening here, in this new neighborhood, when he had only just arrived. Naively, he had hoped to find a brief respite here from the tattle. In fact, he had counted on it, for how in the world was he to help Georgiana, if he was a pariah from the very start?

He unclenched his jaw, inclined his head, and smiled at an old trout bustling by him to claim her cake. He had been introduced to the woman when he had first arrived, before the news of his reputation had made the rounds of the assembled matrons. Then she had simpered and fawned over him, no doubt eyeing him as a possible match for her empty-headed niece. Now she looked thunder at his effrontery in greeting her and muttered under her breath about the decline in morals in the younger generation.

Anthony gazed past her retreating back to where Lady Jane stood waiting with her three sisters, their husbands, Lord and Lady Ryde, and Lady Ryde's young brother, the Earl of Trenwich, for the butler to cut the cake—or rather, cakes. Due to the large number of guests, four large Twelfth Night cakes decorated with crowns and delicate white pastillage were displayed on a large gleaming table decorated with evergreen garlands in the old-fashioned style. On either side of the cakes were large silver bowls full of punch, and next to one of the punch bowls there sat, strangely, a hat.

Most of Lord Ryde's family looked in high spirits and seemed to be enjoying the Twelfth Night revelry, but Lady Jane did not. She did not seem interested in the cutting of the cake or curious to learn who would find the bean and pea. Instead, she gazed rather wistfully at some ugly sprig of green bedecked in ribbon and hanging from the ceiling above a small doorway to her right. Anthony was reminded of his first sight of her, as he had entered Farthingsgate's fine ballroom and spotted her standing with one of her sisters, the dark-haired one, who had been prattling in her ear. He had thought Lady Jane pretty, but not particularly memorable, until he had followed her gaze and realized that she was not, as he had supposed by her sister's animated commentary, watching the entering guests, but instead staring at a rather ugly wall sconce to the left of the doorway. For a moment, an unfamiliar chuckle had burbled in his throat. Then he had noticed the lady's melancholy expression and the bowed line of her pretty shoulders, and all desire to laugh had fled.

The butler finished his ministrations, and Lord Ryde gave the signal for the footmen to begin distributing cake and punch to the guests. Lady Ryde whispered something into her lord's ear that made him laugh and hand her the hat by the punchbowl with a flourish. She took the hat and flashed her husband such a warm smile of affection in return that Anthony felt his shoulders tighten in envy.

Lord Ryde was a lucky man. In Anthony's experience, high-born wives of the *ton* rarely expressed open affection—let alone such warm feeling—toward their husbands. Anthony's gaze moved on to Lord Ryde's sisters. They, too, seemed unfashionably fond of their respective spouses—even the prim and proper blonde one, Lady Maria. Several times during the evening, Anthony had caught her casting warm glances toward her husband when she thought no one was looking. He wondered what the St. John family secret was for domestic bliss. They all seemed so happy—all except the one figure standing apart at the end of the row.

Anthony wished she would look his way.

Earlier, when he had been dancing with his hostess, he had turned to find Lady Jane standing quite near. She had been gazing directly at him, her blue eyes filled with open admiration. It had not been a flirtatious look. Its openness had been entirely unintentional. She had started a little when their eyes had actually met, and a wave of pretty color had washed over her face. Yet that look had quite bowled him over, so much so that he forgot to be wary. He had smiled at her, and she—she had turned her back on him.

Since the debacle of Regina Hepworth, he had grown accustomed to receiving the cut direct from many in the *ton*, even friends of long standing, but somehow receiving it from this stranger had stung deeply. When his hostess had urged him to invite the lady to dance, he had done so reluctantly. Lady Jane, too, had seemed hesitant.

Yet, somehow, when they began to dance, holding her in his arms felt surprisingly right and natural. Which is why he grew so frustrated when her gaze remained tenaciously fixed on his cravat. He reproached her for her discourtesy, and she finally looked up, seeming almost startled by his scold, and for a moment he was knocked off balance. Her blue eyes were large and beautiful and full of hurt. He kept dancing—holding on to her—trying to get his feet back underneath him, but she started to speak, and all he could do was listen and hang on even tighter, for she spoke with an honesty that both terrified and enthralled him.

A passing footman offered Anthony cake and a glass of punch. He accepted them distractedly, watching as Lady Ryde gathered up the married sisters, the contented ones, and carried them off on some secret enterprise involving the hat, leaving poor Lady Jane to stand alone. She, too, held a plate of cake, but she was so abstracted she forgot to eat it. Anthony took a step forward, then stopped. It was not his business to draw her out of her melancholy. She cast another wistful—no, mournful—look at that damn sprig of green hanging over the door again. He took a few more steps forward, but stopped a second time, as Lord Ryde, with the young earl in tow, moved to Lady Jane's side and engaged her in a brief conversation. Then the marquess led his young brother-in-law across the room, and she was once again left alone, and Anthony could bear it no longer.

He crossed to where she stood behind the vast table.

"Lady Jane?" he said, his tone more tentative than he would have wished.

She turned. "Mr. Winston," she replied, greeting him with a smile even more tentative than his tone.

"Have you discovered it yet?"

"Sir?"

"The prize pea in your cake."

She looked down ruefully at the plate in her hand. "I fear I have not yet begun my exploration."

"Then it is high time you made a start."

"Sir, with four whole cakes to hide it in, the odds are very poor that it is in my one small slice."

He shook his head. "On the contrary. I am positive it is there. You had best take a bite."

"I do not know why you should be so certain."

"I am sure, because on this Twelfth Night I will have no other queen."

She stared at him, her smile suddenly emerging like the sun from behind a cloud. "That is nonsense, you know."

"Indeed it is," Lady Ryde remarked, coming up behind them unexpectedly. "I have been informed by no less an authority than my brother Carlton that peas and beans are quite *passé*. Of course, so are many of our decorations, but he has been willing to turn a blind eye to those, if I will accommodate him on tonight's entertainment. To that point, please pick a character." She thrust the hat, now full of curling strips of paper, at him.

He reached into the hat and took one.

Lady Ryde looked sternly at her sister-in-law. "Now you, Jane."

Lady Jane did so, and read the script on the paper out loud. *"Frederica Flirt?"*

Lady Ryde laughed. "And you, Mr. Winston?"

Anthony looked down at the scrap of paper in his hand. He said drily, "Apparently I am to be Jack Flash."

"Excellent. Now the two of you go with Alex—I am sorry, Mr. Winston. Allow me to introduce another of my husband's sisters, Lady Alexandra Alderston. She will show you to your costumes."

The charades were a great success. The guests laughed and clapped and shouted out guesses as to identities with robust good humor. At first, Anthony worried that Lady Jane would be too subdued to enter into the spirit of the playacting comfortably, but after donning a red silk gown that her sister provided her with, she greeted him in his borrowed military kit with a mischievous smile and a snap of her fan. He offered her his arm, and they paraded back to the ballroom—she winking at the gentlemen and he leering at the ladies—both of them in high good humor.

Anthony had, at first, been highly self-conscious to be strutting about as Jack Flash, a military dandy with high collar points and a roving eye, but strangely, playing the role with exaggerated *brio* and for obvious comic effect, he found his neighbors eyeing him with a more benign eye. It was as if the ridiculousness of the role made the tales of his past seem ridiculous as well.

Lady Jane also played her role broadly, and Anthony was both amused and slightly startled to see how convincingly she could play Frederica Flirt, the lovely coquette. This Lady Jane, with her saucy smiles and laughing eyes, was quite a different woman from the melancholy lady he had danced with earlier. After their identities had been shouted out and their parading turn about the room was officially over, Anthony was irritated when he was robbed of Lady Jane's company by a young buck Frederica Flirt had just batted her eyelashes at. As the gentleman led Lady Jane away to dance, Anthony decided to ask her to dance with him again during the next set. In the interim, he retreated to the sidelines to watch the others. His hostess appeared at his side.

"Well done, sir," Lady Ryde congratulated him. "You made an excellent Jack Flash."

He smiled at her. "Thank you, ma'am. I must say, I had some misgivings about playing that particular role, but it seems to have gone better than I had expected."

She nodded. "People do not mean to be unkind, Mr. Winston. It is just that they sometimes forget to judge a person's character for themselves and instead rely too much on the reports of others."

He flashed her a sharp look. Had Lady Ryde purposely offered him the hat when that particular strip of paper was on top? He ventured speculatively, "Lady Jane seems to be enjoying her role as Frederica Flirt."

She gazed in Lady Jane's direction with a fond expression. "Yes, it is good for her to be reminded that she is still young, and that there is still joy in the world."

He stared at his hostess. "Lady Ryde, you leave me speechless."

She grinned. "Why sir, I did not think Jack Flash could ever be that!"

He chuckled. "My lady, thank you for inviting me to join tonight's festivities. It has been a pleasant and unexpected evening."

"Sir, the festivities are not yet over. After the next dance, which is to be a minuet, there will be a parade under the mistletoe."

"Mistletoe?" Anthony had a vague memory of an aged uncle talking about the joys of catching a pretty girl under the mistletoe and stealing a kiss.

"Another Christmas celebration my brother assures me is quite antiquated. However, my husband insists it is a St. John family tradition."

As if on cue, Lord Ryde swept toward them and claimed his wife for the minuet. Anthony, determined to claim Lady Jane before some importunate gentleman could beat him to it, rushed to her side and made her an exaggerated bow. "Miss Flirt, may I have the honor of this dance?"

For a moment, Lady Jane's sky blue eyes regarded him shyly. Then she took his proffered arm, playfully tapped his wrist with her fan, and said, "La, sir! I thought you would never ask."

The dance passed pleasantly and much too quickly, and after it was over, Anthony led Lady Jane over to where the couples were lining up for the parade back to the dining room. Lord and Lady Ryde took their place at the beginning of the line. Anthony and Lady Jane were three couples behind them. The line moved forward amidst laughter and excited chuckles. The ladies eyed their escorts from behind lowered lashes. The gentlemen flashed wolfish grins at the ladies. Anthony directed a sideways glance at Lady Jane, wondering if she regretted dancing the minuet with him, since now she would be partnered with him below the mistletoe. To his great relief, however, she smiled at him. It was a rather dazzling smile.

As they entered the dining room, Anthony realized that Lord and Lady Ryde were headed toward the doorway he had seen Lady Jane eyeing earlier, the doorway hung with the ugly sprig of green decorated with red ribbons.

As the marquess led his lady into the doorway, he wrapped his arms around her tightly, leaned his tall head down, and kissed her while the room erupted in cheers and shouts. To Anthony's surprise, the kiss lasted for a considerable time, and when the couple finally parted, Lord Ryde—who had a rather wide grin on his face—wished everyone a very happy new year.

The next couple was Lord Ryde's dark-haired sister, Lady Charlotte, and her husband, Mr. Crawford. They, too, shared a surprisingly lengthy and enthusiastic embrace. Then came Lady Alexandra and her husband, followed by Lady Maria and her husband.

Finally, Anthony and Lady Jane stepped forward. Anthony, who had been too caught up in the pleasure of the lady's company to really think the thing through, now cursed himself for a fool and wondered how in the world he had managed to get himself in such a situation. The eyes of everyone in the room were on him, for he was the rake and outsider who was about to kiss the sister of the master of the house. Despite the enthusiastic embracing of the married couples that had gone before, he was entitled to no such freedom, and he wondered if there was any sort of kiss he could give Lady Jane that his audience would consider chaste enough.

Then she looked up at him, and he noticed a suspicious glitter in her eyes and a faint hurt quiver near the edges of her mouth. Curse his hesitation! She thought he did not want her. Forgetting his audience, forgetting his reputation, forgetting even that his host would likely pull a horsewhip out and thrash him for what he was about to do, Anthony leaned forward and pressed his mouth to Lady Jane's soft lips.

He meant his kiss to be a gentle salute, a token of his esteem, a chaste demonstration of her appeal, but he had not reckoned on the amazing alchemy of her touch.

When he cupped her face in his hands, the velvet of her skin sent waves of desire spilling down his limbs. When he kissed her, the heat of her mouth sent a spark of fire arcing down his chest. When he deepened the kiss and wrapped his arms around her and pulled her close, he felt as if the very earth beneath his feet were slipping away. And when he belatedly realized the kiss had gone on too long and forced himself to pull away from the taste of her and the sweet intermingling of their breath, he felt as if there were no air left in the world for him to breathe.

He stared down at her in wonder.

She stared back at him, her sky blue eyes huge and wary and infinitely beautiful.

Damn, he thought. *I'm lost.*

www.ingramcontent.com/pod-product-compliance
Lightning Source LLC
Chambersburg PA
CBHW030022180626
46810CB00001B/164